THREE BITES OF THE CHERRY

THREE BITES
OF THE CHERRY

Emma Blair

TIME WARNER
BOOKS

TIME WARNER BOOKS

First published in Great Britain in February 2006
by Time Warner Books

A CIP catalogue record for this book
is available from the British Library.

HARDBACK ISBN 0 316 72984 1
C FORMAT 0 316 72986 8

Typeset in Adobe Garamond by Palimpsest Book Production Limited,
Polmont, Stirlingshire.

Printed and bound in Great Britain by Clays Ltd, St Ives plc

Time Warner Books
An imprint of
Time Warner Book Group UK
Brettenham House
Lancaster Place
London WC2E 7EN

www.twbg.co.uk

Part 1

John

1924–1926

Chapter 1

John Mair came bolt upright as his wife's scream brought him abruptly awake. He stared at her in the darkness of their bedroom. She too was sitting up.

'Dear God, Georgie, what's wrong?' he asked, reaching out and placing a hand on her arm.

The screaming stopped as she shuddered into consciousness.

'Georgie?' he queried softly, feeling her trembling under his touch.

Georgie took a deep breath, followed by another, then seemed to collapse forward on to herself. 'Awful. Terrible,' she muttered in a strangulated voice.

Squirming closer, John put his arm round her shoulders. 'Did you have a nightmare?'

She nodded confirmation.

'Bad, eh?'

Georgie turned to face him, gazing at him out of huge, frightened eyes. 'It was about you.'

'Me?'

'I . . . I . . .' She trailed off, and gulped in more air.

'I'm here, darling. There's no need to be afraid.'

Tears appeared and spilled down her cheeks. Then she was hugging him tightly, clutching at him, as though afraid he might somehow disappear. Vanish in a puff of smoke like some will-o'-the-wisp. John could feel her heart thumping in her chest.

'Tell me, Georgie. Tell me what it was all about.'

'It was terrible,' she said hoarsely.

'You've already said that.'

'I was in a room. A very gloomy room lit only by a couple of candles. And . . .'

'And what?' he prompted when her voice again trailed off.

'Oh, Jesus, John. It was so real. I was convinced it was actually happening. That I was there. With you.'

He frowned. Whatever the dream had been, it had really shaken her. He couldn't remember ever having seen her this upset before. The love he felt for her welled inside him in sympathy. 'What was I doing, then?'

'Nothing. You were dead.'

That rattled him. 'Dead?'

'And in your coffin. Your eyes were closed, your complexion a sort of milky colour. You were wearing your suit, best white shirt and red tie, and your hands were folded in front of you.'

'Bloody hell,' he whispered. She was right. It was horrible.

'I started to scream . . .'

'You did that all right,' he interjected. 'It's what woke me up.'

'You mean I actually did?'

'Oh yes. I can assure you of that.'

A new thought came to her. 'I hope I didn't wake Ian as well. You know how light a sleeper he can be at times.'

Ian was their five-year-old son, and only child so far, sleeping in the kitchen. They both listened, but heard nothing.

'I'd better check,' Georgie said.

John knew there was no point in arguing. She'd never settle down again unless she went to look. He nodded. 'On you go.'

Georgie swung her legs out from under the covers and shrugged into her dark green candlewick dressing gown. Silently she padded from the room.

John lit his bedside candle and reached for his cigarettes. A few moments later he was re-joined by his wife, who slipped back into bed again. 'He's fine,' she announced. 'Sleeping sound as can be.'

'Good.'

'It would be a bad night to disturb him, with his starting school in the morning.'

'Aye,' John agreed.

'Can I have a puff of that fag?'

'Help yourself,' he replied, handing it over.

Georgie took several deep drags, then returned it. 'I needed that. Though you know I don't agree with smoking in bed.'

John smiled wryly. It was an old bone of contention between them. 'Feeling better now?'

'A bit.'

She wiped her face, where the tears had now dried. A glance at the clock on the bedside table informed her it was a little past midnight.

'Dead and in my coffin, eh?' he joked, trying to cheer her up.

She nodded.

'And all dolled up like a dish of fish?'

That annoyed her. 'Stop it, John. It was anything but funny. As I said, it was ever so real.'

'I'm sorry.'

She stared at him. 'No, you're not. I can see it in your face.'

John ground out the remains of his cigarette in the ashtray, thinking how beautiful his wife looked, even distraught as she was. A wave of warmth and tenderness swept through him. Not for the first time he told himself how lucky he was to have met and married Georgina McKeand. If ever a couple were right for one another, they were, in his opinion.

'I wonder why you dreamt what you did,' he said.

She shook her head, not having an answer.

'Well, you know what they say.'

'What?'

'That dreams never come true.'

'Do they really say that?'

'You mean you've never heard it before?'

'No.'

'Well, they do. So there. Anyway,' he tapped his chest, 'just look at me. You'll go a long way to find a healthier specimen. Isn't that so?'

She had to admit it was true. Why, she couldn't even recall the last time he had had a cold, let alone anything worse. 'You're right,' she admitted.

'There then. It was probably that cheese you ate earlier gave you the nightmare. You shouldn't have had it so late on.'

It might well have been the cheese, she reflected. But why that particular nightmare? There was absolutely no reason for it. At least, none she could think of.

Reaching over, he ran the tips of his fingers down her cheek. 'Ready for sleep again?'

'Just about.'

'Would a cuddle help?'

Despite herself, she smiled. 'It always does.'

'Then that's what you shall have.'

They switched off their lights and he snuggled down beside her, his front against her back.

'You said a cuddle, not a grope,' she admonished almost instantly.

He laughed in the darkness. 'A grope's far more interesting.'

'No, it's not. Now behave yourself.'

'Do I have to?'

'Yes, you do.'

He pretended to groan. 'Spoilsport.'

She didn't reply to that, but merely smiled. Closing her eyes, she prayed that the nightmare wouldn't recur. Thankfully, it didn't.

'Aren't you hungry?'

Young Ian, washed and scrubbed and staring dully at his breakfast, shook his head.

Georgie sighed, knowing full well what the trouble was. 'Is it the thought of school?'

He nodded.

'There's nothing to be scared of, you know. Why, I enjoyed myself there. Honestly I did.'

He glanced up at her in disbelief. He'd heard stories from other boys – stories he hadn't liked one little bit. The strap, for example. If you were naughty, you were sent to the headmaster and told to hold your hands out in front of you while he gave you 'six of the best' on alternate palms.

'Well, you'll have to eat something,' Georgie went on. 'You can't start your first day without anything in your stomach. So get on with it.'

Reluctantly, Ian spooned some of the boiled egg in front of him into his mouth. The egg was supposed to be a special treat to mark the occasion. Normally they only ever had eggs at the weekends, and then only sometimes.

Georgie glanced at the clock. Almost time to go. God, she was hating this, despite the brave face she was trying to put on. Her wee son starting school! It didn't bear thinking about. She was going to miss him dreadfully during the day.

'Right,' she declared some minutes later. 'Put your coat on.'

Ian felt sick inside as he dragged himself away from his chair. It seemed to his overactive imagination that he was going to his execution. The world as he knew it was about to change for ever. And not for the better, either.

'Mum?'

'What?'

He opened his mouth to plead to be allowed to stay at home, then shut it again, knowing she'd never agree. Not in a trillion zillion years would she do that.

Outside, Georgie took his hand as they walked along the grey but friendly Glasgow streets to the local school, where Ian's fate awaited him.

Ian turned a strained, anxious face up to his mum. The dreaded moment had finally arrived. They were in the playground together and the bell to call him inside had just been rung.

Georgie took a deep breath. 'I'll have to leave you now, son, as there's the janny about to lock the gates. Now, don't worry. You'll be fine. I promise. And I'll be waiting for you at dinner-time.

Ian's narrow chest began to heave. All he wanted was to stay with his mum, be with her as he always had except when out playing in the street.

'Your pals will be here, so you'll have friends about you,' Georgie declared, attempting a cheerful tone which didn't quite come off. She was as upset as he was. 'Off you go, then.'

Turning, she strode purposefully towards the gate where the janny, the same Mr Green who'd been janitor when she'd been a pupil here, was patiently waiting. They exchanged a friendly word, and then she was outside the gates. She mustn't look back, she told herself. That would only make matters worse. But despite herself, she did.

Ian stood rooted where she'd left him, his gaze fastened on hers. Suddenly he was running towards the fence that surrounded the school until he came up against it, his face awash with tears.

'Mummy, please don't leave me. Please don't leave me,' he screamed hysterically, one arm extended beseechingly through the bars.

'Oh, Christ,' Georgie muttered. This was turning out even worse than she'd expected. She remained where she was. 'Go inside now, Ian,' she said sternly, feeling anything but stern.

'Mummy, please, please!'

There was nothing else for it. Turning away from him, she went on her way with his hysterical screams ringing in her ears.

Ashen-faced, Georgie sank gratefully into a chair, her hands still shaking from the ordeal she'd been through.

'I'll put the kettle on,' her mother Chrissie announced.

'He screamed and screamed, Ma. Even halfway back down the road I could still hear him.'

Chrissie clucked her sympathy. 'Aye, that sort of thing was

never easy. Your sister Lena was the worst I had to deal with. Though I have to admit, she wasn't as bad as that.'

Georgie pulled out her cigarettes and lit up. 'Poor wee soul. It was heart-wrenching, Ma.'

Chrissie, who'd been filling the kettle at the sink, now put it on the stove and lit the gas. 'Children can put you through it, right enough. And I should know, having had five.' She paused for a moment, thinking of the boy who'd died directly after birth. That had been a bitter blow, one it had taken her quite a time to recover from. If, indeed, she ever had. Kenneth, they'd called him, though there hadn't been enough time to have him christened. Even now she occasionally went to visit his grave.

Georgie glanced out of the window. 'Looks like it's going to rain.'

Chrissie followed her gaze. 'I wouldn't be surprised. At least it isn't wash day. That's something.'

Georgie nodded her agreement.

'That's the trouble when you only have the one,' Chrissie went on. 'They're never as tough, to begin with anyway, until others come along.' She regarded Georgie hopefully. 'Any news in that department?'

Georgie shook her head.

Chrissie frowned. 'Five years is a long time. You should have been expecting again by now.'

'Well, it's certainly not for the lack of trying, Ma, before you ask. I can guarantee that.'

Chrissie grunted her approval. 'I wish I could give you a biscuit, but I've none in, I'm afraid.' She patted her ample stomach. 'It won't harm me to do without, and that's a fact.' After five children her figure was not what it had been, although once she'd been as slim as Georgie. Still, her husband, Big Tam, always protested he preferred her with a bit of meat on her bones. A lie, of course, or so she believed, but kind of him. That was the sort of man he was.

Georgie watched Chrissie clatter out some cups and saucers. 'I had a horrible nightmare last night,' she said quietly. 'Woke up screaming, according to John.'

'Oh aye?'

'Fair put the wind up me. Worst nightmare I've ever had.'

Chrissie paused to stare at her daughter. 'Ian screaming, you screaming? Dearie me. What was the nightmare about?'

Georgie told her.

'Sounds terrible, right enough. No wonder it gave you the willies.'

Georgie shook her head at the memory. 'The most frightening thing was that I felt I was actually there. It was ever so real.'

'It would have scared me half to . . .' Chrissie hesitated, then went on, 'I was about to say to death. But that's hardly an appropriate way of putting it.'

Georgie had to smile at that, for it was true enough. 'The one good thing, according to John, is that dreams never come true. Have you heard that?'

'Oh aye.' Chrissie nodded. 'That's what they say. Thank God.'

Something about the way Chrissie said it prompted Georgie to ask, 'Why thank God?'

Chrissie looked embarrassed. 'I was thinking of a dream I had myself some while back. I suppose you could've called that a nightmare too.'

'And?'

'And what?'

'Tell me about it.'

'Och no. I'm sorry I mentioned it now.'

Georgie was intrigued. 'Come on, Ma. Spill the beans.'

'You'll laugh.'

'No, I won't.'

'Oh yes you will. I guarantee it. So I'm not telling.'

Georgie took a deep draw on her cigarette, even more intrigued. 'Suit yourself,' she declared in an off-hand manner, as if it was of no further interest to her. 'Though it's hardly fair.'

'What isn't fair?'

'I told you my nightmare, so it seems only fair you tell me yours. But no matter.'

Chrissie busied herself with the teapot while Georgie,

pretending she'd taken the huff, remained silent. Knowing Chrissie as she did, she was sure her mother would eventually crack.

'Aye, all right then,' Chrissie said at last. 'But you must promise me not to laugh.'

Georgie kept a straight face. 'I promise.'

'Mind you keep it then.'

Georgie waited expectantly while Chrissie took a deep breath. 'Daft, really,' she declared. 'But in my dream I was standing stark naked in the middle of Sauchiehall Street on a Saturday afternoon, when the place was teeming.'

Georgie stared at her mother in amazement. 'Stark naked?' she repeated incredulously.

'Not a stitch on and everyone gaping and pointing at me.'

It was one of the funniest things Georgie had ever heard. Her mother naked in Sauchiehall Street, one of Glasgow's main thoroughfares. Now what on earth had made Chrissie dream that?

Despite her promise, Georgie threw back her head and roared with laughter at the very thought of it.

Chrissie scowled. 'See, I said you'd laugh. But just remember, that didn't come true either.'

Georgie couldn't reply. She was completely convulsed.

'You're home then,' Georgie said when John appeared in the kitchen that evening.

He went to her and kissed her on the cheek. 'What's for tea? I'm starved.'

'Toad in the hole.'

'Fair enough. That'll do.'

'How was work?' she enquired, as she did every time he got back.

'All right. Nothing untoward happened. Ardrossan and return. Slick as you like.'

John was a fireman with the recently formed London, Midland and Scottish Railway. His job was to stoke the engine boiler:

back-breaking graft but a job he enjoyed none the less. It was his great ambition to be a driver one day.

'Good.' Georgie nodded, aware that some shifts could be worse than others, especially if they had trouble with the engine, or, as could happen, it broke down altogether. Fortunately, such occurrences were rare.

From his seat at the table, Ian watched his father cross to the sink and give himself a quick wash.

'So, how was school then?' John asked with a smile when he had finished.

Ian glanced at his mother, who was sworn not to tell his father about the scene in the playground that morning. He muttered something unintelligible.

John raised an eyebrow. 'That good, eh?' he said ironically.

'He met up with a few pals, which made things easier,' Georgie chipped in.

John came and sat at the table facing Ian. 'What's your teacher called?'

'Miss Hamilton.'

'Is she nice?'

'I suppose so.' Reluctantly.

'Just suppose so? Don't you know?'

Ian shrugged.

'I see. Is she young or old?'

'It's hard to say.'

'And why's that?'

Another shrug.

'What did you do at playtime?'

'Someone had a ball and we had a game of footie. I enjoyed that.'

John smiled. 'So school wasn't too awful then?'

'I got a sore bum sitting at my desk. Wood isn't very comfortable.'

'I remember.' John nodded. 'My bum used to get sore as well.'

Ian blushed to hear John use that word. It just didn't seem right coming from his father.

12

'And who are these pals you've met up with?' John went on.

'Just other boys.'

John sighed. He wasn't getting very far here. 'From the street?'

'And round about.'

'Good pals?'

Yet another shrug.

'Was it their first day too?'

'For one of them. The others are already there.'

'They'll be able to show you the ropes, then.'

Ian frowned. 'I don't understand that?'

'Where to go and what to do,' John explained.

'Oh aye.'

'That'll make it easier for you.'

Ian took a deep breath. 'School's useless anyway.'

John glanced at Georgie, then back again at his son. 'Why useless?'

'I spent the whole day there and at the end of it I picked up a book and still couldn't read.'

'You still . . .'

'Useless,' Ian repeated doggedly.

For the second time that day Georgie burst out laughing. So did John. What a thing to come out with! Absolutely priceless. It had the pair of them in stitches.

Chapter 2

'I see you've started on the whisky already.'
Big Tam McKeand glanced over at his wife from where he was sitting beside the fire. 'Are you complaining, woman?'

'No,' she replied drily. 'Just commenting.'

It was early Saturday evening and, as always on a Saturday after his one o'clock finish at McNair's, where he was a foreman moulder in the manufacture of marine pumps, Tam had returned home with a bottle of whisky and eighty cigarettes to last him through the weekend.

'That's all right then,' Tam muttered, and busied himself again with his newspaper.

'Where are you off to tonight, Lena?' Chrissie asked her second oldest, who was applying make-up in front of the mirror that hung above the mantelpiece.

'Don't know, Mum. I'm meeting up with Pet and we'll take it from there.' Pet McQueen was Lena's best friend.

No one in the family ever mentioned the fact, but Lena was as ugly as sin. Not just plain, but downright ugly. She had the sort of face that would have made a good model for a gargoyle. On top of that she had a thin, bony figure with hardly any bust to speak of. It was not surprising, Chrissie thought regretfully, that she had never been very successful with men.

'Probably the pictures,' Lena added as an afterthought.

'What's on?' Chrissie asked.

'No idea. Pet will probably know.'

'Where are you meeting her?'

Lena mentioned a local spot.

'So you're not going into town, then?'

'We haven't planned to.'

Tam swallowed a mouthful of whisky, then placed his glass back on the floor, just as his son Tom came into the room. At eighteen, Tom was still serving his apprenticeship at McNair's, where he worked under his father, and, with his greased-back hair and slightly olive complexion, was the apple of his mother's eye. None of them knew where the olive skin came from, but it certainly didn't run in the family. Not that there was any question of his paternity: the similarity in looks between him and Tam was striking. He had been christened Thomas after his father, but Tam preferred the Scottish version.

'As you're wearing a collar and tie I suppose it's the jigging for you the night.' Chrissie smiled. Tom was dancing mad.

'That's right, Mum. I met a wee lassie last week and am kind of hoping she'll turn up again. She was a smashing dancer. A real twinkletoes.'

'Twinkletoes!' Tam snorted, lighting a cigarette. 'Whoever heard the like?'

Tom smiled, well used to his father's disparaging remarks, and knowing there was no malice in them. It was simply Tam's way. 'Twinkle twinkle,' he said teasingly, doing a fancy shuffle with his feet.

'The lad's an idiot,' Tam muttered.

'He's nothing of the sort,' Chrissie rebuked her husband. 'And you shouldn't say such things. You'll dent his confidence.'

'It'll take a lot more than me to do that,' Tam declared. 'He's got so much bloody confidence the stuff almost oozes out of him. Far too much of it in my opinion.'

'You do talk rot at times, Tam McKeand,' Chrissie admonished him. 'For an intelligent man, that is.'

That pleased Tam. He liked the idea of being thought of as intelligent, having left school at the age of nine. He'd gone to the Ragged School, he always said. No shoes, and your bare arse hanging out of your pants. He'd been brought up in hard times when a boy went to work at the first opportunity to help bring money into the house. A proper education for their sons was something the likes of his parents hadn't been able to afford.

With a most unladylike grunt Lena finished her make-up and returned her bits and pieces to the small bag she kept for that purpose. 'I'll be off then,' she announced.

'Mind how you go,' Chrissie said.

'I always do, Mum. Ta-ra then!' And with that she swept from the kitchen.

Tam stared after his daughter, wondering if she'd ever find a man. He doubted it. Which probably meant she'd never move out and would be with them for the rest of their days: a prospect he wasn't entirely sure he relished.

Tom also left the room to come back a few minutes later wearing his overcoat. 'Don't wait up for me,' he said with a smile. 'I might be late.'

'Don't worry, we won't,' Tam growled, and drank more whisky, enjoying the warmth and bite of it coursing down his throat.

'Are you thinking you might be lumbering this wee lassie you mentioned?' Chrissie enquired, wanting to know whether Tom intended to take the girl home with the possibility of arranging a further meeting.

'Possibly,' Tom reluctantly admitted. 'I've no idea where she lives. There's no point if it's too far away. I don't mind a walk but I've no intention of hiking miles and miles.'

Chrissie could see the sense in that. 'Well, enjoy yourself anyway. See you in the morning.'

'Night, Papa.'

Tam glanced up from his paper. 'Night, son. And good luck.'

'Thanks, Papa.'

'Twinkletoes,' Tam muttered to himself when Tom had gone, and chuckled.

Chrissie waited till Tam had had a few whiskies and was in a mellow mood before coming over to sit facing him.

'There's something I want to talk to you about,' she declared. 'And now's a good time as we're on our own.'

'What's that about then?'

'Mary.'

Tam's face clouded over with displeasure at the mention of their oldest child. 'I'm not in the mood to discuss her and her nonsense,' he growled.

'Things can't go on as they are,' Chrissie persisted. 'We haven't seen her in over a year now. Eighteen months, more like.'

'That's not my fault.'

'It was you started the barney the pair of you had last time she was here.'

'I did nothing of the sort!' he protested.

'Yes, you did. And you know it.'

Tam sat further up in his chair, drained his glass and poured himself another. 'She began spouting religion to me yet again, and I wasn't having it. She's become a complete nutter on the subject.'

'She's still our daughter.'

'Look, woman, she's welcome here whenever she likes, but when she comes in this house I insist she leaves all her preaching and holier than thou business at the door. I don't want to hear any of that guff.' He shook his head. 'Always going on about this sect she's joined, and their meetings she's forever going to. Christ, she's done so much praying I'm amazed her bloody knees haven't worn out.'

Chrissie couldn't help but smile. It was true enough. Mary was always mentioning this meeting she'd attended, or that one, or another. She'd become something of a one-woman crusade, though not for the Church of Scotland, to which the rest of the family belonged.

17

'I don't know how James puts up with it,' Tam went on. James was Mary's husband, and father of her two children. 'I'd have given her a good skite long before now.'

'That's because he's weak and lets Mary walk all over him.'

Tam nodded his agreement. 'Nice enough chap. But, as you say, weak as sugarallywater.'

'But brave. You can't deny that, now.'

There had been a bad fire some years previously at the tannery where James worked. When he was told that his brother was trapped in the burning building he had wrestled clear of those who were trying to stop him and dashed back inside to rescue him. James had received a special citation for bravery.

'No, I can't,' Tam admitted. 'He was a hero when it counted and no one can ever take that away from him.'

Tam drank more whisky and then lit another cigarette. He'd aye liked James Davidson but despised the way he kowtowed to his wife. It upset Tam that he was estranged from Mary whom he'd doted on as a child, she being their firstborn. He wished things could go back to how they'd been before she'd fallen in with those holy rollers and absorbed their weird notions. According to them the world was going to end in twenty-something years' time, and everyone would go to hell who didn't hold to their beliefs and practices. Hence Mary's anxiety to get the rest of the family to join, and therefore be 'saved'. As he'd pointed out to her, it didn't seem very likely that God would destroy the vast majority of mankind and save only those souls who believed the teachings – rantings, more like – of the sect. That wasn't very logical to his way of thinking. Or, or as he'd once put it more succinctly, in his opinion the whole thing was nothing more than a load of old shite.

Chrissie sighed, deciding to drop the subject. For now, anyway. But just for now.

Miss Hamilton stopped to peer over Ian's shoulder. Suddenly acutely aware of her presence, he blushed bright red.

'What a lovely house you've painted, Ian,' she said. 'I'm impressed.'

He thought Miss Hamilton was smashing, and she always smelled wonderful. 'Thank you, miss,' he managed to croak.

She pointed a finger. 'And this little chap here. Is that you?'

'Yes, miss.'

'And the lady?'

'My mum.'

'I see. And what about your dad?' John was noticeably absent.

'He's at work.'

The originality of the reply amused her. 'Is he away at work a lot, then?'

'Yes, miss.'

'What does he do?'

'He's an engine fireman on the railway, miss.'

'How interesting. And such a responsible job.'

'He wants to be a driver one day, miss.'

'Well, I'm sure he will be. Well done, Ian.' She produced a little booklet from which she peeled a gold star, and Ian was fit to burst with pride when the star was stuck to the top of his picture.

He stared after Miss Hamilton in adoration as she continued on down the line of desks.

'Now you're sure you know the way and won't get lost?' Georgie asked anxiously. It was Ian's first day of being allowed to go to school by himself, Georgie having been taking him there and back for the past fortnight.

'I won't get lost,' Ian assured her.

She stooped and straightened his tie, which was already askew. 'Off you go then. And make certain you're careful crossing the roads.'

'I will, Mum, I promise.'

She wasn't too worried about his crossing the roads involved as there was hardly any traffic to speak of. Trams, of course, and the occasional delivery cart and van, but it was rare to encounter a private car. Cars were the preserve of rich people, doctors and the occasional commercial traveller. Nevertheless, Georgie's heart was in her mouth as she kissed Ian on the cheek and ushered him off down the stairs, where he quickly vanished from sight.

How fast they grow up, she reflected, back in the kitchen once more. How very, very fast. She was about to start washing the breakfast dishes when it suddenly came to her what she must do for peace of mind. If she didn't she'd fret every single minute till dinnertime when he was due to come home again. Hurriedly, she snatched up her coat from the hall peg where it lived, and dashed out of the door, locking it behind her.

Down the street she went, following in his footsteps, anxiously scanning the road ahead. He finally came in sight just as he, and lots of others, was entering the school gates.

Safe, she thought with relief. He'd made it safe and sound. It was as though a huge burden had been lifted from her shoulders.

Safe and sound, she thought again, as she began returning the way she'd come. It had been daft of her to chase after him like that. Quite unnecessary.

But he was her son, after all. And she loved him dearly. She'd only done what any mother in her position might.

'I was thinking,' John declared during tea a few weeks later. 'As we seem to be having something of an Indian summer this year what about going to the seaside on Saturday?'

'Aren't you working?' Georgie asked in surprise.

He shook his head. 'Got the weekend off. Not due in again till Tuesday night.'

That explained it. 'You're back on night duty, then?'

'For a while, I'm afraid. No idea how long.'

Georgie hated his being on nights. But it came with the job and had to be done. There was no getting out of it.

Ian was almost squirming with excitement. The seaside! 'Can we take a picnic?' he asked, eyes glowing with eagerness.

'That depends on your mum, son.'

'Mum?'

Georgie smiled at him, noting his enthusiasm. How could she possibly refuse? 'I don't see why not.'

'Yippee!' Ian yelled.

'Providing the weather stays good, that is,' she added, thinking that a picnic would be cheaper than having to buy something there. She began mentally planning what they might take.

'Thanks, Mum.' Ian was beaming.

'Now where shall we go?' John asked. Wherever it was, they'd travel by rail as he had a free pass for himself and family.

They fell to discussing destinations.

Ian sat staring out of the carriage window at the countryside flashing past. The good weather had continued, as he'd desperately hoped it would, and now they were on their way to Helensburgh on the Firth of Clyde.

Georgie glanced at John, who'd dropped off to sleep, which took years off him. What a good man he was, she reflected. She'd been lucky. She only hoped she was as good a wife to him as he was husband to her. And father to Ian.

She smiled as he snorted, changed position and started to snore. Thank goodness they were the only ones in the carriage. She'd have been obliged to wake him if they hadn't been.

'Enjoying yourself so far?' she asked Ian.

'Oh, yes, Mum. But I can't wait to get to the seaside. That's going to be even better.

Georgie couldn't remember when she'd last been so content.

Chrissie was halfway down Buchanan Street when she spotted Mary coming towards her. She pulled up short, wondering what to do.

Mary went white when she saw her mother, hesitated, then carried on walking, only stopping when she reached Chrissie.

'Hello, Ma.'

'Mary. How are you?'

'Fine. Yourself?'

'Not too bad.'

There was a strained silence between them for a few seconds, then Chrissie asked, 'Still going to your meetings?'

Mary immediately bridled. 'Of course,' she snapped. 'Why shouldn't I be?'

Oh dear, Chrissie thought. She'd said the wrong thing. Trust her. 'No reason,' she murmured. 'I was just asking, that's all.'

Mary's expression softened slightly. 'Aye, well, there we are.'

Suddenly Chrissie wanted away from her daughter, who'd quite unnerved her. 'I'd better be getting along,' she declared. 'I've got a lot yet to do.'

'Me too.'

''Bye then, Mary.'

''Bye, Mother.'

A few moments later Chrissie turned to watch Mary's retreating back.

She could have wept.

'Oh, this is glorious,' Georgie sighed, lying prostrate with the sun beating down on her. John was alongside her, Ian happily playing at the water's edge. They didn't have trunks for the boy who was stripped down to his underpants. There were about a dozen other people scattered along the beach, plus an old fisherman sitting outside a hut nearby mending some nets by hand.

'Those egg sandwiches were really tasty,' John muttered, eyes closed, as were Georgie's. 'I don't know what you did to them but they were truly delicious.'

'Good.'

'The fish paste ones weren't bad either. Certainly hit the spot.'

Georgie opened her eyes and rolled over on to her side to stare at him. She'd always thought him a beautiful man, and never more so than at that moment. 'A penny for them?' She smiled.

He was smiling too. 'They're not worth a penny.'

'Oh, come on,' she teased him. 'I'm sure they are.'

'You'd be wrong.'

'Tell me anyway.'

He opened his eyes to gaze at her. 'I was thinking about going back on nights . . .' He stopped when she groaned. 'Told you they weren't worth a penny.'

'How can you think about work on a day like this?' she said accusingly.

'Quite easily actually. It just sort of drifted into my mind.'

Suddenly they both became aware of some sort of commotion. Looking round they saw that the old fisherman was now on his feet and wildly gesticulating.

'The boy, the boy!' the old man shouted. 'He's gone under.'

'Gone under?' John frowned, glancing down at the water's edge.

'Someone do something!' The old man was waddling as quickly as he could in the direction he was pointing.

'Oh, my God!' Georgie breathed, realising there was no sign of Ian. 'It's Ian he's on about.'

The colour drained from John's face as he leapt up. Vaguely, he heard Georgie screaming behind him as he ran to where he'd last seen Ian. Georgie sat petrified with fright, unable to move a muscle. It was as though she'd been turned to stone.

Tiny waves lapped at John's feet and legs as he went rushing into the water, almost instantly spotting his son, lying submerged a yard or two further on. He grabbed him and hauled him out of the water. Ian was limp in his hands, and did not appear to be breathing.

Fearing the worst, John quickly returned to the beach, and laid Ian out face down on the sand.

'Let me,' said the old fisherman, kneeling down beside them. Rough, callused hands immediately began working on Ian's back.

A distraught Georgie joined them, having somehow overcome her paralysis. 'Is he . . . is he . . . ?'

With a gasp, Ian convulsed. Water shot out of his mouth, and he sucked in breath after breath.

The old fisherman gave a sigh of relief and sat back on his haunches. 'He'll be all right now,' he declared to Georgie and John. 'But it was a close thing.'

Georgie sank to her knees and pulled Ian into her embrace. 'Oh, my darling. My darling,' she crooned.

'I slipped, Mum. I slipped and fell in,' Ian explained, shaking all over. 'I'm sorry.'

'We can't thank you enough,' John told the old fisherman. 'We could easily have lost him. I blame myself for not keeping an eye out.'

Georgie turned her head away from Ian, and was violently sick.

Chapter 3

'This is a day I'll never forget for the rest of my life,' Georgie said quietly. It was later that night, and Ian was fast asleep in his recessed bed, having, it seemed, recovered completely from his earlier ordeal.

'Me neither,' John agreed, and had a swallow of whisky from the bottle he'd bought on their way home. An extravagance perhaps, but one he'd declared they were entitled to.

'If that old man hadn't . . .' Georgie broke off, and shuddered. 'It doesn't bear thinking about.'

'No, it doesn't.' John nodded.

Georgie lit a cigarette with a hand that hadn't stopped shaking since the incident.

'Are you still feeling cold?' John queried.

'As ice inside.'

'Shall I put the fire on?'

She thought about that. 'We'll be going to bed soon so it would be a waste. Anyway, it's only me that's cold. The weather's warm enough.'

'I can still light it.'

She smiled at him, the smile disappearing as she thought for the umpteenth time how differently things might have turned out. 'I don't think I'll sleep much tonight.'

John leant across and refilled her glass. 'Try more of that. It might do the trick.'

Georgie doubted it. Despite having already had four large ones she was sober as a judge. Even the whisky hadn't helped warm her insides.

'It was my fault,' John said yet again. 'I should have known better than not to keep watching him.'

'I was just as much to blame as you. More so, as I'm his mother.'

They both glanced over to where Ian lay sleeping soundly, trying not to imagine what it would have been like if he'd drowned. Their wee son. Their only child. Georgie began to cry silently, which she'd been doing on and off since the accident. John rose, went to her and put an arm round her shoulders. He felt like crying himself. 'There there, lassie. There there. That won't help any.'

'I know,' she said huskily. 'But I can't stop myself.'

He gently rocked her back and forth for a few minutes while she continued to cry, gripped by the emotions that were rampaging through them both. Strongest of all was guilt.

'Are you asleep?'

'No.'

'I didn't think you were.' John reached out and took Georgie by the hand, giving it a slight squeeze.

They lay like that for a little while, then she turned and snuggled up to him. 'I'm so empty inside, John,' she whispered. 'So terribly empty.'

'Still cold as well?'

'Yes.' Despite the sheet, four blankets and quilt which covered them. But her coldness had nothing to do with the lack of that kind of comforter.

'John?'

'What, darling?'

'I need . . . Well, you know?'

It surprised him. 'Do you?'

'I appreciate it's late. But please, John. I just need that.'

He was only too willing to comply, and found as much solace in the act as she did.

Finally they both drifted off to sleep.

Chrissie gasped. 'That's too tight, Lena. Far too tight.' She was putting on her new corset for the first time at home, her old one having finally given up the ghost.

Lena relaxed the laces a little. 'How's that?'

'Better.'

'Right then.' Lena tied the laces off and stepped back to admire her handiwork. 'It seems to fit all right.'

'It's far stiffer than I'm used to. But it would be, being new, I suppose.'

Lena grunted her agreement. She thought corsets horrible, constricting things, but, according to fashion, they were almost obligatory once you got older.

Chrissie moved her arms about, to see if they were restricted in any way. They weren't.

'Was it expensive?' Lena asked.

Chrissie told her how much it had cost.

'Enough for what's only a bit of material and a few pieces of whalebone, when all is said and done,' Lena commented.

'Don't forget the labour that goes into the making of it. That has to be paid for as well.'

True enough, Lena thought. She hadn't considered that. She watched as Chrissie slipped into her dress, a green one with large white polka dots that was a long-standing favourite of her mother's. And which, she had to admit, suited Chrissie.

'I haven't told you – or anyone else in the family, come to that – but I bumped into Mary last Saturday while in town shopping.'

'Oh aye? And how's my big sister?'

'Same as always.'

'Still spouting religion all over the place?'

Chrissie nodded miserably. 'I asked her if she was still going to the meetings and she nearly bit my nose off. Well, you know what she's like?'

'Only too well.' Lena sighed. 'A pain in the backside.'

Chrissie couldn't have agreed more. 'I just wish things were different. I know it upsets your papa enormously that we're estranged.'

'I'm not surprised. Mary was always his favourite,' Lena said bitterly.

'Now, you know that's not so.'

'It damn well is. Oh, give him his due, he tried to hide it. But the rest of us could see right through that. She was his favourite by a long shot.'

'Well, she certainly isn't now. He's terribly disappointed in her, though he rarely says.'

'A thaw in relations will come sooner or later. Has to. You'll see.'

'I'm not so sure,' Chrissie replied, her face filled with sadness. 'One thing I'm certain about, any thawing, as you put it, won't come from your father. You know how stubborn he is—'

'As is Mary,' Lena cut in. 'They're so alike, those two. They stick to their guns and won't budge.'

Chrissie sighed. 'If only she'd see some sense. Believe in her religion, if she has to, but shut up about it in front of the rest of us. Stop trying to ram it down our throats.'

'Some hope,' Lena sniffed.

Chrissie eyed her daughter speculatively, finally getting round to why she'd started this conversation in the first place. 'You and she aye got on well in the past.'

'Not too bad,' Lena grudgingly admitted. 'For sisters, that is.'

'You got on far better with her than you ever did with Georgie and Tom. Not that you didn't get on with those two, but you know what I mean.'

'As I recall it was always Georgie and Tom against Mary and me. That pair have always been as thick as thieves.'

'It's an age thing, I suppose.' Chrissie smiled. 'The two youngest ganging up against the two oldest.'

'Huh!' Lena snorted. 'Probably.'

'So I was wondering . . .' She trailed off, looking at Lena in a strange way.

'Wondering what?' Lena queried, slightly alarmed at the expression on her mother's face. It spelt trouble.

'If you'd go and see Mary. Have a word with her. Try to build a few bridges.'

'Me!' Lena exclaimed.

'You're the obvious choice. If she'll listen to anyone she'll listen to you.'

Lena didn't fancy the idea at all. She was as fed up with Mary's religious claptrap as the rest of the family.

'Come on,' Chrissie urged. 'Say you'll go. For my sake if nothing else.'

Lena was still reluctant. 'I don't think it would do any good, Mum. Honestly I don't.'

'You can at least try. Where's the harm?'

'Plenty if my visit ends up in a shouting match.'

'There's no need for that if you keep your temper and don't let rip.'

'And what if she starts?'

'Don't react. Be all sweetness and light itself. Try to make her see reason.' Chrissie hesitated, then added, 'Please, Lena? It would mean so much to me and your papa if we were all reconciled.'

Lena caved in, though visiting her sister was the last thing she wanted to do.

'All right then,' she sighed eventually. 'I'll go.'

Chrissie beamed at her. 'Thank you.'

God, Lena thought. What had she let herself in for? She dreaded to think.

Tam came out of his office at the end of the day's work to find Tom waiting for him, as his son always did. As usual, they would walk home together.

Tom waited till they were clear of McNair's before asking the question he had in mind. 'There was a pile of scrap metal tucked away in a corner out back of the foundry that I noticed has disappeared. Do you know about that, Papa?'

Tam's eyes slid to his son, and then away again. 'You're observant.'

'Not really. Not particularly so. I just happened to notice it's gone.'

'Have you mentioned this to anyone else?'

Tom shook his head. 'No.'

'Then don't.'

Tom was intrigued. 'Can I ask why?'

'Just don't mention it, that's all.'

'If you wish.'

'I do. Now let's drop the subject.'

Tom couldn't help but be puzzled. Why on earth was his father taking that attitude? What if it was theft? There was money to be made in scrap metal. Particularly lead and copper. Good money, too.

And then the penny dropped. His father was at it. He was the one responsible. He was selling the damn stuff on the fly. That had to be the answer, for Tam would have been down like a ton of bricks on anyone else who tried it.

Well well well, Tom mused. This was a new side to his father whom he'd always considered to be above anything untoward.

He just hoped and prayed that Tam never got caught. There again, in Tam's position as gaffer, that was highly unlikely.

The subject was never broached between them again.

'Have you ever contemplated living abroad?' Pet McQueen asked Lena. The two of them were in a café having coffee. Pet had enormous breasts, brassily dyed blonde hair, and lips that she was forever coating in the brightest of bright red lipstick. Together, albeit they were the best of pals, she and Lena made an incongruous pair.

Lena stared at her friend in surprise, then shook her head. 'Whereabouts abroad?'

'Oh, I don't know. Canada maybe. Or America. America

certainly appeals. If it's anything like the movies, that is.'

'America,' Lena mused. 'Do you mean Hollywood?'

'Why not? I've read that's a helluva place to be. Especially if you can break into films.'

'Not much chance of that in my case.' Lena laughed. 'I may be many things but a beauty I'll never be.'

Pet clucked in sympathy. That was true enough. Whereas she, on the other hand, was – at least so she believed. 'You don't have to be a beauty to be in films,' she pointed out. 'There are all sorts of people employed by the studios. Make-up ladies, for example. And many others who never go in front of the cameras, most of whom get paid extremely well.'

Lena thought about her own job. It wouldn't take much to be paid better than she was.

'Just imagine.' Pet sighed dreamily. 'All that sunshine, day after day. And they say fruit just falls off the trees there. You can pick yourself a fresh orange or peach any time you like. That must be absolutely fantastic.'

Lena thought so too. And what a contrast to cold and rainy old Glasgow – not to mention snow. No comparison whatever. 'Are you really thinking of going there?' she demanded with a frown that completely furrowed her forehead.

Pet shrugged. 'I might be.'

'It's awfully far away.'

'So?'

'It would be difficult getting back again.'

'Once there who'd want to come back? I doubt I would. Another thing to consider, there are lots and lots of rich blokes in Hollywood with more dosh than they know what to do with. Driving big flashy cars, living in houses like palaces. All with swimming pools too.' Pet shook her head in wonder. 'It would be the life of Riley right enough.'

Lena had to agree.

Georgie was still finding it strange not having Ian around for most of the day, although he had now settled in at school and was doing well. Why, he was actually keen to get there in the morning because he was enjoying it so much. But it left a large hole in her life.

And then there was John working nights. Home during the day, but asleep in bed which meant she had to pad around quietly so as not to disturb him. Everything had gone topsy turvy in her world.

A glance at the clock told her it was time to put the dinner on as Ian would be back for it in a wee while. Several hours after that she'd have to feed John when he got up. It was a pain they couldn't eat together.

Crossing to the sink she began peeling potatoes, relishing the sunlight streaming through the window above the sink. The Indian summer was still continuing. It seemed as if it would go on for ever.

She smiled lovingly when she heard the sound of snoring coming from the bedroom. Within minutes John was giving it big licks.

Mary opened the door to find Lena standing there. She frowned. 'This is a surprise.'

'Am I welcome?'

'Of course. Come in and I'll put the kettle on.'

Lena stepped nervously into the hallway which was immaculate as usual, as would be the rest of the house. Even the tiniest speck of dust was never allowed to settle, Mary being obsessive about cleaning and polishing.

'So who sent you?' Mary challenged her as she filled the kettle. 'Mum or Papa?'

Lena blinked, having been caught off guard. 'No one,' she stuttered. 'I came of my own accord.'

Mary flashed her a look which plainly showed she didn't believe her, just as three-year-old Cora waddled into the room. She was a fat child, though Mary had always sworn in the past that she didn't overfeed her.

Lena smiled. 'You've grown since I saw you last.' Cora's response was to go and hide behind her mother's skirt.

'You just caught me,' Mary said. 'Another half an hour and I'd be gone. I have a meeting at the hall.'

Lena didn't reply to that. 'You're looking well,' she said instead.

'Am I?'

'I wouldn't have mentioned it otherwise.'

Mary ignored what she considered to be a jibe. 'I have a cake baked. Would you care for a slice?'

'What sort of cake?'

'Getting fussy in our old age, are we?' Mary riposted sharply.

Lena groaned inwardly. Talk about touchy! 'Not in the least. It's simply that there are some kinds of cakes I like, and others I don't. Surely you remember that?'

Mary now did, though she'd temporarily forgotten the fact. 'Pineapple upside down.'

'Oh, lovely!' Lena enthused. 'Yes please!'

'Cora have some too?'

Mary glanced down at her daughter and gave her an indulgent smile. 'I think you can, poppet. Go and sit at the table.'

Cora hurried to comply.

Lena looked round for Mary and James's elder child. 'Where's Rex?'

'Out playing somewhere. But he'll be home shortly to go with us to the meeting.' Mary added ominously, 'He knows better than to forget or be late.'

Poor little sod, Lena thought. It must be torture for children the age of Mary's to sit through interminable religious waffle. She felt for them.

'Did Mother tell you we ran into each other?' Mary asked.

'Yes she did. Buchanan Street, I believe she said.'

'And is that why you're here?'

Careful, Lena warned herself. 'In a way. I thought that if the mountain wouldn't come to Muhammad, then Muhammad better get her skates on.'

Mary had the grace to laugh. 'It has been a while.'

'Too long. We all miss you, you know.'

'Do you?'

33

'Yes, we do, Mary.'

'Even Papa?'

'Especially Papa. Don't forget, you were aye his favourite. Naturally he misses you.'

Mary produced the cake from a tin and began to slice it. One slice was larger than the other two, and she handed it to Cora, who immediately began wolfing it down. Mary had lied about overfeeding the child, Lena thought, if that slice of cake was anything to go by.

Mary snorted, a habit she had in common with her sister. 'That was a long time ago. Do you still take sugar in your tea?'

'Please.'

Mary poured boiling water into the teapot, then laid out cups and saucers.

'Can I say something without you flying off the handle?' Lena asked quietly.

'What?'

'You'd be more than welcome back home if you stopped spouting religion. Nobody expects you to change your beliefs. That's your affair. Just stop talking about it when you're with the family.'

Mary glared at Lena. 'Can't they understand I'm trying to save their souls?'

'Yes, they do. But your beliefs are you own, and theirs are theirs.'

'I wondered when you'd get round to religion,' Mary declared, eyes blazing. 'I just bloody well wondered.'

'Now don't lose your rag. Can't we talk sensibly about this?'

'I am talking sensibly, if only one of you would listen,' Mary replied hotly.

'Sensibly to you, perhaps. But not to us. Can't you accept that?'

'No, I can't!' Mary thundered. 'Nor will I ever give up on any of you. I don't want to see you cast into oblivion, or the fiery pits of hell. Not my own family, my own flesh and blood. I'll do everything in my power to make it otherwise.'

Lena, hearing the vehemence with which the vow had been delivered, felt that she'd failed in her task. But then she hadn't really expected anything else.

'More cake?' Cora asked, seemingly oblivious of the argument raging round her.

'You've had enough,' Mary snapped.

Tears filled Cora's eyes. 'Still hungry.'

'I said you've had enough. So be quiet.'

Just then Rex appeared, no one having heard him enter the house. Lena immediately wrinkled her nose in disgust.

'What's that smell?' Mary demanded.

He shrank in on himself, cowering away from his mother. 'I've had an accident,' he replied in a tiny voice. 'I got so excited playing I've done number twos in my pants.'

Forgetting all about tea and cake, Lena quickly made her excuses and fled.

Chapter 4

'Have you been happy doing the same job all your life, Papa?'
Tam paused in what he was doing to stare at his son in
surprise. 'What makes you ask that?'

'I was just wondering.'

Tam considered the question. 'I honestly don't know. I've never
actually thought about it.'

'You've always seemed happy enough to me,' Chrissie chipped
in.

'So there's your answer,' Tam declared to Tom.

'What put that into your head?' Chrissie queried.

Tom frowned, and took his time in replying. 'It just seems to
me that it must get boring, tedious even, being years and years
in the same job. Going through the same routine day after day,
that sort of thing.'

'Boring doesn't come into it,' Tam responded. 'My generation
are only too pleased to go through the same routine every day
because it means we're in work. Earning, able to look after our
families. There were many didn't have that luxury when I was
younger, and unemployment was rife.'

'True enough,' Chrissie agreed. 'Your papa was considered lucky
to get a start at McNair's. There were lots applied who didn't.'

'You've asked me if I'm happy with my job. Are you?' Tam said quietly.

'Oh aye. I enjoy it. And there's so much to learn. But what about twenty years from now? Or thirty, even? Will I still be enjoying it then? Or will I be wishing I'd been able to experience a bit more in life?'

'Like what, son?' Chrissie asked.

'Well, think about it, Mum. I was born and brought up in this house. Some day I'll probably get married and have a house of my own. A house, no doubt, quite close to here so I can walk to and from McNair's. Is my entire life to be just that? Living in the same area, going to McNair's day in day out? It doesn't seem . . . well, very much.'

Lena, sitting at the table, glanced up from the magazine that had been passed on to her from her friend Pet McQueen. 'Pet feels the same way,' she announced. 'She's considering going to Hollywood to try to be a film star.'

'Dear me!' Chrissie gasped, quite taken aback. 'Whoever gave her that idea?'

'No one. She dreamt it up herself.'

'Hollywood?' Tom mused.

'That's right. To try to be a film star,' Lena repeated.

Chrissie had a sudden alarming thought. 'You're not thinking of going with her, I hope?'

Lena smiled, and shook her head. 'I don't believe I'm exactly film star material, do you?'

Embarrassed, Chrissie glanced away. How could any female who looked like Lena possibly be a film star? She didn't reply.

'Mind you,' Lena went on, 'as Pet pointed out, there are lots of jobs in film studios that don't involve going in front of a camera. A make-up lady, for example.'

'So you are thinking of going?' Chrissie was appalled at the idea. Hollywood was so far away. Why, she'd probably never see her daughter again.

'Who knows?' Lena shrugged. 'Stranger things have happened.'

'Tam, you speak to her this minute. Put your foot down,' Chrissie appealed to him.

'I can't do that. She's old enough to know her own mind. She's not a bairn any more, and no longer under my jurisdiction. If she decides to go then I can't stop her.'

Chrissie opened her mouth to reply, then shut it again. This was terrible.

'They say you can pick a ripe orange or peach from a tree any time you like in California,' Lena continued. 'Imagine that?'

'And it's sunny every day of the week,' Tom added. 'I read that somewhere.'

Tam produced an old pipe and began filling it from an equally old leather pouch.

'Since when have you started on the pipe again?' Chrissie demanded. 'You haven't smoked that for ages.'

'Since today. I found myself missing it. Any objections?'

Chrissie shook her head. 'None at all. In fact, I rather like to see you with a pipe. It makes you look rather distinguished.'

Tam barked out a laugh. Distinguished? What a joke! Still, if that's how Chrissie saw him he wasn't about to disagree.

'You'll never go,' Tom declared to his sister.

'Why not?'

'You aren't the type.'

'And precisely what sort of type am I?' she asked, slightly cross.

'Not that type, and that's for certain. You're not brave enough to take such a leap into the unknown.'

'And you are, I suppose?' she snapped.

'Maybe.'

'Stop it, you two,' Tam admonished them. 'You're giving me a headache.'

'Sorry, Papa,' Tom apologised with a grin, knowing that they were doing no such thing. It was simply one of the things Tam said when he wanted someone to shut up.

Lena, after a final dirty look at Tom, returned to her magazine.

'It would be exciting, though, to go somewhere else for a

while,' Tom reflected aloud. 'Though I have to say California is a bit extreme.'

'And how long before you get bored, then?' Tam asked him, striking a match.

'Aye, how long?' Chrissie was worried. She'd be delighted when they both left home, but not if it meant their going to the far-flung corners of the world. That was something she hadn't anticipated for one moment.

'You're missing the point, Papa. I'm only talking about a bit of a change – an adventure, if you like. Not emigration or anything like that.'

'Then you'd come back and settle down?' Chrissie asked hopefully.

'I presume so.'

'And what if you meet someone while you're away and settle down there because she won't leave?' Tam smiled. 'That can happen.'

Tom didn't have an answer to that.

Lena was still fizzing inside. Not brave enough? What a cheek! How did Tom know what she was capable of? He didn't. He might think he did, but he didn't.

Chrissie picked up her knitting and got on with the pullover she was making for Tom. All this talk about California and the like had quite upset her.

Hollywood indeed! What a right load of nonsense.

'Oh, you're awake!' Georgie exclaimed, when she entered their bedroom to find John staring at the ceiling. 'I've brought you a cup of tea.'

'Thanks, darling,' John said, sitting up in bed and accepting the cup and saucer she handed him. 'I've been awake for ages, actually.'

'Then why didn't you get up? It's well past when you usually do.'

He sighed. 'I've had all the sleep I want, but I'm still tired. Bone weary, to tell the truth. So I just carried on lying here.'

Georgie regarded him with concern. 'It's working nights that's done it,' she said. 'It always upsets the system.'

'It's never made me like this before.'

Georgie racked her memory. He was right: it hadn't. There had been one terrible bout of constipation a few years previously, and an attack of boils before that, but never tiredness. 'Tell you what,' she declared. 'Why don't I go to the chemist's later on and get you a tonic. That might do the trick.'

'Good idea, Georgie. Let's just hope it does.'

'Are you going to get up now?'

He nodded. 'Once I've had this tea.'

'Then I'll get your meal on.'

She wished she could feed him on steak, she reflected as she returned to the kitchen. But, sadly, the price of that was beyond them. John earned a decent enough wage, but it didn't extend to sirloin. More's the pity.

Tom spotted her across the dance floor. Twinkletoes, whom he hadn't run into again since the night they'd danced together weeks and weeks ago. He immediately hurried over.

'Hello.' He smiled. 'Remember me?'

She stared blankly at him. 'Should I?'

His heart sank. Damn and blast, she'd forgotten. 'I was hoping you might. We had a few turns round the floor, but it was a while ago now.'

'Oh.'

He could see she still didn't recall him. 'Would you care to dance?' he asked rather formally.

'If you like.'

Hardly an encouraging reply, he thought. Hardly enthusiastic.

She mustn't get too excited, Georgie warned herself. But it did seem, on the face of it anyway, that she was two months gone. Pregnant again, after all this time.

Elation filled her, and a strange warm feeling she remembered only too well from when she was carrying Ian.

Her parents would be thrilled, she thought. Especially Chrissie, who was dead keen for her to have another child, and Chrissie another grandchild. Mary had given them two, of course, but they never saw Cora or Rex now that they were estranged from Mary. She knew how deeply that hurt the pair of them.

A little boy, or a girl? A girl would be nice, as she and John already had Ian. Oh, the fun she'd have with a wee lassie! Dressing her nicely, fussing with her hair, talking to her, eventually, about feminine things. Having another female in the house.

Georgie smiled broadly, guessing what John's reaction would be when she finally told him. He'd be ecstatic. Over the moon.

But she wasn't telling anyone yet. Not till she'd missed another period and was absolutely sure. Then John would be the first to know.

She gently rubbed her stomach. Yes, no doubt about it. A girl was her preference. But as long as all the baby's bits and pieces were in the right places that was the important thing.

'You really are a terrific dancer, Brigid.' Tom smiled at his partner.

'Thank you very much. You're not bad yourself.'

'Well, thank *you*.'

This was their fourth dance together. She had stayed up with him for that length of time, and as far as he was concerned it was a 'click'.

'Can I ask where you live?'

She stared up at him, being shorter than he. 'Why?'

He flushed slightly. 'Oh, I was just wondering if you were local.'

'You mean come from round here?'

'That's right.'

'Do you?'

'Not that far away. About a ten-minute walk.'

'Same for me.'

Good, he thought. He'd definitely try to lumber her later on. The number came to a finish and everyone on the floor applauded.

'Will you excuse me? I have to go to the ladies,' she said.

'Of course.'

She stared him straight in the eyes for a moment, then, turning, walked away.

Lovely figure, he mused as he left the floor. Quite the bobby-dazzler in his opinion. Taking up a position beside a pillar, he awaited her return.

'Someone's home early,' Chrissie commented on hearing the scrape of a key in the outside door. As it was a Saturday night, both Tom and Lena had gone out earlier.

It turned out to be Tom who was back. And in a bad humour, too, judging from his expression.

'What's up, son?' Chrissie asked.

'Nothing, Mum.'

'Would you like a dram?' Tam queried. 'There's plenty left.'

Tom shook his head. 'Thanks, Papa, but I won't if you don't mind.'

'I don't mind at all. It's all the more for me.'

'I think I'll go to bed,' Tom declared, not wanting to face the quizzing about his night at the dancing which was sure to take place.

Chrissie glanced at the clock. 'Aren't you feeling well?'

'I'm fine, Mum. Don't fash yourself. I just thought I'd have a read, that's all.'

'What's wrong with reading in here?'

'Leave him alone, woman,' Tam said. 'If he wants to read in his own room then let him do so.'

'We'll be having a wee bit supper in a minute or two,' Chrissie told him. 'I've got a tin of salmon in as a special treat. Shall I bring you through a couple of sandwiches?'

'No thanks, Mum. I'm not hungry. Goodnight now.'

'There's something up,' Chrissie declared after he had gone.

'If there is he obviously doesn't want to talk about it. Just let him be.'

'But—'

'I said let him be, Chrissie,' Tam interjected. 'Don't go on. Now why don't you get that supper you mentioned? Tom might not be hungry, but I am.'

Tom slumped on to his bed, not quite sure how he felt. Stupid? Probably. Let down? Without a doubt. And bloody angry too, if he was honest.

Just going to the ladies, she'd said. And he, like a right diddy, had stood there patiently waiting for her to re-join him. She never did.

After a while he'd gone looking. But she was nowhere to be found, which could only mean one thing. She'd bolted, leaving him in the lurch.

He'd liked her, too. A lot.

'Can't you put a sock in it!' James, Mary's husband, said to her in exasperation.

She regarded him with astonishment. It was rare for him, normally so mild-mannered, to have a go at her. 'What's got up your humph tonight?' she retorted.

James sighed. 'Sometimes a man wants just a bit of peace and quiet. Know what I mean? Which there isn't a lot of in this house.'

'I was only reading scripture to the children,' she declared coldly.

'Yet again and again,' he snapped. 'Can't you read them Little Red Riding Hood for a change? Or how about Cinderella?'

Mary's nose wrinkled in scorn. 'That's the most ridiculous suggestion I've ever heard.'

'Is it?'

'Yes, it probably is. Scripture is far more rewarding and instructive than those stupid stories. No value in them whatsoever.'

'But more entertaining I should say. They're only children, Mary. Let them have some childhood, for Pete's sake.'

Mary glared at him. It never entered her mind for one second that he might be right. Without a further word she turned her attention back to Cora and Rex and began reading from where she'd been interrupted.

James groaned, and rolled his eyes heavenwards. There was nothing else for it. He was off to the lavatory, in which sanctuary he groped in a pocket to produce a bar of Highland Toffee, his favourite. Sitting, he undid the wrapper, snapped off a piece and popped it into his mouth.

He didn't leave the lavatory again until he'd eaten the whole bar. Which made him feel a lot, lot better.

Lena glanced up from the ledger she was working on to see Hamish Murchison coming in her direction. When she noted he was carrying a ledger she knew what that probably meant.

So handsome, she reflected. And available too. If only . . . But she was only too horribly aware that she had no chance with such a good-looking chap. Pigs would fly first.

'I've come to ask a favour,' he said quietly on reaching her desk.

'The usual?'

'I'm afraid so. I just can't make these figures add up. I've been trying all morning, and failing miserably.'

'And you want my help?'

He leant closer. 'Please, Lena. You'd be saving my bacon. I'm in bad enough odour with old baldy as it is.' Old baldy was Mr Crerar, their head of department, who was, as his nickname suggested, bald as the proverbial coot.

'Have you ever considered changing jobs, Hamish?' Lena smiled at him. 'You're not really cut out for this one, are you?'

'It's just that you're so clever. Everyone says so. I doubt there's a ledger in the world, no matter how complicated, you couldn't make balance.'

'Flattery will get you everywhere.'

'So will you bail me out?'

Lena took the ledger from him. It was going to be a nuisance, as she had more than enough work of her own to be getting on with, but how could she refuse? One glance into those sexy blue eyes and she was lost. If she'd stood up she'd probably have found she was weak at the knees.

'Of course I will. Come back in an hour or two.'

'Thanks, Lena. You're a darling. I owe you yet again.'

She watched his retreating back, desperately wishing things were different. She'd been called clever Lena at school too, top of the class more often than not. But she'd happily have traded all her so-called cleverness for a new face any day. By God and she would.

'I've come over to apologise.'

Tom turned to find Brigid standing beside him. He couldn't help the scowl that came on to his face. 'Oh aye?'

'Were you cross with me?'

He shrugged.

'You were, then.'

He didn't reply.

'I'm sorry. Truly I am. But let me explain?'

She was pretty, he thought. The figure was as good as he remembered – and he remembered only too well. 'Go on.'

She glanced around. 'Can we find somewhere a little less crowded?'

Tom couldn't see why not.

'Over there,' she said, pointing, and moved off. He followed her. When they reached the quiet corner she'd indicated, she turned to face him.

'This is embarrassing,' she declared, and took a deep breath. 'I had an upset stomach last Saturday night. When I left you to go to the ladies I . . .' She took another deep breath. 'I had terrible diarrhoea.'

He was immediately sympathetic, his face softening.

'I was in there for absolutely ages,' she went on. 'Then, when I was finished, all I could think of was getting home as soon as possible in case there was a recurrence. My stomach really was giving me gyp. Griping like mad.'

'It must have been awful for you,' he said sincerely.

'It was. Believe me. Luckily it cleared up over the rest of the weekend and I was able to go back to work on Monday. So do you forgive me for being so apparently rude?'

'Completely.' He smiled.

'Leaving you standing has been on my conscience all week. I can only imagine what you must have thought of me.'

'Well, let's just say it wasn't very complimentary. I felt a proper charlie.'

Her smile matched his. 'I know it's not a woman's place to ask, but now that's out of the way do you want to dance?'

'With you? I can't think of anything I'd like to do more.'

Hooking an arm round hers, he led her on to the floor.

Her mouth was soft, and warm, and by far the nicest he'd ever kissed. It was sheer heaven.

'Hmm,' he murmured when it was over.

'I'd better go on up,' she whispered. 'It's late.'

'Just one more?'

'Just one then,' she agreed.

Magic, he thought when he finally left her to walk off down the street.

That's what she was. Magic.

Chapter 5

'This tea in bed business is becoming something of a habit,' Georgie teased John, who was wriggling into a sitting position.

'And one I rather like. Why, are you complaining?' he asked, tongue in cheek.

She handed him the cup and saucer. 'Not really.'

'Good.'

She stepped back a pace and studied him. 'That tonic I gave you has really worked wonders. You look healthier than you've done in years.'

'I feel it. And not a trace of tiredness when I shouldn't be feeling that way. I'm a new man.'

She leant forward and kissed him on the cheek. 'Hungry?'

'Starving, woman. I could eat a horse.'

She laughed. 'Well, I'll try to do better than that. How do sausages sound?'

'Wonderful.'

'With mash, peas and onion gravy.'

'Better still.'

'And lots of it.'

'Can't wait.' He patted the bed. 'Sit with me for a minute or two.'

She sat where he'd patted. 'Any news yet of you coming off nights?'

John shook his head. 'Afraid not. I'll have another month to do at least.'

She pulled a face.

'Can't be helped, darling. You know that.'

'Of course I do. It just turns things topsy turvy, that's all.'

'I was talking to one of the drivers the other night. Lucky bugger owns a cottage in the country.'

'How did he manage that?' Georgie queried in surprise. Drivers were well paid, but not that well!

'A relative died and left it to him. He and his family go there on holiday. The rest of the time he's only too pleased to let it out. Which made me wonder, why don't we take it? Next Easter, perhaps, when Ian's off school.'

The idea gripped her, filling her with excitement. 'Where-abouts in the country?'

'Perthshire, he said. It's lovely there, I believe.'

Georgie's eyes glowed with enthusiasm. A real holiday in the country would be absolutely fantastic and it would do them all the power of good to get away: away from Glasgow, though she loved it dearly, with all its smoke and grime; away from soot-blackened tenements stretching off in all directions; away from general heaving humanity and all that went with it.

Away from . . . And then it struck her. April? She did a quick mental calculation. No no, that was fine. April wasn't a problem.

'So, how about it?' John demanded.

'Oh, yes, please. If we can afford it, that is.'

'We'll manage somehow. It's just too good an opportunity to pass up.'

'Ian will love it,' Georgie said rapturously. 'Simply adore it.'

'I'll arrange time off well in advance,' John said. 'Shouldn't be too hard to organise. And of course we'll get there and back free on the railway. So that's a saving.'

Georgie beamed at him, and he beamed back.

'I think we should celebrate,' he suggested.

'How?'

'Why don't you take your clothes off and get into bed?'

'In the middle of the day?' she exclaimed, genuinely shocked.

'Why not?'

Why not indeed, she thought. There were no rules against it after all. And it would be rather exciting. Naughty, even.

'It's been a while,' John reminded her. 'Too long. This night shift nonsense has been getting in the way.'

She took his cup and saucer from him, and went back to the kitchen, where she removed various pots that had been slowly coming to the boil. Then she returned to the bedroom, stripped, and slipped in beside him.

'You're the best thing that's ever happened to me, Georgie,' he said softly, suddenly serious.

'And you me.'

Moments later they melted into one another.

'Take your time,' Chrissie admonished. 'You'll give yourself indigestion eating as quickly as that.'

'Sorry, Mum,' Tom apologised. 'But I'm going out, which is why I'm in a bit of a rush.'

Chrissie glanced at her husband. This was unusual, as Tom normally stayed in during the week. 'Can I ask where to?'

Tom coloured slightly. 'The pictures.'

'The pictures, eh?' Chrissie mused. 'I take it there's a lassie involved?'

'That's right.'

'What's her name?' Tam asked, amused at his son's obvious discomfiture.

'Does it matter what her name is?' Tom retorted, shifting uncomfortably on his chair. 'She's just a lassie I met at the dancing, that's all.'

'How mysterious,' Lena commented with a smile.

'There's nothing mysterious about it,' Tom replied hotly.

'Then why no name?'

Tom shot Lena a murderous glance. 'I don't pry into your affairs, so stop trying to pry into mine.'

'Now now, don't talk to your sister like that,' Chrissie rebuked him. 'She doesn't mean anything.'

'What's on anyway?' Tam enquired. He liked a good picture himself, though he didn't go all that often as Chrissie wasn't so keen.

'Don't know. We'll find out when we get there.'

'The back seats, of course,' Lena teased. 'Where all the winching couples go.'

Tom coloured again. 'Maybe,' he reluctantly admitted.

'Lots of kisses and cuddles, eh?'

'That's enough, Lena,' Chrissie chided her. 'Leave the lad alone. Can't you see you're embarrassing him?'

Tom hastily finished the little left on his plate. 'Can I leave the table, Papa? I want to get on.'

'You're excused.'

'Thanks. That was lovely, Mum. Thank you.' And with that he hurried from the room.

'Are you enjoying it?' Tom whispered.

'Oh aye, it's great.'

The film was *Safety Last* starring Harold Lloyd who, as usual, was performing all his own terrifying, death-defying stunts. Brigid gave a sudden gasp and her hand flew to her mouth as Lloyd looked as though he was about to topple from the roof of a skyscraper. A moment later she relaxed when he performed yet another amazing acrobatic feat to save himself.

Tom, whose own heart was pumping for reasons that had nothing to do with the film, curled an arm nonchalantly round Brigid's shoulders while he continued to watch the screen. He waited tensely to see if she'd object, but she didn't. There was not even a glance to acknowledge what he'd done.

Tom heaved a small sigh of relief. So far so good. The next step was kissing, which some of the other couples in the back row were already doing. He needn't have worried. Before he could make his next move she turned to face him, closing her eyes invitingly.

The night was a great success, and they agreed to meet up at the dancing the following Saturday.

'Oh no!' Georgie exclaimed softly, bending over in pain. A sharp pain had lanced through her stomach. 'Please, no.' Horribly aware of what was happening, she began to cry.

Through in the bedroom John started to snore.

'So was it a period or did you miscarry?' Chrissie queried, having heard Georgie's tale of woe.

Georgie shook her head. 'I honestly don't know, Mum. I mean, I couldn't rightly look in case . . .' She trailed off. 'I simply cleaned up without paying too much attention and came straight over.'

'You don't usually miss periods, do you?'

'No, never. That's why I was convinced I was pregnant. There again, there's always a first time, I suppose.'

Chrissie wished she had a little whisky or brandy in the house for Georgie. She could always nip out and get some. It wouldn't take long. 'Oh, Georgie,' she sighed. 'I'm so sorry.'

Not as sorry as she was, Georgie thought bitterly. She'd been so looking forward to having another child, to giving her parents another grandchild.

'Where's John now?'

'In bed asleep.' Georgie glanced at the clock. 'I can't stay too long, or Ian will be home for his dinner.'

'And John didn't know you were pregnant?'

'I was waiting to be absolutely certain before breaking the news. Just as well I didn't.'

'But you must tell him,' Chrissie urged.

'No, Mum. It would only upset him and I don't want that. You're not to say anything either, promise?'

'If you wish.'

'I do. Now promise.'

Chrissie nodded. 'I promise.'

Tears welled yet again in Georgie's eyes, and she attempted to brush them away with her hanky. 'I feel so terrible, Mum. So let down.'

'I can understand that. It must be awful for you.' Crossing to her daughter Chrissie raised her out of the chair she was sitting in and hugged her tight. 'You'll get over it,' she crooned. 'It'll just take time. You'll see.'

When Georgie was gone Chrissie broke down and cried herself. The world could be so cruel. She couldn't help but sit and think of the child she'd lost all those long years ago.

So very cruel.

'I've made up my mind. I am going to Hollywood,' Pet McQueen announced.

Lena studied her friend. They were in their favourite café having coffee, and Pet meant it all right. That was obvious from her expression. 'It'll cost you to get there. Won't be cheap.'

'I've already thought of that, and I'm going to start saving right away. I shall also be looking for a part-time job for evenings or weekends. The money from that will help.'

Lena's heart sank. If Pet succeeded in finding more work then she wouldn't be seeing her as much as she usually did. And Pet was her one and only close friend. The pair of them had been pals for years and years. 'I see,' she murmured.

Pet lit a cigarette. 'No more of these either. This is my last packet. They cost far too much anyway.'

'Any idea what sort of job you'll go after?'

Pet shook her head. 'Not yet. But I'll find something in the paper or on the grapevine.'

Pet's day job was in a large department store where she worked on the perfume counter. A glamorous job, Lena had always thought. Certainly far more glamorous than poring over ledgers all day long. That could be tedious, to say the least.

'Hollywood,' Pet mused, a faraway look in her eyes. 'It'll be fantastic.'

Lena regarded her with envy. No doubt it would be.

'So why don't you come along?' Pet demanded. 'Give it a go, same as me.'

Lena smiled. 'I must say I'm tempted. It would be a wonderful experience, if nothing else.'

'Does that mean yes?' Pet said excitedly.

'Not exactly. I'll certainly think about it, though.' This time her smile was rueful. 'My brother Tom says I haven't got the courage to up sticks and go abroad.'

'Nonsense!' Pet exclaimed. 'Of course you have. Don't listen to his prattling on. What does he knew?'

'I keep imagining those orange and peach trees you mentioned when we talked about this before.'

'What about them?'

Lena shook her head in amazement. 'The very idea seems out of this world.'

'Not out of this world.' Pet laughed. 'But in California where the sun shines all the time, and lots of men are loaded.' Her eyes gleamed. 'And when I say loaded, I mean exactly that.'

Not that she'd have much chance with one of those, Lena reflected. But the idea of a life in films, even behind the camera, was certainly very appealing.

'How will you get there?' she asked curiously.

'Boat from the Clyde to New York, I suppose,' Pet replied. 'Then train all the way across America. A long train ride, eh?'

'You can say that again.'

'It takes days, apparently. But eventually it arrives, and there you are. Bob's your uncle!'

Lena glanced out of the café window and saw that it was teeming down again. The Indian summer they'd had was long gone.

Oh, she was tempted all right. Truly tempted.

'Is something wrong?' John asked, watching Georgie making the sandwiches he'd take with him on duty.

Ian was sitting on the floor playing with an array of ancient lead soldiers, most of them missing paint and otherwise damaged in some way. He adored his soldiers and liked nothing more than to play 'battles'. It was his dream that one day he'd have a toy fort to go with them. In the meantime he made do with a cardboard box.

'No,' Georgie replied, looking over. 'Why?'

'It's just . . . well, you've seemed a bit down in the dumps lately. Nothing to do with me, I hope?'

'Of course not, silly.'

He hesitated. 'So, what is bothering you?'

She couldn't tell him about the baby she'd lost, knowing how much it would upset him. She'd convinced herself since the event that she had miscarried and it hadn't simply been a late, and extremely heavy, period.

'Nothing. Nothing at all.'

'Then why the long face?'

She shrugged. 'I wasn't aware I've had one.'

He stared at her in concern, wondering if it had just been his imagination? No, it hadn't been. She'd definitely been out of sorts for the past few weeks. Not at all her usual cheery self. 'Maybe you should prescribe yourself a tonic as you did for me?'

Georgie smiled at him. 'Maybe I will. Certainly wouldn't do me any harm.'

'Buck you up perhaps.'

'The fact this is your last night duty will buck me up more than anything.'

'Aye.' A warm feeling swept through him. 'My last night. Back to normal Monday morning. I can't wait.'

She glanced at Ian and saw he was absorbed with his game. 'Neither can I. It gets lonely in that bed when you're on your own.'

John couldn't have agreed more.

'I start next Wednesday night,' Pet finished triumphantly.

'As a cocktail waitress?' Lena sounded as astonished as she felt.

'That's right. Wednesday, Thursday and Friday straight from

work. Saturdays start at six till the finish. Good money, too –
plus tips. Apparently there are lots of those.'

'You really have landed on your feet.' Lena said. 'But what
about food? If you go to this nightclub straight from work when
will you eat?'

'You're forgetting we have a canteen at the store. I'll just eat a
lot more at dinnertime there and that'll see me through. I'll possibly
be able to grab a sandwich or something at the club, but I'll have
to wait and find out. I forgot to ask about that at the interview.'

'Well well,' Lena mused, highly delighted for her friend.

'I have to wear a costume which is skimpy to say the least.
All revealing legs and upthrust bust.'

Pet hardly needed the latter, Lena thought, her bust being
the more than generous size it was. Unlike Lena's own modest
endowment.

'I'll have my fare saved in no time,' Pet enthused. 'Particularly
if the tips are as good as I was told.'

'The club must be frequented by toffs,' Lena guessed.

'So I believe. Rich toffs, too, at the prices it charges. Talk
about daylight robbery!'

'That expensive, eh?'

'When I say daylight robbery I mean precisely that. I'm just
surprised they don't have the waitresses wearing black masks and
carrying horse pistols.'

They both laughed.

On her way home Lena realised she was envious as hell.
Absolutely pea green with it.

Georgie glanced over at Ian, fast asleep in his recessed bed. The
wee soul had pleaded to stay up and see the New Year in with
them and she had agreed, knowing full well he'd never last that
long. He'd done well though, and it had been nearly ten before
John had lifted him from where he'd dozed off and slipped him
under the sheets.

'Only a few minutes to go,' John commented, looking at the
clock. 'I'd better pour us a drink.'

'Lemonade with mine, don't forget.'

He smiled lovingly at her. 'How could I forget how my wife likes her whisky after all these years of marriage?'

Georgie lit a cigarette while John did the honours. 'Ta,' she murmured when he handed her a glass.

'I wonder what the new year will bring?' he mused.

'Who knows?'

'Happiness and prosperity, I hope.'

'We already have the happiness, John. And we don't do too badly on the money front. Better than many.'

'True,' he agreed.

Another baby, Georgie thought. If she could have a wish granted that's what it would be. A little girl. Bonny as a picture.

Somewhere bells rang out. The new year had arrived. They stared at one another, then John raised his glass in a toast. 'Here's to us in 1925, lass.'

'Us in 1925,' she echoed.

They both drank.

'Now how about a kiss?' he suggested.

'Why stop there?' she teased.

John laughed, laid his glass aside and took her into his arms. The ensuing kiss was long and deep.

'I do love you,' she whispered when it was finally over.

'And I you.'

'Do you think we'll have any first foots?'

'It isn't likely.'

'Then why don't we drink up and go on through?'

Which is precisely what they did.

Chapter 6

Every Sunday morning Tam went for a walk along the banks of the nearby canal. It was something he'd been doing for years. On this particular Sunday Lena had asked to accompany him, which she'd never done before.

It was a bitter January day with the hint of snow in the air. Both of them were wrapped up warm.

'So what do you want to talk about?' Tam enquired as they strolled along.

'What makes you think I want to talk about anything?'

'Why else would you want to come with me? I can't think of any other reason.'

'Perhaps I just like being with you,' she teased.

He smiled. 'Pull the other one, Lena. I'm not daft, you know.'

'I didn't think you were.'

He halted and lit his pipe. 'So, what's on your mind?' he asked as they continued on their way.

'You remember I told you Pet McQueen is going to America? Hollywood actually. She's saving every penny for the fare.'

He nodded. 'I remember.'

'She's dead keen for me to go with her.'

Tam's eyes slid sideways to fasten on his daughter. 'Do you wish to?'

'I have to admit it's tempting, Papa. It would be a whole new world for me.'

'Aye, it would that,' he agreed.

'And what is there for me here? Not a lot. A boring old job . . .'

'Which you're good at,' he interjected.

'But that's not the point. It's still boring, good at it or not. And it's not as if there are any prospects. I'm a woman, don't forget. Being a ledger clerk is as high as I can get in the company.'

'Which is a pity,' Tam murmured. 'You've a good brain in your head. You could go far if they'd let you.'

'But they won't – as you well know. Only men can progress further up the ladder. It's the same in most fields.'

'Do you think you could do better in Hollywood?' Tam asked slowly.

'There are certainly opportunities there, the Americans being more progressive than us. And if I did get into the film industry, behind the scenes that is, then anything's possible.'

'Where did you get this information?'

'Magazines mainly,' she admitted. 'Pet buys lots and always passes them on. You've seen me reading them.'

'And you believe everything in there is gospel?'

'Of course not, Papa. I'm sure some of the stories are exaggerated. But there must be a core of truth in those articles. It can't all be baloney.'

He considered that. 'It seems to me that magazines are a rather flimsy basis on which to change your entire life. Don't you agree?'

Reluctantly she did.

'If you were to ask me for advice,' he went on, 'I'd look into this more thoroughly. Do some proper homework on the subject. I've no idea how you'd go about that, but you'll find a way.'

Lena had to admit it was good advice. 'You're right, Papa. I will.'

'Fine.'

'Let's say I do the homework and still decide to go. How would you and Mum feel about it?'

Tam stopped and put another match to his pipe, which was in danger of going out. 'Well, your mother wouldn't be best pleased for a start. In fact she'd be downright devastated.'

Lena's face fell, although it was more or less what she'd expected to hear. 'And you, Papa?'

'The same,' he said quietly.

They walked a little way in silence before Tam spoke again. 'Parents expect their children to grow up and move out. That's perfectly normal. What they don't expect them to do is leave not only the family home, but the country as well. To go so far away they might be on the moon for all it matters. Perhaps never see them again.'

'I know,' Lena murmured.

'But it's your life to do with as you wish,' Tam continued. 'That's your right. What you mustn't do is let your mother and me hold you back, no matter what the pain involved. If you want to go, then you must. All I ask is that you think long and hard before reaching a decision.'

Lena took a deep breath. 'I will, Papa. I promise.'

Tam stopped again and looked out over the canal. 'I swear that water gets filthier by the week. God help anyone who ever falls in and swallows any. It would kill them stone cold dead.'

Lena took her father by the hand and squeezed it. 'Thanks, Papa.'

John placed the blade of his shovel on the footplate and used it for support as he sucked in breath after breath.

Willie Winning, his driver, frowned at him. 'What's up, John?'

'Came over all funny there for a moment or two. My head spun, and I was suddenly short of breath.'

'That's unlike you.' Willie continued to frown.

John straightened and ran the sleeve of one arm over his face and eyes. 'It must be age,' he joked. 'I'm getting old.'

'Nonsense, man. You're not even thirty yet. *I'm* old. Fifty-eight last birthday.'

'And don't look a day over seventy!'

'Get away with you! None of your cheek, now.'

John grinned. He and Willie were good mates, having often worked together. 'Cheek, me? Never!' he protested.

Willie smiled. 'Only another half-hour and we'll be back in Glasgow and knocking off. Not long to go then.'

Using his shovel John tipped open the fire door and began heaving more coal inside, the breathlessness forgotten.

'The tips are brilliant,' Pet McQueen enthused. It was the first time she had seen Lena since she'd started at the Green Slipper Club. 'Why, only last week this old chap had a good feel of my arse, then gave me a fiver for the privilege.'

'A fiver!' Lena exclaimed in awe.

'A nice crisp white one. Of course the customers aren't supposed to take liberties, but he or anyone else can feel my arse any time for a fiver. Darn tootin'!'

Lena laughed. 'Tell me more?'

'Usually the tips are in the region of a couple of bob, or half a crown. Occasionally you get a ten bob note, and once in a while a quid. It soon adds up, I can tell you. And the tips are on top of my wages, which are bloody good to start with.'

'And the customers, what are they like?'

'All sorts really. But all well off. They have to be to be able to afford that place. As I said to you before, it's damned expensive.'

'You're enjoying yourself, then?'

'Immensely. It certainly knocks selling perfume into a cocked hat.'

Lena could well believe that, thinking of the drudgery of her own job, the never-ending entries that had to be made, the columns that had to be added. 'Do you get any single men there?' she asked. 'I mean younger ones?'

'A few. Not many. Mainly they come with their girlfriends or wives on a night out. You know the sort of thing.'

'I can imagine.' It was all she could do, as she'd never been asked out by a member of the opposite sex. Not once. 'What about the clothes these females wear?'

'Expensive, like the prices. There was one woman the other night in an emerald green dress which was simply stunning. Rather short and showing quite a lot of cleavage, which I thought a bit daring. She certainly got a lot of admiring glances.' Pet described the dress in detail, down to the seed pearls that had been sewn into its waist.

'Gosh,' Lena murmured.

'She was very pleasant, too, when I spoke to her. Some of them turn their noses up at you because you're a waitress, but not her.'

Lena watched as Pet lit up. 'I thought you were stopping smoking?'

'I intended to before I realised how much money I'd be earning. Absolute pots, darling. Absolute pots.'

Lena laughed at the upper-class accent her friend had affected. Not a bad impression, she thought. Pet might have talent as an actress after all.

'Still intending to go to Hollywood?'

'You bet. Soon as possible too. Once I have enough cash it'll be toodle-oo! I'm on my way.' Pet eyed Lena speculatively. 'Any further thoughts on that yourself?'

'Well, one thing's certain: I won't be going with you. I'd never be able to save enough in time, not the way you're raking it in.'

'We could still meet out there though,' Pet declared. 'You having followed on later like.'

'There's always that possibility.' Lena smiled. She wondered what it would be like to have a man feel your backside? Rather nice, she decided. Even if he was old.

John was washing at the sink, having just come off shift, when Georgie exclaimed and pointed at his arm. 'How on earth did you get that bruise? It's massive.'

'What bruise, darling?' he asked, turning to face her.

'That one there.'

He glanced down to where she was pointing, and frowned. Georgie was right, it was a big one. 'No idea,' he declared, shaking his head. 'I must have banged it without realising.'

Georgie went over to him. 'Is it sore?'

He touched it gingerly. 'A little. Though I haven't felt it up until now.'

'You'll have to be more careful, John,' she chided. 'I can't have you coming home all black and blue.'

'I'm hardly that.'

'It must have been some whack,' Georgie commented.

'Well, anyway, there's nothing to be done but let it heal of its own accord. Now, what's for tea?'

Tom gaped at the scene which met his eyes. Brigid had persuaded him to a different dance hall from the one he normally used, but she hadn't mentioned this.

There were only four members to the band: brass, piano, drums and vocalist, and the number they were playing – albeit Tom didn't know it at the time – was 'Livery Stable Blues'.

'It's jazz,' he breathed.

'Have you never heard jazz before?' Brigid asked, smiling.

'Once or twice. It's very different.'

'It's meant to be. Quite a change from the traditional stuff you're used to, eh?'

Tom could only agree. Quite different indeed. He studied the dancers, the steps unlike anything he knew.

'I've been coming here for a while,' Brigid told him. 'That's why I wasn't at the other place every Saturday night.'

'Well, the waltz and foxtrot it certainly isn't.'

Brigid laughed. 'You'll soon pick it up. I'll teach you.'

'Are those women supposed to be flappers?'

'They're not supposed to be. They are.'

Most of the dresses on view were skimpy and exuberant. Some had long fringes, many were worn with ropes of gaudily coloured beads. A number of the women sported narrow bandeaux across their foreheads.

The men's attire was varied. Lounge suits were in evidence, such as Tom was wearing, which put him at his ease as he wouldn't stand out. But to his amazement a scattering of men had on sleeveless jerseys atop plus-fours, while a few were clad in Oxford bags which he thought looked truly hideous.

'It's more like a carnival than anything else,' he commented wryly.

'The Bright Young Things is what the *Daily Mail* calls them,' Brigid informed him. 'They're all the rage.'

The number came to an end, and almost instantly the band swung into a new one, this time the 'Dixie Jazz Band One-step'.

'Do you fancy having a go?' Brigid queried. 'And don't worry, I'll talk you through it.'

'I don't want to look a fool,' Tom replied, uncertain.

'You won't. Don't forget we've all got to learn.'

'But so publicly?'

'I'm telling you, it won't matter.'

'All right then,' he agreed, following her on to the floor.

At the end of the night he had to admit he'd thoroughly enjoyed himself, while Brigid complimented him on how quickly he'd picked up many of the steps.

'What's all this?' Chrissie demanded as Tam and Tom came through the door carrying a large, boxlike object.

'What does it look like?' Tam replied sarcastically. 'It's a wireless set.'

'Dear me.' Chrissie gasped. 'Where did you get it?'

Tam gave her a fly wink. 'Ask no questions, get no lies. Understand, woman?'

She was shocked. 'Do you mean it's stolen?'

The two men placed the wireless on top of the kitchen table. 'Not at all,' Tam lied. 'Somebody at work owed me a favour and gave it to me to sort of pay that off.'

'Oh!' Chrissie exclaimed, believing him.

Tam had told Tom the same story, but after the incident of the scrap metal Tom wasn't so naive as to take that explanation at its face value. However, he'd said nothing to the contrary, but given the impression of accepting what his father had said.

'Now, where shall we put it?' Tam wondered, glancing round.

When Lena returned from work she was amazed to be greeted by the evening news when she entered the kitchen. It distracted her for a little while, but after tea she fell to brooding again on what had happened at work that day.

She had spotted Hamish Murchison making in her direction and was relieved to note he wasn't carrying a ledger. She had more than enough on her plate as it was.

'How are you today?' He was beaming as he reached her desk.

'Fine. Yourself?'

'In the pink, actually.'

'Oh?'

'You might congratulate me.' He was still beaming.

She had no idea what he was on about. 'Why should I do that?'

'Haven't you heard?'

Lena shook her head. 'About what?'

'I've been promoted into a junior management position, starting next month. A rung up the ladder and more money to boot.'

She stared at him. 'Junior management?'

'That's right.'

She was incredulous. The man was incompetent, to say the least. Why, it wasn't that long ago she'd suggested he find himself another job as he was absolutely useless in the one he had. Now he'd been promoted!

'Well?' he prompted.

'Congratulations,' she replied through gritted teeth.

'Thank you, Lena. I appreciate that.'

He had a few more words with her and then went blithely on his way, while she stared daggers at his retreating back. If anyone should have been promoted it was she. But there was fat chance of that, being a woman.

Bitterness churned inside her, and she actually felt sick. How unfair it all was. How bloody unfair! She might not have minded so much if it had been someone deserving of promotion. But Hamish Murchison!

It wasn't till later she found out Hamish belonged to the same golf club as the chairman, and that the two of them regularly had cosy little chats in the clubhouse, where Hamish had no doubt indulged in some serious brown-nosing.

The news had completely ruined the rest of her day. And now it set her thinking, yet again, about Hollywood, and America in general.

'Look, Mum. Look!' Ian exclaimed excitedly, and pulled Georgie towards the window of a toy shop they were passing.

His eyes grew wide as he stared at the fort on display. It was a cracker, festooned with gaily coloured knights and men-at-arms.

'Very nice.' Georgie smiled, eyeing the price. Nice it might be, but it certainly wasn't cheap.

Ian's mind was racing, imagining himself playing with the fort, and all the fun he would have.

She must speak to John, Georgie decided. He'd said ages ago he'd make a fort for the lad, but had simply never got round to it. She must remind him. On the other hand, Ian's birthday was on the horizon. Perhaps they could buy this one and give it to the lad. Expensive, yes. But maybe they could stretch that far.

She'd have a word later that evening.

'He offered me twenty quid to sleep with him.'

'My God,' Lena exclaimed. 'Someone actually propositioned you?'

'The same old chap who felt my arse. Said we could do it in a swish hotel he'd choose. Bold as brass he was.'

'You turned him down, of course?'

'Of course,' Pet replied indignantly. 'What do you take me for? I wouldn't consider such a thing for a single moment.'

Lena, noticing a glint in her friend's eyes, wasn't sure she believed that. 'Did you report him to your boss?'

Pet shook her head. 'He'd have been barred, which would have been a pity. He's rather a pleasant old coot.'

'Married?'

'He doesn't wear a wedding ring. At least, not in the club. Though who knows? Not all men do, and anyway he might take it off on coming in.'

Twenty pounds, Lena mused. An awful lot of money when you thought about it. It would certainly have boosted Pet's savings, if it hadn't been completely out of the question. You only slept with a man when you were married and he was your lawful husband.

'I still don't mind him feeling my arse though,' Pet said, and giggled. 'As long as I get a fiver afterwards. As far as I'm concerned he can have a good grope any time he likes.'

Lena wasn't at all sure she approved of that. But she could see Pet's point. 'How's the bankbook coming along?' she enquired.

'Handsomely. At a rate of knots. In fact so well I've decided to stay on at the club to make enough to have something solid behind me when I go to the States.'

Lena nodded her approval. 'Good idea.'

'It's so when I arrive there I won't have to rush into anything but will be able to take my time. Where I decide to live, for example. That kind of thing.'

Lena wished she could get a job at the Green Slipper Club and do as well as Pet. But that was a non-starter. They'd never employ anyone with a face like hers. They wanted to attract customers, not scare them away.

'I was wondering . . .' Pet began, and trailed off.

'Wondering what?'

'If he'll up his offer. Twenty-five, thirty. Possibly more. It depends how much he fancies me.'

'Pet!' Lena exclaimed.

'Oh, don't worry,' Pet replied hastily. 'I wouldn't take him up on it. Not even for a hundred quid. I'm just curious, that's all.'

'Well let it stay that way. I don't want to be friends with an immoral woman.'

Pet laughed.

'What's so funny?'

'You saying "an immoral woman". You sounded just like a minister preaching in church. Though God knows, it's been a long long time since I was in one of those.'

'Have you been to the consulate yet to get your immigration forms?'

'Actually, I have. Spoke to a nice bloke there who was very helpful. Explained the forms to me in detail.'

'When do you intend lodging them?'

'Shortly. When I get round to filling them in. The chap told me it can take a while for an application to be processed.'

On her way home Lena thought about their conversation, and Pet's being propositioned by a customer.

She hated to admit it, but why didn't she entirely believe that Pet had turned him down? Or would in the future should the stakes be raised?

She was ashamed of herself for thinking that. But, sadly, she did. Though she'd never find out the truth of the matter. Not in a million years.

Chapter 7

'Just smell that air!' Georgie enthused. 'So clean and pure it almost makes me dizzy.' They were on holiday at the cottage in Perthshire belonging to John's railway colleague.

'It is that,' John agreed.

'Chalk and cheese compared to Glasgow air. No comparison whatsoever.'

'Well, there are no chimneys belching smoke here,' John pointed out. 'Industrial and otherwise.'

'The water's the same. Pure as can be.'

He smiled. 'So you're enjoying yourself then?'

'You know I am. And you?'

'Having a whale of a time. I honestly believe I could stay on for ever. Except I have to go back to work and bring in the pennies.'

Georgie glanced out of the window she was standing in front of. 'I don't know if I could live here. I think I'd miss the bustle of Glasgow too much. Not to mention my family and friends.'

'Aye, there is that.'

Georgie spotted Ian playing amongst a stand of trees. There was no doubt he was loving it, even if he didn't have any of his wee pals to play with. Still, both she and John had tried to fill in for the missing friends and played with him quite a lot. They'd also taken him for long walks, including one to a nearby loch where John had constructed a simple fishing rod for him to try to catch brown trout. Success would have been unexpected, as the hook was in reality just an open safety pin with a worm on it, but Ian had thoroughly enjoyed himself none the less, which was the main thing.

'Do you mind if I go to the village pub for a couple of pints?' John asked. The village was about a quarter of a mile away.

'Not at all. I'll get dinner started while you're there.'

John's face lit up. 'Say an hour?'

'Fine by me.'

'Shall I bring a couple of bottles back for us to have later?'

'Why not? I'd like that.'

Just then the door burst open and Ian flew in. 'I came across a deer in the woods!' he exclaimed. 'Honestly I did. A real live deer. When it saw me it ran away.'

Both John and Georgie laughed. 'Ran away, eh?' John repeated.

'That's right, Dad. It sort of wiggled its ears and then ran off.'

'Well well.' Georgie smiled. 'You have had an adventure. That'll be something to tell them when you return to school.'

Ian's eyes gleamed. 'Miss Hamilton might ask me to stand up in front of the class and tell them about it.'

'Will that bother you?' John asked out of curiosity. Basically a shy man, he would certainly have hated being asked to do something similar.

'Oh no,' Ian replied. 'I've stood up and told a story before.'

'About what?' Georgie queried.

'Engines. Dad's told me lots about them and I just repeated what he said.'

That amused John, as it did Georgie. He ruffled Ian's hair, then made for the open door. 'Won't be long,' he said, giving them both a small wave.

'Can I come, Dad?'

''Fraid not, son. I'm off to the pub and you're not allowed in there.'

Ian turned to Georgie.' When will I be allowed, Mum?'

'Not for years and years yet. Not until you're eighteen.'

Ian's face fell. 'That's old.'

Georgie had to smile. 'Not too old, I can assure you.'

'I wish I was eighteen now,' Ian declared.

'Don't wish your life away, son. Life's short enough as it is. Eighteen'll come round soon enough, you'll see.'

He wasn't at all convinced.

'You've been going out with this lassie quite a while now,' Chrissie said to Tom one evening.

'That's right, Mum.'

'And we still don't even know her name. Is it a secret or something?'

Tom squirmed in his chair. 'No secret.'

'Then why won't you tell us?'

'Yes, why won't you tell us?' Lena chimed in.

Tom shot his sister a murderous look. 'You keep your nose out of what doesn't concern you. Hear?'

'My my.' Lena smiled. 'We are touchy.'

'I'm nothing of the sort.'

Lena raised an eyebrow. 'No?'

Tam glanced up from his newspaper. 'Will you two stop it?'

Lena gave a twisted smile. 'Sorry, Papa.'

'Tom?'

'Sorry, Papa.'

Lena lit a cigarette, her eyes dancing with merriment.

'I thought you might like to bring her to tea one evening,' Chrissie said casually after a few seconds' silence. 'It's high time we met her.'

Tom was acutely aware of Lena watching him, waiting for his answer. God, how his sister irritated him on occasion. He knew only too well she did it on purpose.

'I'll mention it to her,' he replied evasively.

'Has she got horns or something?' Chrissie smiled, attempting to be funny.

'Of course not, Mum. She's just an ordinary lassie, that's all.'

'Without a name,' Lena teased, which earned her a disapproving look from Tam.

'I said I'll mention it. Now can we please leave it at that?'

Chrissie rose from her chair. 'I think I'll put the kettle on. Who's for a cup of tea?'

They were on one of their walks when John suddenly came up short. 'Hang on a minute, Georgie, till I catch my breath.'

She stopped to stare at him in concern. It was not the first time this had happened. Going to him, she put an arm round his waist, noticing how pale he was. 'Are you all right?'

'Just a bit breathless. Nothing to worry about.'

She gestured towards a fallen tree. 'Can you make it over there for a sit-down?'

'What's wrong, Dad?' an anxious Ian wanted to know.

'Wheesht now,' Georgie admonished him. 'There's nothing wrong.'

'Then why's Dad all bent over?'

Georgie ignored that as she helped John to the tree, where he slumped on to the trunk.

'Came on without warning,' he said eventually, voice rasping in his throat.

'Maybe you're smoking too much?' Georgie suggested.

'Aye, it could well be that. I must cut down.' He gulped in several more breaths. 'That's better now.'

'Are you sure?'

'Stop fussing, woman. I tell you I'm fine.'

He didn't look it, she thought. Was the light playing tricks or did he have the start of dark bags under his eyes?

'We'd better get back,' she said.

'Nonsense. We'll go on.'

Georgie glanced up at the sky where, thankfully, ominous clouds had appeared. 'I think it might rain and I don't want us all to get soaked. Especially Ian. It would be a shame to end his holiday with a stinking cold.'

John could see the sense in that. 'Right, home it is then,' he declared, coming to his feet.

They had just reached the cottage and gone inside when the heavens opened.

'What do you think?'

Lena gaped at her friend, who'd turned up to their meeting wearing the most beautiful fur coat. 'My God,' she breathed. 'Where did you get that?'

'Bought it, of course.'

'It must have cost a fortune.'

Pet laughed. 'It's musquash by the way. Like?'

Lena could only shake her head in wonder and admiration. 'It's gorgeous, Pet. Absolutely gorgeous. I'd die for a coat like that.'

'I was told it suited my colouring. Do you agree?'

Lena's mind was whirling. Women like them didn't go out and buy fur coats. It was unheard of. Fur coats were for the rich. 'Yes, I do. It certainly does. But where did you get the money from?'

'My savings, naturally.'

'Your savings?' Lena was incredulous.

'I've told you how much I'm making in tips at the club. I'm coining it.'

'Even so . . .' Lena trailed off. A fur coat. Bloody hell! 'What about Hollywood? I thought you were saving up to go there?'

'I still am,' Pet protested. 'But I got to thinking, wouldn't it be better if I arrived there with a decent wardrobe in tow. That way I'll hopefully make an instant impression with the casting directors. The people who hire and fire actors and actresses.'

That sounded reasonable to Lena. A good idea, actually.

'As regards the coat, I didn't pay anything like the retail cost. I got it trade and a discount on top as well. It was just too good an opportunity to pass up.'

'And how did you manage that?' Lena asked.

'The little man who feels my arse turned out to be a furrier.

We got chatting one night and he said if I dropped by his shop he'd see what he could do for me. So I did.'

Lena was beginning to smell a very large rat. In her experience people rarely did something for nothing. There was usually a price to be paid. 'And what did you do for him?'

'Nothing at all. I swear.'

Lena looked into Pet's eyes but couldn't see any duplicity there. Either she was telling the truth or she was going to be very good at the profession she intended getting into.

'Not a thing?'

Pet smiled. 'Well, a little bum feel on the way out each time I went there. But where's the harm in that?'

Lena reached across and ran a palm down the fur. As she'd said, it was gorgeous. 'I'm envious,' she admitted.

Pet was delighted. 'Can't you just imagine me parading down Hollywood Boulevard wearing this? Wow, eh?'

'You'll look sensational, and no mistake.'

Pet almost purred with pleasure. 'Now what have you been up to since I saw you last?'

Lena gave her a wry smile. 'Well, certainly not buying myself a fur coat.'

'Come on, wake up. You can't still be tired.'

John yawned. 'What time is it?'

Georgie told him.

'I am getting lazy, aren't I?'

'You can say that again. I've never known you spend so much time in bed.'

'It's the air.' He smiled. 'I'm just not used to it.'

Georgie noticed that the dark bags under his eyes were even more pronounced than they had been, which was worrying. And another bruise had appeared only the other day, this one on his back. Again he'd said he must have knocked himself without realising.

'Will you do me a favour, John?'

'Name it.'

'Will you go and see the doctor when we get home?'

He frowned at her. 'What ever for?'

'Something's not right. You just haven't been yourself for a while now. It's beginning to worry me.'

He took one of her hands in his and gently squeezed it. 'There's nothing wrong, Georgie. I've been a bit off colour, that's all. I'll be right as rain again before you know it.'

'Maybe so,' she conceded. 'But I'd be a lot happier if you went and spoke to the doctor. Please?'

He decided to humour her. Where was the harm in visiting the doctor? None that he could see, apart from the waste of time it would undoubtedly be. 'All right,' he agreed.

'Good. Now, are you going to get up for your cup of tea, or shall I bring it through?'

'I'll get up,' he replied.

'Then I'll go and pour.'

He swung his feet out of bed after she'd left him. It was their last day at the cottage and they'd had a wonderful time. If they could afford it he'd bring them back the following year, he promised himself. That would be something to look forward to.

Lena was cutting Chrissie's hair, which she did every month or so. Although completely untrained she showed great skill where hair was concerned. Tam and Tom were both working late on a big project which had a deadline to meet.

'Have you seen Pet McQueen recently?' Chrissie asked.

Lena stepped back to appraise what she'd done so far. 'Only the other night, as a matter of fact. You'll never guess what she's gone and bought herself?'

'What's that?'

'A musquash fur coat.'

'Dear me,' Chrissie breathed, visibly impressed.

'She's earning pots of money at this club where she's cocktail waitressing. She says the tips are fabulous.'

'They must be if she can afford a fur coat.'

Lena decided not to elaborate on the story. It was best her mother didn't know about the furrier.

'Is she still intending to go to America?'

'So she says.'

Chrissie hesitated, then asked casually, 'And what about you? Have you made any decisions yet?'

Lena stopped to stare at the back of her mother's head. The question might have sounded casual but she knew there was a lot more to it than that.

'No decisions yet, Mum,' she said softly.

'Will you make your mind up soon?'

'I honestly don't know. What I do know is if I do decide to go it will take me ages to save up for my fare.'

'I see,' Chrissie murmured.

'I promise you one thing, though. When I do make up my mind, one way or the other, you'll be the first to be told. All right?'

'All right, lass. Thank you.'

John breezed into the kitchen carrying various lengths of wood which he placed on the table.

'Well?' Georgie demanded anxiously.

'Fit as a fiddle. The doctor said there was absolutely nothing wrong with me and that you've been worrying about nothing.'

Georgie frowned. 'Did he examine you?'

'Oh aye, the full stethoscope thing. Front and back.'

'What's the wood for, Dad?'

John beamed down at his son. 'Guess what? I'm going to make you a fort – a real humdinger of a fort. But before I start it you and I are going to sit down together and design it.'

'Oh, Dad!' Ian exclaimed, almost beside himself with excitement.

'Was it old Dr McCulloch you saw?' Georgie was still frowning.

'No. He retired recently, apparently. It's a new chap now, Dr Corrie. Young, but seemed to know his stuff. I found him quite affable and easy to talk to, which Dr McCulloch wasn't always, if you recall.'

'And he didn't find anything at all wrong with you? Come on, John, be honest.'

'He did advise I cut down smoking. Just as you did when we were away.'

'Nothing else?'

'No. And that's the God's truth.'

'So how did he explain the breathlessness, the bruising and the bags under your eyes?'

'He didn't. Simply said I was in perfect health, and that was that.'

'You did tell him about those things, didn't you?' she persisted.

'Of course.'

'And he still said there was nothing wrong with you?'

'He did. Now will you please stop fussing. The doctor wouldn't be wrong now, would he?'

'Did you also mention the tiredness?'

John let out an exasperated sigh, not wanting to admit he'd forgotten about that. 'Yes,' he lied.

Georgie stared at him, perplexed. She'd been so certain that something was wrong, but it would seem she'd been worrying unnecessarily.

'Now, we need paper and a couple of pencils,' John declared, turning to a hovering Ian.

'In that drawer,' Georgie informed them, pointing. Ian immediately hurried over and opened it, finding the paper and pencils at once. Georgie went back to her chores, unsure whether or not she was relieved. She still found it hard to accept the doctor's verdict.

'Look what I found on top of the wardrobe when I was looking for something earlier,' Chrissie said, handing Tam a photograph album.

He recognised the album and knew what was inside. Photos of Mary and James's wedding. He stared at it for a few seconds, then slowly opened it, a lump coming into his throat at the sight of the first picture: Mary and James by themselves.

'Seems like only yesterday, doesn't it?' Chrissie smiled.

Before she'd joined that bloody sect, Tam thought. When their firstborn had still been his golden lassie, and apple of his eye.

Lena and Tom watched their father, wondering how he was going to react.

'I said it seems like only yesterday,' Chrissie repeated.

Tam didn't reply. Instead, he turned to the next picture, which was a group one of the family. He'd aged, he reflected. He hadn't been quite as bald then, and he'd certainly been slimmer. Chrissie too had aged, and put on weight. Happier days, he thought. Far happier, at least where Mary was concerned.

'Tam?'

'It was a fine wedding,' he declared at last, in a quiet, reflective voice. 'James looks very smart and upstanding. Quite the bridegroom.

'I never did like that dress I'm wearing,' Chrissie commented. 'I don't know why I bought it.'

Tam fought back the emotion that was suddenly threatening to overwhelm him. When he next spoke his voice was cracked. 'Bloody religion. It's caused far more harm than good in this world.'

Tom went cold inside to hear him say that. It made him feel sick.

Tam snapped the album shut and stared into space, his mind full of memories of times long gone. Then he startled them all by suddenly coming to his feet and tossing the album on to his chair. 'I'm off down the pub for a couple of drams,' he declared. 'I won't be too long.'

'It was a mistake showing him that, Mum,' Lena said after Tam had left them.

Chrissie didn't reply, but picked up the album with the intention of returning it to the top of the wardrobe.

'I'm going out for a walk,' Tom said, and got up. He went to a pub as well, but not the one his father frequented.

He knew what had to be done. And it was the last thing in the world he wanted to do.

Chapter 8

'What are you doing?' Georgie asked.

'I would have thought that was obvious.' John smiled back at her. 'Putting another hole in my belt.' With a grunt, he finally managed to push the awl he was using through the leather, and began wiggling it about to enlarge the hole he had made.

'Have you lost weight or something?'

'Must have,' John replied. 'Otherwise I don't suppose I'd need the extra hole.'

'Stand up a minute.'

'Wait till I'm finished here, woman.'

When the job was finally done to his satisfaction he came to his feet and threaded the belt through the loops on his trousers. Georgie studied him. Yes, he definitely had lost weight, and she could only wonder why she hadn't noticed. In fact, he'd become quite thin, though not alarmingly so.

He was eating as much as he always did, she reflected, which wasn't all that much as he'd never been a great eater at the best of times. Unlike her brother Tom, who Chrissie often complained ate them out of house and home.

'There,' John declared, fastening the belt. 'That's better. My trousers were getting so loose on me I was scared they might fall down.' He laughed. 'Imagine that happening in the middle of

Sauchiehall Street. I'd probably be arrested for indecent exposure or something.'

If he meant to make Georgie smile he failed to do so. Not a flicker cracked her face.

'Now don't you go worrying again,' John went on, wagging a finger at her. 'I'm absolutely fine. All right?'

'If you say so.'

'I do. Now why don't you get the lad ready for bed and we'll have a nice cup of tea after he's dropped off. How does that sound?'

'Lovely.'

His eyes twinkled. 'Just the two of us, if you get my meaning?'

'What *are* you suggesting?' she teased him.

'As if you didn't know.'

'I don't want to go to bed,' protested Ian, who was in the middle of a game with his old lead soldiers, pretending they were cowboys and Indians.

'You never do.'

'Can't I just stay up a wee while longer? Please, Mummy?'

''Fraid not, Ian. You've got school in the morning, don't forget.'

'Tell you what, son,' John chipped in. 'We'll let you stay up later on Friday night as you don't have school next day. How's that?'

'I suppose so,' Ian replied, knowing there was no use in any further pleading. It had to be bed.

'And I'll have another go at the fort during the weekend,' John promised.

'Can I help?'

'Of course you can. I'd expect you to.'

Mollified, Ian began stripping.

'Did you ever ask that lassie of yours about coming to tea?' Chrissie asked.

Tom looked over at her. 'She's not my lassie any more. We split up.'

Chrissie's expression changed to one of concern. 'I'm sorry to hear that. The pair of you were going out for quite some time. I thought there might have been something in it.'

'Give you the elbow, did she?' Lena taunted, unable to stop herself having a dig.

Tom glared at her. 'No, she didn't. It simply wouldn't have worked out, that's all.'

'And why's that?'

'Just because.'

Lena sniggered. 'Just because!' she mimicked. 'How pathetic is that?'

'Will you shut it!' Tom snarled.

'Enough,' Tam growled from his chair. 'You're forever bickering, the pair of you. Why can't you just try and get on for a change?'

'It isn't my fault,' Tom protested. 'She always starts it.'

'No she doesn't,' Tam contradicted him. 'You're each as bad as the other.'

'The mystery girl with no name,' Lena mused, and lit a cigarette.

'She does have a name,' Tom snapped back.

Lena raised an eyebrow.

'Well, if you must know, her name is Brigid O'Reilly. Which probably tells you why we split.'

Tam, who was putting new soles on a pair of his work boots using the cobbler's last he kept for that purpose, focused on his son. 'What did you say her name is?'

'You heard me, Papa. Brigid O'Reilly. And yes, she is a Catholic. A Fenian.'

'Dear me,' Chrissie breathed. So that was why Tom had always refused to give the lassie a name. It all made sense now.

'And you've split up?' Tam went on, having been only half listening to the conversation while he was intent on his cobbling.

'That's right.'

'Just as well. It could never have got anywhere.'

Lena glanced away, embarrassed to have been the instigator of this revelation, and wishing now she hadn't.

'Not in Glasgow anyway,' Tam added.

'Don't you think I'm aware of that, Papa?'

'Catholics and Protestants don't mix, son. And as for marriage, that's completely out of the question. Try that lark and your lives would have been made hell.'

Chrissie eyed her son shrewdly. 'So it was serious, then?'

Tom nodded.

'I see.'

'You did the right thing by nipping it in the bud,' said Tam. 'And I'm pleased you've finally told us.'

'Brigid and I talked it over,' Tom said slowly, 'and we both came to the same conclusion. She said I'd have to turn Catholic before she'd ever consider marrying me. Which of course I could never do.'

'Quite right, son. It's unthinkable.'

Chrissie's heart was softer than that, though she knew what her husband was saying. She truly felt for Tom. She'd speak to him alone at some point and explain how sympathetic she was.

'Catholics and Protestants.' Tom shook his head. 'Why can't they just get on? It's the same religion, after all. We're all Christian.'

'It's all to do with history,' Tam said. 'And there's a lot more to it than I know about. But as things stand each side hates, despises and mistrusts the other, and many a person has died in the past because of it.'

'Anyway, it's over now,' Tom said wistfully. 'Finished.'

'You'll find someone else,' Chrissie declared. 'You'll see. As they say, there's plenty more fish in the sea.'

'Aye, that's true,' Tam agreed.

Were there? Tom wondered. At that moment he couldn't have cared less, for he was missing Brigid more than he would ever have admitted. His sense of loss was profound.

Willie Winning took the controls back from John. 'You're really getting the hang of it now,' he declared. 'You'll be a good driver when you finally get promotion.'

John had thoroughly enjoyed his lesson. It was the custom for drivers to train up firemen to the point where they could apply for promotion, and Willie found John a keen and observant pupil, who caught on quickly and was easy to teach. The engine they were on was a Jones goods engine, number 108, the first 4–6–0 ever to be built in Britain.

'How long do you think I'll have to wait?' John asked.

'You're relatively young yet. A few more years, I'd say. Then make your application.'

'I'll do that.'

'In the meantime I'll let you build up experience. Give you lots of practice and advice.'

'Thanks, Willie.'

'Don't mention it. I remember my days as a fireman. It was my big dream to become a driver, and no doubt it's the same with you.'

John picked up his shovel and flipped open the door to the firebox. Bending to his task, he began to heave in lumps of coal and shale till the inside of the box looked like the gate to hell itself.

Sweat was running off him in rivers.

'I've been meaning to speak to you,' Tam said, when he and Tom were on their way to McNair's.

'What about, Papa?'

'That lassie of yours.'

Tom glanced sideways at his father but didn't reply, waiting for Tam to go on.

'Mary and her religion is bad enough for one family to have to contend with. But if you'd gone ahead and married this Brigid lass . . .' He broke off and shook his head.

'I realised that, Papa,' Tom said softly.

'All I want to say is how sorry I am for you.'

'Thanks.'

Tam sighed. 'Life can be a right bastard at times, and no mistake.'

'What if I had gone ahead, married Brigid and turned. What then, Papa?'

'You'd have been a fool, son.'

'But what would have happened?' Tom persisted.

Tam took his time in replying. 'We'd all have suffered the consequences. Believe me.'

Lena was depressed. She sat at her desk staring blindly at a ledger, thinking about how miserable she was when she should have been hard at work.

It was the same old thing that came back to haunt her time after time. Would she ever meet a man who'd be interested in her? Perhaps even love her? She gave a wry smile. Pigs would fly first.

She loved children, but was probably never going to have any. She might not appear on the surface to be the maternal type, but deep down she was, and she positively ached to have a baby of her own.

Enough of this! she scolded herself. She was becoming maudlin, and that would never do.

Pushing the ledger away she rose and headed for the ladies. She needed a fag, and there she could have one.

John suddenly choked, his eyes bulging, his hand going to his throat.

Georgie looked across the table at him in alarm. 'What's wrong?'

He pushed his chair back and ran to the sink, where he vomited violently into the basin, staring in horror at the bright red blood which spattered its sides. Again and again he threw up, till at last there was nothing left to come.

'Dear God!' Georgie was standing at his side. What was going on?

Finally John finished being sick. Straightening, he sucked in breath after breath.

'Here, let me,' Georgie said, voice shaking, and began wiping the blood from his lips and chin. Ian was sitting staring at his father as if John had suddenly sprouted horns.

'I'm fine now,' John declared, taking the towel from Georgie and finishing the job himself.

'What brought that on?'

He shook his head. 'Absolutely no idea. I suddenly felt very queasy, and then this.' He glanced down at the blood-spattered sink. 'Fucking hell!' he muttered to himself.

'It's back to the doctor for you this very night,' Georgie said firmly. 'And I don't want any argument about it.'

'All right,' a thoroughly shaken John agreed. That had given him the fright of his life.

'And what's more, I'm coming with you.'

'What about Ian?'

'We'll drop him off at my mum's, and pick him up again later.'

'Just give me a few minutes to pull myself together,' John said. Woozily he made his way back to his chair and slumped on to it. His face had gone completely white, the dark bags under his eyes more accentuated than ever.

Ian, still staring at his father, burst into tears.

'So what did the doctor say?' Chrissie demanded when Georgie and John returned from the surgery. Tam, Lena and Tom were anxiously looking on, their concern obvious.

'He's making an appointment for John to see a specialist,' Georgie replied.

'Has he no idea what the problem is?' Tam asked.

Georgie shook her head. 'If he has he wouldn't be drawn. Just said seeing a specialist was the best thing.'

'Can I sit down?' John queried, attempting a smile that didn't quite come off.

Tom was instantly on his feet. 'Sit here.'

'Thanks.'

'How are you feeling now?' asked Lena.

'Absolutely terrible. I'm so tired it took all my willpower to walk back from the surgery.'

Lena didn't like the sound of that one little bit. None of them did.

'Would a cup of tea help?' Chrissie suggested.

'It certainly wouldn't do any harm.'

'I'll put the kettle on,' Lena volunteered, and set about the task.

'So, when do you think you'll be seeing this specialist?' Tam queried.

'The doctor couldn't be specific,' Georgie answered for John. 'But he did say it should be some time soon.'

'That's good.' Tam nodded.

'And in the meantime he's to stay off work,' Georgie added.

'I don't know about that,' John protested, glancing over at her.

'You'll do as the doctor told you,' Georgie snapped back.

'But my wages . . .'

'We'll manage,' she interjected, her expression resolute.

John sighed. When Georgie spoke in that tone of voice there was no gainsaying her.

'I'll have to let them know at the station.'

'Don't you worry about that. I'll go there tomorrow morning directly after Ian's left for school.' She shuddered inwardly, remembering the mess in the sink which she'd have to clear up when they got home. That wasn't going to be exactly pleasant.

'How about a bite to eat, John?' Chrissie asked. 'I've got some nice newly made scones.'

He shook his head. 'No thanks.'

'Are you sure?'

'They are lovely,' Tom told him, having wolfed down four earlier.

'Honestly, I couldn't.'

When it was time to leave Tom went with them to give assistance to John should it be needed, while Lena cleared the tea things and Tam and Chrissie sat wrapped in their anxious thoughts.

'What do you think?' Tam asked later as he and Chrissie were getting ready for bed.

'He's lost so much weight since I saw him last. I was quite shocked by his appearance.'

'Aye.' Tam nodded. 'I noticed that myself.'

'He's nothing but skin and bone.'

'Georgie must be worried sick.'

'I know I would be if it was you.'

Tam sat on the edge of the bed and put on his pyjama top. 'I wonder what is wrong with him? Could be almost anything.'

'Whatever, I just hope it isn't serious.'

'It looks serious enough to me, girl, and I'm no doctor.' Tam slowly shook his head. 'Vomiting blood. Lots of it. Not to mention the weight loss and permanent tiredness. Makes me wonder if it isn't consumption. There's always a lot of that about in Glasgow.'

'Oh, please God it isn't. That would be terrible.'

'He seems to have all the symptoms that I've heard of.'

Consumption! That would be more or less a death sentence. Some did survive, but precious few. She'd even heard of entire families being taken off by that dreadful scourge.

'Well, all we can do is wait and hear what the specialist has to say.' Tam yawned.

'I'll drop by on them tomorrow morning,' Chrissie declared. 'Georgie might need some help.'

'Good idea. You do that.'

When she was curled up at Tam's broad back Chrissie closed her eyes and prayed for John; prayed he'd soon get over whatever it was and be back to full health again.

'How did you get on?' John asked when Georgie returned from the station next morning.

'I saw the manager, Mr Laidlaw, and explained the situation to him. He was very sympathetic and sent you his best wishes.'

'Aye, he's a decent man is Laidlaw.' John, who was propped up in bed, where Georgie had insisted he stay, nodded.

'He also said that if you're off for more than a fortnight he'll speak to the Union, and they'll probably send someone round.'

'Good. But I hope it doesn't come to that.'

'Now,' Georgie declared, suddenly businesslike. 'How about some breakfast? I could make you a poached egg. Does that appeal?'

He shook his head. 'I'm simply not hungry, lass.'

'Well, you must have something. What do you fancy?'

'Nothing, Georgie, honestly.'

'Won't you just try, for my sake?' she pleaded.

He took a deep breath. 'All right. A poached egg it is then.'

'Coming right up.' And with that Georgie swept from their bedroom.

In the event John only managed a few mouthfuls before saying he couldn't take any more. He wasn't sure he would, but he did somehow succeed in keeping those few mouthfuls down.

The day had finally arrived for John to be told the results of the extensive tests that had been carried out on him. At the appointed time he and Georgie presented themselves at the specialist's office.

Dr Abrams was considered one of the top men in his field. He was tall and thin, with a sallow complexion and a beak of a nose. His dark brown eyes had an intense penetrating quality about them as if he was visually dissecting you.

'Please sit down,' he said, indicating chairs in front of his desk. Nervously, John and Georgie sat as instructed. Once they had done so, Abrams also seated himself.

'Your results are in, and conclusive,' he said gently. 'And they're not good, I'm afraid.'

The breath caught in Georgie's throat, and her mouth began to move as she offered up a silent prayer.

'You have leukaemia, Mr Mair. And as I said, the tests are conclusive.'

John swallowed hard.

Stunned, Georgie stopped praying. 'What's the treatment?' she asked hoarsely at last.

'Sadly, there isn't one.'

'There must be!'

'I'm afraid not. Once diagnosed all we can do is let the condition take its course.'

John blinked, and blinked again. 'Am I going to die?'

'Yes. That will be the outcome.'

Georgie sagged. This was her worst nightmare come true.

'How . . .' John swallowed hard. 'How long?'

'That I can't be specific about. But your condition is well advanced, Mr Mair. A year at most. Perhaps only months.' He paused, then added softly, 'I'm terribly sorry.'

John could only smile ruefully at that. 'Not half as sorry as I am, Doctor. Not half as sorry.'

Chapter 9

It was at Pet's request that she and Lena went for a walk in the park. She desperately needed to get some fresh air about her, she explained, after nights of working in a smoky nightclub. She came quickly to the point.

'Well, my immigration papers have come through at last,' she announced. 'They arrived in yesterday's post.'

'Congratulations!' Lena beamed. 'You must be excited!'

'Oh, I am. Thrilled to bits actually. Hollywood, here I come with bells on.'

Lena laughed at the picture that conjured up.

'Next thing is to book my passage, which I'll do as soon as possible.'

'You have enough money in the bank, then?'

'Enough, with pots to spare. The Green Slipper Club has been very good to me.'

'And the man who feels your bum?'

'Of course. Which, I'm happy to report, he does regularly at a fiver a grope. God bless the lecherous sod.'

Lena still thought there might be more to it than that, but had never pressed her friend on the subject. If Pet had taken it further then that was her affair.

'Still not made up your mind?' Pet asked.

'I'm afraid not. There are times when I'm keen as mustard, other times when I think it would be a big mistake. For me, anyway.'

'Well, if you do decide to come I'll always be there waiting with a place for you to stay.'

Lena smiled. 'Thanks, Pet. I'm going to miss you, you know.'

'And I'll miss you, Lena. Not that we'll lose touch. I shall be writing regularly.'

'And I shall be replying regularly. You have my word.'

They walked a little way in silence, each deep in thought.

'Can I ask you a favour?' Pet said eventually.

'Naturally. What is it?'

'Will you come and see me off? I'd like that.'

Lena hesitated for a moment. What if it was during the week when she should be at work? Oh, to hell with it, she decided. She'd lie about being unwell on the day. It was a special occasion, after all.

'I'll be there Pet. Waving from the quayside when the boat pulls away.'

'Thanks. I appreciate that.'

'Who else will be coming along?'

'My parents.'

'It'll be a sad day for them.'

'Aye, it will that. But it can't be helped. I'm on my way and nothing will stop me.'

Lena heard the note of fierce determination in her friend's voice which told her that was only too true.

'I'm off to the land of peach and orange trees,' Pet enthused. 'Hollywood and all its glory.'

How wonderful, Lena thought. How utterly wonderful.

Georgie opened the door to find her sister Mary standing there clutching a sheaf of religious pamphlets and papers published by the sect, and inwardly groaned.

'Mary!' she exclaimed. 'This is a surprise. Come on in.'

'I'm ever so sorry to hear about John,' Mary said as they entered the kitchen. 'You must be devastated.'

Georgie nodded. 'That's one way of putting it.'

'How is he?'

'Not too well, I'm afraid.'

'I thought I might speak to him?'

Shit, Georgie thought. That wasn't a good idea at all. Like the rest of the family John had no time for Mary's religious megalomania.

'It's important,' Mary added, grasping Georgie by the arm.

'How did you hear about him anyway?' Georgie asked.

'One of my neighbours works out of the same station as John. His wife mentioned it a few days ago during a natter we had in the street.'

'Would you like a cup of tea while you're here?'

Mary shook her head. 'Not for me, thanks. Can I see John?'

Oh dear, Georgie thought. This was difficult. 'I don't think that's possible, Mary. He's very frail, and asleep most of the time. I wouldn't want him to get agitated in any way.'

Mary's eyes gleamed with fervour. 'If he's dying, Georgie, I must show him the light before he goes. Save his soul from eternal damnation, for only those who believe will be saved by the good Lord, God Almighty.'

'John has his own beliefs,' Georgie stated quietly. 'And now is not the time or place to challenge those.'

'Nonsense. It's the perfect time!'

Georgie was beginning to get irritated by her older sister. How dare she come crashing in here like this on her so-called holy mission? 'I say it's not, and that's an end of it.'

'You'd send his soul to eternal damnation? The man you purportedly love?' Mary almost screeched.

'Enough of this claptrap,' Georgie replied harshly. 'I want you to leave before you wake John. He needs all the sleep he can get.'

Mary changed tack. 'Please, Georgie? Please let me see and talk to him?' She was squeezing Georgie's arm so hard it hurt.

'No, and that's final. Now on your way, Mary.' And with that Georgie began pushing her from the room.

'At least let me leave this literature and promise me you'll get him to read it.'

'You can leave it. But whether or not he reads it is up to him.'

They were at the front door now. Georgie managed to open it, and with a final push they were both out on the landing.

'Here, take them,' Mary said, thrusting the pamphlets and papers into Georgie's hand. Georgie tore herself free, immediately stepping back inside the house and slamming the door in Mary's face. She's completely off her chump, she thought. A madwoman if ever there was one.

Returning to the kitchen, she threw the pamphlets and papers into the bin. The best place for them, she thought with grim satisfaction.

'It's a lovely cabin,' Lena said, glancing round.

'It'll do me.' Pet opened the suitcase the steward had put on top of her bunk, her musquash coat already hung up on the rail provided.

Lena went to the porthole and peered out at the river and far bank where other ships were moored. 'It's a pity your parents couldn't come,' she said.

Pet sighed. 'They just didn't feel up to it. Wanted to say their goodbyes at home. Ma said she was afraid of making a spectacle of herself by blubbing all over the place in public. As for Da, he said it would break his heart to stand there and watch me steam away out of their lives for ever.'

'I can understand that.' Lena nodded. 'It would have been very hard for both of them.'

'I would still have liked them here.' Pet smiled. 'But there we are, maybe it's for the best they aren't.'

Lena glanced again through the porthole, wondering what she'd feel like if she was the one off to America. Excited, no doubt. And probably terrified as well. It was an awfully big step Pet was taking. A giant leap into the unknown.

'Tell you what,' she said, turning to face her friend again. 'The steward said we could have a cup of coffee and some sandwiches in the salon if we wished. As there's two hours to sailing time why don't we do that and then we'll come back here and I'll help you get settled in?'

Lena had watched the ropes being cast off, and now the ship was beginning to stir, seemingly eager, although that could simply be her imagination, to begin its long voyage.

The TSS *Ulysses* was a cargo vessel of roughly eight thousand tons carrying a maximum of six passengers. On this particular trip, it was headed for the Port of New York with a cargo of whisky and Shetland ponies, and four passengers.

It was a chilly day, and blowy, with a hint of possible snow or sleet in the air. Lena shivered and pulled the collar of her coat tighter round her neck.

The ship started moving away from the quayside, twin screws churning the water at its rear. Overhead, seagulls were raucously crying as they swooped and soared high above the deck.

There was a huge lump in Lena's throat as she stared at her friend who was gazing back, wearing her musquash coat to keep out the cold.

The ship's horn blew, then blew again, and the ship moved forward on its way down the Clyde to the Atlantic.

'Goodbye! Good luck!' Lena yelled, and frantically waved.

Pet waved back, and seemed to be yelling something as well, which Lena couldn't make out, the words being carried away by the wind, as no doubt hers were as well.

'Good luck, Pet!' Lena repeated in a whisper, a hollow emptiness filling her. Pet was the only close friend she had had in her life, and now she was gone.

After a while she turned and headed for the stop from where a tram would take her home, tears rolling down her cheeks as she walked. The parting had been much worse than she'd anticipated. An awful lot worse.

John came awake to the sound of the front door being shut. A few moments later Chrissie came into the bedroom.

'Oh, you're awake then?' She smiled.

'Just.'

'Georgie won't be long. She's gone out to get the messages. Would you like me to sit with you for a while?'

'That would be nice.'

Chrissie pulled over a chair.

'I was having such strange dreams,' John said in a weak voice.

'Nightmares?'

'Not really. Dreams. I was back with my parents when I was young. They had a newsagent's shop, you know, down Scotland Street. Did very well out of it too. God bless them.' He drew in a deep breath. 'Long gone now, of course. My parents, I mean.'

'It is some years back,' Chrissie agreed.

'Well, they were already getting on when they rescued me from the orphanage, and adopted me. The two of them must have been in their mid-fifties. Never had any children of their own, and then at that age decided to adopt one and I was chosen.'

'They were very nice people, from all accounts.'

'They were. I think you'd have liked them, and they you and Tam. They certainly would have adored Georgie. But sadly they were already gone by the time I met her.' John's eyes misted over in memory. 'Did Georgie ever mention that I'm English?' he asked eventually.

Chrissie frowned. 'No, she hasn't.'

'Well it's true. Though I've no idea whereabouts in England I was born. I've always suspected it was Newcastle, though I've no proof of that.'

'Your parents never told you?'

'I never even knew I was adopted until after they were dead. It was quite a shock when it came to light, I can tell you.' He suddenly smiled. 'But finding out I was actually English was an even bigger one!'

'I can well imagine!'

'English!' He laughed, and shook his head.

'But you're Scots now,' Chrissie declared. 'At least, that's how you've been brought up. And with a good Scots tongue in your head.'

'My surname was Miller, apparently,' he went on. 'So I would have been John Miller and not John Mair.'

'Have you any idea what happened to your original parents?'

'None at all, Chrissie. There was no reference to either of them.' He glanced at her, and guessed what she was thinking. 'Yes, I could well be illegitimate. A bastard. I simply have no way of knowing.'

'That's often the case,' Chrissie mused. 'A lassie has a child out of wedlock and puts it into an orphanage, or some other such institution. Wisely in my opinion. Though it's probably hard on both of them.'

'Aye,' John agreed. 'It probably is. A woman carrying a bastard isn't exactly highly thought of.'

'However, you don't know what your circumstances were. It's all supposition on your part. You might have been placed in the orphanage as the result of some tragedy or other. Don't forget the great influenza epidemics of years ago. Perhaps both your real parents died as a result of one of those.'

'Maybe,' John said quietly.

'One thing I do know: you've been a damn good husband to Georgina, and a fine son-in-law to Tam and me. We're proud of you.'

He closed his eyes for a second or so. 'Thank you,' he whispered.

'Now, how about a cup of tea? Georgie said you might like one when you woke up.'

'That would be lovely.'

'You just stay where you are and I'll put the kettle on.'

He had to smile. 'I'm hardly going anywhere, now am I?'

That made her smile too. 'I won't be two ticks.'

'Of a lamb's tail,' he called after her as she left the bedroom, and heard her chuckle.

Tom was standing outside the dance hall where Brigid had taken him to hear jazz. The place the Bright Young Things frequented. He had intended to go inside, but now he was here he had doubts. What if he should run into Brigid? What then? If she was there he'd have to speak to her; to do otherwise would be rude. But a conversation would only be painful for the pair of them.

Then a new thought struck him. What if she was there with someone else? Someone she'd met since he and she had broken up? That would be unbearable – and highly embarrassing. He'd probably go all red in the face and look a right charlie.

If only he still didn't miss her so much. Not a day went by when he didn't think of her. Recall their times together. The fun they'd had. What a superb dancer she was. How good the pair of them were together.

Hell, he just missed her company.

Gritting his teeth, Tom turned away. He wouldn't go in. Not now, or ever. Instead, he headed for the nearest pub to drown his sorrows. And at the bottom of every glass Brigid's face stared back at him.

'Is Daddy going to die?'

Georgie stopped what she was doing, the question stabbing her like a knife.

'Is he, Mum?'

Georgie sighed. Ian had to be answered. And truthfully too. He had to be told at some point, and now was as good a time as any. But that didn't make it any easier.

'Come and sit down, son,' she said. Taking him by the hand she led him to a chair, and squatted down beside him. God, but this was going to be difficult. She stroked his hair – hair the same colour as his dad's. Then she looked into eyes that also reminded her of John. 'You know your dad's very ill, don't you?'

Ian nodded.

'He's suffering from something called leukaemia.'

'Leukaemia,' Ian repeated, stumbling slightly over the unfamiliar word. 'What's that?'

'It's to do with Dad's blood. It isn't working properly.'

Ian frowned. 'You mean it's gone bad?'

'That's right.'

'So why don't they fix it?'

Georgie longed for a cigarette, but didn't want to move away to get it. 'They just can't, I'm afraid.'

Ian's eyes grew wide. 'So Dad is going to die?'

'Yes, he is. There's absolutely nothing the doctors can do.'

'When is he going to die?'

'We don't know. It could be any time.' Georgie sighed, then took Ian into her arms and hugged him tight, his little chest heaving in her embrace.

'I don't want my dad to die,' he whispered in her ear.

'Neither do I. None of us do. It's simply the way things are.'

She was certain he would cry. But, to her surprise, he didn't, though he was clearly extremely distressed.

'Can I go out and play?' he asked when she eventually released him.

That surprised her too. 'If you wish. Just don't stay out too long. Don't forget you've got school in the morning.'

At the door to the kitchen he stopped. 'Does Dad know he's going to die?'

'Yes, son, he does.'

Ian ran down the stairs as fast as he was able, and then along the street in the same way. There was a secret spot he knew: an old building currently lying empty which you could access through a window that had been left unlocked. And there he went to curl up in a corner all by himself, and stayed until it was time to go home again.

'Do you think he'd like a bottle of whisky? A dram might do him a power of good.'

'I doubt it, Tam. But take one along if you like. I could be wrong.'

Tam nodded that he understood.

Chrissie hesitated, then said, 'You haven't seen him for a wee while, so be prepared for a shock. He's lost even more weight, though I wouldn't have thought it possible. He's now only skin and bone.'

Tam stared grimly at his wife. 'That bad, eh?'

'Worse. Believe me.'

He turned to Lena. 'Are you sure you won't come with us?'

She shook her head. 'I'll visit another night, Papa. Three of us there might be too much for him.'

That wasn't her real reason for not going. She was terrified of death, and had been for a long time. To have been in the presence of someone so close to it would have given her the willies. It was something she shared with her sister Mary.

'Well, we'd better be getting along then,' said Tam.

He bought the bottle en route, but, as Chrissie had anticipated, John declined to have a dram. Even a weak one was beyond him, he informed them. Chrissie had also been right about Tam's emotions at the sight of his son-in-law. He was shocked beyond belief.

Lena eagerly ripped open the letter bearing the Hollywood postmark. It was the first she had received since Pet had left.

Quickly she scanned the three pages the envelope contained. Pet had arrived safely and soon found a nice place to stay, even if it was a little expensive. It was all true about the peach and orange trees, especially the orange ones. They were everywhere. In fact she had two in her back garden, which for some reason the Americans called 'the yard'.

Within a couple of days of arrival she'd registered with Central Casting who supplied extras to all the films. So far she hadn't been given any work, but it was early days yet.

The weather was glorious, the sky a permanent duck egg blue, with an occasional deeper shade of that colour. She'd already acquired something of a tan, though she was being careful not to get too much of one as it might go against her when casting was taking place.

Oh, but she was enjoying herself. Revelling in the experience. Ever so glad she'd come. It had been a good move, and no mistake.

She didn't miss rainy, cold Glasgow one little bit.

After she'd finished the letter Lena re-read it, then laid it aside. She let out a huge sigh, envious to the very core of her being.

Chapter 10

'I'm Miss Hamilton,' the lady at the front door explained with a smile. She was holding an obviously upset Ian by the hand.

'Come in,' Georgie said quickly. 'Is something wrong?'

'Ian's had a bit of an accident,' Miss Hamilton informed her. 'Nothing serious. Simply didn't make it to the lavatory in time.'

Ian hung his head in shame.

'I see.'

'Sorry, Mum,' Ian mumbled.

'Then we'd better get you sorted out, hadn't we?'

Ian nodded.

'Thank you for bringing him home, Miss Hamilton. That was kind of you.'

'Not at all. But while I'm here I would like a little bit of a chat.'

'Oh? Well, of course. Why don't you take a seat while I attend to Ian in our room? We can have a cup of tea when I get back.'

'Lovely.'

Georgie took Ian through to the bedroom, where John was fast asleep. 'What happened?' she asked.

'Are you angry with me, Mum?'

'Of course not. Accidents happen. That's all it was, wasn't it?'

Ian nodded.

'Right then. Get those wet things off and I'll look out some fresh.'

Georgie handed him a towel, then went about producing clean shorts and underwear. She made sure Ian was dry before allowing him to put them on.

'There.' She smiled. 'Good as new.'

'Can I go back to school now?'

'Let's see what Miss Hamilton has to say, shall we?'

Miss Hamilton welcomed the idea of Ian's returning to school as it allowed her to speak to Georgie in private. 'See you again shortly,' she said to him.

'Say thank you for bringing me home, Miss Hamilton,' Georgie instructed him.

'Say thank you for bringing me home, Miss Hamilton. I'm sorry for what happened.'

'Don't you worry about that, Ian. Now off you go.'

When Ian had left them a puzzled Georgie returned to the kitchen and put the kettle on. 'That's most unlike Ian,' she apologised. 'In fact I can't remember him wetting himself since coming out of nappies. He's always been excellent where that's concerned.'

'I must say I was surprised as well. There's been no indication of anything like this since he started with us.'

Miss Hamilton was a good-looking woman whom Georgie judged to be in her mid to late twenties. She seemed to radiate some sort of inner glow which shone from her face. Georgie had taken an instant liking to her, and was certain she was a very good teacher.

'I have some chocolate biscuits in.' Georgie smiled, wondering what this was all about. 'Would you care for one?'

'Oh, yes, please. I adore chocolate biscuits of any kind. And to be honest, if I'm not careful chocolate itself will be my downfall one of these fine days.'

Georgie laughed. 'I know what you mean. I have to be careful in that direction myself.'

'Anyway,' Miss Hamilton went on, becoming serious. 'This

has given me the opportunity to talk to you. I was going to pay you a visit shortly, and Ian's little accident just gave me the excuse to make it sooner.'

Georgie studied her guest. 'Is something wrong?'

'It's Ian's behaviour. He's always been such a sunny little chap. Outgoing, and keen on his lessons. But all that has changed recently. He's become moody and introverted. Sullen, you could even say. And not the least interested in his schoolwork any more. Frankly, he's worrying me, so I've come to ask if there's anything wrong at home. Anything I should be aware of.'

'Do you mind if I smoke?'

'No, go ahead. I don't myself but it doesn't bother me.'

Georgie lit up, and inhaled deeply. She'd had no idea, not an inkling, that Ian was acting up at school, but it was under-standable really when you thought about it. Her heart went out to her son. 'It's Ian's dad,' she said slowly. 'My husband.' She told Miss Hamilton what the situation was.

'How awful,' said Miss Hamilton, when Georgie had finished. 'No wonder the wee lad's the way he is.'

'Now you understand.'

'Fully.'

'He . . .' Georgie hesitated, and took a deep breath. 'He's been quite good about it at home, though he has been more reserved than usual. I should have thought about school, though, and perhaps called in and spoken to the headmistress. But to be honest, it just never crossed my mind.'

'And why should it when you've already got so much on your plate,' Miss Hamilton said sympathetically. 'It must be terrible for you. Absolutely ghastly.'

Georgie nodded, emotion suddenly almost overwhelming her. 'Excuse me,' she croaked, and turned away so Miss Hamilton couldn't see the anguish flooding her face.

'Why don't you sit down and I'll make the tea?' Miss Hamilton offered.

Georgie took her up on it.

*　*　*

'How are you doing for money, lass?' Tam asked a few days later.

'We're all right, Papa. The Union, God bless them, are taking care of things.'

'I thought that would be the case, but I just wanted to make sure. You never know. And what about . . .' He shifted uneasily in his chair, thinking this might sound ghoulish. But it had to be asked none the less. He cleared his throat. 'Expenses for . . . well, when it happens.'

'You mean the funeral?'

'Aye.'

'The Union will also take care of that. It's John's due being a fully paid-up member. I've had a representative round here on several occasions. A nice man called Mr Duncan. He's assured me there'll also be a pension. A small one, but welcome anyway.'

'That's something of a relief for you.'

'I'll have to go out and work as the pension won't cover everything. But we'll deal with that bridge when we come to it.'

'It's a dreadful business,' Tam muttered, shaking his head. 'I can't imagine what you're going through. Hell, no doubt.'

That was putting it mildy, Georgie thought. Every time she looked in the mirror it was as if she'd aged even more. At this rate she was going to be an old crone before long.

'Just remember,' Tam went on, 'your mother and I are there if there's anything you need help with.'

'I know that, Papa. Thank you.' She looked away, suddenly overwhelmed by a kind of anger. Why John, she inwardly raged. Why him? He was such a good, upstanding man. Good husband. Good father. Why take him when there were so many rotten bastards around who were being allowed to carry on with their lives? It was so wrong. What was God thinking of to let such a thing happen? 'Oh, Papa!' she wailed.

Quickly going to her, Tam took her into his arms. 'There there, lass,' he crooned in a throaty voice. 'There there.'

She sobbed against his shoulder, filled with a combination of anger and grief.

'Someone once told me life isn't fair,' Tam said quietly. 'How right they were.'

It was as if he'd read her thoughts, Georgie reflected. Just like Papa to do that. She agreed wholeheartedly with what he'd just said. Life was anything but fair.

Lightning lit up the inside of the bedroom, followed a few moments later by a heavy crack of thunder. Rain was lashing against the window.

John threw one arm out, then the other. His body began writhing as though he was fighting invisible demons.

More lightning, more thunder. Rain was driving even harder against the window. Georgie didn't know what time it was, and didn't care. All she wanted was for the storm to stop. It was beginning to scare her.

A flailing arm caught her a blow across the chest, causing her to grunt with pain. That had hurt. Perhaps she should wake him? But deep down she didn't have the heart to – at least not yet. Hopefully he'd soon calm down again.

This time it was a glancing blow across her cheek which knocked her head sideways. A nail had caught her cheek, ripping it slightly to draw a trickle of blood.

She cringed when there was another peal of thunder, this one seemingly directly overhead. What a night, she thought.

'Georgie?'

She was startled, for he'd been sleeping only seconds previously. 'What is it, John?'

'I was having a nightmare.'

'I know. You were thrashing about something terrible.'

'Did I wake you?'

'No, the storm did.' In fact it was a combination of both that had wakened her.

'Listen to that,' he said as another peal of thunder banged out. 'Loud, isn't it?'

'Very.' She hesitated, then asked, 'What was your nightmare about? Can you remember?'

'Oh yes,' he replied very softly.

'Well?' she prompted when he didn't elaborate.

'I don't think I should tell you. You'd only get upset.'

All that did was intrigue her. Now she definitely did want to hear. 'What if I promise not to get upset?'

'You will anyway.'

She wondered what persuasive line of argument she could take. 'John, we're man and wife and as such are supposed to share things. The good and the bad.'

He laughed drily in the darkness. 'I know your game, Georgie. You're trying to weasel it out of me. Well, it won't work.'

'Oh, come on, John. I'm a big girl. Let's hear it.'

He relented, though he knew he shouldn't. 'Give me your hand, Georgie.'

She took hold of his, a hand once plump and strong, now skeletal with protruding bones. A hand that was only a shadow of what it had once been.

'I was dead, Georgie,' he whispered. 'Dead, but alive at the same time. Or at least aware of what was happening.'

She could hear her heart thumping in her chest. 'Aware of what?'

'Worms eating my flesh.'

The picture conjured up in her mind filled her with terror. She wished now she hadn't pursued the subject.

'Nibbling away. My flesh vanishing morsel by morsel, bit by bit. I was screaming for help, but there was no one there. I was in my coffin, deep under the earth. Buried alive.

'Oh, John,' she whispered, not knowing what to say.

'Worms,' he repeated. 'Nasty, slimy things.' He paused for a second, then said, 'Do you know the worst thing about my nightmare?'

'What?' she croaked.

'All the while they were burrowing and nibbling the little bastards were laughing at me. They thought it was terribly funny.'

Outside, the loudest peal of thunder yet boomed out as the

storm gathered even more momentum. Neither of them slept again that night.

Miss Hamilton stared in surprise as Ian suddenly got up from his desk in the middle of lessons and headed for the classroom door.

'Ian?'

He neither looked at her nor replied.

'Ian, where are you going?'

He went straight out of the door and down the corridor. He knew the gates to the playground would be shut and locked, but there was another way out of the school and he made for that. Mr Green, the janitor, had a small room where he kept all manner of things: mops, pails, brushes, ladders and the like. There was also a window there, easily opened, from where it was only a short drop to the street.

Minutes later Ian was on the pavement and walking in the direction of his secret spot. He wanted to be alone. No more Miss Hamilton, no more other pupils. Just himself.

Once inside the empty house he lay down and curled up in the same corner as before. Putting a thumb into his mouth, he began to suck.

Lena was delighted to receive another letter from Pet. Sent, as Pet wrote in it, from the land of eternal sunshine.

Work as a film extra was coming in regularly now, and she was employed most days of the week. She'd already made lots of friends amongst the other extras and come to know a few 'important people': in other words, people who could help her with her career. One of them had recommended she take voice lessons with the prime objective of losing her strong Scottish accent. Such lessons would be expensive but she was determined to have them come what may.

She hadn't actually met any of the big stars so far, but she had been in close proximity to several, including Douglas Fairbanks and John Gilbert, no less. Both men were absolutely gorgeous, dishy as could be and, from what she'd heard, extremely pleasant. The actresses were a different kettle of fish entirely. Most of them were out-and-out bitches, who were just as nasty to each other as they were to the female extras they encountered. She'd been advised to stay away from them whenever possible as the one thing they hated most of all was another pretty female, star or otherwise.

Pet had found a better and more convenient place to stay, an apartment which she was sharing with another extra called Jolene. The two of them were getting along famously.

Pet had kept the juiciest bit for last. She'd met a guy called Dwayne. They'd been out together once, and would shortly be going out again. She'd let Lena know more about Dwayne in her next letter.

'What are you doing up?' Georgie demanded when John appeared in the kitchen carrying Ian's fort.

He grinned. 'Is it against the rules?'

'No, of course not. But you're supposed to be in bed.'

'The doctor never said I had to stay there. Certainly not in my presence.'

She had to admit it was true. The doctor had never actually said that. 'Well, you'd better sit down and I'll put the kettle on.'

John did as instructed. 'Know what I'd really like?'

'What?'

'A proper drink.' He sighed. 'Pity there's none in the house.'

Georgie smiled. 'But there is. The remains of that whisky Papa brought some time back.'

'The very dab. I'll have a dram,' he enthused.

Georgie frowned at him. 'You seem very sprightly all of a sudden.'

'I don't know why but I'm full of beans. That's why I decided to come on through and finish Ian's fort. There's not a lot left to do and I want to get it done.'

Georgie poured his whisky, then one for herself. It was lovely having him up and about like this. A real treat.

'Slainte!' John toasted her when she'd handed him his glass. She returned the gesture. 'Now,' he went on. 'I need glue, that sharp knife I use, and the paints and brushes.'

'You just sit there and I'll get them for you.'

He gazed lovingly at her as she moved about, wishing with all his heart that things could have been different. If he'd done one wise thing in his life it was marrying Georgie. He could never have chosen better, not in a thousand years. The pair of them just fitted.

John glanced at the recessed bed where Ian lay fast asleep. The wee fella would take it badly when he was gone. But Ian was young, and the young recovered quickly. At least, he hoped and prayed that would be the case.

Georgie spread newspaper in front of John, and began placing the items he'd requested on it. Soon he was hard at work.

'I'm amazed you're keeping that whisky down,' she commented after a while. 'You've hardly kept any food in your stomach for ages now.'

'Yes, it is a bit of a miracle, isn't it? Just don't knock it, that's all.'

'I'm not!' she protested.

'Fine,' he replied cheerily. 'In fact, that first dram was so good I think I'll have another. If you don't mind, that is?'

'Are you sure, John?'

'Absolutely.'

Georgie rose from the table to refill his glass, while he concentrated on the task in hand.

'I've been meaning to speak to you for some time now,' he said casually a few minutes later.

'About what?'

'Us.'

'What about us?'

'Well actually, it's really about you.'

She was puzzled. What was he driving at? 'I'm listening.'

He cleared his throat, then bent again to the fort. 'You're still a young woman, Georgie. Too young to stay a widow for the rest of your life. I wouldn't want that.'

It was as though she'd been punched in the midriff. 'Go on.'

'I'm hoping, if the right man happens along, that you'll eventually remarry. I would approve of that.'

'Never!' she exclaimed fiercely. 'That will never happen.'

He stopped to stare at her. 'Don't be silly, Georgie. I'm trying to be practical about this.'

'I will never remarry, John, not even if Prince Charming came along. And that's final.'

'There's Ian to consider, don't forget. He'll need a father, or at least a father figure. Surely you wouldn't deny him that?'

'There's Papa. He'll be all the father figure Ian will need. I'll see to it.'

'It's not the same, Georgie. Not by a long chalk, and you know it. What you want is someone who lives in the same house and takes a day-to-day interest in the lad. Tam, with the best will in the world, just couldn't do that.'

Georgie, reluctantly, had to concede he had a point there. But at the moment she simply couldn't think about what he was proposing. 'I'll never find anyone to take your place, John.'

He smiled. 'I'm flattered. But it wouldn't be to take my place. It would be a whole new relationship. Nothing whatsoever to do with me.'

'Nonsense.'

'It isn't nonsense at all,' he protested.

'Yes, it is.'

'No, it is not!'

Georgie lit a cigarette, cross with him, and hurt too. 'I don't want to talk about this any more.'

'Then we won't.'

She smoked in silence, then stubbed out the remains. 'Would you remarry if the positions were reversed?' she asked softly.

'Yes. If I met the right woman, that is. Life goes on for those left behind, after all. And that's a fact, harsh as it may sound.'

She bit back her disappointment. 'You really would?'

'If the right woman came along,' he repeated. 'I may be many things, but I'm not a bloody martyr. And neither should you be.

109

If I'm up there with the angels then I'll heartily approve if you find another bloke. Believe me.' He paused to stare at her, his eyes unblinking. 'And the reason for that is because I love you so much. I'd want you to be happy.'

A lump came into her throat. 'Oh, John,' she whispered.

'There!' he announced with a flourish, laying a small paint-brush aside. 'Finished at last. What do you think?'

'I think it's lovely. Ian will be ever so pleased. Shall we leave it there so he can see it first thing in the morning?'

'Good idea.'

John saw off what was left in his glass, considered having a third, then decided against it.

'I'm suddenly tired again,' he said. 'It's back to bed for me.'

'I'll help you through.'

'I can manage,' he declared, coming to his feet. At the door he hesitated, then said over his shoulder, 'I want you to think about what we were discussing. Promise me?'

'I promise.'

He was smiling as he continued on through to the bedroom.

The next morning when she woke Georgie found John lying dead beside her.

Part 2

Charlie

1929–1932

Chapter 11

Tam and Tom were bursting with it when they arrived in from work, Tam's face flushed with excitement. 'We've done it. We've bloody well done it!' he yelled and, taking Chrissie by the waist, whirled her round.

Chrissie laughed, as delighted by the news as her menfolk. 'I never thought I'd see the day when we had a Labour government,' she declared when Tam set her down again.

'But only with the help of the Liberals,' Lena pointed out. 'Labour has no overall Commons majority.'

'The fact is we're forming a government, which is all that matters.' Tam was beaming, shaking his head in happy disbelief. This was a dream come true as far as he was concerned.

A curious Ian was looking from person to person, wondering what all the fuss was about. What was Labour?

'Ramsay MacDonald will make a brilliant prime minister. Just you wait and see,' Tom enthused.

'Damn right he will.' Tam nodded. 'And he's a Scotsman too! That's the icing on the cake.'

'Anything to keep that Welshman out,' Tom added.

'Imagine MacDonald appointing a woman as Minister of Labour,' Chrissie said. 'That's a turn-up for the book.'

'I'm not sure I approve.' Tam frowned momentarily. 'But I

have to say Margaret Bondfield does have a good reputation.'

'And why shouldn't he appoint a woman minister?' Lena sniffed. 'Honestly, Papa, some of your ideas and prejudices belong in the ark.'

'I quite agree,' Chrissie declared. 'It's high time women got a say in running the country. Let's hope she's just the first of many.'

Tam remained sceptical, but decided not to pursue the argument.

'They said on the wireless that reducing unemployment is to be MacDonald's top priority,' Chrissie informed the men.

'Good idea,' Tam replied. 'It would be my top priority as well if I had the job.'

Georgie arrived to pick up Ian as she did every evening after work. Now that she had a job as a packer in a bleach factory Ian came to his granny's on leaving school to wait for her.

'Have you heard the news, lass?' Tam boomed.

'Aye, I have. It swept round the factory earlier. A few of the girls were actually jumping up and down when they heard.'

Tam laughed. 'Great for them.'

'The manager wasn't too pleased, though. I'm sure he's a Tory.'

'He probably is if he's a boss.' Tam nodded. 'Scum of the earth, that lot.'

'As bad as the Liberals, if not worse,' Tom agreed.

'I've got nothing but contempt for both of them,' Tam declared. 'But it's all change now, thank God. From here on in the working man will get a fair crack of the whip.'

'Anyway, Ian and I will get down the road and leave you to it,' Georgie said, indicating to Ian to collect his things.

They said their goodbyes, and went on their way, Ian quizzing her about what Labour was, and she doing her best to explain. As they walked she noticed him scratching, and when they got home she asked, 'Is your skin acting up again?'

He nodded.

Georgie stared at him in dismay. Ian had developed eczema shortly after his father's death and nothing the doctor had prescribed or suggested had managed to cure it. The skin disease was a continuing bane of both their lives. Thankfully, for the past few months it hadn't been troublesome, but now it would seem to have flared once more.

'Take your shirt off and I'll put some ointment on,' she said. 'And when I've done that try not to scratch.'

All the ointment did was soothe the patches, but at least that was something. It made life more bearable for the lad.

Lena looked up and saw Hamish Murchison heading towards her. She frowned. What did he want? She rarely saw him nowadays since he'd been given his own small department.

He stopped in front of her desk and smiled. 'Hello, Lena. How are things?'

'Fine. And with you?'

'Excellent. Certainly can't complain.'

'Still golfing?' she enquired, her voice dripping sarcasm.

'Of course. Every weekend.'

She could have made a jibe about the chairman, but decided not to. 'So, how can I help? You obviously want something.'

Hamish laughed. 'What makes you think that?'

'Because the only time you ever speak to me is when you do. So, what is it?'

He leant over her desk, his eyes twinkling. 'I was wondering if you'd like to have a drink with me after work?'

That stunned her. 'A drink?' she stuttered.

'That's right. Just the two of us.'

The handsome Hamish asking her out? She couldn't quite take it in.

'Well?'

She nodded, not trusting herself to speak.

'Good. Do you know the Swan Hotel?'

Of course she knew the Swan. It was just down the street. 'Uh-huh.'

'We'll meet in reception. All right?'

Again she nodded.

'See you there then.'

She watched him walk away in complete and utter disbelief.

It was a thoroughly nervous Lena who presented herself in the reception area of the Swan Hotel. To her relief she found him already there and waiting.

He rose to his feet on spotting her. 'You made it.' He smiled.

'And to prove it I'm here,' she replied, with would-be lightness.

He laughed at the typical example of Glasgow humour. 'Shall we go on through?'

It was a lovely feeling when he took her by the arm to guide her. It was the first time any man had ever done that.

'What would you like?' he asked when she was seated at a table.

'A gin and tonic would be nice.'

'Coming right up.'

She still couldn't believe this was actually happening. Halfway through the afternoon she'd almost convinced herself she'd imagined the invitation. At one point her hands had started to shake so badly in anticipation that she'd had to put her pen down and wait for them to stop.

Lena gazed around. She had never been in the Swan before, let alone in the lounge. It was tastefully decorated, she decided. Quite posh, really. A lot of leather, a patterned red carpet, very expensive-looking wallpaper. She had no doubt the drinks would be expensive too. She lit a cigarette, thrilled to bits to be there with someone as good-looking as Hamish Murchison. She silently prayed she wouldn't start shaking again when he re-joined her.

'There we are.' Hamish placed her drink on the table. He'd elected to have whisky and soda. 'I rather like it here, don't you? Beats a smelly old pub any time.'

Lena poured tonic into her gin, then had a sip.

'Cheers!' he said, eyeing her over the rim of his glass as he drank.

'How's the new job coming along?' she enquired politely.

'Not too bad. A few teething problems, though, which I intend to iron out.'

'Oh?'

'And that's where you come in.'

'I don't follow?' She frowned.

He stared at her. 'Lena, you're the best damned ledger clerk in the entire building. Certainly for my money anyway. Which is why I'd like you to consider joining me in my department.'

Her nerves vanished, replaced by the dull ache of disappointment. She'd thought . . . but she'd been wrong, apparently. It would seem this wasn't a social occasion after all. How stupid of her to think otherwise. She should have known better.

'Go on,' she said harshly.

'I want you to be my sort of chief clerk, though without that designation. The company would never wear it.'

Lena knew that to be true enough. All the managers and chief clerks were men.

'If you agree,' Hamish went on, 'I could arrange more money for you. Say ten bob a week. How does that sound?'

'Fifteen bob would sound better.'

'Hmm,' he demurred, not at all certain he could go that far. She was asking a lot.

'Anyway, all this is hypothetical,' she declared. 'Old baldy would never let me go.'

'I believe I can persuade him,' Hamish replied. 'There are certain pressures I can bring to bear that would make him agree to the move.'

The chairman again, Lena thought bitterly. No wonder Hamish was so optimistic.

'So what do you say?' he demanded eagerly.

Work under him? Lena thought. The man was an incompetent who should never have been employed by the company in the first place. There again, there was the money to consider. The rise was a sweet enticement which would add to her growing savings, for she still hadn't given up the idea of going to Hollywood where Pet was doing extremely well, thank you very much.

'I'd still want fifteen shillings a week extra,' she declared. 'Ten isn't enough.' It actually was, but she wasn't about to admit that.

'If I can get you fifteen will you agree?'

She studied him through cigarette smoke, angry with herself for thinking he'd actually been asking her out on some sort of 'date', as Pet put it in her letters.

'Let me think about it.' She smiled thinly. 'I don't want to make a decision here and now.'

Hamish heard the finality in her tone, and knew there was no point in discussing the matter further.

'So where have you been? You're late,' Chrissie demanded when Lena arrived home.

'Sorry, Mum. I had a drink in an hotel with a head of department who wanted a chat.'

Tom nearly made a derogatory remark, but didn't. 'What sort of chat?' he queried instead.

Lena told them while Chrissie put her tea on the table.

'An extra fifteen bob a week!' Tam exclaimed, and whistled softly. 'I hope you grabbed it.'

'Not yet, Papa.'

'Well, you should have done, my girl. That's a lot of money.'

Lena had already made up her mind to accept the offer, providing old baldy let her go and there was fifteen shillings on top of her current weekly wage. But she wouldn't let on to Hamish until he came back and assured her that both these conditions were in place. Meanwhile, let him worry she wouldn't accept. One thing was certain, for she knew Hamish only too well in some respects: he wasn't doing this out of the kindness of his heart. He needed her.

Later, she sat on the edge of her bed thinking about the day's events, still angry with herself for being so stupid as to think Hamish had asked her out for her own sake.

Would a man never ask her out for that? Not for what she could do for them, but for herself? Black despair filled her, because she doubted one ever would. She was going to die a frustrated old maid, a virgin. She would never know what it was like to have sex, or to be married and have children, all three of which she desperately wanted.

Falling backwards on to her bed, she began to weep, tears running down her face. A face she hated, loathed and detested with a fierce intensity.

It was a fortnight before Hamish again appeared at her desk, smiling like the proverbial cat who'd scoffed the cream.

'It's all fixed,' he announced. 'Old baldy has agreed to let you go and the cashier to the extra cash. All I need now is to hear you'll take the job and you can start the first Monday of next month.'

'You pulled it off, then?'

'I did. It wasn't easy, mind you, but I got what I wanted in the end.'

How pleased with himself he was, she mused. She wouldn't have been at all surprised if he'd thrown back his head and crowed.

'Well?' he demanded.

'I'll present myself in your department on the first Monday of next month,' she replied with a smile, jubilant inside at the fifteen shillings' rise she would be paid every week – or three pounds a month as she was salaried – and pleased she'd stuck out for fifteen and not accepted the ten he'd initially proposed.

He beamed. 'See you then, Lena.'

'See you then.'

He badly needed her in his department, she reflected. Otherwise why go to all the trouble he had?

She bent again to her work, meticulously carrying on where she'd left off.

Georgie glanced over at Ian, nicely tucked up and sleeping in his bed. How lonely her nights had been since John died, she thought. Oh, there were occasions when her mother dropped by, and sometimes Lena. But usually she spent the nights on her own after Ian had gone to bed.

How she missed John, even after so long. She still half expected him to come in through the door, a cheery smile on his face, demanding to know what was for tea. But most of all she missed his presence in bed, the comfort of his arms, and knowing she was safe and sound while he was there.

She thought back to the little holiday they'd had, and how wonderful it had been. Happy days, true enough. And then how ill he'd been towards the end; dreadfully so. Thin beyond belief. In pain, but never complaining. And then that last evening when he'd come into the kitchen and drunk whisky while finishing off Ian's fort. It was almost as if he'd known he'd never make morning and that was their last chance to be together in this life.

Georgie sighed. Dear John. Dear, lovely, adorable John. Rising from her chair, she went to put the kettle on.

Lena ripped open her latest letter from Pet, or Dawn Ryder as Pet was now known, having been given a new name by the studio. As usual it was full of show business gossip: who was making what film, a rumour about so and so; things of that nature. Pet's latest film had just been released, in which she played a supporting role – a terrific part as a wicked woman. The film was due to come out in Britain the following year, and she, Lena, must go and see it.

In fact Lena had seen Pet – or Dawn Ryder as she must think of her – in several pictures to date. It still amused her to hear Pet speak with an American accent. Though, she had to admit, the accent was good and sounded authentic enough – at least to her ear, anyway.

Pet went on to say the studio had ordered her to diet as she'd gained a little weight recently, so on a diet she was. She remained unattached, though had been out on a number of 'dates' of late. Nothing serious. More to get her face in the movie magazines than anything else.

On finishing the letter Lena refolded it and returned it to its envelope. The same old irresistible Pet who never changed. Good for her. Stardom might not be that far away after all.

Now that would be something.

'Goodnight.'

'Goodnight, Tom.'

More out of courtesy than anything else he kissed the girl, whose name was Alison and who smelt strongly of cheap scent.

'Will I see you again?' she asked when the kiss was over.

'I'll be at the same dancing next Saturday night. I'll probably run into you then.'

'Oh,' she replied, clearly disappointed.

She was rather pretty, he thought, studying her in the moonlight. 'Ta-ra then.'

'Ta-ra, Tom. See you next Saturday.'

'I'll be looking for you,' he lied, and headed off down the street.

Now why had he walked her home, he wondered. He couldn't really say, for he'd known all along he really didn't fancy her. She was nice enough, with a good figure and a sunny nature. By rights he should have been interested enough to take it further, but he wasn't. He knew what the problem was, of course. Brigid. He'd never really got over her.

He'd tried time and time again with the lassies, even taking a few out several times, but in the end Brigid's ghost always came back to haunt him. To get in the way. The strange thing was he'd never spotted Brigid at the dancing since they'd broken up. He'd been certain he'd run into her at some stage, but it had just never happened.

For what must have been the millionth time in the intervening years he wondered how she was and what she was up to. Was she engaged, or even married? Or still single like himself? Whatever, he hoped she was happy.

Though the thought that she might be happy with someone

else was something he found almost impossible to bear. Why oh why had she been a bloody Catholic! Everything could have been so different otherwise.

'I'm just nipping out, Lena. Hold the fort for me if you will.'

Lena watched Hamish clap a bowler hat on his head and make smartly for the door. It was the same every morning: he'd be gone a good two hours at least. And the same in the afternoon.

She knew where he was off to. In a nearby street there was a tobacconist's which had a coffee shop at the rear. That's where he spent his time, either reading the newspaper or chatting with other customers – all men, for it was a strictly male province.

On other occasions he'd announce he was off to a meeting upstairs, meetings she knew to be pure fantasy because she'd checked. It was simply another excuse to skive away from his desk.

The department was running as smoothly as clockwork, thanks entirely to her. It was certainly nothing to do with Hamish, who was one of the laziest men Lena had ever come across. There were four other female clerks whom she'd been put in charge of, all of them diligent workers and good at their job since she had whipped them into shape during her first few weeks in the department.

Lena glanced down at the ledger she was currently bringing up to date. Re-insurance was boring at the best of times, and when it was to do with farming, which was what the department dealt with, it was positively soporific. At least with old baldy there had been some interest, certainly when it came to shipping which she'd rather enjoyed. Shipping had some romance about it: all those different cargoes going to every corner of the world; even the ships themselves with their at times exotic names.

She considered going to the ladies for a cigarette. Why not, when Hamish could disappear off for hours on end? A few stolen minutes in the toilet was nothing by comparison.

Then she remembered she didn't have any cigarettes, having forgotten to buy some on the way in to work. 'Damn!' she muttered. She couldn't even borrow off one of the other girls as none of them smoked.

At least Hamish was easy to get along with, she reflected, unlike old baldy who'd watched everyone like a hawk, and never had a word of praise for anyone. Miserable sod.

Re-insurance. An insurance company takes on a huge risk, then, to ensure they don't come a cropper should they have to pay out an enormous sum, offloads a percentage of that risk on to the re-insurers, paying the proportionate percentage of the original premium to do so.

Re-insurance. Boring as hell. Dry as dust. Non-stop slog with pen, paper and figures – never-ending figures that just went on and on and on till you wanted to scream at the sight of them.

Lena suddenly giggled to herself. What did Hamish look like in that bowler hat? Absolutely ridiculous, in her opinion. A real city-type clown. Quite, quite absurd.

She quickly pulled herself together when she saw one of the other clerks staring at her in astonishment, no doubt because she'd giggled. It was completely out of character.

Oh, but she could murder for a fag!

Chapter 12

Georgie was on her morning tea break, chatting away to Daisy Somerville who worked alongside her, when it happened. One moment they were talking, the next an enormous explosion threw all the women present higgledy-piggledy.

Georgie lay there, stunned, groggily wondering what on earth had happened. Then she heard the screams coming from the factory floor.

Daisy was unconscious, having banged her head when going down. A thin trickle of blood was running from her mouth.

'Jesus Christ!' one of the fallen girls exclaimed, struggling to her feet. Judging from the sounds now coming from the factory floor, pandemonium had broken loose.

'Daisy! Daisy! Wake up,' Georgie muttered, gently slapping Daisy's face.

Daisy groaned, and opened her eyes. 'What happened?'

'Don't know yet. Are you hurt?'

Daisy gingerly felt her body. 'Don't think so.'

'You were knocked out.' Georgie coughed as dust clogged her throat. Glancing up she saw that the dust, and there was a lot of it, was falling in a white shower. She also noticed that a great crack had appeared in the ceiling. 'We've got to get out of here,' she croaked, fearful the ceiling might collapse.

One of the other girls opened the door leading on to the factory floor, and gasped when she saw what confronted her. A huge conflagration was blazing over to her right. And then they smelt it: the pungent aroma of bleach wafting into the room. Within seconds they were all spluttering, their eyes streaming. Another, smaller, explosion further widened the crack in the ceiling.

The girl who'd opened the door stumbled out of it, quickly followed by others as they fled the room. Georgie helped Daisy to her feet, and Daisy cursed as her legs immediately buckled under her.

'Can hardly see,' she whispered, as the bleach fumes grew steadily stronger.

Georgie's lungs seemed to be on fire as she half dragged, half pulled Daisy towards the door. When they reached it the sight that greeted them was of a raging inferno, flames roaring and hissing as the conflagration advanced, trying to encompass and consume everything in its way. The stench was unbelievable, the noxious smell of bleach even stronger than it had been in the room where they'd been having their tea break.

Georgie bent over and coughed violently, her sides heaving as she coughed again and again. Behind her, the ceiling caved in with an almighty crash.

Daisy was staring in horror at the body of a lassie lying prostrate across one of the packing benches. The girl was clearly dead. Daisy recognised her as Ishbel Campbell, a seventeen-year-old. From that distance Daisy couldn't tell what had caused Ishbel's death.

Women were still screaming, while in the distance Georgie thought she could hear the clamour of a fire engine. 'Can you walk yet?' she gasped to Daisy, who nodded that she could. 'Then let's go.'

Daisy started to shake. 'We're all going to die! We're all going to die!' she exclaimed hysterically.

'Shut it. Let's get a move on. Don't just stand there.'

'Can't!' Daisy was still hysterical.

'Can't bloody what?' Despite herself, Georgie was beginning to get angry with her workmate.

'Can't go into that. Too scared.'

Georgie's right hand flashed to crack across Daisy's cheek, a real humdinger of a blow. 'Get a grip, Daisy. For God's sake get a bloody grip. You'll die for certain if you don't make a run for it. Now come on!'

'That hurt.' Daisy's voice was hoarse.

'I was trying to knock some sense into you.'

Daisy's hand went to her throat, then her eyes rolled upwards and she collapsed to the floor, overcome by the fumes.

'Daisy!' Kneeling, Georgie grasped Daisy by the shoulders and roughly shook her, to no avail.

Georgie forced herself to stay calm. What to do? She certainly couldn't carry Daisy; her workmate was far too heavy for that. Nor could she leave her here like this.

Then she thought of Ian. He'd already lost his dad. It was up to her to see he didn't lose his mother as well. She had to save herself for his sake, if nothing else. And that meant leaving Daisy behind.

She gave her friend another shake, but there was still no response. Daisy was out like a light.

'I'm sorry,' she whispered. 'I really am. But there's nothing else I can do.'

Forcing herself to her feet again she stumbled in the direction of the main factory doors.

She was in some sort of dream world which didn't make any sense at all.

'Is that one alive, Charlie?'

'Aye, she is.'

'Then you'd better get her the hell out of here.'

Georgie's eyes fluttered open to stare into the face of a fireman bending over her. He immediately smiled.

'Not to worry, hen. Charlie's here. You're going to be all right.'

She tried to reply, but couldn't. What a lovely face he had, she thought woozily. The face of a cherub.

'Let's be having you now,' Charlie said, lifting her into a sitting position.

The next thing Georgie knew she was slung over his shoulder, vaguely aware of what might have been gunfire but was, in reality, exploding bottles.

Then she passed out again.

'She's awake,' a female voice declared.

Georgie found herself gazing up at a pristine white ceiling. She had a dreadful headache, her temples pounding. She was also desperately thirsty.

'How do you feel, Mrs Mair?'

The speaker was an elderly nurse whose expression was one of deep concern.

'Water,' Georgie finally managed to croak after several unsuccessful attempts.

A porcelain spout was manoeuvred into her mouth, and she swallowed greedily at the water flowing from it.

'That's enough for now,' the nurse told her, removing the spout. 'I can't give you any more till doctor's seen you, which will be shortly.'

Closing her eyes Georgie thought of Daisy whom she'd abandoned, and who was now probably dead. There was nothing else she could have done, she reminded herself. There was simply nothing else she could have done in the circumstances.

But that didn't make her feel any better. She'd still left Daisy behind to her fate.

'You're a very lucky woman, Mrs Mair,' Dr Almond declared, when he had finished examining Georgie. 'Even a few more minutes in that toxic environment might have proved fatal.'

Georgie gasped for breath, her throat feeling red raw and constricted. 'How many . . . ?' She trailed off to swallow saliva.

'Died?'

'Yes.'

'The figure isn't yet known. Or I should say finalised. But fourteen bodies have so far been recovered.'

Dear God, Georgie thought. She wondered who they all were, for it was a small factory and she'd known everybody by sight, and most by name.

'We have three more women here like yourself. Two with bad burns and inhalation damage, the other, like yourself, with inhalation damage.'

At least she hadn't been burnt, Georgie reflected. That was something.

'Now it's best you don't try to speak,' Dr Almond went on. 'Not for a day or two anyway.'

'Son,' Georgie croaked. 'My son.'

'You want to see him?'

'Please.'

'Tomorrow at visiting time, then. I'll have a word with the police and they'll arrange it. But no speaking, mind. Promise?'

'Promise.'

'You just rest. That's the best thing for you at the moment. Let nature take her course.' He added wryly, 'She's often a better doctor than any of us.'

'Thank you.'

'No more speaking.' He wagged a finger at her. 'If you need a bedpan catch the eye of a passing nurse and make this sign.' He demonstrated for her. 'Understand?'

She gave him the smallest of nods, and even that hurt.

She closed her eyes after he'd gone. But there was no peace for her. Over and over, in her mind's eye, she relived the terrible happenings in the factory.

'So how are you today, lass?' Chrissie had been one of the first into the ward when the bell had been rung announcing visiting hour. It was Georgie's tenth day in hospital, and her condition had steadily improved.

'Fine, Mum. I've got good news. Dr Almond has told me I can go home tomorrow,' Georgie replied, her voice newly husky as a result of the fumes she'd inhaled.

'That's wonderful.' Chrissie beamed.

'They're discharging me at ten a.m.'

'I'll be waiting for you.'

'They did offer an ambulance, but I didn't think that was necessary.'

'Are you sure?' Chrissie frowned.

'I'll be all right, honest. There's nothing wrong with my legs, after all. And we'll be in a tram for most of the way.'

'If you're absolutely certain.'

'I am, Mum.' Georgie smiled. 'I can't tell you how keen I am to get out of here. They've all been terribly nice, and the treatment's been excellent. But you know how it is?'

'Oh aye.' Chrissie nodded. 'Home's always best.' She took a deep breath. 'Now, you've not to worry about anything. I'll be there every day to do whatever needs done. Shopping, cleaning, that sort of thing. What's important is for you to get some more rest until you're really fit again.'

'Thanks, Mum.'

Chrissie dropped her gaze a little. 'They're having most of the funerals today. I thought you'd like to know.' At the final count seventeen people had died in the fire.

'Is Daisy Somerville one of them?'

'Yes. She's being buried this afternoon.'

Georgie hadn't told a soul that she'd had to leave Daisy behind. She didn't know if she ever would. Guilt hung heavily within her, and would probably remain there for the rest of her life.

'Such a tragic business, the whole thing,' Chrissie said softly, and shook her head.

'I would have been among the dead if it hadn't been for a fireman called Charlie,' Georgie declared. It was the first time she'd mentioned him. 'I would certainly have never made it out on my own.'

'God bless him,' Chrissie said, extremely grateful to Charlie, whoever he was.

'Aye, God bless him,' Georgie repeated, remembering that cherub-like face staring down at her. 'When I get home I think I'll write him a letter expressing my gratitude.'

'Good idea,' Chrissie approved.

Yes, Georgie thought. She'd do just that.

'I'm nipping out for a little while,' Hamish declared. 'Hold the fort as usual, all right?'

Lena nodded. Right on time for the coffee shop. It was getting so you could have set your watch by him. His leaving, that is – not always his return.

Hamish hesitated. 'I only heard earlier this morning that your sister was involved in that terrible fire which was in all the newspapers. Is that true?'

'Yes, Georgie was in it. Ended up in hospital as a result.'

Hamish cleared his throat. 'She survived then. Was she burnt?'

'Thankfully, no. She suffered from fume inhalation, which was nasty enough. She's home now and making a good recovery.'

'I'm delighted to hear that,' Hamish said sincerely. 'It must have been a big scare for you and your family. Is she married?'

'Widowed, with a little boy of ten. Her husband died of leukaemia a few years ago.'

'Poor woman. And poor lad. I've lost both my parents. Dad in the Great War, Mum a few years later to influenza. Though in my case I was a lot older than ten when my mum went.'

'I'm sorry to hear that. You losing your parents, I mean.'

Hamish's eyes took on a faraway look. 'I still miss them. Quite a bit actually. But there we are. What's happened has happened and nothing can change that.' He took a deep breath. 'Anyway, I'm off now. And I'm pleased to hear your sister is going to be fine.'

He wasn't such a bad old stick after all, Lena mused when he was gone, wondering if he was presently going out with anyone. Probably, she thought, though he hadn't mentioned it. There again, he rarely talked about anything concerning his private life. All she knew was that he was neither married nor engaged, and, now, that both his parents had passed on. Everything else remained a mystery.

* * *

130

Chrissie sat on the edge of their bed, put her face in her hands and burst into tears.

Tam stared at her in astonishment, then went quickly over. Sitting beside her he put a comforting arm round her shoulders. 'What's wrong, lass? What's wrong?'

Chrissie's entire upper torso was heaving. 'It just suddenly got to me, that's all,' she sobbed.

'What did?'

'Thinking about how close we came to losing Georgie.'

'Aye,' he said slowly. 'It was a near-run thing right enough. The doctor told her that even a few more minutes might have been fatal.'

'The thought of it. The very thought of it . . .' Chrissie trailed off, her mind filled with the horror of what it would have been like if Georgie had died.

'We'll simply have to put it behind us,' Tam counselled. 'That's the best thing.'

'And wee Ian. What would have happened to him?'

'He'd have come here, of course, and we'd have had another bairn to bring up. There would have been nothing else for it. But, as it is, everything's worked out all right.'

'I got such a fright when the polisman told us, Tam. I went cold inside.'

'I think we all did, lass.' He shook his head. 'As they say, you just never know the moment till the moment after.'

'No, you don't,' Chrissie agreed. 'Can you get me a hanky from that drawer over there?'

Tam did so, and handed it to her.

Chrissie sniffed as she dabbed at her eyes. 'Sorry about that. I'm better now.'

'There's nothing to be sorry about. It's perfectly normal. There have been times since the fire when I've been choked with emotion myself.'

Chrissie smiled at him. 'But you didn't cry. Glasgow men don't. They don't consider it manly.'

Tam matched her smile. He had cried, but waited till he was

alone before doing so. Not that he would ever let on. Not even to Chrissie.

As she'd said, Glasgow men weren't supposed to be soft.

A new dance hall called La Scala had opened in town and Tom had decided to pay it a visit. He was there with two pals from work, one of whom, from the looks of it, had already 'got off' with a lassie, a tall redhead with a stunning figure.

Tom liked the new dance hall, reckoning that no expense had been spared in doing it out. In the centre of the ceiling a many-faceted crystal ball was revolving, sending off what seemed like a thousand shafts of light in all directions, reflections from the spotlights directed on it.

And then he saw Brigid. In the arms of another man, she was laughing at what the chap was saying, the pair of them apparently very much at ease in one another's company.

Tom was consumed with jealousy. Though, he reminded himself, he had absolutely no right to be. Brigid was nothing to him any more. Only a distant memory. History.

Was she with the chap? Or were they only up for a dance together, having just met? He'd soon find out.

Four dances later when they still hadn't come off the floor Tom was forced to the conclusion that she was with him, though whether the chap was her boyfriend or they'd only just met he couldn't say.

He finally forced himself to take his eyes off her. His night out was completely ruined. He had to get out of there before she saw *him*, he decided. There was nothing else for it.

Ten minutes later he was in a nearby pub drinking pints and chasers, and feeling sick to the pit of his stomach.

Georgie answered a knock on the door to find a smartly dressed man carrying a briefcase standing there. 'Can I help you?'

'Are you Mrs Mair?'

'I am.'

'Let me introduce myself. I'm Mr Brown from Salamander Insurance. May I come in?'

Georgie couldn't think why this Mr Brown wanted to talk to her. She was mystified. 'What's this all about?'

'The fire you were involved in at your place of work, Mrs Mair. My company covered the factory.'

'I see,' she murmured, still uncertain about the reason for his presence here. 'Then you had better come in.'

On entering the kitchen Brown glanced swiftly around, then focused on Georgie. 'You've been in hospital, I understand?'

'That's correct.'

'For?'

She frowned. 'For what?'

'Why were you in hospital?'

'Because of the fumes I inhaled during the fire.'

'Uh-huh.' He nodded. 'And are you now fully recovered?'

Talk about twenty questions, Georgie thought. 'Not quite. I'm still suffering from a sore chest and, as you can hear, my voice has gone all husky. Dr Almond, the specialist who took care of me, says it's entirely possible my voice will remain this way.'

'And your chest?'

'Will be all right given time. I've been prescribed a mixture to help clear it up.'

'Do you mind?' Brown asked, indicating that he wanted to put his briefcase on the table.

'Help yourself.'

'Then let's get down to business, shall we?'

Lena laid down the form, which she'd read from beginning to end. 'This is easy enough to fill in. Do you want me to do it for you?'

'Please.' Georgie smiled. 'You're the expert on insurance.'

'How much will she get?' Chrissie queried from across the room.

'Hard to say, Mum. It all depends. But certainly something; I can almost vouch for that.'

Compensation, Georgie thought with glee. It had never crossed her mind until Mr Brown's visit. Now it seemed she was in for a windfall.

'Have you heard of this Salamander Insurance?' Tam asked Lena.

'Oh aye. They're a very good and respected company. A Scottish company, too, with their head office in Bath Street.'

Tam nodded his approval. The fact they were a Scottish company was recommendation enough for him.

'Right,' Lena declared. 'No time like the present. Just let me get a pen and we'll make a start.'

Half an hour later the claim form was filled in, ready for Georgie to post back to Mr Brown.

Chapter 13

'Excuse me, does someone called Charlie work here?'

The fireman Georgie had addressed stared at her for a moment or two before replying. 'Would that be Charlie Gunn?'

'I'm afraid I don't know his surname. But I'd like to speak to him, if that's possible.'

'Can I tell him who's asking?'

'Mrs Mair. But that probably won't mean anything even if it is the man I'm looking for.'

'I see,' the fireman murmured. 'Aye, all right. You hang on there, hen, and I'll send Charlie down to you.' And with that the fireman vanished up a flight of stairs.

Georgie glanced at the sky. Damn! she thought. It was going to rain. She'd get soaked if she wasn't careful.

There was a clattering of boots on the stairs, and then her Charlie appeared. He frowned when he saw her.

'Don't you recognise me?' she asked shyly, noting his puzzlement.

'I . . .' And then the penny dropped. 'You're the lassie from the fire at the bleach factory, aren't you?'

'That's right. I've come to say thank you for saving my life.'

Charlie stared at her in astonishment. 'Well! This is the first time anyone's ever done that.'

'I was going to write you a letter till it dawned on me I didn't know your surname or which station you worked at. This is the second station I've called in to enquire about you. The other one had a Charlie as well, but obviously he wasn't you.'

Charlie was tickled pink, and thought she was a lot better-looking than he recalled. There again, she'd hardly been at her best when he'd picked her up off the floor.

'I honestly don't know what to say,' he admitted, still amazed at her having sought him out.

'You don't have to say anything. Just thanks again. I'd have died that day if it wasn't for you.'

Charlie was about to reply when the heavens suddenly opened and it began to bucket down. 'Here, come inside,' he said, and Georgie hurriedly did so.

'Would you like to come upstairs and meet the rest of the lads?' Charlie asked. 'And if you've got time you can have a cup of coffee. At least stay until the rain stops.'

Georgie hesitated. This was the last thing she'd been expecting.

'Oh, come on,' Charlie urged. 'We don't bite.'

'Are you sure it'll be all right?'

'Of course. I wouldn't have asked you otherwise.'

'A cup of coffee sounds wonderful, then. Thanks.'

She followed him up the stairs into a room where the men of Charlie's watch were taking their ease, waiting for the next call-out. Some were playing cards, others reading, while one chap was sitting in a large comfy chair fast asleep.

Georgie was introduced all round, and the men were delighted when they heard why she'd called in to see Charlie. She thanked them as a group, for they too had attended the fire. Then Charlie ushered her to a chair and fetched her a cup of coffee from a pot already made. He sat opposite her and smiled while she had a sip from the cup he'd handed her.

'Fag?' he offered, holding out his packet.

Georgie shook her head. 'I do smoke, or used to anyway, but haven't had one since the fire. It's my chest, you see. One puff and it's agony.'

'Due to fume inhalation?'

'That's right.'

'I'm sorry to hear it. Were you burnt at all?'

'No, you got me out before that happened.'

'Good. Though fume inhalation is bad enough. How long were you in hospital for?'

Georgie told him. 'This husky voice is another after-effect of the inhalation. My specialist said I might have it for the rest of my life.'

'Well, I like it.' Charlie beamed at her. 'It's sexy.'

Georgie coloured, and glanced away, thinking that the remark was a bit forward on such a short acquaintance.

'Mr Mair must have been . . . how shall I put it? Relieved to say the least that you survived.'

'My husband is dead,' Georgie replied softly. 'He died a few years back from leukaemia.'

'I'm sorry.' Charlie looked stricken. 'Trust me to put my two big feet in it.'

'Don't worry. You weren't to know.'

Charlie sighed. 'As a matter of fact I'm a widower myself. My wife tripped going down the tenement stairs where we live, fell and broke her neck. Died instantly.'

Georgie expressed her sympathy.

'Left me with my daughter Avril to bring up. Which hasn't been easy considering the shifts I do.'

Georgie could well imagine. 'How old is she?'

'Ten.'

'Same as my son Ian. He's ten as well.'

'Really? Now there's a coincidence. It would seem we have a lot in common.

They sat in silence for a few moments, until Charlie asked, 'Does it bother you if I smoke?'

'Of course not. Go ahead.'

She watched him as he lit up. He wasn't exactly a handsome man, but she found his cherubic face most appealing.

'So how do you manage with Avril?' she queried. 'Surely she's too young to be at home alone overnight? You do work night shifts on occasion, I take it?'

'Oh aye. As many night shifts as day ones. I would have had to change my job if it wasn't for my married sister Betty, who lives just round the corner. She takes care of Avril when I'm not there. She also does our washing and ironing, for which I pay her. Betty's been a godsend, I can tell you.'

Georgie finished her coffee, then glanced at a nearby window. 'It's stopped raining,' she observed. 'I'd better be going.'

'What's your first name, by the way?' Charlie asked.

'Georgie. Short for Georgina.'

'Georgie,' he repeated. 'I like it. It suits you.'

'Thank you.'

'It's been a pleasure meeting you, Georgie.'

'And you, Charlie. I'm glad I came.'

'And I'm glad you did. As I said, you're the first one who's ever taken the trouble to say thank you. I'm touched.'

She laid her cup and saucer on the floor, then rose. He did the same.

'I'll see you out,' he declared.

Georgie said goodbye to the rest of the lads, thinking what a nice, friendly lot they were. Then Charlie escorted her down the stairs. At the entrance to the station they halted.

'Goodbye then, Charlie.'

'Goodbye, Georgie. Good luck.'

She extended a hand, and they shook.

'You take care now. Don't get caught up in any more fires,' he joked.

'I'll try not to.'

Turning, she strode away. She'd only gone a few yards when he called after her. Then he was there at her side. 'I was wondering,' he said, and cleared his throat, 'if you'd care to go to the pictures with me on Saturday night?'

She was completely taken aback. 'You mean go out with you?'

'That's right. To the pictures. And we could have fish suppers afterwards if you like?'

'I . . . er . . .'

He mistook her hesitation for a refusal. 'Don't worry,' he apologised. 'It was just a thought.'

Her initial instinct had been to say no. Now she wasn't so sure. 'Can I be honest with you?'

'Of course.'

'I haven't been out with anyone since John died.'

'Coincidence again. I haven't been out with anyone either since Agnes broke her neck. So why don't we give it a go together, eh?'

Her heart was in her mouth as she made a decision. 'Where shall we meet?'

He named a place in the centre of Glasgow, and suggested a time.

'I'll be there,' she promised.

'I'm really looking forward to it.'

'Till then.'

'Till then, Georgie.'

'Going out with a man!' Chrissie exclaimed.

'Well, it would hardly be another woman,' Tom commented, laughing.

'The man who saved my life, don't forget,' Georgie reminded her mother.

'I appreciate that.'

'I, for one, approve.' Tam nodded. 'It's high time you got out and enjoyed yourself again instead of being stuck in that house night after night.'

'Quite right,' Tom agreed.

Georgie glanced down at the floor. 'John told me the night he died that I was too young not to consider marrying again. He was quite insistent about that.'

'Why, are you thinking of marrying this Charlie?' Chrissie asked in alarm.

'Of course not, Mum. I've only just met him. But in order to remarry some day, should it ever come to that, I have to start somewhere. And going to the flicks with Charlie seems as good a point as any.'

Lena was listening, trying to control the jealousy she felt. Her sister had lost one man, and now it would appear she might have found another. Bitterness gnawed inside her as she thought about her own bleak situation.

'So will you look after Ian on Saturday night, Mum?'

'I'd be delighted to, lass. He can bed down in Tom's room and you can collect him Sunday morning.'

Georgie turned to Ian standing by her side. 'You don't mind staying with Granny and Grandpa Saturday night, do you?'

Ian was idly scratching a patch of itchy skin. 'Why can't I come to the pictures with you and this Charlie?' he queried with a frown.

Georgie suppressed a smile. 'Oh, we'll be out far too late for someone your age. You'll be all tucked up and long in the land of nod before I get home.'

Tam winked at his grandson. 'You'll enjoy it here, Ian. We can listen to the wireless. You like listening to the wireless, don't you?'

Ian nodded.

'And I'll bake a cake,' Chrissie declared.

'A chocolate one?' Ian asked eagerly.

'If that's what you want.'

'Oh yes please, Granny!'

Georgie smiled. 'Thanks, Mum. Thanks, Papa.'

'You can tell us all about it on Sunday,' Tom teased her. 'All the gory details, if you know what I mean?'

'Get lost,' she snapped back good-naturedly.

Tom laughed.

On Saturday afternoon Georgie stood by the graveside staring at John's headstone. Ian was already at his granny and grandpa's, and she had felt she had to come and make her peace with John before going out with Charlie later.

'It was your idea, John,' she said softly, as though speaking to him face to face. 'You did give me permission.' She paused, and took a deep breath. 'So I know you'll understand why I'm doing this even though I still love you, and always will.'

Wind rustled in a nearby stand of trees, while overhead two crows cawed raucously.

'Always will,' she repeated.

She was wiping away tears as she left the graveside and made for the main gate out of the cemetery. Daisy Somerville's grave would still be unmarked, or she would have visited Daisy too, and apologised again for leaving her behind in the fire.

'Good God!' Georgie exclaimed.

Charlie turned to her. 'What's wrong?' he whispered.

'I know that woman,' she whispered back.

'What woman?'

'The one who's just come on screen. She's a friend of my sister's who went to Hollywood to become an actress. And there she is.'

Charlie glanced at the screen. 'Which one?'

'The one on the left.' Wait till she told Lena about this, Georgie thought gleefully. She couldn't wait.

'This fish supper is the best I've ever tasted,' she exclaimed later, as Charlie walked her to her tram stop after the film.

'I told you it would be. That one's the best fish and chip shop in all Glasgow.'

She smiled at him. 'So how do you know about it?'

He tapped his nose. 'We firemen get to hear all manner of things. You'd be surprised.'

'Such as?'

'The best fish and chip shop in Glasgow, for example,' he teased.

'And?'

'Which pubs will let you in the back door after hours for another.'

Georgie laughed. 'Trust a man to count that as important.'

She was thoroughly enjoying her night out, finding Charlie easy and relaxing to be with. The more she knew him the more she liked him.

'Can I ask you a question, Georgie?'

'Which is?'

'What did your husband do for a living?'

'Same as you. He was a fireman.'

'Really!' Charlie exclaimed. 'Another coincidence.'

'But he wasn't the same type of fireman as you. He worked on the railway – LMS.'

'Oh, I see.' Charlie nodded. 'He kept the firebox going. Like a stoker on a ship?'

'It was John's great ambition to one day be promoted to engine driver. But he died before that could happen.'

Charlie glanced at her, wondering if it was wise to ask his next question. He decided he would. 'Do you still miss him?'

She took her time in replying. 'Yes, I do, to tell the truth. We were very close. But he's dead, and life goes on. What about you?'

'Do you mean regarding Agnes?'

'Uh-huh.'

'Not really. It wasn't exactly the happiest of marriages. We rowed a lot. It sounds callous to say this, but it was actually something of a relief when she fell down those stairs.'

Georgie was slightly shocked, though she wasn't sure why. She was well aware that not everyone had as happy a marriage as she and John.

'Do you think me terrible for admitting such a thing?' Charlie asked softly.

'No, not really. If that was the case then that was the case. No point in pretending otherwise.'

'Good.'

They continued chatting until they reached the tram stop, disposing of their fish and chip wrappings on the way. They were the only ones at the stop.

'There should be a tram along in a minute.' Georgie smiled at him.

'Have you enjoyed yourself?'

'Oh aye.'

'Me too. A lot, actually.' He spotted a tramcar in the distance. 'You were right about one being along in a minute.'

'If it's mine, that is.'

'Georgie, would you like to go out with me again?'

She'd already decided on her answer, should the question be asked. 'Yes.' She smiled.

'It'll have to be in the week because of my shifts. How would Tuesday night suit?'

'I don't see why not.'

'There's a little restaurant I know. Nothing fancy, mind. Plain cooking, but it is licensed. How about that?'

'Sounds wonderful.'

They quickly arranged a time and place to meet, and then the tram, which was Georgie's, drew alongside.

'Thanks for tonight, Charlie.'

As Georgie moved to board the tram Charlie pecked her on the cheek. 'Thank you, Georgie. 'Bye for now.'

When the tram had moved away Georgie touched the spot where he'd kissed her. To her amazement she didn't feel the least bit guilty.

Tam sighed as he dropped his newspaper on to his lap.

'What's wrong?' Chrissie queried.

'I don't like what I'm reading nowadays. There are hard times ahead, lass, you mark my words.'

'How so?'

Tom glanced up from what he was doing. 'Yeah, how so, Papa?'

'It would seem industry is beginning to feel the knock-on effect of the Wall Street crash last October.'

'But that was in America!' Tom exclaimed.

'None the less, it's going to affect us. We could be in for a bad slump.'

'But we've a Labour government in power,' Chrissie declared. 'Surely they won't let anything happen here?'

'They may not be able to do anything about it,' Tam said.

'Unemployment could just rise and rise. That's how these things work.'

'What about McNair's?' Tom queried, alarmed.

'Who knows?' Tam shrugged. 'We might be all right. There again, maybe not. What do you say, Lena? You're the brains in the family.'

'You're right, things aren't looking too good. Our economy was already fragile before the crash. What I do know is the volume of business at work has been steadily decreasing of late, causing concern amongst the management. It's early days yet, but if I was asked to give a prediction it would have to be a gloomy one. Perhaps even worse than that.'

'Unemployment,' Chrissie whispered fearfully. It was the nightmare of every working-class housewife.

'We'll just have to wait and see,' Tam declared. 'We may be worrying for nothing.'

Maybe, Lena thought to herself.

Georgie's eyes literally bulged when she saw the size of the cheque that had been enclosed with Mr Brown's letter. Two hundred and ten pounds was an absolute fortune to her. A king's ransom.

She shook her head in disbelief. Surely there had been some mistake? There had to be. She'd been hoping for some decent money, twenty or thirty quid perhaps. But two hundred and ten pounds! She'd never dreamt she'd ever have so much.

Raising the cheque to her mouth she kissed it, her mind whirling. What a windfall! What an absolutely marvellous bloody windfall!

First things first, she told herself. She had to get this cheque into a bank, which meant opening an account as she didn't have one. Neither had John, when he was alive. They had lived from one pay day to the next, same as all the families she knew. The sole exception was Lena.

Her hands were shaking as she slipped on her coat, trying to remember where the nearest bank was. Minutes later she was hurrying down the road, the precious cheque secure in her purse.

Chapter 14

It was the second week Hamish had been off with a badly sprained ankle, leaving Lena in charge of the department. She was thoroughly enjoying the responsibility, and as far as she was concerned he could stay away as long as he liked.

She closed the ledger she'd been working on, which brought her own work up to date. She glanced at the other girls, all beavering away, and wondered what to do next. She considered going to the ladies for a fly fag, but decided against it. She'd leave that till later.

Then she remembered something she'd been puzzled about for a long time. Hamish kept several ledgers in a desk drawer which only he ever dealt with. Now why would he do that?

On a whim she decided to investigate. With Hamish off, who was to gainsay her, after all? Curiosity had simply got the better of her. Or downright nosiness, as her mother would have called it. Rising, she went to Hamish's office and went inside, closing the door firmly behind her. With the door shut no one could see what she was up to.

She found the ledgers easily enough, none of the drawers in the desk being locked. Placing them on the desktop, she stared at them. They seemed ordinary enough. No different from the many which passed through her hands. So why did Hamish keep them to himself? It was completely out of character for him to do any work when there were others he could pass it on to.

Sitting at the desk, Lena drew the first ledger to her, and opened it.

Lena was in Hamish's office for well over an hour before she closed the second ledger and sat back in his chair. She was absolutely stunned. Hamish was cooking the books, at least where these entries were concerned.

No doubt about it. He was embezzling. Oh, not a huge amount. But fifty quid a month was embezzlement all the same. No wonder he kept these ledgers in his desk and did all the book-keeping himself. The bugger was at it!

She had to think about this, Lena told herself. Embezzlement was a very serious offence. Not only would Hamish be sacked if she reported him, he could also go to prison.

Replacing the ledgers where she'd found them she left the office and went straight to the ladies, where she lit up. Who would have thought it? Certainly not her. Hamish on the fiddle! If it wasn't so serious she'd have laughed. This was a side to the incompetent Hamish she'd never have dreamt existed.

'Davey McIlwham has been laid off,' Chrissie announced to Tam when he and Tom returned from McNair's that evening. Davey and his family lived up the same close as the McKeands.

Tam regarded his wife grimly. 'How many altogether?'

'Fifteen, I was told.'

Davey was employed in a sheet metal factory where he'd grafted man and boy. If Tam's recollection was correct the factory employed about thirty men, which meant half the workforce had been laid off. This was bad news indeed. A portent of things to come?

'How are he and Doreen taking it?' he asked.

'You can imagine. Doreen's beside herself. They've got three children to feed, don't forget.'

Tam took a deep breath. 'I'll go down and have a sympathetic

146

word with him later. Not that it'll do much good, but it's the least a neighbour can do.'

'Aye.' Chrissie nodded. 'You do that, Tam.'

'Now, what's for tea, woman? I'm starving.'

Lena was lying on her bed staring at the ceiling, thinking about what she'd discovered earlier in the day and the difficult position it put her in.

She was hardly over-enamoured with Hamish, but at the same time she had nothing personal against him. On the contrary, in many ways she'd become fond of the sod. What on earth had made him do it? He must be paid a reasonable wage after all as head of a department, albeit a small one. Nor did he have a wife and family to provide for.

Idiot! she thought. Bloody idiot! In her mind's eye she gave him a good kick up the backside for being so incredibly stupid.

It seemed to her she had two options. One was to keep quiet about the whole thing and let matters go on as they had. The only trouble there was what if he got found out in future by someone other than herself? That was always a possibility, even though he did keep those ledgers apart from the others that went through the department. Any sharp-eyed clerk would soon pick up on what he was doing, just as she had. Then it would definitely be the sack for him and maybe prison.

The alternative was to report him and let him suffer the consequences, which she was hesitant to do.

Then a third possibility struck her. She could tell him what she'd discovered and offer to re-do the books so the embezzlement would never be found, the proviso being his promise never to do anything so stupid again. She could save his bacon, in other words.

Out of the blue an idea came to her. An idea so outrageous it simply took her breath away and made her go cold all over. Swinging her feet on to the floor she lit a cigarette with hands that were suddenly trembling.

She couldn't. No, she couldn't. Or . . . could she?

*   *   *

Georgie let herself into the house after another evening out with Charlie. Yet again she'd thoroughly enjoyed his company. The pair of them got on like a house on fire. Things were beginning to get serious, she told herself. The idea pleased her a great deal.

That night she dreamt about Charlie, and in the morning she woke with a huge smile on her face.

'How's the ankle?' Lena enquired when Hamish presented himself. He had been off for three full weeks.

'A lot better, thank you.'

'How did you sprain it in the first place?'

'Haring after a bus, believe it or not. It sort of turned under me, and that was that. Minutes later it was swollen to the size of a tennis ball. Painful as hell, I can tell you. I was in agony.'

Lena nodded her sympathy. 'Well, before you ask, everything's fine here. Up to date and running like clockwork.'

He beamed at her. 'I expected nothing else with you in charge, Lena. You're a treasure right enough.' And with that he went into his office and closed the door behind him.

Later, Lena glanced at the wall clock. Half an hour to go, and she still hadn't made her move. Several times she'd been about to, then changed her mind at the last moment and sat down again.

She didn't have to do it today, she reminded herself. He was only just back, after all. But in her heart of hearts she knew that to be the lamest of excuses. Tom was right when he'd told her she lacked guts. She always had been that way.

But not now. Not bloody now!

Rising, she went to his closed door, knocked, and went in. Hamish looked up in surprise.

'What can I do for you, Lena?'

'I think you and I should have a drink in the Swan tonight.'

He stared at her in puzzlement. 'What? Why?'

'Because I have something important to say to you.'

'Can't you say it here?'

'No. It's too personal for that.'

He continued staring at her, his puzzlement deepening. 'I don't understand.'

'You will. Right after work. That suit?'

'If you insist.'

'I do, Hamish. I most certainly do.'

His forehead crinkled in a frown as she swept away.

Hamish placed a large gin and tonic in front of Lena, who had deliberately chosen an out-of-the-way table where they wouldn't be overheard. 'Now what's this all about?'

She waited till he was seated before replying. 'You're a fool, Hamish Murchison. A damned fool.'

He blinked at her. 'I beg your pardon?'

'You heard me, Hamish. You're a fool.' Surprised by her own calmness, she had a sip of her drink, then lit a cigarette, while he stared at her in astonishment.

'Perhaps you'd care to explain that?' There was a trace of anger in his voice.

'Did you really think you could defraud the company and get away with it?'

His face drained of colour until it was left a pasty shade of white, his eyes out on stalks. 'That's . . . that's . . .' he stuttered.

'Don't try to deny it, Hamish. While you were off I had a look at those ledgers you keep in your desk, which told the story. You've been at it since shortly after becoming head of department to the tune of roughly fifty pounds a month.' She found she was rather enjoying this. His expression was a mixture of terror and sheer incredulity.

'How dare you go through my desk,' he choked at last.

'Not exactly ethical, I admit. But what I found was most illuminating.'

'It's a damned lie!'

She sighed. 'No, it isn't, Hamish. As you're well aware. You've been cooking the books. Thieving, in other words. For which you can be sacked, and most likely sent to prison.' She watched in amusement while he picked up the whisky he'd ordered for himself and drank it in one go. 'Such sloppy book-keeping, too. What you were up to almost leapt off the page at me.'

'What . . .' He swallowed. 'What are you going to do? Are you going to report me?'

She puffed on her cigarette and deliberately didn't reply for a few moments, making him suffer. 'That depends,' she drawled eventually.

'On what?'

'Whether or not we come to an arrangement.'

He was sweating now, trickles of it running down his forehead. 'What sort of an arrangement?' he croaked.

'Embezzlement,' she mused, shaking her head. 'I'd never have thought it of you, Hamish.'

'What arrangement?' he almost screamed.

'Control yourself, man,' she chided. 'You don't want to draw attention to yourself now, do you?'

He quickly glanced round the room, but no one was watching. 'No.'

'Why don't you go and get yourself another whisky? You look as though you could use one.'

He hesitated, desperate to hear what this arrangement was, but his need for another drink momentarily overrode all other considerations. Getting to his feet he strode swiftly back to the bar. Lena was amused to see him ordering two doubles, the first of which he threw down his throat before returning to the table carrying the second.

'This arrangement?'

'I don't think you'd like prison, Hamish. Nasty places, I understand. Then, when you came out, who would employ you? You'd probably end up doing something manual, which doesn't strike me as being you at all.'

He gritted his teeth in fear and frustration. 'What's the arrangement, Lena. Come on, out with it.'

'I'm not exactly a pretty woman, am I?'

He glanced away.

'Well? Be honest.'

150

'No, you're not,' he admitted.

'Haven't got much of a figure either.'

He didn't reply to that.

'You know what my big dread in life is, Hamish?'

'What?'

'Ending up an old maid. Unmarried, unloved and never having known a man in the biblical sense.'

Dear God, he thought in alarm. Was she about to propose marriage? The idea of being married to Lena McKeand made him feel sick inside. She was the original dog.

'Well, now I'm in a position to sort out one of these things,' she said slowly.

He opened his mouth, shut it. Then opened it again. This was a living nightmare. 'Which one?'

She treated him to a razored smile, the look of a bird of prey about to pounce on its victim. 'The arrangement is that you sleep with me once a month. That's all I ask. That arrangement to last until the day you get married, at which time it's dissolved. As a bonus for you, and to make this more palatable, I'll allow you to keep on doing what you've been doing, but in the meantime will show you how to do it in a way whereby your chances of being caught in the future are absolutely minimal. And, if you take my advice, you'll re-do the ledgers already in existence in the same manner. In other words, make new books to replace those in your drawer.'

Lena sat back in her chair and studied him. There, it was done. She'd had the courage after all. And, surprisingly, she'd rather enjoyed herself in the process.

'This is blackmail,' he accused hoarsely, mind reeling.

'Yes, isn't it just.' She smiled.

He tried to imagine what it would be like in prison, how it would be to be surrounded by hardened criminals. And, as Lena had pointed out, what would he do for employment on his release? Dig ditches? Him, Hamish Murchison! The very idea made him cringe.

'Well?' Lena prompted.

'You don't give me much choice.'

'Well, it's either one thing or the other. I imagine your golf pal, the chairman, wouldn't be very happy to be informed of your little sideline. It would be the end of a beautiful friendship. Of course, if he doesn't find out, then I would think there's further promotion in the pipeline for you, wouldn't you say?'

'Bitch,' he snarled.

'Sticks and stones, Hamish. Sticks and stones.' She finished her drink and pushed her glass across the table. 'I'll have another, please.'

He glared at her before picking up the empty glass and returning to the bar. She lit a second cigarette, considering the prospect of being in bed with the handsome Hamish. The images flashing through her mind aroused her, causing her to shift in her chair.

'Thank you,' she said when he returned with another large gin.

'Just once a month?'

'That's right.'

'And the arrangement stops the day I get married?'

She nodded.

'And you'll show me how—'

'Yes, yes,' Lena cut in. 'We've been through all that. You know exactly what the proposition is. So, take it or leave it.'

He stared at her, trying to find something even vaguely attractive in that face of hers. He failed.

'I agree,' he said woodenly.

'The first Saturday of every month,' she said. 'And I leave it to you to fix up where our meetings will take place.'

'All right.'

She'd pulled it off, Lena thought with glee. She smiled at Hamish, who didn't smile back.

Georgie was thoroughly enjoying herself, but then she always did when she was with Charlie. They were at a dinner dance, the first she'd ever been to.

'That was lovely,' she declared, pushing her plate slightly away from herself.

'It is good, isn't it? More wine?'

'Please.' Georgie giggled as he refilled her glass. 'I'm not used to wine. It's making me feel all girly.'

'I like that.'

'Do you?'

'Uh-huh.'

He had gorgeous eyes, she thought. Kind, warm, tender. Occasionally when she caught him looking at her it made her shiver.

He smiled. 'You're an excellent dancer.'

'Thank you. But I'm not nearly as good as my brother Tom. Now he really can dance. He's got magical feet, that one. Fairy feet, my mum says.'

Charlie laughed. 'I don't think I'd like to be told I had fairy feet. Whoever heard of a fireman with those?'

'Or a moulder, which is what Tom does. But that's what Mum says.'

Charlie regarded her over the rim of his glass. 'They sound a wonderful family. Perhaps I should meet them some time?'

'Would you like to?'

'Very much so.'

'Well, I'm sure that can be arranged.'

'I'll look forward to the occasion.' Reaching across the table he laid a hand on hers. 'I'm glad you came to the station that day.'

'So am I.'

'Whoever thought it would develop into this?'

Georgie merely smiled.

'Shall we?' he asked as the band struck up again.

'Of course.'

She sighed with pleasure as he took her into his arms, feeling completely at home there. At home, and totally safe.

Lena took a deep breath before knocking Hamish's door. He opened it almost immediately.

'Hello,' she said, a slight nervous catch in her voice.

'Hello. Come on in.'

153

Knowing that he lived on his own, his parents being dead, she'd been expecting a right old tip. To her amazement the inside of the house gleamed like a new pin.

'Gin and tonic?'

'Please.'

As he poured she noticed that the bottle of malt on display was one of the very best. And expensive.

'I thought we'd have a few drinks before . . .' He trailed off, and coughed.

'Good idea.'

She sat, and gazed around. 'If you don't mind me asking, how does a bachelor keep his place so neat and tidy?'

Hamish grinned. 'That's easy. He hires a neighbour, who's a middle-aged widow, to "do" for him. Dust, clean, polish and so on. She also washes and irons, sews, and does other repairs.'

'I see. And you can afford her, plus the best whisky, because of you-know-what?'

'Exactly. It also pays for better clothes than I could normally afford, and lots besides.' Hamish dropped his gaze to stare at the floor. 'Lena, before we go any further I've a confession to make.'

'And what's that?'

'I've never . . . well, to put it bluntly I've never been to bed with a woman. All this will be new to me.'

It pleased her enormously. 'That makes two of us. So it'll be all right then.'

He nodded his relief, feeling a lot better after his admission. He wouldn't be expected to perform like some expert. They had their several drinks, which gradually relaxed them both. 'Shall we go through to the bedroom?' he suggested after a while.

Lena rose, only too eager to do so, yet apprehensive at the same time.

When, later, she left Hamish to walk off down the road she was wearing the broadest of smiles. What had happened had been a bit of a grope and fumble. But they'd got there in the end.

And she wasn't a virgin any more.

Chapter 15

'What an exceptionally nice chap,' Chrissie enthused after Georgie and Charlie had left them. Charlie had been invited for Sunday dinner.

'Decent of him to bring a bottle of whisky along,' Tam commented warmly, and decided to have another dram from what was left.

'They make a good couple, don't you think?' Chrissie asked Lena.

'Aye, I thought so as well.' Lena wasn't nearly as jealous of her sister as she would have been before her arrangement with Hamish. At least, now, she wasn't completely left out of things.

'What did you think, Tom?' asked Chrissie.

'I quite took to him. He's certainly charming enough.'

Ian, who had elected to spend the afternoon with his grandparents, was in a corner playing with an old tin tray, not listening to the conversation.

'Do you imagine it's wedding bells?' Tom mused.

Chrissie looked at Tam, who shrugged. 'Might be.'

'She could certainly do a lot worse.' Chrissie nodded, keen on the idea.

'Ian seemed to take a shine to him,' Tom commented.

'Maybe that's because Charlie brought him sweets,' Lena pointed out cynically.

'No, there was more to it than that. At least I thought so.'
Tom was sticking to his guns.

'If nothing else, I'm glad we've met the man who saved
Georgie's life,' Tam declared. 'We all owe him a lot for that.'

'No one more than Georgie,' Chrissie muttered.

'Aye,' Tam agreed, sipping the dram he'd just poured. That
was true enough.

'Let's just hope she's fallen on her feet and met another as
good and kind as John, God rest his soul,' said Chrissie.

Tam's face clouded at the reminder of John, whom he'd liked
enormously. What a tragedy that had been.

'Well, I for one approve,' Chrissie went on. 'If they do decide
to wed I only hope they make each other happy.'

'I'm sure they will.' Lena smiled.

'What? Get married or make each other happy if they do?'
said Tom.

'Both.'

Tam produced his pipe and lit up, thinking about Charlie and
what his first impression had been. One thing was certain, it
hadn't been a bad one; quite the contrary. That was enough for
Tam, who considered himself an excellent judge of character.

'Come on, Lena, let's get these dishes done,' Chrissie urged.
'I'll wash, you dry.'

Lena rose and joined her mother at the sink, while Tam began
reading those parts of the Sunday paper he so far hadn't, and
Tom fell asleep. The excitement over, it was a normal Sunday
afternoon at home.

'How did I do?' Charlie demanded of Georgie the moment they
were down the stairs and out on the street.

She linked his arm. 'They liked you.'

'Are you sure?'

'Oh aye, I am that. They all took to you. Thought you were
terrific.'

'How about Ian?'

'Bringing him sweets helped. It was a good idea, that.'

'Bribery and corruption, eh?' Charlie laughed.

'A wee bit bribery perhaps, but hardly corruption.'

They smiled at one another. Then, acting on impulse, Charlie kissed her swiftly on the mouth.

'Not in the street!' Georgie exclaimed, pretending to be scandalised. 'What will the neighbours think?'

'Bugger the neighbours. They shouldn't be peeping out from behind their curtains anyway.'

Georgie laughed. 'You'll never stop them doing that. They're a right nosy lot round here.'

'Well, they should find better things to do than spy on each other.'

Georgie pulled herself even closer to him as they headed for Charlie's tram stop. 'When am I going to see you again?'

'How about this Saturday? You can come to my house and meet Avril. How does that sound?'

'Fine by me.'

'She already knows about you so it won't be a bolt out of the blue. Would you like to bring Ian along?'

'Yes, why not?'

'That's agreed, then.'

She stared lovingly into his eyes, and this time it was she who kissed him swiftly on the mouth.

'What about the neighbours!' he exclaimed, tongue firmly in cheek.

'Bugger them. With knobs on.'

They laughed uproariously as they continued on their way.

'Lena, can you come into my office for a minute?'

She glanced up from what she was doing, then got to her feet and followed him.

'Shut the door, will you?' Hamish produced a ledger which he placed on his desktop. 'This is the first of the two I'm redoing. Will you tell me what you think?'

Lena lifted the ledger, opened it at random, and studied the figures on that page.

He'd learnt well, she thought, although he had not been the easiest of people to teach, not being exactly the sharpest knife in the drawer. He had about as much aptitude for figures as she had for glamour modelling. She flipped over some pages and again studied the figures, while Hamish looked anxiously on.

'It'll do,' she declared at last.

Hamish gave a sigh of relief.

'Where's the one it's replacing?'

'Don't worry, it's at my house. I'll destroy it now you've given that one the all clear.'

'And the second ledger?'

'I shall be starting on that right away. The sooner I've covered my tracks the better, eh?'

She nodded her approval. 'I'll get back to work, then.'

'So must I. Lots to do.'

Like going to the coffee house, Lena thought cynically. At the door she paused. 'You haven't forgotten this Saturday is the first in the month?'

He met her steady gaze. 'I haven't forgotten, Lena. I'll be waiting.'

And she'd be there. Dead on time. She was already counting the days.

'Hello, Avril. I'm delighted to meet you.' Georgie smiled at the curly-golden-haired girl looking up at her. What a beauty, she thought. If Charlie's face was cherubic then Avril's was angelic. She was the prettiest wee lassie Georgie had seen in a long time.

'Hello, Mrs Mair,' Avril replied solemnly, extending a thin white hand.

Georgie had already thought about this introduction, and made a decision. 'I think Mrs Mair is a little formal,' she said, shaking with Avril. 'Why don't you just call me Georgie?'

'If you wish, Georgie.'

Georgie's smile became a beam. 'That's far better. And this is my son Ian.'

Ian already hated this house. He didn't like the way it smelt, or the unfamiliar furniture. He disliked everything about it, particularly the fact that although it was sunny out, it was dark inside. He would later learn that the inside of the house was permanently gloomy which was why the gas mantles were on all the time when anybody was at home.

'Hello, Ian. Nice to meet you.'

'And you, Avril.'

How sweet, Georgie thought. They weren't acting like children but like rather diminutive grown-ups. She thought it touching.

'Why don't you take Ian through and show him your bedroom?' Charlie suggested.

Ian didn't want to visit a lassie's bedroom. It was probably full of dolls and other daft feminine things. Nor did Avril want to take him there. Her bedroom was her private place.

'What a good idea,' Georgie enthused, hoping the youngsters were going to get on together.

Avril glanced at her father and saw the look in his eyes. She'd have to obey. 'All right then,' she declared. 'Come on, Ian.'

Reluctantly, almost dragging his feet, he followed her.

'That seems to have got off to a good start,' Charlie commented.

Georgie thought so too. 'They'll soon warm to one another, you'll see.'

'They're just shy, that's all. Quite natural.'

Georgie dismissed the subject. 'Now, what are we having for dinner?'

'I'm not much of a cook, I'm afraid, Georgie. So if you don't mind, it's just mince and potatoes.'

'My favourite,' Georgie lied. 'And you don't have to worry about cooking. I'll do that. Just show me where everything is.'

He'd been hoping she'd volunteer. 'That's very good of you.'

'Don't mention it.'

'I swear that's the best mince and potatoes I've ever tasted,' Charlie declared, pushing his plate away.

'Thank you,' Georgie acknowledged. 'Are you enjoying it, Avril?'

The wee girl stared at her, face expressionless. 'My mummy was a good cook. Isn't that so, Daddy?'

'Yes, she was, hen. A very good cook,' Charlie replied, eyes flicking to Georgie to see what she was making of this.

'You must miss your mummy a lot, Avril,' Georgie said quietly.

'Can I get down now, Daddy?'

'Not yet. Ian and Georgie haven't finished.'

'I have,' Ian muttered, pushing his plate away as well, wondering when they were going to leave this place and go home. The sooner the better as far as he was concerned.

At that moment there was the scrape of a key in a lock. 'That'll be my sister Betty,' Charlie explained. 'She said she'd drop by.'

The woman who entered the room was unmistakably related to Charlie, having the same cherubic face and similar colouring. 'You must be the Georgie I've heard so much about?' She smiled. 'I'm pleased I get to meet you at last.'

Georgie rose from her chair and shook hands with the newcomer. 'And I'm pleased to meet you. I would have recognised you anywhere as Charlie's sister.'

'Aye, people have always said we look alike.' She glanced at the table. 'Am I interrupting?'

'No, no,' Charlie assured her, coming to his feet. 'We'd just finished.'

Georgie introduced Ian, who got up to shake hands and then more or less hid behind his mother.

'Georgie cooked the dinner,' Charlie informed his sister.

'That's nice.'

'Charlie peeled the potatoes,' Georgie added, feeling awkward.

'That's right, you keep him up to scratch, Georgie. He can be a lazy sod at times. That so, Charlie?'

'According to you, anyway. No one else has ever complained.'

'Agnes did. All the time.' Betty's hand flew to her mouth. 'Sorry. Maybe I shouldn't have said that.'

'No offence taken,' Georgie said, forcing a smile on to her face. 'She was Charlie's wife, after all.'

* * *

'Georgie has a funny voice,' Avril said after the visitors had gone.

'That's because the fumes from the fire I saved her from damaged her throat,' Charlie explained.

Avril's expression was one of sheer admiration. 'Were you a hero, Daddy?'

'Of course.'

'You're always a hero, aren't you?'

This was a favourite conversation of theirs. He nodded. 'Always.'

'I love you, Daddy.'

'And I love you, pet. You know that.'

She went to him and buried her head in his lap. 'You won't ever leave me, will you, Daddy?'

'Never,' he assured her.

There was a few minutes' silence, then Avril said, 'Ian has got horrid skin. Did you notice?'

'He has some sort of skin problem. Georgie has mentioned it in the past. The doctors are hoping he'll grow out of it as he gets older.'

'It's still horrid.'

'Tell me, what did you think of Georgie? Did you like her?'

Avril didn't reply.

'Well?'

'Her mince wasn't as good as Mummy's.'

And that's all Charlie could get out of his daughter on the subject.

Lena's eyes opened wide as she gave a loud moan of pleasure. So this is what it's meant to be like with a man, she thought.

And then she found she was mistaken. There was more. Throwing back her head she screamed in reaction to the sensation exploding through her insides.

'That really was something,' Hamish said a few minutes later. Lena was lying staring catlike at him.

'I think we got it right this time,' she said.

He laughed. 'I think so too.'

Lena closed her eyes, reliving what had just taken place, aware that her entire body was glowing in a way it never had before.

'More champagne?'

'Please.'

She sat up when he handed her a glass, her eyes locking on to his over its rim when she drank.

'We seem to have learned rather quickly,' he commented.

Lena couldn't have agreed more.

Tam was pleased with himself – or dead chuffed as he might well have put it. Another deal with Groves, the scrapman, had been completed, with even more profit than usual as he'd been able to include rolls of copper wire, the price of which was currently extremely high.

Life as a foreman certainly had its perks, Tam reflected. If you were prepared to take the risks, that is. As long as McNair's never found out mind. And he was damned careful they never would.

He kept fingering the extra notes in his pocket as he and Tom made their way home at the end of their day's work.

Lena laid down the latest letter she'd had from Pet. The big news was that Pet was going out with a famous Mexican actor called Ricardo Martinez, who'd starred in many films as the romantic lead. Pet was terribly excited about this latest liaison, even hinting that it might lead to marriage if things continued as they were. She'd also landed a plum part in a new movie, with shooting due to start in a few weeks' time. She was terribly excited about that too.

As usual Pet ended the letter by demanding to know when Lena was going to join her in Hollywood. Surely Lena had saved up enough money by now to make the trip?

Lena thought about Hamish and their monthly get-togethers. She'd be mad to give those up. Completely insane. It might not be much, but it meant a great deal to her. It was an arrangement she wasn't going to jettison in a hurry. As far as she was concerned Hollywood was now completely off the agenda. And when she replied to Pet's letter she'd tell Pet so. She'd explain that she too was in a relationship, though there would be no mention of how that relationship had come about.

Blackmail.

'I've got some wonderful news,' Georgie announced. She had just arrived at her parents' house with a pale-faced Ian in tow.

'And what's that?' Chrissie wanted to know.

'Charlie and I are getting married.'

Tam nodded. 'Aye, we thought that might happen. Congratulations, lass.'

'Oh, Georgie,' Chrissie breathed, delighted. 'I'm ever so happy for you.'

The entire family crowded round to make a fuss of Georgie, all talking nineteen to the dozen while a silent Ian looked on.

'So, when's the big day?' Tom demanded.

'We haven't settled on that yet, but we will shortly. It'll be the register office, of course, as we've both been married before. And only the immediate family to be there so as to keep down the cost.'

'Very sensible,' Tam acknowledged.

'Does that mean you're now engaged?' Lena queried, glancing at her sister's left hand to see if there was a new ring on the third finger.

'We decided to forgo that. It'll be marriage plain and simple, with no strings attached.'

'I think this calls for a drink. If I give you the money will you go and get a bottle, Tom?'

'Of course, Papa. The usual?'

'Aye.'

'He's a lovely chap. I quite took to him,' Chrissie enthused. 'You'll be giving up your own house then, I take it?'

'That's right, Mum. I'll speak to the factor as soon as we've settled on a date.'

'A second bite of the cherry, eh?' Lena commented. 'You're lucky.'

'Oh, I know that. I never thought I'd find anyone after John, and here I have. Lucky right enough.'

'So where did he propose?' Chrissie demanded. 'Sit down. I want to hear all the details.'

'In the park, Mum. We went for a walk and he proposed in the middle of it.'

'In the park,' Chrissie repeated. 'How romantic.'

Tam couldn't see how proposing in the park was any more romantic than anywhere else. But then, what did he know? He was only a man.

Ian was in floods of tears. 'I don't want to leave here,' he sobbed. 'And I don't want to change schools either.'

'There there, son. There there. Don't get so upset.' Georgie was upset herself.

'I hate that house. It isn't nice.'

That baffled her. 'What do you mean, it isn't nice?'

'It just isn't.'

'You'll soon get used to it, I promise you. It might be a bit strange to begin with, but that'll soon wear off.'

'And I don't like Avril. She hurt me when we were in her bedroom.'

'How did she do that?'

'She nipped my arm really hard. It was sore.'

Georgie wasn't sure whether or not she believed him. Why on earth would Avril nip Ian's arm? It didn't make sense. 'Are you certain?'

Ian stared at her as the tears continued to roll down his face. 'I'm not fibbing, Mum. I'm not. She was horrible to me.'

If it was true then it was something that would have to be sorted out, Georgie thought. The two children would just have to learn to get along. There was nothing else for it.

'Can't we stay here, Mum? Please?'

'No, we can't, son. I'm marrying Charlie and I'll be living with him in his house. So will you.'

'But I don't want to!'

He was rapidly becoming hysterical, Georgie realised. Well, she couldn't have that. 'If you don't calm down this instant, then big boy or not, I'm going to spank you. Understand?'

Ian stared at his mother in disbelief. She'd never spanked him. Not ever. And now she was threatening to. It was all that Charlie's fault. And that horrible Avril.

He couldn't have articulated it as such, but he felt as if his entire, secure world was crumbling all around him.

'I now pronounce you man and wife. You may kiss the bride.'

Georgie closed her eyes as Charlie's lips pressed down on hers. Her husband's lips. The lips of the man who'd saved her life, and whom she'd come to love.

As Lena had once said, she was extraordinarily lucky to have a second bite of the cherry.

Chapter 16

Chrissie glanced round in surprise when she heard a key in the lock, and a few moments later Tam and Tom trooped into the kitchen. 'What are you doing home so early?' she demanded. 'Dinner won't be ready for another couple of hours yet.'

'Three-quarters of the workforce has been laid off until further notice,' a grim-faced Tam announced.

Chrissie's jaw dropped. This was awful, though not exactly unexpected. People were being laid off all over the country. And by that she meant Britain and not just Scotland.

'Both of you?' she croaked.

Tam shook his head. 'I'm still there, but only for three days a week as we're now more or less reduced to a skeleton staff. I picked the men in the foundry who got the bullet, and had to choose Tom to be amongst them. You can imagine what would have been said if I hadn't.'

'Three days,' Chrissie repeated. 'Less money, I take it?'

'Oh aye.'

Tom flung himself into a chair. 'Nobody has any idea how long it'll be before we're called back. Weeks. Months. Who knows?'

'Lack of orders, you see, Chrissie. They've been getting less and less of late. And now, apparently, they're on the verge of drying up altogether.' Tam shook his head. 'We've got the Yanks to thank for this. Them and their damned Wall Street crash. Greed was behind that. Sheer bloody greed.'

'You'd have thought the government would have been able to do something,' Chrissie muttered.

'I've no doubt they tried,' Tam replied bitterly. 'But they couldn't.'

Thank God for Lena's pay packet coming in, Chrissie thought, her mind whirling as she wondered how she was going to cope. And Tam's three days, she reminded herself. They'd get by, somehow. But it wasn't going to be easy.

Tam took out his pipe, and lit up. Then he removed it from his mouth and stared at it. 'No more tobacco or fags for me after this lot,' he said. 'Won't be able to afford them. Or my whisky at the weekends. That's something else I'll have to do without.'

Chrissie's heart went out to him, knowing how much he loved his smoke and dram. But he was right, they were both luxuries for which there would be very little cash from now on.

'Maybe I can find another job somewhere?' Tom said hopefully, well aware of how unlikely that was. There again, looking on the bright side, miracles did sometimes happen.

Georgie glanced at the clock, wondering how long it would be before Charlie got home. He had gone out for a drink with some of his pals, while she'd been sitting worrying about her family, who were struggling because of the reduced amount of money coming into the house.

She'd spoken to Charlie about the possibility of his being laid off and he'd laughed, saying that they'd never lay off firemen. Do that and the entire city could burn down. His reassurance had been a big comfort to her. They, at least, were safe from the general slump.

Half an hour later Charlie still hadn't returned. Had something untoward happened, she wondered. Glasgow was a violent place, after all. And then there he was, falling into the room, red-faced, eyes glazed, swaying from side to side. It was the first time Georgie had ever seen him drunk, and it wasn't a pretty sight.

Charlie staggered to the nearest chair and slumped into it. 'I'm pished as a rat,' he slurred. 'I hope you're not going to complain, woman?'

Georgie frowned, not liking his aggressive tone. 'What makes you think I would?'

'Agnes always did. But then she was a bitch. Not sweet-natured like you, eh?'

'I think I should get you through to your bed, Charlie.'

'I want another drink.'

'There's none in the house.'

He gave her a peculiar, leery smile. 'Oh aye there is. Hidden. Planked, you ken.'

This was news to her. 'Where exactly?'

He told her. And, sure enough, when she went to investigate she found a half-full bottle of whisky.

'Pour me a dram,' he instructed her when she returned with the bottle. 'And make it a big one.'

'Why hide the bottle, Charlie? There's no need for that.'

'Habit, you undershtand. From the old days. Had to hide it otherwise Agnes would have had it.'

'You mean she'd have drunk it?'

'And licked the inside of the bottle too if that had been possible.'

'Really?' This was also news.

'Aye, really. She loved the gargle did Agnes.'

She handed him a generously charged glass which he stared at for a few moments before throwing its contents down his throat. He belched loudly.

'Another one, hen. And quickly.'

Georgie wasn't impressed by this side of Charlie. Not one little bit.

He insisted on finishing the bottle before she could get him into bed, where he snored, and intermittently broke wind, throughout the night.

*   *   *

168

Tom lay in his bed listening to his father and sister getting ready for work. Black despair filled him. He felt useless not working himself. A drain on the family finances because he wasn't earning. A parasite, in other words.

He knew he should get up and join them, but just couldn't bring himself to do so. He didn't feel able to face them when they were employed and he wasn't. He'd been looking everywhere for a job, but there was simply none to be had. Not even the sniff of one.

He'd go for a walk later on, he decided. At least that was something to do.

'Lena, can you please come into my office for a moment?'

Damn, she thought. She was in the middle of a difficult computation which she'd now have to leave and come back to. Most irritating.

'Close the door,' Hamish said when she joined him. Then he sighed, and perched on the edge of his desk, a most unusual informality for him. 'I've had orders from on high.'

'Oh?'

'I've to get rid of one of the girls in the department and I want you to tell me which one.'

That was a jolt. 'I see.'

'You know them and their abilities better than I do. Don't you agree?'

She nodded. That was true enough.

'It's a bad business having to let someone go, but orders are orders.'

'Are the other departments also getting rid of personnel?'

'So I understand. Harsh times, Lena. Harsh times, I'm afraid. Let's just hope and pray it doesn't get to the stage where you and I are also given the boot.'

She smiled thinly. 'I doubt you'd ever be given the boot, Hamish. Your golfing friend, the chairman, wouldn't allow it.'

Hamish had the grace to blush. 'Think about it, and let me know your decision before we leave this evening.'

He was still blushing as Lena returned to her computation.

*   *   *

169

'Bread and dripping,' Tam said quietly, looking at what Chrissie had placed before him for tea.

'I'm afraid that's all we can afford, Tam. You can't really complain. You had a couple of sausages and mash for dinner, after all.'

Tom stared at his plate in disgust. He absolutely loathed bread and dripping. But he was going to have to eat it; either that or go without.

The so-called meal made up Lena's mind for her. She'd visit the bank the following day.

Chrissie gazed at the wad of notes Lena had handed her as if it was manna from heaven.

'My savings, Mum.'

'You mean . . . your Hollywood money?'

Lena nodded. 'It's needed here rather than lying in the bank.'

Chrissie felt a choke in her throat. 'I never wanted you to go to Hollywood, you must have known that. There again, I don't want your dream to end like this.'

'I'd already made up my mind not to go, Mum, so it's not the end of any dream. I promise you.'

Chrissie raised the notes to her mouth, and kissed them. 'Thank you, lass.'

'Thanks aren't needed, Mum. Don't forget, I'm in this present pickle as well. It's just fortunate that I'm able to help out a bit.'

Chrissie took a deep breath. 'Wait till I tell your father. He'll be right proud of you.'

Lena didn't think pride came into it. But necessity did.

Ian and Avril were on their way to school when she suddenly gripped him by the arm, forcing him to stop.

'You smell,' she said quietly, eyes glittering with amusement. And with that she went running off up the street roaring with laughter, leaving a stricken Ian staring after her.

*　*　*

Georgie had become friends with Gladys Renton, her next-door neighbour, and was now in her house having a cup of tea and a natter.

'Can I ask you a question, Gladys?'

'Aye, sure. What is it?'

Georgie slowly stirred her tea. 'I take it you knew Agnes, my predecessor?'

'Not too well, I have to say. She kept to herself a lot.'

'So you don't know what she was like?'

Gladys stared at Georgie, then nodded. 'I suppose that must interest you. Stands to reason. I know I'd be curious in your circumstances.'

'Well?'

'She was pleasant enough, when sober. Which wasn't often.'

'She drank a lot, then?' Gladys's words bore out what Charlie had said.

'Like the proverbial fish. Whenever she had the money, that was.' Gladys shook her head. 'She'd drink anything alcoholic, that woman. You name it, she'd pour it down her throat. When she was really desperate she'd go on the cheap red wine. And I mean cheap. Other times it would be strong cider. On occasion she'd mix them both, wine and cider in the same glass.'

'How horrible,' Georgie breathed. 'That must have been lethal.'

'That was the whole point, don't you see? It was a surefire quick way for her to get out of her skull.'

Georgie hesitated. 'Was she pretty?'

'Might well have been when she was younger. But if so the drink had put paid to that. She was anything but pretty when she died.'

'Fell down the stairs, I understand?'

'Pissed when it happened. They say she tripped, and no wonder, the state she was in. I'd had a brief word with her earlier that day and she was already incoherent. Couldn't get any sense out of her whatever. She was standing there staring at me with dribbles of spit running down her chin. Awful it was. And then later took her tumble. Probably fell over her own feet.'

Poor Charlie, Georgie thought. Imagine being married to a woman like that.

Tom stopped outside a soup kitchen to stare grimly at the queue which had formed there. Poor bastards, he thought. They were really on their uppers. How humiliating having to accept charity.

Most of them would be on the dole, he presumed, though from what he understood the Public Assistance only paid out measly sums. He'd heard somewhere that a married couple with three children got one pound nine shillings and threepence a week. How on God's earth were they expected to live on that? And anything they did manage to earn was instantly deducted from their entitlement. Even a few pence from a child's paper round would be taken off.

At least he and the rest of the family hadn't been reduced to these pitiful levels, thanks to Lena's job, her cash contribution, and his father's short-time. Yes, when you looked at it that way they had a lot to be thankful for.

'What's wrong with you, son?' Georgie asked anxiously at the tea table. Something clearly was.

Ian shook his head, and didn't reply.

'Are you feeling ill?'

'No, Mum,' he answered in a small voice.

'Is it your skin?'

'No, Mum.'

'Then what?'

Avril pushed her plate away. 'I'm going to my Aunt Betty's,' she announced, sliding from her chair.

'I don't want you going there. Your father will be home shortly,' said Georgie.

Avril stared defiantly at her stepmother. 'I'm going to Aunt Betty's. She's a lot more fun than you.'

'No you're . . .' Georgie trailed off when Avril suddenly dashed from the room, banging the outside door closed behind her.

What a difficult child, Georgie thought. Was she never going to win her over? Their relationship was rapidly becoming a problem she didn't know how to solve. She felt a complete and utter failure where Avril was concerned. Avril, who doted on her father as if he was some kind of god.

'There's something different about you lately, and I can't quite put my finger on it,' Chrissie declared.

'Different?' Lena queried.

'Aye, different. What do you think, Tam?'

He glanced over at his daughter, frowning as he studied her. He'd been thinking that he could've murdered a pipeful of tobacco, or a fag, for he was still having terrible trouble trying to conquer the urge. Chrissie had refused to give him any of Lena's money to satisfy his craving, saying they had no idea how long the money was going to have to last, so in the meantime he would just have to go without. He'd thought it mean of Chrissie, but in his heart he knew she was right.

'She looks the same to me.'

'She's put on weight,' Tom said.

'You know, I think you have,' Chrissie agreed, having appraised her daughter again.

Lena ran her hands over her hips, which did seem fuller than they had been. Fuller, and rounder. Her bras had been hurting a bit recently, too, which would make sense if her breasts had become larger.

'Your skin's changed as well,' Chrissie commented. 'It's got more colour to it than usual.'

Lena suddenly smiled as the penny dropped. Going to bed with Hamish, albeit only once a month, was having a beneficial effect on her physicality, which delighted her.

'What's causing it, I wonder,' Chrissie said.

'I have absolutely no idea,' Lena lied. 'None at all.' She began humming as she got on with what she'd been doing. Thank you, Hamish Murchison, she thought gleefully. Thank you very much indeed. She was looking forward to the coming

Saturday's session even more now she realised what sex was doing for her.

Charlie had come off duty with a splitting headache, the result of banging his head hard while attending a fire. All he wanted was something to eat and an early night.

'I'd like to talk to you,' Georgie told him as he tucked into his meal.

'What about?'

'Ian. He's being bullied at school.'

Charlie glanced across to where Ian was sitting watching them. Avril was still at her Aunt Betty's. 'Is that right, Ian?'

Ian nodded.

Charlie sighed. He really didn't need this at the moment. 'What are they doing to you? Or is it only one child?'

'It's three boys,' Georgie declared.

Charlie grunted. 'Can't he speak for himself?'

'Ian?' Georgie prompted.

'It's three big boys.'

'And what do they do to you?'

'Hit me. Chase me round the playground. Spit on me.'

'Do you think I should go to the headmaster?' Georgie asked.

'That would only make matters worse. He'd be called a mummy's boy. You don't want that, do you?'

Georgie bit her lip. 'No,' she admitted.

Charlie had another mouthful of food, but he had suddenly lost his appetite. His head was really killing him. Sitting back in his chair, he sighed again.

'It is a rather rough school,' Georgie said.

Charlie stared at her. 'Rough? How do you mean rough?'

'They all seem to be toughies there.'

'And I suppose the school he went to before was a lot nicer?'

'It was actually,' Georgie replied, not noticing the sudden glint of anger in Charlie's eyes.

'Does that mean you think this area isn't as nice as where you used to live?'

'Well, it isn't,' she admitted honestly. 'Surely you can see that?'

'Are you telling me it isn't good enough for you and your son?'

Alarm flared in her. 'No, of course not, Charlie. I didn't mean that at all.' She was unsure of herself now, having heard the aggressive tone in her husband's voice.

'I would remind you,' Charlie almost hissed, 'that my Avril goes to this school you say is full of so-called toughies. She's only a wee defenceless lassie but she gets on perfectly well there. She doesn't get bullied like your precious son.'

'I didn't mean you to take offence,' Georgie retorted swiftly. What was wrong with the man to make him react like this?

Charlie swivelled his gaze on to Ian. 'You say these big boys chase you round the playground. Is that because you run away?'

'Yes,' Ian confessed in a whisper.

The lad's a coward, Charlie thought with contempt. A bloody little coward. No wonder he was being bullied. At school, cowards and the weak usually were. It was the way of things.

'Then don't,' Charlie snapped. 'Stand your ground. If they hit you, then hit back. That's the only thing they'll understand. Hit back and they'll soon stop the bullying. It won't be so much fun for them then.'

'But there are three of them,' Ian protested in a scared voice.

'So?'

'They'll . . .' Ian broke off, the implication clear.

'Knock spots off you maybe. But that's something you'll just have to take until they get the message that you're going to defend yourself.'

'I'm not sure I approve of that,' said a horrified Georgie, having visions of Ian coming home covered in blood and bruises – maybe even with a broken limb.

Charlie decided he'd had enough, and got to his feet. 'I'm going through to bed. So I'll leave you with this little coward of yours.'

Georgie stared at her husband in astonishment and fury. 'How dare you call Ian a coward!' she protested.

'Oh, bugger off, the pair of you,' Charlie snarled, and left them.

Ian started to shake, and then burst into tears.

'Hey, Tom, wait up!'

Tom turned to find Danny Peterson hurrying towards him. Danny was a pal of his from McNair's.

'I was just thinking about you this morning,' Danny announced.

'Oh aye, why's that?'

'Have you found another job yet?'

Tom shook his head. 'And it's not for the lack of trying, I can tell you.'

'Then I might have something that's just the very dab.'

Tom frowned. 'Are you working yourself?'

'Nope.'

'Then why aren't you after whatever it is?'

Danny's face broke into a huge smile. 'Because I've got two left feet, that's why.'

He went on to explain.

Chapter 17

Mrs Simpson, short, plump, immaculately dressed and coiffured, was manageress of the Belgrave, a private club. Her accent was Kelvinside, which is to say Glasgow posh, and her hazel-coloured eyes shone with intelligence.

She studied Tom, sizing him up. Good-looking, she thought. That was in his favour, as was being of middle height. And he had a nice, easy manner about him.

She smiled. 'All right, Tom, let's see what you can do.' She came to stand directly in front of him. 'Shall we start with the waltz? You lead, of course.'

'But there's no music to dance to.'

Mrs Simpson laughed. 'Which makes it all the more difficult, wouldn't you say?'

It certainly did, Tom reflected ruefully.

'Now take me in your arms.'

He did so.

'And off we go.'

In rapid succession they went through the foxtrot, quickstep, polka, and various other steps that came under the general heading of Old Time Dancing.

Eventually Mrs Simpson stopped and broke away. 'Well, you move all right, I'll give you that.'

'I wasn't really at my best,' he apologised. 'It was the lack of music, I'm afraid.'

'Do you own a lounge suit?'

'I do.'

'A decent pair of dancing shoes?'

'Yes.'

'And are you reliable?'

'How do you mean?'

'Will you turn up every night?'

'Oh yes.' Tom smiled. 'You can count on it. I need the money, you see.'

That was good enough for her.

Tom burst into the kitchen to find the others already sitting down and having their tea.

'Where have you been? You're late,' said Chrissie.

'I've got a job, Mum!' Tom informed her jubilantly.

Chrissie clapped her hands in delight. 'That's wonderful news, son. Absolutely wonderful.'

'Doing what?' Tam asked, impressed that Tom had been able to find employment in the current slump when millions of men were laid off throughout the length and breadth of Britain.

'Promise you won't laugh?'

'Of course I won't laugh,' Tam replied. 'Why would I do that?'

'Because the job's that of a professional dancer.'

Tam stared at his son in astonishment. 'Bloody hell!' he muttered.

'What sort of professional dancer?' Lena asked, amused.

'In a private club called the Belgrave. It's a club for older people where they can have a drink, or whatever. Quite a number of widows, and women whose husbands are away on business, go there, as well as couples, of course. There are four men and three young women employed to dance with the patrons when requested. Money for old rope if you ask me.'

'You'll be dancing with older women?' Chrissie repeated with a frown, not sure if she liked the idea of that.

'It's all above board, Mum. There's no hanky panky or anything of that nature. I just sit there until asked to dance, which I then do. Simple really.'

'What's the pay?' Tam enquired, bemused.

'Almost as much as I was getting from McNair's. And just for dancing, which I enjoy anyway. I can't believe my luck.'

'And the hours?' Lena asked.

'Sunday and Monday off. Tuesday through till Saturday night. Start at six thirty, finish at midnight.'

'I don't know what to say,' Chrissie told him, shaking her head. 'What a bolt out the blue.'

'I've Danny Peterson to thank,' Tom said to his father. 'He put me on to it. There was no use his applying as he can't dance for toffee. I begin next Tuesday.' He sat at the table. 'This means I'll be earning again and not a drain on the family. That's the main thing.'

'Aye,' Chrissie agreed. 'That's the main thing.'

Georgie hadn't laughed so much in a long time. They were at the table, Charlie cracking joke after joke, all of which were extremely funny and some hilariously so.

'Stop it, Charlie,' she gasped at last. 'You'll give me a seizure if you keep on.'

'A last one then.'

It was the funniest of the lot, and brought tears into Georgie's eyes. Ian sat solemn-faced, not having understood any of the jokes. Avril wasn't present; she seemed to be spending most of her time at her Aunt Betty's recently. Georgie hadn't objected, continuing to find the child wilful and difficult. If Avril wanted to be with her Aunt Betty, then so be it.

'I have other ones I could have told you,' Charlie said, a mischievous smile curling his lips. 'But not with Ian here, I'm afraid.' Georgie knew he meant dirty jokes, of which he had a vast repertoire. 'Another time,' he added, and winked at her.

He rose and stretched. 'I'm off out for a couple of pints with my pals from the station. That all right?'

Georgie instantly sobered. 'I thought you were staying in tonight?'

'I never said so.'

'I presumed you were.'

'It'll only be for a wee while, Georgie. I'll be back before you know it.'

She tried to hide her disappointment. This going out with his pals for a drink was becoming more and more frequent. Not that she entirely disapproved; it was just that it would have been nicer if he'd spent more time with her and Ian.

Coming round the table he kissed her on the cheek. 'Did I mention you're looking lovely this evening?'

She was flattered, as she knew she was meant to be. 'Less of the old flannel, Charlie.'

'But you are!' he insisted, and proceeded to blow into her ear, which made her giggle and jerk her head away.

'Not with Ian here,' she admonished him.

'Later, then,' he promised in a whisper.

At the door he turned and winked at her again, before leaving for the pub.

Georgie came awake when the bedroom door opened. God knew what time it was as it had already been late, well past pub closing, when she'd come to bed.

She listened to Charlie stumble into the room, curse when he banged into a piece of furniture then begin to remove his clothes. Moments later he crawled in beside her and immediately started lifting the bottom of her nightdress.

'Are you awake, Georgie?' he slurred.

'I am now. I thought you were coming home early?'

'Forgot it was one of the lad's birthday. We made a bit of a night of it.'

'But the pubs shut ages ago.'

'I told you once I know where to get a drink after hours. That's where we went.'

She squirmed as his hand found her crotch. 'I'm tired, Charlie. Honestly I am.'

'You'll not deny me, will you?'

He stank of booze, the sour fumes from his mouth washing over her. She turned her face away to escape them, and was about to reply when a probing finger found her.

'Charlie!' she hissed.

But it was no use. He was insistent, and she had to let him have his way.

Afterwards she was pleased she had. Despite everything, it had been lovely. Something she'd never have admitted to a living soul, and hardly did to herself, was that Charlie was a far better lover than John had ever been.

Lena sniffed the air. There it was again, the unmistakable smell of perfume. And expensive perfume too if she was any judge. Not hers, of course, as she only occasionally wore a splash of lavender water.

Jealousy at the thought that Hamish must have had another woman in his house stabbed through her. Unjustly so, she reminded herself. Her arrangement with Hamish didn't exclude his seeing other females. But she was jealous none the less.

Hamish, wearing only his dressing gown, re-entered the bedroom carrying two cups of coffee. He smiled. 'All right?'

'Fine.' She regarded him speculatively. If the woman had been in his bedroom did that mean they'd slept together? She rather thought it did. Which probably meant he'd been seeing her for some time.

'Good one, eh?' He handed her her coffee.

'Very.'

'I'll say this for you, Lena. You really enjoy it.'

'So do you.'

'No doubt about that.'

Lena wondered why she hadn't smelt the perfume earlier. Perhaps because her mind had been on other things – like a desperate need for sex. 'Tell me something,' she said.

'What's that?'

'I don't really have the right to ask, but do you have a girl-friend?'

A look of embarrassment crept across Hamish's face. 'What's that got to do with us?'

'Nothing. I'm simply curious, that's all.'

He stared at her, undecided about whether or not to tell the truth. Then he made up his mind he would. Lena would find out eventually, so why not now? 'Yes, I do.'

Lena lit a cigarette, partially turning away from him so he wouldn't see her expression. 'Is it serious?'

Hamish cleared his throat. 'We plan to get engaged next month after I buy the ring.'

Lena felt as though she'd been punched in the stomach, remembering all too clearly that she'd promised these visits of hers would stop when he got married. 'I see,' she murmured, hoping it was going to be a long engagement. 'What's her name?'

'Celia. Celia Cunningham.'

It took a few moments for the penny to drop. 'The chairman's daughter?' she queried in astonishment.

'That's right.'

Realising her mouth had dropped open, she shut it again. 'How on earth did you meet her?'

'The chairman invited some of his golfing friends round for a meal one night and I was placed next to Celia at the table. We got on like a house on fire during the meal, and afterwards. Before leaving I took her aside to ask if she'd like to go out one evening, and she agreed. That's how it started.'

'Is she pretty?'

Hamish was even more embarrassed. 'Extremely.'

'Yes, I'd heard that. They say she's very glamorous.' Unlike herself, Lena thought bitterly. Laying her coffee aside she rose from the bed. 'I'd better get dressed.'

'You're not too upset, are you?'

What a stupid question, she thought. Of course she was upset, and would probably be a lot more so once the news had properly sunk in. 'Not in the least,' she lied with a smile. 'It was bound to happen one day. Though, I have to say, I never for one moment imagined it would be the chairman's daughter.' She added acidly, 'You do aim high, don't you?'

'It wasn't like that, Lena. I swear.'

'No?'

He shook his head.

'But once the opportunity arose you were only too quick to take advantage of it?'

'That's not true.' He was lying now.

'Think of the promotions that'll be coming your way. Why, one day you might even be chairman yourself. Don't tell me that hasn't crossed your mind?'

He didn't reply.

'Do you love her, Hamish? I certainly hope you don't intend marrying her unless you do.'

'Of course I love her,' he replied unconvincingly, blushing as he spoke.

Lena laughed. 'Liar!'

'I am nothing of the sort,' he protested vehemently.

'Oh yes you are, Hamish Murchison. You're lying in your teeth. It's obvious. To me, anyway.'

Again he didn't reply, just stood there watching Lena putting on her clothes.

'Will you be coming back?' he asked when she was fully dressed.

'Damn right I will,' she replied sweetly. 'This doesn't alter matters. Not for the present, anyway.'

To his surprise he found he was rather pleased about that. Though why he should be escaped him.

Tom was nervous as hell when he reported for his first night at the Belgrave, but he began to relax a little after Mrs Simpson had introduced him to the other men and women doing the same job.

Two of the men were considerably older, in their forties Tom judged. Of the women, two were roughly his age while one was, again, in her forties, or thereabouts.

'It's dead jammy here,' Derek, the other younger man, confided to Tom. 'I love it.'

'Money for old rope as far as I'm concerned.' Tom smiled amiably. 'What are the customers like?'

'All posh and monied. It costs a fortune to join the Belgrave, so there isn't any riff-raff.'

Tom nodded that he understood, then gazed out over the main club area, part of which was a dance floor. The decor was gold and heavy tapestry wallpaper. Dotted about were various statues and other items, including huge flower arrangements, that lent, or were supposed to lend, character to the place. The lighting was subdued, giving everything a soft hue.

A few minutes later a three-piece band in black tie arrived. They began arranging and tuning their instruments and when everything was to their satisfaction they struck up.

'There are rooms off here where customers can go and sit in peace, or have a conversation, should they so choose,' Derek informed Tom. 'Not all of them come to dance, you see.'

'So how does a club like this make a profit?' Tom asked, thinking there must be more to it than simply dancing.

'Well, for a start, the drinks are horrendously expensive. Secondly, and keep this to yourself, there's a gaming room where customers often play for high stakes.'

'Ah!' Tom exclaimed. Now it was beginning to make sense.

'Mrs Simpson's a real sweetie,' Derek went on. 'Unless you cross her, that is. Then it's easy to see why she was made manageress. She rules with a rod of iron, but she's fair with it. You do your job well, keep your nose clean, and Mrs Simpson will be your best friend.'

'I'll remember that.' He would too, not having any wish to lose this godsend of a chance to earn.

People had already been arriving, and now even more appeared. Five minutes later Tom was asked by a middle-aged lady to dance.

'Mum, you shouldn't have waited up!' Tom exclaimed. He'd reached home in the small hours, having walked from the club.

'Oh, hold your wheesht. I wanted to know how you got on.'
Chrissie took a deep breath. 'Well?'

'It was brilliant, Mum. I thoroughly enjoyed myself.'

'You did?'

'The time just flew past once we got going.' He laughed. 'Some
of those women are terrible dancers, truly awful. Others very
good indeed. But they were, without exception, nice people.'

'None of them tried to . . . well, make advances?'

'Of course not. I told you, the club is strictly above board.
No shenanigans whatsoever.' He regarded her with amusement.
'I must say, I'm surprised you thought of such a thing.'

Chrissie snorted. 'I may be your mother but I'm not unaware
of what goes on in the world, you know. I didn't come up the
Clyde on a bicycle.'

Clearly she hadn't. 'I'll tell you what though. I could murder
a cup of tea.'

'Then I'll make you one. I could use a cup myself.'

While Chrissie filled the kettle and set it on to boil he told
her about his night, describing some of the women he'd danced
with, mentioning Derek and the others employed as partners,
and couples who'd caught his attention.

'I'll tell you something,' he said when Chrissie handed him his
tea. 'It sure as hell beats grafting in the foundry, and that's a fact.'

Chrissie didn't doubt it for a minute.

'Ian! Ian!'

Ian, who'd just come out on to the playground, was startled
to hear his name being called. With astonishment he saw it was
Charlie doing the calling, and that Charlie had a fire engine with
him. Engine and crew.

'Can you get out of there?' Charlie asked when Ian ran over
to join him at the railings.

A wide-eyed Ian nodded, wondering what this was all about.

'Go on then. I'll wait for you.'

Ian was well aware he wasn't supposed to leave the playground,
but surely this was different.

When he got to the engine a group of pupils had gathered at the spot where he'd spoken to Charlie, all visibly impressed by the sight of the firemen and their machine.

'Right,' Charlie declared. 'Let's put you up in the driving seat, shall we?' And with that he lifted Ian and swung him into the cabin. A fireman already there plonked a helmet on to Ian's head.

Ian was in seventh heaven as he grasped the wheel and pretended to steer. This was magic. Especially as he was being watched by the others gathered on the other side of the railings, a crowd which continued to grow with every passing second.

Charlie took Ian all over the engine, showing him where everything was, and even raising the ladder a bit and allowing Ian to climb a few rungs. The fun only ended with the sound of the bell announcing that playtime had ended.

'Thanks, Charlie.'

'Think nothing of it, son. Now hurry back before you get into trouble.'

Ian had one last look at the engine as it moved away before re-entering the school building, where he soon discovered he'd become something of a hero.

'Oh, Charlie, that was wonderful of you,' Georgie said later that night when Charlie arrived home. 'Ian's been talking of nothing else ever since he got in.'

'Aye, well, there was a reason for it.'

She frowned. 'What reason?'

'It'll make him somebody at school, somebody to be envied and even looked up to. That's my reasoning, anyway. It might just stop him being bullied if we're lucky.'

Georgie wasn't sure about that, but thought it extremely kind of her husband. 'What can I say? Except thank you.'

'My pleasure, I can assure you. The idea came to me as we were heading back from a call-out. The timing couldn't have been better. We were just passing the school as playtime was starting. A quick word with the lads, and Bob's your uncle.'

She pecked him on the cheek. 'You're a lovely man, Charlie Gunn, and I'm glad I married you.'

'And I'm glad I married *you.*'

In the event his reasoning proved to be correct. Ian was never bullied again. Whatever it was went through the three boys' minds, from that point on they kept their distance.

Chapter 18

Lena glanced up as an elegant young woman swept in her direction, instinctively knowing who the stranger was.

The newcomer stopped at Lena's desk, and smiled. 'If Mr Murchison is free can you please tell him Miss Cunningham is here to see him?'

They hadn't lied about her being a beauty, Lena thought bitterly. The bitch was stunning. Sickeningly so.

'He's alone, so why not just go straight on in,' she replied, forcing herself to be pleasant.

'Thank you.'

Lena watched as Celia tapped the door, then went inside.

'Darling!' she heard Hamish exclaim in surprise. And then the door was shut again.

Those clothes had cost a pretty penny, Lena reflected. And, from the style of them, they might even have come from London's Bond Street itself.

She seethed with jealousy.

'Are you all right?' Hamish asked her later, after Celia had gone.

'I'm fine, thank you.'

'I had no idea she was coming. Sorry.'

'There's nothing to be sorry about.'

'Celia was just reminding me I'm to meet her during lunch hour to buy the engagement ring.'

That was something she didn't need to know, Lena thought angrily. Honestly, had the man no tact! 'How nice for the pair of you,' she replied tartly.

'So if I'm late back you'll know what's holding me up.'

She knew what she'd like to hold him up with. A rope with a noose on the end. 'Why don't you take the rest of the day off?' she suggested. 'We can manage well enough without you.'

'Are you sure?'

They could always manage without him, she thought, he being about as useful as a chocolate teapot. It was she who ran the department, not Hamish. Most of his so-called work simply involved signing things.

'Of course I'm sure.'

'Then I'll do that.'

She smiled to herself as he crossed to the hat stand and removed his bowler. One of these days she'd tell him he looked a proper idiot in it, she thought.

There again, maybe she wouldn't.

'Here you are, Mum, my first pay packet from the new job.' Tom grinned, handing Chrissie a small brown envelope.

'Thank you, son.'

Using a finger she opened it and extracted the contents, notes and coins which she swiftly counted. He'd been right; it was only a little less than he'd been earning at McNair's.

Chrissie peeled off several of the notes and returned them to him, keeping the rest. 'You'll be wanting your breakfast now?'

'Please, Mum. I'm starving.'

'I've bought you an egg in anticipation of your wages coming in, so I'll do that for you. Fried or boiled?'

'Boiled. With soldiers if you don't mind.'

Lena, already at the table, snorted. 'Honest to God, soldiers at your age. How pathetic!'

'Leave him alone,' Tam growled.

'But I ask you, Papa!'

'It's always her who starts it,' Tom declared piously. 'And nobody believes me when I say that.'

'You're both at fault,' Chrissie stated. 'Anyway, Tom, you should know better than to rise to the bait. I must have told you that a million times.'

Tam was wondering what to do with the rest of the day. His days off were becoming more and more of a problem for him.

'Now that we've almost as much coming into the house as before I think you can start smoking again, Tam,' said Chrissie.

His face lit up. 'Can I?'

'I just said so.'

'What about whisky at the weekends?'

She glanced over at him. 'Half a bottle instead of a whole one.'

That was better than nothing, he reflected. He hadn't tasted a dram or a pint in months. Nor smoked his pipe or had a fag, come to that. Thank God life, for them anyway, was getting back to normal.

'Look at the time!' Lena exclaimed. 'I'd better be going or I'll be late.'

'Which would never do,' Tom smirked, for no other reason than to annoy his sister.

As she passed him Lena retaliated by giving him a sharp elbow in the ribs.

'That hurt!' he shouted after her.

'It was meant to.'

Chrissie shook her head in a combination of exasperation and disbelief.

'I've hardly sat down all night,' Tom commented to Derek. 'I've been up and down like a demented yo-yo.'

'It gets like that sometimes,' Derek replied. 'But better that than twiddling your thumbs.'

Tom nodded. 'True.' He suddenly became aware of a middle-aged woman, by herself at one of the tables, staring intently at him. He smiled at her, but she didn't smile back, simply continued staring at him. How odd, he thought. And a little disturbing too.

Moments later he was again asked to dance. He glanced to where the staring woman had been, only to find the table empty.

'There's someone here to see you, Lena,' a beaming Chrissie announced, having answered a knock at the door.

Lena stared in astonishment at the figure who brushed past Chrissie. A figure who was almost unrecognisable from the last time she'd seen her.

'Hiya, kid, howya doin'?'

'Pet,' Lena stuttered.

'In the flesh.'

The two women flew into each other's arms, hugging one another tightly.

'And it's not Pet any more,' she declared when they'd disengaged. 'It's Dawn.'

'You'll always be Pet to me. But . . . what are you doing here?'

'Visiting. But first, let me mind my manners.' She went to Tam, gave him a big kiss and had a few words, and then did the same to the hovering Chrissie.

'Where's Tom?' she asked. 'Out on the razzle?'

'He's working,' Lena said. 'I'll explain about that later.' She eyed her friend up and down. 'You look wonderful,' she breathed. 'A real Hollywood star.'

Pet was wearing a grey, waisted suit with a creamy frilled blouse underneath; her shoes were black patent. A simple ensemble, but stunning in its execution.

'Why thanks, honey.'

Lena noted that the once brassy blonde hair had been considerably toned down, and the breasts were not quite so prominent, no doubt due to the bra Pet was wearing. 'So what brings you here?' she demanded, still unable to take in that Pet had just turned up like this.

'It's a long story, hon. Basically, I'm on my way to Europe for a vacation, and stopped off in London to do some promotion for my new movie. And while in London I simply had to come up to Glasgow for a few days to see my folks. And you, of course,' she added with a smile.

'Would you like a cup of tea, dear?' Chrissie asked.

'No thank you, Mrs M. I've only got a few minutes. In fact I've got a taxi waiting downstairs.'

Lena's face fell. 'Only a few minutes?'

'Which is why I thought we might have lunch tomorrow. A long lunch over which we can catch up. What do you say?'

Christ, Lena thought. The next day was her Saturday with Hamish, and she certainly didn't want to miss that. Not the way she was feeling.

'Does it have to be lunch?' she queried. 'How about an evening meal instead?'

'That's OK by me, hon. Where do you suggest, and what time?'

Where? She wasn't used to going to restaurants. Then she remembered the Swan Hotel.

'Seven o'clock then,' Pet agreed. 'I'll be there with bells on. Now I must rush.'

'I'll see you out,' Lena volunteered.

At the door they embraced again, each kissing the other on the cheek.

'Tomorrow night.' Pet smiled.

'Tomorrow night,' Lena repeated.

And then Pet was gone, clattering off down the stairs.

''Bye, Dawn!' Lena couldn't help but call out, thinking it funny. 'Well, well, imagine that,' she went on, returning to the kitchen. 'What a bombshell.'

Hamish during the day, Pet at night. It was going to be one hell of a Saturday!

Charlie arrived home with a face like thunder. 'They sprung it on us just as we were coming off watch. The fucking bastards!' he snarled.

Georgie glanced at Ian and Avril. No matter what had

happened, she didn't approve of such language in front of the children, and would take Charlie to task once he'd calmed down.

'Sprung what on you?' she said.

His eyes were blazing when he answered. 'Remember I told you they would never lay firemen off?'

She nodded. 'I remember.'

'Well they've done something else instead. As from next week our pay has been cut by almost half.'

'Oh dear,' Georgie muttered. This was terrible. 'Is there nothing you can do about it?'

'The Union will have something to say, I can tell you. But with the country in such a state at the moment I doubt any argument they might make will have any impact.'

Almost half, Georgie thought. That was indeed a body blow. She didn't know how they were going to manage, but they'd just have to. If the worst came to the worst she always had her insurance money in the bank.

Charlie threw himself into a chair, then jumped out of it again. 'I don't want any tea tonight,' he declared.

'But it's already made. A lovely stew with dumplings.'

'I said I don't want any, woman! What have you got, cloth ears?'

Georgie bit her lip, and didn't respond.

Charlie glanced at his daughter, who unflinchingly gazed right back at him. He grunted. 'What I do want is a drink. And lots of it. By Christ and I do.'

'Shouldn't we be watching what we spend from now on?' Georgie said in a small voice.

'Not tonight. Not tonight! Tonight I'm getting pissed out of my head. Stocious. Hear me?'

'I hear you, Charlie.' She knew there was no arguing with him when he was like this. The way he was at the moment she could easily get a clout if she did. Not that Charlie had ever hit her, but there was always a first time. 'On you go then,' she said, attempting a brave smile. 'I won't wait up if you don't mind.'

Charlie stormed from the house.

*　　*　　*

Lena opened her eyes to stare at a sweat-slicked Hamish lying beside her. 'It doesn't get much better,' she sighed, with a smile of complete satisfaction.

'No,' he agreed. 'It doesn't.' Reaching across he fondled the breast nearer him. 'These are getting bigger,' he observed.

'You approve?'

'Very much so.' He idly flicked a nipple. Then flicked it again.

'Are you playing a game, or what?' she queried drily.

'I'm just wondering if I can go again if we wait a while,' he answered.

She glanced at his bedside clock. Plenty of time yet before her meeting with Pet. But did she want to go again, as he put it? Truth was, he'd already given her such a pounding she was rather sore. On the other hand, why look a gift horse in the mouth, as the saying went. She also had to remember that these trysts wouldn't go on for ever. Best to get as much as she could while it was available. There would be long lonely years ahead after she finished seeing Hamish, unless someone else came along, which she doubted very much indeed.

'I hope you can,' she purred. Swinging her legs out of bed, she picked up her cigarettes. 'There's something I want to talk to you about,' she said after she'd lit up. 'More of a suggestion really.'

'Oh?'

'Now that you're engaged to the boss's daughter don't you think it would be best to stop fiddling those accounts? I would certainly recommend it.'

Hamish slowly nodded. 'You're right, of course. I'd be daft to continue.'

'I doubt anyone would ever find out. But if they did, well, I don't have to spell out the consequences. Your future's made, Hamish; there's absolutely no need to go on fiddling. Why risk it?'

He stared at her, thinking it was a pity she was so bloody ugly. In other circumstances she would have had a lot to offer. 'Would you like a drink?'

'A little white wine would be nice.'

'No gin?'

'I don't want to get tipsy. I'm having a meal with a famous Hollywood star tonight.'

His eyes opened wide. 'You're taking the mickey, aren't you?'

'Not at all.' She went on to explain about Pet and how they had been the best of pals before Pet had gone to Hollywood in search of stardom.

'Dawn Ryder,' Hamish mused. 'I've seen her in pictures.'

Lena reeled off a list of those Pet had been in, and then the names of some of Pet's starry boyfriends.

'Imagine you knowing her,' Hamish declared, somewhat awed. 'Who would have believed it?'

'We're going to the Swan. It was the only place I could think of when she asked me to recommend somewhere.'

He laughed. 'Bloody hell! Dawn Ryder in the Swan. I'm almost tempted to turn up just to have a peek. But sadly I . . .' He trailed off, suddenly embarrassed. 'I'll get you that wine.' And with that he hurried from the room.

Lena could guess what he'd been about to say. He was seeing Celia later on. The thought put rather a damper on what had been a lovely couple of hours. Still, she hung on till he was ready again, and exacted a little revenge by clawing his back, and leaving scratches.

Let him explain those to the beautiful Celia, she gloated. If he dared.

'I'd forgotten how much Glasgow smells,' Pet declared quietly after they'd ordered. 'It stinks.'

Lena was immediately up in arms in the defence of her beloved city. 'It does nothing of the sort. It's your imagination,' she snapped in reply.

'It does too, honey. Believe me.'

'It's just a big industrial city, Pet. Not an orange grove, which is the sort of thing I suppose you're used to now.'

It was obvious to Pet that her friend was miffed by what she'd said. 'I didn't mean to offend, kid. Sorry,' she apologised.

Lena shrugged. 'That's all right. No offence taken.' There had been, but she wasn't about to pursue the subject and spoil their night out together.

'Sure?'

Lena nodded.

'OK. Now, tell me what's new with you?'

'I don't want to talk about me. I want to hear about you,' Lena protested. 'So come on.'

'I told you I was going on vacation to Europe, right?'

'You did.'

'What I didn't mention was that it was at the invitation of an Italian count. How about that, eh?'

Lena was completely taken aback. 'A genuine count?'

'As genuine as they come.' Pet laughed. 'Count Mario Tesccheti, no less. A count and a bachelor worth millions. And I mean good ole Yankee greenbacks when I say that.'

'Wow!' Lena breathed.

'He has a yacht in Cannes, France, on which I'll be joining him and a few others. The plan is that we cruise in the Med, and possibly even the Aegean.'

'Sounds . . . well, amazing.'

'He isn't exactly the best-looking guy around, but who the hell cares?'

'How did you meet him?' Lena asked, thinking it was like a fairy story come to life.

'In Hollywood, natch. I went to a party thrown by Charlie Chaplin, and there he was. We dated for a while, and then he had to return home on business. But before leaving he pleaded with me to join him in Cannes, which is what I'm going to do.'

'Lucky cow,' Lena said good-humouredly. 'Trust you to meet someone like that.'

'I'm not due to start my next movie for several months yet, which gave me the opportunity to get my ass over here. And when I told the studio they asked me to do some promotion in London, so part of my trip is a busman's holiday, the rest . . .'

Her eyes twinkled. 'Sheer unadulterated pleasure. And I say that from experience. He's a real knockout between the sheets. And I mean knockout.'

They stopped speaking for a few moments while their starters were placed before them.

'You've slept with him, then?' Lena said quietly after the waiter had left.

'Darn tootin', kid. On the night we met, the temptation being just too great to resist. Don't forget, it's Hollywood after all; everyone's at it like rabbits. It's how half the female actresses get cast in that town. Putting out to producers, directors and the like.'

'Putting out?' Lena frowned.

'Shagging, honey. The casting couch is no myth, believe me. I could tell you stories that would make your hair stand on end.'

'Does that mean you've been with lots of men?' Lena queried, jealous as anything.

'And some women too, if the truth be known.'

Lena truly was shocked. 'You don't mean that?'

'I do.'

Pet went on to regale Lena with more tales of life in Hollywood, and the goings-on there. Lena, for the main part, listened in rapt silence.

'But enough of me,' Pet eventually declared. 'What's been happening here on the home front?'

Somewhere along the line Lena had decided to lie. To bolster herself in the eyes of her friend. Well, she reasoned, it wouldn't all be a fib. Part of it was true, if embellished.

'I have a boyfriend too,'

Pet sat back in her chair. 'Really? What's his name?'

'Hamish. Hamish Murchison. He's my boss, head of the department. And, you might not believe this, gorgeous as hell.'

Pet was amazed. 'Go on.'

'It's a real love match. He absolutely dotes on me, and I on him. We also . . .' She cleared her throat, then confessed in a whisper, '. . . sleep together.'

Pet was flabbergasted. 'You do?'

'He has his own place, you see. That's where we go. He swears he can't get enough of me.'

'Well, good for you, kid,' Pet managed to say at last. 'Are we talking marriage here?'

'Possibly,' Lena said, managing to blush. 'Though nothing has been said yet.'

'And you're sleeping with him?' Pet frowned, remembering this was staid, Calvinistic Scotland, where morality ruled.

'As often as we can. It's marvellous.'

'Hot damn!' Pet breathed. 'You do surprise me, Lena. You really do.'

It hadn't all been one way, Lena reflected later as she made for her tram stop, having seen Pet off in a taxi. She'd kept her end up, and not been the sad, lonely virgin Pet had been expecting.

At least that was true enough. She certainly wasn't a virgin any more. A fact of which she was extremely proud.

Chapter 19

Georgie arrived home from shopping to find Charlie sitting with Ian bent over his knees, leathering the poor boy's backside with his belt. Ian was screaming his head off, while a smug-faced Avril was watching the proceedings.

'What the hell are you doing?' Georgie shrieked as another blow descended with a loud crack.

'He was naughty,' Avril stated, eyes gleaming.

'Stop that at once, Charlie,' Georgie shouted. Rushing forward, she attempted to pull Ian off Charlie's lap.

Charlie hadn't been there when she'd gone out. Now, from the smell of alcohol emanating from him, she knew where he had been. To the pub. Yet again.

Charlie grunted, and released Ian. 'Be thankful your mother's got back or there would have been more of that,' he snarled at the lad.

Ian, clutching his bottom, tears streaming down his face, was hopping up and down.

'What did he do to deserve this?' Georgie demanded. If she'd been a man she'd have flattened her husband there and then.

'Tell her, Avril,' Charlie slurred.

'He pulled down my knickers and looked at me,' Avril replied, as though butter wouldn't melt in her mouth.

'I didn't,' Ian stuttered.

'Yes, you did.'

'She asked me to look,' Ian wailed. 'She pulled down her own knickers and asked me to look.'

'Liar!' Charlie shouted. 'My Avril wouldn't do such a thing. She's a good girl.'

'She did!'

'Did not,' Avril said, shaking her head.

Georgie knew which one she believed. 'Whatever, it was no reason for you to be so hard on the boy,' she hissed at Charlie, wondering how many strokes of the belt Ian had had before she'd arrived on the scene.

'Dirty little bastard, trying to interfere with my daughter. I'll have none of that in my house, by Christ and I won't.'

'I'm sore, Mummy. I'm sore,' Ian blubbered, still hopping on the spot.

Georgie suddenly realised she was shaking, and no wonder. 'Never, ever lay a hand on Ian again,' she spat. 'If there's any punishing to be done then I'll do it.'

Charlie regarded her with contempt. 'You're far too easy-going with him. If you're not careful he'll grow up to be a big soft nelly. Or worse, a raving fucking poofter.'

'Don't swear in front of the children,' Georgie said savagely. 'You hear? And what's more, you're drunk again. Drink we can't afford.'

Charlie brandished his belt at her. 'Maybe you'd like a few good wallops across your arse as well! I've a damned good mind to do just that.'

It was the first time he'd ever truly scared her. 'You wouldn't dare!'

'No? Just try me, woman. Just bloody well try me.'

Georgie noticed that Avril was smirking. Little bitch. It was she who'd caused all this trouble. And intentionally so – Georgie had no doubt about that. Avril had laid a trap for Ian and he'd fallen right into it.

'Come on, son, let's go through to your bedroom. Mummy will take care of you there.'

She was certain she heard a snigger from Avril as they left the room, but she did not react. Closing the door of the bedroom behind them, she turned to Ian. 'Right,' she said. 'Take your shorts and undies off, then lie down on the bed so I can see what's what.'

'I'm sore, Mummy,' he sniffled, his tears now drying up.

'I'm sure you are. Now do as I say.'

'My God,' she whispered to herself when she examined his bare bottom. What a thrashing he'd had. The flesh was red hot, wealed in places – weals that would very soon turn black and blue. There was even a small dribble of blood where the skin had been cut.

'My poor darling,' she murmured. 'You just lie there until I get some cream that'll soothe it for you.'

'I hate him,' Ian muttered, still sniffling. 'I hate him.'

Georgie had no reply to that.

There she was again, Tom noticed. The staring woman back for the fourth time. Why didn't she speak, ask for a dance, or something? This continual staring was beginning to faze him.

Perhaps he should go over and engage her in conversation? Then he thought better of it. That might cause trouble of some sort, which was the last thing he wanted. Then, to his surprise, she suddenly came to her feet and headed towards him.

'Can I have a dance, please?' she asked, her accent Kelvinside.

'Of course.' He led her on to the floor and they began to waltz. 'I'm Tom, by the way,' he went on.

'I'm Mrs Mulherron.'

'Nice to meet you, Mrs Mulherron.'

'And you, Tom.'

She wasn't a bad dancer, he soon realised. He'd certainly come across far worse. 'I've noticed you looking at me,' he said.

She blushed. 'Oh dear. Has it been that obvious?'

'I'm afraid so. Is there a reason?'

She glanced away, then back at him. 'Yes, there is. You remind me of someone.'

'Oh? Someone nice, I hope?'

'My son Robert.' She hesitated, then added in a tight voice, 'He was killed at Ypres during the war.'

'I am sorry,' Tom said sympathetically.

'The resemblance is quite remarkable. In fact, now I'm close to you it's even more so. Except for the skin – yours is darker-toned than his was. But, apart from that, you could be two peas in a pod.'

That explained the staring, Tom thought. How extraordinary.

'It was a friend of mine who comes here regularly who first spotted you,' Mrs Mulherron went on. 'When she told me I simply had to come and see for myself. And how right she was. It was as if . . . well, it was as if Robert had come back to life.'

Tom didn't know what to say.

Mrs Mulherron suddenly stopped dancing. 'Excuse me,' she choked. 'I've come over all emotional.' And with that she walked swiftly away in the direction of the ladies' room. It was the last Tom saw of her that night.

Tam ran a hand wearily over his forehead. He was worried, and scared too. Another section of men had been laid off at McNair's, to the point where production had almost ceased altogether.

What if they closed the foundry down entirely? That was him out of a job till production started up again, and God knew when that might be. The great slump continued, was going on and on, with no end in sight. No wonder he was scared. In fact, if he was honest with himself, he was downright terrified of joining the ranks of unemployed. The shame would be awful for a chap like him.

They way things stood he couldn't even do a 'trick' by selling off scrap as he had in the past. There simply wasn't enough of it at present due to the cut-backs. And even if there had been, conversely, the reduction of staff meant there were far too many eyes about now to risk anything along those lines. Before, it had all been hustle and bustle, whereas now people had time on their hands. Time to notice things.

Tam sighed. At least Lena had her job and Tom had his, which was something to be thankful for if the worst came to the worst.

Lena wondered what was wrong with Hamish. He'd been agitated in the extreme since coming to work that morning. To put it bluntly, he had a right case of the fidgets.

'What's wrong with you today?' she asked when she had to go into his office. 'Have you got ants in your pants?'

Hamish didn't laugh, or even smile. 'I have to talk to you, Lena. Can we meet after work in the Swan?'

'Talk about what?'

'Not here. In the Swan.'

'Fine.' She nodded. 'I'll be there.'

'Good.'

But he remained agitated for the rest of the day.

'So what's this all about?' she demanded as Hamish laid a drink in front of her.

He sat, but wouldn't look her in the eye. 'I'm sorry, but there's no easy way to say this. Celia and I are eloping at the weekend.'

She stared at him in shock. 'You're what?'

'Eloping at the weekend to Gretna Green where we'll be staying as long as it takes to get married and have a short honeymoon.'

Lena had a swift gulp of gin and tonic, then fumbled for her cigarettes. 'I thought . . . I thought, or rather hoped, you'd be having a long engagement. A year, say, or even more.'

'That was what Celia and I had planned. But the plan has had to be suddenly changed out of necessity.'

It dawned on Lena what he was getting at. There was only one explanation that she could think of. 'Is Celia up the duff?'

Hamish nodded, his expression one of sheer misery.

'Is she certain?'

'Absolutely. It's been confirmed by a doctor.'

'You bloody fool,' Lena angrily hissed. 'How could you be so stupid? Didn't you use a French letter like you do with me?'

'We did,' Hamish protested. 'Always. But on one occasion it split. We didn't realise until it was over, and by then the damage was done. At the time we didn't worry too much. I mean, it only happened once, after all. But once was enough.'

Lena stared grimly at him, though part of her was sympathetic. What had occurred was damned bad luck.

'Celia had hysterics when she was told,' Hamish went on. 'We even discussed an abortion – there are places where these things can be arranged. But, in the end, she decided she wanted the baby. Or, to put it another way, she didn't want an abortion in case something went wrong.'

This weekend, Lena thought in despair. That meant their monthly trysts were over. She felt a sudden dull ache in the pit of her stomach, an ache that grew with every passing second.

'Have you told the chairman and his wife?' she asked.

'Good God no! There'd be hell to pay if we did. Celia and I have talked it all through and decided eloping is the best way out for us. We'll leave a note behind, and then just leave. We'll say we simply couldn't wait any longer to be married, and so we're off to Gretna. Hopefully, they'll think it all rather romantic.'

'How far gone is Celia?'

'Two and a half months.'

Lena raised an eyebrow. 'So, the baby's going to be premature, I take it?'

He nodded.

'Surely the hospital will know to the contrary?'

'We'll sort that somehow. Celia can be most resourceful when she wants to be. The main thing is that her parents don't find out the truth.' He hesitated, then said, 'I'm sure we can pull it off.'

'Excuse me a moment,' Lena apologised and, leaving him, went to the ladies, where she threw up.

Lena lay in the darkness of her bedroom staring at the ceiling, still trying to come to terms with the bombshell Hamish had dropped earlier that evening in the Swan.

It was over, she thought for the umpteenth time. Finished. No more visits to Hamish's house for nookie. From now on sex would only be a memory. Something to be remembered with pleasure, and sadness too.

'Christ!' she whispered to herself. Life could be so bloody unfair. Why did she have to have been born so ugly that she repelled men? For she did, and had known it for almost as long as she could remember.

It was going to be awful continuing to work alongside Hamish day in, day out. Seeing him, thinking of him going home to the beautiful Celia.

Then she had an idea. Perhaps she could get a transfer out of his department into another? Yes, that would help. She certainly couldn't, in the current slump, leave the company altogether. That would be madness with jobs so thin on the ground.

Then she had an even better idea. Perhaps she couldn't leave the company, but she could leave the country. Why not? Hollywood was still there. Pet would surely help her get something when she turned up.

The only drawback was money. She had no savings left, having given them all to her mother, so she'd have to start again from the beginning which would take years the way things were.

Or would it? Dare she? It frightened her to even think about it. But it could be done. Quite easily, too, given her skill and ability as a ledger clerk.

Hamish had got away with it, after all, to the tune of fifty pounds a month. Why, if she embezzled the same amount, in six months she'd have more than enough and could be on her way.

She mustn't rush into this, she warned herself. She must carefully think it through.

A new start. A new beginning. By God and she was tempted.

'I'm sorry I can't offer you a biscuit, or a piece of cake,' Georgie apologised. Gladys Renton had dropped by for a natter and a cup of tea.

'That's all right. I perfectly understand. So how are you doing anyway?' It had been nearly a week since they'd last spoken.

'Fine. Feeling the pinch like everyone else.'

'Aye, aren't we just.' Gladys nodded.

'But you're all right, surely? Your Sammy's still in work.' Sammy was a night watchman whose job was more or less guaranteed as the firm he was employed by feared night-time break-ins by out-of-work opportunists trying to steal whatever. The lead on the company's roof was a particularly tempting target for thieves.

'No, no, I didn't mean Sammy and me,' Gladys hastily corrected herself. 'I meant the country as a whole.'

'Damn,' Georgie swore. 'I'm out of sugar again. Can you take it without?'

'Oh aye. As long as it's hot and wet I'll not complain.'

Georgie hesitated, then said quietly, 'There's something I've been meaning to ask you.'

'What's that?'

'It's about Charlie's wife Agnes. Did he ever . . . well, did he ever hit her?'

Gladys eyed Georgie speculatively. 'Has he been hitting you then, hen?'

Georgie shook her head. 'But he does have a terrible temper, which has made me wonder at times if he's capable of it.'

'I can honestly say I don't know. I never saw any signs that he had, and Agnes never mentioned it. Not to me anyway.'

That was a relief, Georgie thought. 'Thanks, Gladys. I just wanted to know.' She poured boiling water into the teapot. She'd have to go shopping later, she thought. Which meant more money out of the bank to cover the household expenses as she was seeing less and less of Charlie's pay packet at the end of the week. The majority of his wages went down his throat, leaving her very little to try to manage on.

'There again,' Gladys went on, 'there are some men who hit their women where it can't be seen. On the body like. Some of the bastards can be dead crafty when it comes to hammering the wife, believe me.'

Georgie digested that. 'I see,' she murmured. Had that been the case with Agnes? It was always a possibility.

'While we're asking questions, what do you make of Charlie's sister Betty?'

Georgie took a deep breath, and looked sideways at Gladys who was watching her intently. 'The truth? I can't stand the woman. There's something about her makes my flesh creep.'

'She and Agnes didn't get on, I can tell you that.'

'Oh?'

'Agnes couldn't bear her sister-in-law who, apparently, thought Charlie had married beneath him. Which is a laugh when you think about it. No offence meant, but he's only a fireman after all. Hardly special.'

'I wonder why Betty thought that?'

'Who knows? She's a queer fish right enough. There was talk at the time . . .' Gladys broke off, and bit her lip.

'Talk at what time?'

Gladys sighed. 'Well, I may as well tell you. There was talk at the time, pure speculation mind, that Agnes might not have tripped when she fell down the stairs.'

'I don't understand.' Georgie frowned.

Gladys stared her straight in the eye. 'The talk was that Agnes might have been pushed after some sort of row.'

'Dear God,' Georgie breathed, shocked.

'Betty had been in your house that day. I don't know why, but she'd definitely been there before the accident. I saw her myself. But no one spotted her leaving or knows what time that was.'

'That would have been murder,' Georgie declared, thoroughly shaken.

'There's absolutely no proof it was that. But it's a hard fact the two women loathed each other. And Betty . . . as I said, she's a queer fish. And very nasty with it. A little shove at the right moment, and hey! An accident.'

'She's always been friendly enough to me,' Georgie said. 'Or appeared to be friendly enough. I just don't like her, that's all. She gives me the willies.'

'What I told you is strictly between the pair of us, all right? It was only talk, after all.'

'Strictly between the pair of us,' Georgie agreed. She was still shaken by what she'd just learnt.

'I'm sorry for running away last time,' Mrs Mulherron apologised. 'I was just simply overcome. Please forgive me.'

'There's nothing to forgive.' Tom smiled. 'I understood.'

She gazed into his face, then away again. 'The resemblance really is quite uncanny.'

'Must have been a handsome devil, your son,' Tom joked.

Mrs Mulherron laughed. 'There were those who thought he was. As did I, though I have to admit to being prejudiced.'

'A mother's privilege.'

'Indeed it is.'

'Was Robert an officer?'

'A captain when he was killed. He was with the artillery.'

'You must miss him dreadfully,' Tom sympathised.

'I do. Very much.'

'As must your husband?'

'I'm afraid Freddy's also dead. He passed on several years after the war ended. He never really got over Robert, you see. That was a terrible blow to him.'

'Do you have other children?' Tom was curious.

'No, Robert was our one and only. The apple of Freddy's eye. And mine too, of course.'

The dance came to an end and they politely clapped. 'Can you stay up for another?' she asked hopefully.

'Yes, but only one more. Two at a time is the maximum. House rules.'

'Which is why I have a favour to ask.'

'Which is?'

'I presume you have the days free?'

'That's right.'

'I'd love to have a really good chat with you, which I obviously can't do here, and I was wondering if you'd care to come to lunch next week?'

He was taken aback. 'Lunch?'

'I'd be very grateful if you could. I'd like to show you Robert's photograph so you can see the likeness for yourself.'

Chrissie's warnings about predatory women flashed through Tom's mind. But he couldn't believe Mrs Mulherron was one of those.

Mrs Mulherron noticed his look of concern, and guessed what it was about. 'Don't worry, Tom, we won't be alone. The staff will be in attendance, I promise you.'

Before the dance was over Tom had agreed to go to her house for lunch the following Wednesday.

Lena was hurrying home from work when she was brought up short by a street billboard advertising that evening's newspaper. The headline written on it screamed in large black letters: TRAGEDY AT SEA. FAMOUS HOLLYWOOD ACTRESS DROWNED.

Lena's heart was in her mouth as she bought a copy of the paper and quickly scanned the front page.

The actress was Dawn Ryder.

Chapter 20

'Pet's dead,' Lena announced to the family when she got in. She waved the newspaper at them. 'It's here on the front page.'

'Dead?' Chrissie repeated, shocked. 'How?'

'The paper says she drowned while swimming off the yacht she was holidaying on. It happened yesterday, apparently.'

Tam shook his head in disbelief. He'd always had a soft spot for Pet McQueen.

'I must go and see her parents,' Lena declared. 'They'll be devastated.'

'You'll have your tea first though?'

'I couldn't eat a thing, Mum. I'm just so upset. She and I were . . . well, you know. The best of pals.'

'I'm sorry, sis,' Tom sympathised. He'd also liked Pet.

'I'll just have a tidy up and then be on my way.' Lena suddenly staggered, and had to lean on the table for support. 'Sorry,' she croaked. 'As I said, I'm just so upset.'

'Understandable, lass.' Chrissie nodded.

Lena took a deep breath, and did her best to pull herself together. Leaving them, she went to her bedroom where, within minutes, she broke down and cried.

Poor Pet. Poor, poor Pet. The one consolation was, Lena

reflected through her tears, she'd been a Hollywood star when she died. Her dream had come true.

Tom stared in awe at the house where Mrs Mulherron lived. It was more of a mansion than a house, he thought – it was absolutely huge.

Go on, he mentally urged himself. Ring the bell. You are invited, after all. Screwing up his courage, and feeling completely out of place, he mounted a few stone steps and did just that.

There was the sound of footsteps, then the door was opened to reveal a rather ancient butler.

'My name's Tom McKeand,' Tom stuttered. 'Mrs Mulherron is expecting me.'

The butler was staring at Tom as though he'd opened the door to a ghost. 'Quite so, Mr McKeand,' he replied at last. 'Do come in. Mrs Mulherron is in the morning room. If you'll kindly follow me I'll show you the way.'

Tom gazed about him as he walked behind the butler, if anything even more awed than he'd been out in the street. There were antiques everywhere, and gilt-framed paintings on the walls. He had no idea who the painters were, but he presumed they were famous.

Mrs Mulherron rose to her feet the moment he was ushered into the room. 'Ah, there you are, Tom. How kind of you to come.'

He wasn't sure what to do next, being completely out of his depth. He elected to go to her and shake her by the hand. She looked older in daylight, he noticed. The lighting at the the Belgrave was far kinder, particularly for women of a certain age. Which, of course, was the intention.

He smiled. 'I'm delighted to be here.'

'Well, what do you think, Smith? Was I right or wrong?'

'You were right, madam,' the butler replied. 'When I opened the front door I would have sworn it was the young master himself standing there.'

Mrs Mulherron turned her attention again to Tom. 'Now, I'm

having a pre-lunch sherry. Would you care for one? Or perhaps something else. A whisky maybe?'

'Whisky would be lovely.'

'Would you care for it neat, sir, or with water or soda?'

'Soda, please,' Tom replied, knowing that was how many of the nobs took it.

'Certainly, sir.'

Mrs Mulherron gestured to the white marble mantelpiece. 'I've laid out a few photographs for you to look at.'

Tom crossed to the mantelpiece to stare at the largest photo, which was set in a silver frame: Robert Mulherron wearing his military uniform. Tom presumed that the photograph had been taken just before his departure to the Front.

He might have been gazing into a mirror. Robert was him to a T. A younger version, but him to a T.

'Do you see the resemblance?' Mrs Mulherron queried with a sad smile.

'Oh, yes. We might have been brothers.'

'You might have been twins,' she corrected.

'Indeed,' Tom mused. They might well have been.

The other photographs were of Robert at various stages in his short life. The resemblance in the younger ones wasn't quite so noticeable, but it increased as Robert grew up. Tom found the whole thing rather spooky.

'How did he die?' he asked quietly.

'Blown up, I was told. One moment he was there, the next gone. He and the entire gun crew.' She paused to compose herself. 'At least it was quick. He wouldn't have known what happened, or felt any pain.'

'That must have been a consolation.'

'Yes, it was. And still is.'

Smith returned with Tom's whisky and soda, offering it to him on a tray. 'Thank you,' Tom said, accepting the drink.

'I don't normally, but I'll have another sherry, I think,' Mrs Mulherron told the butler.

'Certainly, madam.'

'Smith's been with us for years and years,' she explained to Tom when the man had gone. 'He was very fond of Robert. Very fond.'

'He strikes me as a nice man, Mrs Mulherron.'

'Oh, he is. But enough of this Mrs Mulherron business. Far too formal. My Christian name is Dorcas, believe it or not. I hate it. From some Shakespearean play, I understand, and quite the silliest name imaginable. I prefer Dolly, and have insisted on being called that since very early on.'

Tom grinned. 'Then Dolly it is.'

'Good. Are you hungry, Tom?'

'Fairly so.'

'Then we shall shortly go on through.'

The starter was pâté, which Tom had never eaten before, the main course a fish dish which he thoroughly enjoyed. The pudding was something named brûlée, again thoroughly enjoyable, and the meal was accompanied by a choice of red or white wine. Dolly elected to drink white, Tom red.

'If it's not rude to say so, I'm most impressed by your house,' Tom commented halfway through the pudding. He felt quite relaxed, Dolly being the easiest of company. There were certainly no airs or graces about her.

'It is lovely, isn't it?' Dolly sighed. 'I should move to something smaller now that I'm on my own, but I can't bring myself to do so. There are far too many happy memories for me here.'

'Yes, I can understand that.'

Dolly's eyes took on a wistful, faraway look. She was clearly lost in memory.

'Can I ask what your husband did?' Tom was dying to know. Nosy, as Chrissie would have said.

Dolly came out of her reverie. 'Freddy was a manufacturer of nuts and bolts, a very successful one. I sold the business after he died on advice from my advocate. A wise decision, I've always thought. Freddy was the dynamism behind the company. Without him . . . well, who knows what might have happened.'

'Nuts and bolts,' Tom repeated, amused. 'He must have been turning them out by the millions to afford a house like this.'

'Oh, he was. Supplying firms not only in this country, but abroad.'

Tom finished his brûlée, laid his spoon aside, and had a sip of wine.

'Now, tell me about yourself,' Dolly said. 'I want to know everything about you and your family.'

'Everything?'

'Absolutely.'

'That's a tall order,' Tom joked.

'We've got all afternoon, don't forget.'

He shrugged. 'To be honest, there's not that much to tell, really. We're a pretty ordinary family to whom not much happens.'

'Nevertheless, on you go.'

So he did.

'This is Robert's bedroom, which I've left exactly as it was the day he went off to France.'

Tom glanced around. It was certainly a comfortable bedroom, with books and all sorts of mementos scattered around. 'Which school did Robert go to?'

'Glasgow Academy, where he did very well. He was quite bright, if I say so myself.'

'Well that's something I'm not.'

'Oh, I wouldn't say that.' Dolly smiled. 'You strike me as a very intelligent young man. In different circumstances you might have gone far, indeed you might.'

Tom couldn't see it himself. He picked up a rugby ball, throwing it a few inches into the air and catching it again.

'Have you played?' Dolly enquired.

'No.' Tom laughed. 'That's strictly a posh game. It was football with me. In the playground and on the street. Gangs of us at times. It was great fun.'

Dolly had a sudden idea which caused her to wrinkle her forehead. Why not? she thought. Better they did some good than just hang there in the wardrobe. As long as Tom didn't take offence, that was.

When she made her suggestion, he didn't.

'That must have cost a pretty penny,' Chrissie said, fingering the cloth of the overcoat Tom had brought home with him. 'A real Crombie too,' she added, noting the label.

'Just look at these suits,' Tom demanded, pulling one from the suitcase he'd also brought back.

Chrissie whistled silently. She knew quality when she saw it.

'Three suits and six shirts.' Tom grinned. 'Not bad, eh?'

'I should say so. And that suitcase is crocodile skin. That wouldn't have come cheap either.'

'I've to return the suitcase,' Tom explained. 'She said that way I have to visit her again.'

The clothes were all in excellent condition, Chrissie observed. Almost brand new.

'I was offered shoes as well, but had to turn them down as Robert's feet were smaller than mine.'

'And do these suits fit?'

'Dolly and I both thought so. If I do need an alteration or two I'm sure Lena will help. You know how good she is at that sort of thing.'

'Dolly, eh?' Chrissie smiled. 'On first-name terms now, are we?'

'She insisted. Said Mrs Mulherron was far too formal.'

'And you actually do look like her son?'

'I'm a dead ringer, Mum. We might have been twins.'

Chrissie thought about that. 'What was the house like?'

'Ah!' Tom exclaimed. 'Now you're talking.' He went on to describe the house in detail, inside and out.

'This Mrs Mulherron must be filthy rich,' Chrissie commented when he'd finally finished.

'As Croesus. She even has a butler called Smith. Not to mention a cook, a chauffeur cum handyman, and several maids. That lot must cost more than a couple of quid a week.'

Chrissie could only agree.

Dolly was sitting on the edge of Robert's bed staring at his wardrobe. She'd been right to give Tom those clothes, she thought. Better he had them, and made use of them, than they just continued to hang there.

She hadn't said so to Tom, but the suit he wore at the Belgrave had seen better days. And it couldn't be very nice wearing the same suit night after night. It would wear out in no time, but to buy a new one would be a big lay-out for Tom, who couldn't be on that much money a week.

Now that she'd made a start should she get rid of the rest of Robert's things? She'd avoided doing so since his death, wanting to keep the room exactly as it had been. It would break her heart to do it, but perhaps it would be best in the long run. Coming in here to sit, from time to time, was downright morbid now she thought about it. But she wouldn't make a decision there and then. What if she came to regret chucking everything out?

'Oh, Robert,' she whispered. 'Oh, Freddy.'

How she missed them both.

'Can you please try not to hurt me like that,' Georgie said.

Charlie was surprised. 'Did I?'

'There's no need to grab and squeeze. A little gentleness is what's called for.'

'I'm sorry, Georgie,' he apologised. 'I wasn't aware I was doing that.'

'Well you were. At one point I thought you were going to pull my tit right off.'

'Sorry again. I'll be more careful next time.'

This roughness was a recent thing, Georgie reflected. It hadn't been like that when they were first married. Like everything else in their marriage, lovemaking had deteriorated.

Turning away from him she thought of John. Dear, lovely

John. That night she dreamt of him, and how it had once been between them.

A smiling Hamish came breezing into the department on his first day back after the elopement. 'Morning, everyone!' he declared, heading straight for his office. 'Lena, can you please join me for a few moments?'

She mustn't let her feelings show, she thought. She had no right to be angry, or jealous, after all. He'd kept his part of the bargain so she could hardly complain.

His expression was grave when she entered his office and closed the door. 'First of all let me say how sorry I am about your friend Dawn Ryder. It must have been a terrible shock for you.'

Lena hadn't expected this. 'Yes, it was. How did you find out?'

'It was in the newspapers.'

Of course. She should have thought of that. He read the papers like everyone else.

'Well, I'm sorry, and I wanted you to know that.'

'Thanks, Hamish.'

He took a deep breath. 'Anyway, to business. Has everything been all right here? No problems?'

'No problems,' Lena assured him. She didn't add that there wouldn't be with her in charge.

'And my absence, has that been explained in any way?'

'The chairman sent down a memo saying you'd taken unexpected leave, and to carry on as usual until your return. Elopement or marriage wasn't mentioned.'

'Fine.' Hamish nodded.

'Have you seen Celia's parents since your return?'

'We only got in late last night, and I decided it was best to come straight to work this morning. So the answer's no.'

Lena cleared her throat. She didn't want to ask the question, but felt driven to do so. 'How did it all go?'

He stared at her, then, embarrassed, glanced away. 'As planned. We had the ceremony, which took longer to organise than I'd realised, then had a short honeymoon. I wish I could say the weather was wonderful, but it wasn't. In fact it rained nearly all the time we were there.'

Lena took some grim satisfaction from that. 'Too bad.'

'Still, it could have been worse, I suppose.'

'So now Celia is officially Mrs Hamish Murchison.'

Was it her imagination or did Hamish squirm ever so slightly in his chair?

'That's right. And has a gold band on her finger to prove it.'

'Then I wish the pair of you all the very best.' It wasn't true, but she felt obliged to say it.

'Thank you.'

'There's something else, Hamish.'

'What's that?'

'I'd like a transfer to another department. I'm sure you can understand why.'

He stared at her, aghast. 'You don't mean that?'

'I'm afraid I do.'

'But I rely on you so much, Lena. You know that,' he spluttered. 'You're my right hand. I don't know what I'd do without you.'

'Manage somehow,' she replied, giving him her razored smile.

Hamish came to his feet, walked to the window and stared out. 'Is this some sort of revenge?' he asked quietly over his shoulder.

'Not revenge, Hamish,' she answered. 'But I think it would be for the best, don't you?'

'No I bloody well do not!' he exploded, whirling on her. 'I refuse to transfer you. Absolutely refuse.' He held up a hand. 'And there will be no further discussion or argument about that. Do you hear?'

'What if I went above your head?' she queried, the same arctic smile on her face.

'You can't, Lena. You're forgetting I'm the chairman's son-in-law now. If I say you stay, then you stay.' He glared at her. 'And don't even think of threatening me with out little secret. Because if I go down I'd swear you were in on it. That it was your idea in the first place. Then we'd both be sunk.'

'I had no intention of threatening you,' Lena replied quietly. 'You kept your part of the bargain, and I'll keep mine. Now, is there anything else?'

He shook his head.

A little later he left for the coffee shop, not even looking at her as he strode past.

Tom and Dolly applauded politely at the end of the dance. It had been her second with him, which meant she now had to relinquish him to another partner.

'You seem very perky tonight,' Tom complimented her, having noted the spring in her step, and the twinkle in her eye.

'I feel it.'

'Any particular reason?'

'None that I can think of. I simply woke up in an excellent mood this morning and it has continued throughout the day.'

He smiled at her. 'Will we be dancing again later?'

'Of course. But in the meantime I thought I'd chance my luck in the gaming room.'

'Really? I didn't know you gambled.'

'On occasion, when the opportunity presents itself. Freddy and I used to . . .' She broke off. 'But that's another story which I'll tell you some time.'

Tom re-joined Derek, who'd also just sat down. 'Is the gambling here on the level?' he asked in a whisper.

'As far as I know,' Derek replied.

'Good.'

An hour later Dolly was back asking for another dance, and Tom was only too happy to oblige. He'd become quite fond of Dolly Mulherron, in a friendly sort of way.

'So how did you get on?' he enquired as they took to the floor.

'I played blackjack and won.'

'Good for you!'

'Nearly two hundred pounds.' She giggled. 'Not bad, eh?'

'Not bad at all. I'm impressed.'

The next moment several gaming chips were slipped into his breast pocket. 'Your cut,' she said, smiling.

'But I didn't do anything to deserve a cut!'

'You're getting one anyway.'

From then on, whenever Dolly won in the gaming room, which was often, she shared her winnings with Tom.

Chapter 21

'Thanks for calling round. I'll see you again soon, no doubt.'
''Bye then, Georgie.'
''Bye, Betty.'

Georgie closed the front door and let out a sigh of relief. That had been an unexpected visit from Charlie's sister, and she hadn't enjoyed it one little bit. The woman really did give her the willies. She couldn't have said why, since Betty was always agreeable enough. But there was something in her eyes Georgie found most disturbing.

Had Betty pushed Agnes down the stairs? One thing was certain: Georgie believed her quite capable of it. That was a harsh verdict, perhaps, particularly when there was no proof of any sort, but Georgie believed her capable all right. She found herself watching her back when Betty was around, and being politeness itself.

She shivered as gooseflesh suddenly erupted all over her body. That was the effect Betty had on her.

'I wonder what she's like?' Derek mused. He was referring to the new young female dancer who was taking over that night from her predecessor, who'd had to leave for personal reasons.

Tom shrugged. 'Search me. As long as she's pleasant, that's all I care about.'

'Aye, true enough.' Derek nodded. All the dancers got on well together, and were hoping the newcomer would fit in. 'There's Mrs Simpson now.'

The manageress had appeared at the far side of the hall, accompanied by a much younger woman.

The newcomer was almost halfway towards them before Tom recognised her. He simply couldn't believe his eyes. It was Brigid. *His* Brigid. The one he'd broken his heart over when they'd split up.

'I'd like you all to meet Miss O'Reilly,' Mrs Simpson announced on reaching the dancers, and immediately began introducing them to Brigid. Tom didn't know what to do. Did he acknowledge Brigid as an old friend, or not mention the fact? He'd be led by her, he decided.

'Brigid, this is Tom McKeand.'

'Pleased to meet you, Tom,' she said formally.

There it was, he'd take his cue from that. 'And I'm pleased to meet you, Brigid.'

'You'll soon get to know everyone,' Mrs Simpson said to Brigid, escorting her back up the line to where she'd be sitting with the two older women.

'Are you all right, Tom?' Derek frowned. 'You look dreadful.'

'Do I?' Tom queried, pretending innocence.

'You've suddenly gone all white and . . . well, I don't know. You just look dreadful.'

'A sudden attack of wind,' Tom lied in a whisper. 'It'll soon pass.'

'Not in my direction, I hope!'

Tom forced a laugh. 'I'll be careful about that.'

His mind was reeling when he sat down again. Brigid! After all these years. It hardly seemed credible. And yet there she was, sitting no more than a dozen feet away, as gorgeous as ever.

During the evening he watched her as she danced, noting she hadn't lost any of her skill and ability. Once he caught her glancing in his direction, looking quickly away again when their eyes met.

He couldn't wait to talk to her when he had the chance.

* * *

Tom took his coat from its peg and hurried after Brigid, whom he'd let go on slightly ahead. Out in the street he caught her up.

'Brigid!'

She stopped and turned to face him.

'That was a shock,' he said, joining her.

'For me too. I had no idea you worked there.'

'Have done for a while now.' They resumed walking. 'I got laid off at McNair's and was lucky enough to be told by a pal that the Belgrave was looking for someone. What about you?'

'Same thing. I got laid off too, and heard about the Belgrave only yesterday. I saw Mrs Simpson, and started tonight.'

'God, it's good to see you again,' he breathed.

She glanced sideways at him, then away again. 'How have you been?'

Why hadn't she said she was glad to see *him*? Maybe because she wasn't. 'Fine. You?'

'All right.'

'I must say you're looking well. You've hardly changed at all.'

'Thank you.'

Hardly enthusiastic, he thought glumly. 'And what about me? Have I changed much?'

'Not really.'

'Well, that's nice to know.' This wasn't going at all well. Making conversation was like getting blood out of the proverbial stone.

'What's it like at the Belgrave?' she asked after a moment.

'Terrific. I thoroughly enjoy working there. If you can call dancing work, that is.' He shook his head. 'I still find it hard to believe I get paid for it. It sure as hell beats the hard graft at McNair's. Money for old rope.'

She smiled at that. 'So it would seem. But tell me, is there anything I should know?'

'Like what?'

'The blokes who ask me to dance. Are any of them going to proposition me? That was my worry.'

'Not a chance,' Tom assured her. 'It's a very respectable place. If anyone ever does try it on just tell Mrs Simpson and he'll be chucked out double quick. Mrs Simpson doesn't stand for any nonsense.'

Brigid looked relieved.

'My mother had the same worry when I started there,' Tom went on. 'It quite surprised me that she would think of such a thing, but she did. I was soon able to put her mind at rest.'

'I suppose it gets hectic Fridays and Saturdays?'

'It can do. There are some nights when you never get to have a breather from start to finish. On your feet all the time.'

'The other dancers seem nice enough,' Brigid commented.

'They are. A good bunch. You won't have any trouble there either.'

She smiled at him. 'It seems I've fallen on my feet then.'

He smiled back. 'Literally.'

That made her laugh.

When they came to a corner she stopped. 'I go this way,' she said.

'I know.'

'So . . .'

'I thought I'd walk you home,' he interrupted. 'It's not that far out of my way, after all.'

'I'm quite capable of looking after myself, Tom,' she said firmly. 'Nothing will happen to me, even at this time of night. I'll be fine.'

'No doubt, Brigid. I just thought . . . well, I'd like to. There's no harm in it, is there?'

'Are you sure?'

'Absolutely. We are old friends, don't forget. It's not as if I'm going to try to chat you up or anything.'

She stared hard at him, then nodded. 'All right.' They continued on their way.

'I saw you at the dancing once,' he told her. 'Years ago. You were with a chap I presumed was your boyfriend.'

'And why would you presume that?'

Tom was suddenly embarrassed, wishing now he hadn't referred to the occasion. 'You had three or four dances in a row.'

'I see.' She glanced at him again. 'And?'

'And what?'

'What happened after the three or four dances?'

'I don't know. I left.'

'Because of me?'

'No,' he lied. 'I simply decided to go elsewhere.'

She knew he was fibbing; she could hear it in his voice. Tom had always been something of an open book to her. She wanted to say she hoped it hadn't distressed him, but decided not to.

Tom looked up at the sky. 'I think it might rain. It seems to be threatening.'

Brigid also looked up. It didn't look threatening to her. 'I imagined you'd have been engaged or married by now?' He wasn't wearing a ring, but there again, some men didn't.

''Fraid not,' he answered vaguely.

'Nor am I, before you ask.'

He grinned. 'I'm aware of that. I had a dekko at your left hand earlier to see if you were. I know it's none of my business, Brigid, but are you going out with anyone?'

She hesitated. 'I was, until recently.'

'What happened?'

She decided to be honest. 'He didn't want to see me any more. I think he'd met someone else.'

'The man's an idiot,' Tom muttered.

'What did you say? I didn't catch that.'

'I said the man's an idiot. A bloody fool for giving you up.'

She was pleased. He still cared. 'What about you?'

'No one at the moment.'

For some reason that pleased her as well. She would have been . . . She frowned when she realised what she'd been about to admit to herself. She'd have been jealous.

Tom pulled out his cigarettes and offered her one.

'Not in the street, thank you very much,' she said.

'The street's empty. Who's to know?'

She had to admit she was tempted. She'd have loved a fag, but had been brought up to believe decent women didn't smoke in the street.

'Go on,' he urged. 'No one will see you.'

She gave in to temptation. 'All right, then.'

He struck a match and held it to her cigarette, then his own. He flicked the match to send it spiralling away.

Brigid sucked in a deep lungful of smoke, then slowly blew it out. 'I've cut down to only a couple a day,' she told him.

'Lack of money?'

'That's it.'

'Well, you'll be able to afford more than that once you get your first pay packet.'

'Thank God. That and other things I've had to go without since being laid off.'

Tom realised they had relaxed together somewhere during their walk. They were at ease with one another again. The fact delighted him. They continued chatting, catching up with one another, till eventually they reached her close, where she stopped and turned to face him.

What to do next? he wondered. Peck her on the cheek? Shake her by the hand? No, that would be ridiculous. Just walk away after saying goodnight? That seemed the safest bet. Though he would much have preferred the kiss on the cheek.

'I'll see you tomorrow night, then, Brigid,' he declared somewhat awkwardly.

She smiled at him. 'Thanks for walking me home, Tom. It was kind of you.'

'Don't mention it. It was nothing of the sort. It was a pleasure, believe me.'

She had enjoyed it too. 'There's just one thing, Tom.'

'And what's that?'

'Don't get any ideas. I'm still Catholic, and this is still Glasgow.'

'I know,' he whispered sadly.

'Goodnight then.'

'Goodnight.'

She was dead right, he thought morosely as he strolled away. She was still Catholic, and this was still Glasgow.

Nothing anyone could do would ever change that.

*　　*　　*

226

'What's wrong with you tonight?' Chrissie asked. She and Tam were alone, Tom at work and Lena in her room.

'I've been thinking, that's all.'

'About what?'

'Mary.'

Chrissie sighed, and dropped her knitting on to her lap. She was using wool from an old cardigan she'd unpicked to knit socks for Tam and Tom.

'It's been so long since we've seen her,' Tam went on. 'Years now.'

Chrissie also missed their eldest daughter. Dreadfully so at times. She couldn't help but feel it was wrong for them to be estranged as they were. She nodded. 'Aye. It is that.'

'The children must have grown quite a bit.'

'I suppose so.'

'And we know nothing of their circumstances. Is James still in work, or has he been laid off too, like so many?'

'I've heard nothing. If I had you'd have been the first to be told.'

Tam wished it was the weekend so he could have had some whisky. But it was still only Thursday. He'd have to wait.

'Do you want to go and see her?' Chrissie asked softly.

Tam glanced sharply at her, then away again. He didn't reply. 'Tam?'

He took a deep breath, then slowly exhaled. 'No, I don't. It's her place to come to us.'

'She won't do that unless she's allowed to try to win us over to her religious views. And you won't allow that.'

'Damn right I won't! If she comes it's as a daughter to her parents without all that guff she spouts about the so-called sect.'

'Then things will just have to remain as they are, I suppose,' Chrissie said, a great weariness in her voice.

The subject was closed.

It was the quietest Tuesday Tom had ever known at the Belgrave. Since his arrival several hours earlier he hadn't been asked up once to dance, nor had any of the others. He was sure they must be as bored as he was.

Derek, sitting beside him, yawned. 'I nearly dropped off there. Mrs Simpson wouldn't have liked that at all.'

'She'd have given you a right flea in your ear.'

Derek grinned his agreement.

Tom had a sudden idea. Why not? He didn't think the manageress would object. On the contrary, she'd probably approve as they were so quiet. He decided to chance it.

Getting to his feet he went to where Brigid was sitting. 'Do you fancy a birl round the floor?' he asked.

She frowned. 'Is that allowed?'

'I don't see why not. The place is all but empty.'

'I'm not sure, Tom. I don't want to get into any trouble.'

'You won't. Now come on.'

Brigid stood up and together they went on to the dance floor. 'It's been a long time,' Tom said quietly as she came into his arms.

'Yes, it has.'

Not that you would have thought it, Tom reflected a few minutes later. It was as if . . . well, it was as if they'd never been apart.

When it came to dancing, anyway.

'So, how's Charlie been lately?' Chrissie queried. Georgie had called in to pay her a visit.

'Much improved, I have to say. He's really been making an effort. Not drinking nearly as much as he was. Nicer too.'

'That's good.'

'Avril's still a right little cow. But then, that'll never change. I've no doubt she'll still be a cow when she grows up. She's that type.'

'And Ian?'

'He's fine. His skin has cleared up a lot recently. Though why, I've no idea. He's getting on quite well at school too, which pleases me.'

'No more thrashings, I take it?'

Georgie's expression became grim. 'No. I'll never forgive Charlie for doing that. Or Avril for instigating it.'

'It was a bad business right enough.' Chrissie shook her head.

'It took Ian a long time to get over it, I can tell you. He's still wary of Charlie. He doesn't say, but I know he is. And I don't blame him either.'

'And you? Are you wary of him?'

'In a way,' Georgie reluctantly admitted. 'He's never yet laid a hand on me. But I always have the feeling it could happen.'

'And if he ever does?'

Georgie shrugged. 'I don't honestly know. I might leave him. There again, that would create a lot of problems. Where would I go, for instance?'

'Here,' Chrissie stated firmly. 'You could have your old bed back in what's now Lena's room. And we could arrange something in Tom's for Ian. We'd cope.'

Georgie's eyes shone with gratitude. 'Thanks, Mum. I'll remember that.'

'See you do.' Chrissie hesitated, then asked, 'Do you regret marrying him?'

Georgie took her time in replying. 'He's certainly not the man I thought I was marrying, and that's the truth. I believed him to be kind and gentle – which he can be, when it suits him. But I wasn't aware of his drinking. That came as quite a shock.'

'You haven't answered my question, Georgie.'

That was because it wasn't a question she wanted to answer. She didn't even want to admit the answer to herself. She stared at her mother, her expression stricken.

'Yes,' she finally admitted. 'I do.'

'What do you do with your days?' Tom asked, having walked Brigid home after work.

'Not a lot, really,' she answered. 'I always have a lie-in during the week, after which I help my mother round the house. Sometimes I go shopping for her. That sort of thing. What about you?'

'Not a lot either. Which is why I was wondering, how about us meeting up?'

'What for?'

'Well, I could buy you lunch for a start.'

Brigid couldn't help but laugh. 'Lunch!' she mocked. 'Since when has it become that? It was always dinner when I knew you before.'

Tom blushed.

'Taking on airs and graces, are we?'

'No, it's not like that. I suppose I used the word because of Mrs Mulherron.'

'And who's Mrs Mulherron when she's at home?'

God, but he wanted to kiss her. That and more, if she'd have let him. 'It's a long story, Brigid, which I can tell you over lunch. So how about it?'

'I don't know,' she replied reluctantly. 'It might not be such a good idea.'

'Of course it's a good idea. You're at a loose end, and so am I. Spending a little time together takes up a bit of slack. It'll be fun. And look on the bright side: you'll get to hear all about Mrs Mulherron. Or Dolly as she insists I call her.'

Brigid was intrigued, as Tom had hoped she'd be. 'Well, maybe,' she prevaricated.

'Which day shall we meet then?' he asked hopefully.

'Hold your horses. I haven't agreed yet,' she protested.

'You name the day and time, and I'll pick you up here.'

Suddenly her resistance crumbled. She could think of nothing she'd like more than to have lunch, as he called it, with Tom. 'No funny business now, right?'

'Right.'

'Sure?'

'Cross my heart and hope to die if I damn well tell a lie.'

She laughed again, then named a day and time as requested. 'I'll be standing here waiting for you.'

What had she got herself into, she wondered as she climbed

the stairs to her house. She didn't quite know. But of one thing she was certain: she was looking forward to it.

'Go straight on through, Mrs Murchison,' Lena said, putting on her best smile. 'Your husband's free.'

'Thank you. Miss McKeand, isn't it?'

'That's correct.'

Celia matched Lena's smile before moving ponderously towards Hamish's office.

My God, Lena thought. What a size! Celia was big enough to be carrying a baby elephant rather than a human child. Lena had never seen a pregnant woman so large. And there was still months to go before the birth! As for Celia's bosom, it was simply ginormous, straining at the dress she was wearing. It was going to take Celia a long, long time to get her figure back, Lena glee-fully reflected. If she ever did, that was. And after her milk dried she was going to have tits down to her knees.

Oh, life was not all bad, Lena told herself. There was some justice in the world after all.

Chapter 22

It seemed to happen as though by magic. One moment Tom was saying goodnight to Brigid, having walked her home after work yet again, the next they were in one another's arms kissing passionately.

'Oh, Brigid,' Tom breathed when the kiss was finally over. 'That was fantastic.' To his astonishment she broke away from him and burst into tears. 'Brigid, what's wrong?'

'You are. We are,' she sobbed. 'I didn't want this to happen. And it's all my fault for letting it.'

Perplexed, he stared at her. 'I'm sorry. I . . . I don't know what came over me.' He broke off in confusion.

She groped in a coat pocket to produce a handkerchief which she used to dab at her tears. She was furious with herself.

'Can I . . .' He moved towards her and she immediately backed away.

'Damn you, Tom McKeand,' she shouted. 'Damn you. Why did you ever have to come back into my life again? After all these years of trying to forget you and then . . . The bloody Belgrave. It just isn't fair.'

'You spent years trying to forget me?' he repeated wonderingly.

'Yes, I did. I thought I'd succeeded, too.'

'And I spent years trying to forget you, but never could. You were always there, somewhere, in my mind and thoughts.'

She hiccuped. 'Was I?'

'I never stopped loving you, Brigid. And that's the truth.'

That brought on a fresh outbreak of tears. 'Well, I hate you,' she wailed. 'Hate you for kissing me like that. And saying what you just did.'

Now he was bewildered. 'You hate me for loving you?'

'Yes.'

'But why?'

'Because I'm still in love with you. That's why.'

She hated and loved him at the same time? How could that be? An impossibility, surely. And then it dawned on him what she'd just confessed, and his heart leapt within him.

'You still love me?' he repeated in awe.

'And now we're going to have to go through it all again.'

'Go through what?'

'Breaking up, dope. What else?'

He had no answer to give her, knowing her to be right. What had he been thinking of? What had been going through his mind since she'd turned up at the Belgrave?

'It can't be,' she cried. 'No matter how much we want it, it just can't be. I've already told you, I'm still Catholic, and this is still Glasgow.'

And with that she turned and fled up her close.

It had been a lovely night out for the pair of them, Georgie reflected as she and Ian made their way home from the pictures. He'd had a good report from school and, as a reward, she'd taken him to see a cowboys and Indians film which he'd absolutely adored. When they came out of the cinema she'd bought them a bag of chips each as a special treat, and they'd just eaten the last ones.

On arriving at their front door she produced her key and opened it. She was still smiling as she entered the kitchen in front of Ian, but what she saw there seemed to turn her blood ice cold, and made the smile vanish abruptly from her face.

Charlie was sitting with a sleeping Avril on his lap. The child was totally naked, and Charlie's half-closed eyes told her just how drunk he was. But it was what he was doing that made her want to scream in horror. His flies were open and he was . . . With Avril on his lap!

Remembering Ian was behind her Georgie reacted swiftly. 'Let's get out of here,' she croaked, turning round and bundling him back in the direction they'd come. In the street again she had to stop for a few seconds in order to throw up in the gutter.

She couldn't believe what she'd just witnessed. It couldn't be true.

But it was.

She re-joined her parents, still in a state of shock. 'Ian's asleep now,' she said.

Chrissie, Tam and Lena still didn't quite know what had happened, only that it was something dreadful. Georgie's garbled story hadn't made much sense, but she had been clear about wanting to stay the night, which Chrissie had readily agreed to.

'Now, what's this all about?' Tam demanded, upset to see his daughter in such a state.

Georgie slumped into a chair. She felt embarrassed about telling her parents and Lena what she'd seen, but tell them she must. They listened incredulously while she described what she'd walked in on.

'Dear God in Heaven,' Chrissie whispered, when Georgie had finished.

Tam's hands were formed into fists. If Charlie had been present, drunk or not, he'd have beaten the bastard senseless.

'The wee lassie was totally naked?' Lena repeated.

'Stark, and asleep.'

'And he was . . .' Chrissie made a gesture.

'That's right, Mum.'

'He's a pervert, that's what he is. A bloody pervert. He should be stuck in jail and the key thrown away,' Tam declared angrily.

'I can't go back there, Mum. I just can't.'

'Of course not,' Chrissie agreed instantly. 'I said only recently that you were always welcome here if anything should happen, and now it has.'

'Thanks, Mum. Thanks, Papa.'

'I'll put the kettle on,' said Chrissie, moving off to fill it. A cup of tea was her panacea for everything.

'I always worried about him hitting me,' Georgie went on. 'I know he's got it in him. But that! Never in a million years!'

'Did Ian see what he was doing?' Lena asked.

'I don't know. He might have. But maybe not because of the angle and him being a lot smaller. He certainly didn't say anything on the way here, and I didn't probe.'

'Let's hope he didn't,' Lena said. 'It could have an awful effect on him if he did.' She shuddered, her heart going out to her sister and nephew.

'What a mess,' Georgie said quietly. 'What a mess.'

Georgie took a deep breath before inserting her key in the lock. Beside her were Tam and Tom, who had come to help her remove her and Ian's things.

'It's all right, lass, we're with you,' Tam said grimly. 'There's no need to fash yourself.'

They went into the house to discover it empty, as Georgie had predicted. She had known Charlie was supposed to be on duty, but it was always possible he'd taken time off work, or somehow changed his shifts, though the latter was most unlikely.

'You go and do what you have to and we'll wait here,' Tam told her.

Half an hour later they were on a tram heading home again, Georgie's last act on leaving the house having been to post her key through the letter box. She'd have no further need of it, since she never intended to go back there again. As far as she was concerned, hell would freeze over first. In the meantime, at her father's insistence, she was going to have a word with the police.

* * *

235

'I'll leave you here then,' said Brigid, when they reached the street corner where she turned off. Since the night of the kiss she hadn't allowed Tom to walk her all the way home.

'Goodnight, Brigid. You take care now.'

'And you, Tom. Goodnight.'

There was an old tin can a little further down the street ahead of Tom. On reaching it he gave it a good kick to send it clattering away. It didn't help.

He was feeling no better when he went to Dolly's for lunch the following day.

'Why so glum?' she asked, as he pushed yet another half-eaten plateful away from him. 'You've hardly said a word since you arrived.'

Tom sighed. 'Sorry, Dolly. I didn't mean to be rude.'

'Not rude, Tom.' She smiled. 'Introspective, shall we say. Now, what's the problem? For it seems to me you must have one.'

He shrugged. 'It's personal, Dolly.'

'Then it's none of my business.' She paused for a moment. 'Though sharing a problem, personal or otherwise, often helps.'

He suddenly decided he would tell her what was bothering him. It would be good to talk, get it off his chest.

Dolly listened intently as he explained about Brigid and himself, only occasionally interrupting to clarify some point or other.

'I see,' she murmured when he'd finally finished. 'No wonder you're so down in the mouth.'

Tom had a gulp of wine, then another. 'There's simply no solution. None whatsoever. Brigid and I both agree on that.'

'Have you considered leaving Glasgow altogether and going elsewhere? A town where the religious thing wouldn't count?'

Tom smiled thinly. 'Don't forget there's a slump on that affects the entire country. At least in Glasgow Brigid and I have work.'

The latter was certainly true, Dolly mused. It was still an idea, though. 'Are you sure you love her, Tom?'

'Oh aye, there's no doubt in my mind about that.'

'And that she loves you?'

'She told me so only the other night.'

She'd have to think about this, Dolly decided.

'So how was school today?' Georgie asked.

'I'm pleased to be back there, Mum,' Ian enthused. 'It's a far nicer school with far nicer teachers.'

'Good.' She smiled. 'You don't miss the old one then?'

'No,' he declared emphatically. 'I don't miss it at all, and I don't miss Charlie's house either. I hated it there.' He stared at his mother through suddenly soulful eyes. 'I hated it there. And I hated him.'

Georgie could have wept.

Smith ushered Tom and Brigid into the morning room, where Dolly was waiting for them. Tom immediately introduced Brigid to her.

'I'm delighted to meet you, Brigid.'

'And I'm pleased to meet you, Mrs Mulherron.'

'Dolly, please. Now, what would you like to drink? I'm having my usual sherry.'

'That would be lovely.'

'Smith, a sherry for the young lady and, I presume, whisky for Tom?'

'Please.'

'Do sit down,' Dolly said, indicating chairs.

Brigid was overawed by the size of the house, and the quality of its contents. Tom had told her what to expect, but she'd still been taken aback by the actual reality.

'It's most kind of you to come.' Dolly smiled at Brigid when all three of them were seated.

'Not at all. It's kind of you to invite me. Though, I have to say, I can't think why you have.'

'Ah!' Dolly's expression was one of amusement. 'Because I have a proposition to put to the pair of you.'

'Proposition?' Tom frowned. 'What sort of proposition, Dolly?'

Dolly insisted on waiting till their drinks had been brought before explaining. Then she said, 'On Tom's last visit here he told me all about the problem he has in marrying you, Brigid, because of the religious differences, which I fully understand.' She paused to have a sip of sherry, thoroughly enjoying herself. 'You also stated, Tom, that there is a general slump throughout the length and breadth of Britain. Which isn't quite true. It's Scotland and the north of England that are mainly affected. Places where they rely on heavy industry for work, which they don't so much in the south.'

A flicker of hope fluttered in Tom's breast. Was Dolly about to pull a rabbit out of the hat?

Dolly went on, 'My late husband Freddy, God rest his soul, had many business friends and contacts, one of whom I took the liberty of writing to. Ford, the motor car people, have built a new production line factory in Dagenham, Essex, where they eventually plan to employ seven thousand workers. Freddy's friend is in top-level management there. A man of some importance, you might say.'

Brigid glanced at Tom, then focused again on Dolly.

'I explained the situation to Freddy's friend, who has agreed to take you both on. Tom will be trained up as a foreman of the assembly line, while you, Brigid, will work on that assembly line. Not only that, but if you agree to go he'll arrange accommodation for you to move straight into on your arrival. I may also mention, Tom, that the foreman's pay is very generous in today's climate.'

Tom was stunned. He didn't know what to think. The offer had come completely out of the blue.

'No doubt you'll want to talk it over.' Dolly smiled. 'I'll give you my telephone number before you leave, Tom, and you can ring me when the two of you have come to a decision.'

Tom opened his mouth to speak, but nothing came out. He was literally speechless.

'Go and live in England!' an appalled Chrissie exclaimed. 'You can't do that.'

'Why not, Mum?'

'Because . . . well, it's full of English.' She said the last word as though they were all lepers.

Tom laughed. 'I'm sure many of them are very nice people once you get to know them.'

Chrissie wasn't at all certain about that. The English were the historical enemy, after all. 'I don't know what your father's going to say,' she declared, shaking her head.

'It's the only way I can marry Brigid,' Tom explained. 'And I do want to marry her.'

'I never even knew you were seeing the lassie again. You never said.'

'There was no reason to. I haven't exactly been seeing her as such, not in that way anyway. We simply, quite by chance, ended up working together.'

'Just you wait until your father gets home,' Chrissie muttered.

'It's my life, Mum, and I'm over twenty-one. I can do as I like.'

'But England, son! It's so far away,' she protested.

'It's not the end of the earth. There'll be visits, I'm sure of that.'

Chrissie took a deep breath. 'You haven't made a final decision, though?'

'Brigid will be talking to her parents, and we'll speak again tonight after work.'

'And this Mrs Mulherron is arranging it all?'

'That's right.'

'But why is she going to so much trouble?'

'Because of her dead son, I would imagine. The one whom I'm the spit of. Besides, she genuinely likes me and no doubt wants to help.'

Tears came into Chrissie's eyes. 'Well, you must do whatever you think's best, son.'

'I will, Mum,' he assured her. 'I will.'

'So what did your parents say?' Tom asked Brigid the moment they were out of the Belgrave later that night.

'They weren't exactly pleased, I'll tell you that. And yours?'

'Papa took it more calmly than I thought he would, considering you're a Catholic, that is. In the end both he and Mum agreed the decision was up to me, and if I did decide to go it would be with their blessing.'

'Mine, eventually, said more or less the same. Though they are terribly disappointed I'm not marrying a Catholic, and that it won't be in church. We can't do that with you being a Prod.' She stopped and turned to face him. 'Will you convert, Tom?'

He smiled at her in the darkness. 'I'll do anything it takes if I can have you as my wife. Obviously I can't convert right away. I would imagine that takes time. But once I have converted perhaps we can have another ceremony, this time in a pineapple.'

Brigid laughed, knowing that pineapple was rhyming slang for chapel, which Catholic churches were often called in Glasgow. 'I'll hold you to that, Tom McKeand.'

'Is it agreed, then? We get married as soon as possible, after which it's straight down to this Dagenham place?'

'It's agreed,' she replied, eyes shining.

'Oh, Brigid,' he breathed. 'We're going to be ever so happy together. I just know we are.'

'We've waited a long time for one another, and it certainly hasn't been easy.'

'No, it hasn't. But everything's come right now and that's all that matters.'

Dolly cradled her phone and smiled a little sadly. Tom and Brigid's decision was the one she'd hoped to hear, but she was going to miss dancing with Tom at the Belgrave, and his visits for lunch.

Crossing to the mantelpiece she picked up Robert's picture, the last he'd had taken before going off to France.

Her son, and only child. How cruel and stupid war was. Ask any mother.

Fortunately Tam was home when it happened, otherwise the outcome might have been completely different.

'I wonder who that is?' Chrissie queried when there was a sudden urgent knocking on the front door.

'Well, the best way to find out is to answer it,' Tam said drily, thinking it must be one of the neighbours.

Chrissie hurried off, while Georgie got on with the business of making dinner. She stopped what she was doing when she heard raised voices.

'Tam, it's Charlie insisting on seeing Georgie,' Chrissie called out in a panic.

'Oh, Christ,' Georgie muttered.

'Do you want to see him, lass?'

Georgie glanced over at her father and shook her head. 'No. Never again. I have nothing to say to him. Not now. Not ever.'

'I want to see my fucking wife!' Charlie shouted. 'It's my fucking right. Get your arse out here, woman!'

'He's drunk,' Georgie stated unnecessarily.

Tam rose slowly to his feet, his expression murderous. How dare the pervert come to his house behaving like this?

'Be careful, Papa. He might get violent.'

Tam reached down and picked up the hammer kept on the hearth for breaking large lumps of coal. Holding it in his right hand, he strode from the kitchen. 'Go back through,' he told Chrissie when he reached the door.

Charlie was in a rage, his face puce, the veins standing out. He stank of alcohol. 'I want to see my fucking wife!' he demanded.

Tam never told either Chrissie or Georgie what he said to Charlie that day. Only that no blows had been exchanged.

But Georgie never saw or heard from Charlie again.

'Well, that's that then. We're on our way,' an excited Tom declared, pulling on the leather strap to raise the compartment window and securing the strap on the brass knob provided for that purpose.

Only Chrissie and Dolly had come to see them off. Tam and Lena were at work, and the O'Reillys had declined, saying it would have been too painful for them.

'What an adventure, eh, Mrs McKeand?' Tom beamed at Brigid as he sat beside her. They were the only two passengers in the compartment.

'It certainly is, Mr McKeand.'

It had been a quiet civil wedding, with only Tom's family, the O'Reillys and Dolly in attendance. Dolly had insisted on taking them all out for a meal afterwards.

Tom reached into his inside jacket pocket and extracted an envelope. 'Dolly gave me this in the station,' he told Brigid. 'Said I wasn't to open it till the train was under way.'

'Probably a card,' Brigid suggested.

'Doesn't feel like one.' He ripped open the envelope and took out the single piece of paper it contained. 'Bloody hell!' he exclaimed when he saw what the piece of paper was.

A cheque for one thousand pounds.

Part 3

Bill Bailey

1935–

Chapter 23

'So what does Tom say?' Chrissie asked anxiously.

Georgie sighed, and started to fold up her brother's letter, which she'd just read. 'There's no problem about getting Ian work. Tom can arrange something for him as soon as he shows up in Dagenham. He also suggests Ian stay with him and Brigid until other suitable accommodation can be arranged.'

'That's great, Mum,' Ian enthused. Then, noting her concerned expression, he added, 'Isn't it?'

'I suppose so.'

'Well, I can't get any work round here. You know that. I've tried and tried. Even Grandpa can't get me an apprenticeship at McNair's.'

Ian, now sixteen, had left school earlier that year, and had been scouting round for employment ever since, to no avail. There simply weren't any jobs to be had.

'It's for the best,' Tam declared from where he was sitting. 'The lad has to earn his keep now he's old enough.'

Georgie couldn't help the lump that came into her throat at the thought of losing her son. Once he left Glasgow, who knew when he might return? If ever. 'Aye, Papa, you're right,' she agreed quietly.

Tam shook his head. 'When will this slump end, that's what I'd like to know. It just goes on and on.'

'But not in some places down south it seems,' Chrissie commented bitterly.

'We should be thankful the south has given Tom employment,' said Tam. 'And now Ian. Better he's in Dagenham than idle here. Better by far. It's a chance for him and he must grab it while it's going.' He swivelled his attention on to Georgie. 'It'll be hard for you, lass, we all appreciate that.'

'Tom will look after Ian all right,' Chrissie assured her. 'You've no worries there.'

Georgie had hated writing to Tom with her request, and had only done so at Ian's insistence. The idea had been Ian's in the first place, and now his eyes were sparkling. 'When shall I leave, Mum?' he queried.

'I'll reply to Tom telling him to expect you. Give it a couple of days and you can be on your way.' Why prolong the agony of his departure? Best get it over and done with.

Tam closed his eyes. Georgie wasn't the only one who'd miss the boy. He and Ian had become quite close since Georgie and her son had come back to live with them. He'd tried desperately to get the lad an apprenticeship at McNair's, but despite his best efforts, including a lot of string-pulling, he hadn't been able to do so. McNair's itself was slowly recovering, now operating at a little over half capacity, and many of the old workers had been reinstated as a result. But there was still a long way to go before it was back to what it had been pre-slump.

'Are you all right, Tam?'

He opened his eyes to smile at Chrissie. 'Absolutely fine, woman. Absolutely fine.' He took out his pipe and began repacking it.

'I can't wait to go.' Ian beamed at Georgie. 'It's going to be fun.'

Georgie made an excuse and left the kitchen.

'You're new!' Georgie exclaimed in surprise. The delivery man who'd appeared in the shop was not the regular one. 'Where's Wally?'

'Broke his leg, so I've been taken on as a replacement. I don't think you'll be seeing him again, either. I'm told he's retirement age, so that's probably what'll happen.'

Georgie was disappointed. She and Wally had been great pals since she'd landed the job at Templeton's, a licenced grocer, nearly two years before.

The new delivery man nodded down at the large wooden tray he was carrying. 'Where shall I put this?'

'In the rear. Come on through and I'll show you.'

'Thanks. I'm Bill, by the way.'

'Pleased to meet you, Bill. I'm Georgie.'

'Pleased to meet you too.'

He seemed a pleasant enough chap, Georgie thought as she led the way. Early forties, she'd have guessed. Maybe a little older.

'So who's this then?' Mr Templeton demanded, making an appearance. 'Where's Wally?'

Bill explained a second time what had happened, and the two men introduced themselves.

'Would you like a cup of tea and a bun?' Georgie asked Bill when he'd completed his delivery. 'Wally always did.'

'In which case I don't mind if I do,' he said cheerfully.

She led him into the rear of the shop and put the kettle on. In the event, she didn't get much of a chance to chat with Bill while he had his tea, for an influx of customers demanded her attention. She just had time to wave in acknowledgement when Bill said goodbye, thank you very much, and see you again later in the week, as he left.

'Aye, I felt exactly the same way the day I saw Tom off on this very platform,' Chrissie sympathised, seeing Georgie's face was wet with tears. In the distance the train carrying Ian down to England swept round a bend and vanished from sight.

Georgie took a hanky from her pocket and dabbed her eyes. 'He just seems so young to be going away.'

'Young, but already a man. A young man to be proud of. He's got a good head on his shoulders, lass; he won't come to any trouble. Certainly not with Tom keeping an eye on him.'

'I know that, Mum. I expected him to leave home one day, but not to leave Glasgow for the south. Away from me altogether.'

Chrissie thought of Tom, whom she hadn't seen since his departure. He and Brigid had a little boy now, whom they called Robin. An endearing little chap, according to Tom's letters. How she would have loved to see and hold her new grandchild. Maybe one day, God willing. 'Aye, it's hard right enough,' she said. 'But I suppose it's just one of these things in life a body has to put up with.'

'Thanks for coming with me, Mum. I appreciate it. And now I'd better get back to the shop.'

Chrissie pulled her daughter closer and kissed her on the cheek, close to tears herself. 'I'll see you later, then.'

Georgie drew in a deep breath, trying to compose herself. 'At least Ian's skin has been a lot better of late,' she said hollowly. 'That's something.'

'Aye,' Chrissie agreed. 'That's something.'

Tea that evening was a subdued affair, everyone round the table only too aware of the empty chair that had been Ian's, and no one more so than Georgie.

'I'd like you to do me a favour, Lena, if you will.'

She stared at her father in surprise. Asking favours was most unlike him. 'Of course, Papa.'

Tam cleared his throat. He was finding this difficult, feeling it showed a certain weakness on his part. 'I've been thinking a lot about your sister recently,' he began quietly.

'Georgie?'

'No, Mary.'

Lena was more surprised than ever. 'I see.'

Tam gave a heartfelt sigh. 'It doesn't seem right that we've lost touch like we have. It's been bothering me for quite some time.' His expression became grim. 'Why in the name of the wee man did she ever have to get mixed up with that sect of hers and go all holier than thou? They've caused nothing but trouble in this family.'

Lena couldn't have agreed more.

'Your mother hasn't said anything, but I know she worries as well.'

'So what do you want me to do, Papa?'

'Go and see her, lass. You've done it before. Find out what's what.'

'I would imagine things are the same, Papa. Mary up to her neck in religion and spouting non-stop.'

Tam sighed again. 'Probably.'

'If she is, then what?'

'To be honest, lass, I don't know. I really don't. But it would be nice, a relief you might say, to know she and her family are all right. That would at least be something.'

Lena could well understand that. 'Why don't I pay a visit at the weekend? Saturday afternoon say?'

'Thanks.' Then, hastily, 'Just don't let on you're there on my behalf. Pretend otherwise.'

She smiled, knowing her father didn't want to be seen to be backing down in any way. It was typical of him. 'I won't, Papa. That's a promise.' She hesitated, then asked, 'Does Mum know about this?'

Tam shook his head. 'No.'

'Are you going to tell her?'

He crossed to the window and stared out. It was a lovely day, the sun shining brightly. In his mind's eye he was picturing Mary as a child, a child he'd loved very, very much. 'That depends on what you report when you get back,' he said slowly. 'I might. Or there again, I might not. As I said, it all depends.'

'Saturday afternoon it is then, Papa.'

Lena stopped outside Mary's close and looked up at the grey, scarred building. A typical Glasgow tenement. She wondered what Mary was like nowadays. Had she put on weight, lost some, aged a lot? Well, she would shortly find out.

She plunged into the close mouth, which smelt of boiled cabbage tinged with strong bleach, and began to climb the stairs.

*　　*　　*

Tam sat upright in his chair when he heard the sound of a key in the front door. Chrissie had gone shopping in town half an hour previously, which meant, he hoped, that this was Lena returned from her visit. It was.

'Well?' he demanded when she entered the kitchen. 'How did you get on?'

This was going to be difficult, Lena thought. It would break her father's heart. And her mother's. Damn Mary for doing what she had. Damn her to hell.

'They emigrated two years ago,' she stated bluntly.

The shock on Tam's face was palpable. 'They've what?'

'Emigrated two years ago,' she repeated. 'A neighbour told me, Papa.'

Tam shook his head in bewilderment. This was unbelievable. 'Where to?' he demanded harshly.

'Canada. Toronto to be precise, according to the neighbour. They just upped sticks and left.'

'But why?'

'It was something to do with the sect which is, apparently, quite big in Toronto. The neighbour had no idea where they got the money from, though she did know James had a job to go to.'

Tam suddenly felt crushed, and old. Older than Methuselah. 'And she never said goodbye,' he managed to whisper at last. 'Just went, without a word.'

'I'm sorry, Papa. Truly I am. But that's Mary all over as far as I'm concerned. Selfish to the core.'

'Don't speak like that about your sister,' Tam said sharply, even though he knew what Lena said to be true.

Lena didn't want to argue, not in these circumstances. Taking out her cigarettes, she lit up. She was furious with Mary for what she had done, the hurt it was causing her father, and the hurt it would cause Chrissie when, inevitably, she found out. To leave the country without saying goodbye. It was despicable!

'I still can't believe it,' Tam said, shaking his head again. 'How could she do such a thing?'

Lena didn't answer, noticing that her father had gone very pale. The pallor was quite a contrast to his normally healthy, slightly ruddy complexion.

Reaching down to the floor Tam picked up his Saturday bottle of whisky and the glass he'd been using. His hands were trembling as he poured himself a stiff one. 'Lena?'

She shook her head. 'Not for me, Papa.'

Tam swallowed half the whisky in his glass, took a breath, then saw off the remainder. 'Your mother's going to be devastated,' he said in a tight voice.

'You'll tell her, then?'

'I have to. I can't keep something like this from her.'

'When?'

Tam considered. 'Are you and Georgie in tonight?'

Lena smiled wryly. When did she ever go out of an evening? Never. And it was the same for Georgie. 'I suppose so.'

'Then I'll tell your mother when we're alone in bed. God help me.'

'I could tell her if you wish.'

He immediately shook his head. 'No, that's my responsibility, Lena. I'm her husband, after all. Mary's our daughter.'

Lena watched as he poured himself more whisky. 'Don't get drunk now, Papa. That won't help anything.'

'I've no intention of getting drunk, I assure you.'

'Just go easy, though.'

His eyes became introspective. 'Canada,' he mused. 'A fine country from what I've heard. Lots of opportunities there. They should do well.'

Lena didn't care whether they did well or not. She'd never forgive Mary for what she'd done. Never in a thousand years.

Tam drank his whisky, then came to his feet. 'I think I'll go on through and have a wee lie-down,' he declared. 'I'm suddenly feeling tired.'

'You do that, Papa. It'll be good for you.'

'Aye,' he agreed.

As he left the kitchen it was with a shock that Lena saw he

was walking with a stoop. It was something she'd never previously noticed.

'Is there something wrong, Tam?'

He glanced nervously across at his wife. 'What makes you ask that?'

'You've been fidgeting all night. Up and down, up and down. Crossing your legs, uncrossing them. That sort of thing. Not like you at all.'

Tam looked at the clock on the mantelpiece. Still ages to go yet before bedtime. He was absolutely dreading telling Chrissie about Mary.

'There is something different about you tonight, Papa,' Georgie chipped in. 'I noticed it earlier.'

'And you hardly ate any tea at all,' Chrissie went on. 'Even though it was one of your favourites.'

Tam fumbled with his pipe, wondering what to reply. Lena took the initiative. It was best her father talk to her mother now.

'Georgie, can you come through to my room for a bit?'

Georgie raised an eyebrow at this unusual request. She'd been sharing Lena's bedroom until Ian had left, when she'd moved into the one he'd been occupying, which had been Tom's before that. 'What for?' she queried.

'Just come through, will you? I'll explain there.'

Georgie shrugged. 'If you want.'

'I do,' Lena stated emphatically, and left the kitchen, giving Tam a slight nod. A puzzled Georgie followed on behind.

'What was all that about?' Chrissie asked.

Tam cleared his throat. 'I've got some bad news, I'm afraid, lass,' he said quietly, and began recounting the tale of Lena's visit to what had been Mary's house.

'Emigrated to Canada!' an amazed Georgie repeated.

'Two years ago, apparently.'

'Without saying goodbye to Mum and Papa, far less her sisters?'

Lena nodded. 'That's right.'

'The cow. The bloody bitch!' Georgie exploded. 'Isn't that just like her.'

'I said as much to Papa and he told me off for speaking ill of my sister. But you know what he's like where Mary's concerned. She could never do anything wrong. Apart from her religious mania, that is.'

Georgie glanced at the bedroom door. 'I wonder how Mum's taking it?'

'How do you think? Badly, of course. Bound to.'

Georgie sat on the edge of Lena's bed. It was a bombshell right enough. All right, they hadn't seen or spoken to Mary for years. But they'd believed her to be still in Glasgow, not all that far away, easily contactable if need be. And while Mary remained in Glasgow a reconciliation was always possible. But now there would never be one.

'I just can't get over it,' Georgie declared.

'Me neither. Not really.' Lena suddenly laughed. 'All those years Mum had to put up with the idea of me going to Hollywood, which didn't happen. Now it's Mary who's buggered off to Canada.' She shook her head. 'Ironic.'

Tam came awake to the sound of quiet weeping. Reaching out, he took hold of Chrissie's hand.

'Have I wakened you, Tam? I'm sorry.'

'Not to worry, lass. Not to worry.' He squeezed her hand, hoping to comfort her a little.

'The family's breaking up,' Chrissie said, still weeping. 'First of all it was Tom down to England, then Ian, and now Mary and her lot to Canada. We'll probably never see any of them again.'

'We might,' Tam replied. 'Nothing is ever set in stone. You should know that.'

There was a silence. Then Tam went on, 'I blame myself for this. If I hadn't fallen out with Mary then we would at least have got to say goodbye.'

'You mustn't blame yourself, Tam. How were you to know this would happen?'

He had no reply.

'She might have written us a letter,' Chrissie went on. 'If only to tell us of her intentions. We are her parents, after all. That wouldn't have been such a hard thing to do, surely?'

'No,' he agreed. 'It wouldn't. But the fact remains, she didn't.' He added angrily, 'So much for her precious religious beliefs. Honour thy father and mother, that sort of thing. Even if you disagree with them.'

'Perhaps she'll write some time in the future?' Chrissie speculated hopefully.

'I doubt it, Chrissie. She's been gone two years already, don't forget. Plenty of time to put pen to paper. No, she won't be writing. She's cut us out of her life for good, which we're just going to have to accept.'

Neither of them got much sleep for the remainder of the night.

Hamish's office door was slightly ajar so Lena went straight in without knocking to find him sitting behind his desk with his head in his hands. He looked up when she closed the door behind her.

'What's wrong?' she asked.

'Nothing. I've got a bit of a headache, that's all,' he lied.

'Shall I get you something?'

'I've already taken a powder. But thanks for asking.'

She studied him, thinking how terrible he looked. Like a man at the end of his tether. 'Are you sure it's just a headache?' she queried. 'If it's something else I'll be happy to talk about it with you, if that would help.'

'It's a headache.' He was still lying, for it wasn't that at all which was bothering him. He suddenly smiled. 'You're a good friend, Lena. I've always appreciated that.'

'Why, thank you.'

'I mean it. A damn good friend. Not to mention an excellent colleague. I couldn't ask for better.'

There was more to this than met the eye, Lena thought. She knew Hamish only too well after all these years, and the intimacies they'd once shared. Something was wrong somewhere if she wasn't mistaken, which she was sure she wasn't.

'How are Celia and the twins?' she asked casually.

'Fine, fine. Never better.'

Again she detected that in his voice which was unconvincing. Trouble at home, perhaps? If so, it was none of her business. He'd made his bed and could now lie in it with the beautiful Celia.

'So, what can I do for you?' he queried.

'I need your signature on these papers.'

'Of course. Right away.'

She wondered if it was money worries that were troubling him. Celia had struck her as the sort who could quite easily spend more than he earned.

She returned to her desk, putting Hamish, and the headache she didn't believe existed, from her mind.

Chapter 24

Georgie smiled when Bill Bailey appeared in the doorway of Templeton's carrying a heavily laden tray. He smiled back at her.

'You're just in time. It's my tea break as well,' she informed him.

'Oh, good oh!'

Georgie turned to Janet, one of the several part-time assistants. 'Can you cover for me while I put the kettle on and have my break? Just give me a shout if it gets busy.'

'All right, Georgie. On you go.'

When she reached the back shop the first thing Georgie did was to light a cigarette. She'd been gasping. Then the kettle was filled and placed on the gas ring Mr Templeton had made available. She was sitting drinking her cuppa when Bill finally joined her, having completed his delivery. 'How are you today?' she greeted him.

'Fine. Yourself?'

'No complaints. Help yourself to a doughnut if you want. Those jammy ones are delicious.'

'How many have you had so far?' he teased.

'Twenty-four,' she replied instantly. They both laughed.

Bill selected a doughnut and sat on an upturned box. 'It's cold out there today,' he commented affably.

'Aye, it is.'

He took a bite from his doughnut. 'You're right, these are good,' he enthused.

'So, how are you settling in with your job?' she asked, genuinely interested.

'No trouble. It's a bit of a doddle actually. Easy as pie.'

That surprised her. 'Really? Wally used to be forever moaning about how hard it was.'

'So I've heard,' Bill replied non-committally.

'Maybe he was just like that.'

'Maybe.'

She realised he wasn't going to be drawn on the subject, which she rather admired him for. He must hear loads of gossip about all sorts of things while doing his rounds.

'Tell me, how did you get the job?' she enquired. 'Did someone tip you off when Wally broke his leg?'

Bill shrugged. 'Luck, pure and simple. I just happened to be in the right place at the right time. Not a moment too soon, either. I was about to give up looking for work and go back into the army.'

'The army!' Georgie exclaimed. Now that she came to think about it there was something military about his bearing.

'I joined as a lad, but over the last few years I'd become tired of it all and decided to come out and try civvy street. Which is what I did some months ago, returning to live with my widowed mum. I had army money which has seen me through, but that was about to run out when this delivery lark came up. So now I don't have to go back in.'

'What sort of rank did you hold?' Georgie asked.

'Corporal.'

'You weren't an officer then?' she teased.

He laughed. 'Not likely. I'm neither posh enough nor intelligent enough for that. Being an NCO suited me just dandy.'

Georgie glanced through to the front shop and saw that Janet was serving a single customer, so there was hardly a rush on. She decided to have another cup of tea. 'Were you in the Great War, Bill?'

His face immediately clouded, becoming pained. 'Oh aye. But I don't want to talk about that if you don't mind. The memories aren't exactly good ones.'

She could well understand that. Many of the soldiers who'd fought in the carnage of the Great War never wanted to speak of it.

'I was in India for quite a spell,' Bill went on. 'Filthy place, but also exciting. Not to mention colourful. Spent nearly six years there in all.'

Georgie was fascinated. 'Where else have you been?'

For the next ten minutes or so he regaled her with tales of life in the army, then had to excuse himself to get on with his round.

What a nice chap, Georgie reflected after he'd gone. She'd thoroughly enjoyed their chat and was looking forward to having more with him.

Tom arrived home from work to be greeted by a beaming Brigid. 'There's someone here to see you,' she announced.

'Oh! Who?'

'Go on through and find out.'

'Sounds mysterious,' he commented as he hung up his coat.

Brigid didn't reply, simply beamed some more.

'Dolly!' he exclaimed in surprised delight on entering their sitting room. 'How wonderful to see you again!'

Dolly rose from the chair she was sitting on and went to Tom, who put his arms round her, then kissed her cheek.

'You're looking well,' she declared.

'And you. Younger than ever.'

Dolly laughed. 'Flatterer.'

'No no, I mean it. Honestly I do.'

His words pleased her enormously. 'Then thank you.'

He released her. 'So, what brings you down to Dagenham?'

'I'm actually on my way to London to do some shopping.' She winked at the hovering Brigid. '*Serious* shopping.' Then she looked back at Tom. 'And I thought, why not make a slight detour and call in to see you all. So here I am.'

'Dolly's agreed to stay to tea,' Brigid told him.

'That's great.'

'I've explained it's nothing fancy. A little bit of plain home cooking, that's all.'

'I'm sure it'll be lovely.' Dolly smiled.

'Where are you staying?' Tom asked. 'We can easily put you up here if you wish.'

'That's kind of you, but I've already booked into an hotel. Brooks and I did that before coming on here.'

'Where is Brooks, by the way?' Tom asked, looking around for the chauffeur.

'I've given him some time off. He'll call back here and collect me later.'

'I'll be in the kitchen if you want me,' Brigid declared, and left them.

Dolly crossed over to the playpen where Robin, now a toddler, was sitting watching them. 'What a gorgeous little lad your son is,' she enthused. 'You must be proud.'

'Oh, I am. Very proud.'

'It makes me feel . . .' Dolly hesitated, then said so softly it was almost a whisper, 'like a grandmother.'

'Then that's how you must think of yourself, Dolly. One of Robin's grandmothers.'

A glint of tears came into her eyes. 'Thank you, Tom,' she said huskily. 'It's very kind of you.'

'Not at all.'

Dolly sniffed, then straightened herself. 'According to your letters you're doing well at Ford.'

'I thoroughly enjoy it there, especially being a foreman. You were certainly right about the company paying well. I simply can't thank you enough for getting me the job.'

She waved a dismissive hand. 'It was the least I can do. I was only too delighted to be able to help.'

'And of course without the move south I wouldn't be married to Brigid, and there wouldn't be a Robin in that playpen. As I said, I can't thank you enough.' He corrected himself. 'Neither

Brigid nor I can thank you enough. You're an angel in disguise.'

Dolly laughed. 'Hardly an angel, Tom. I've led far too . . .' She broke off. 'Well, we won't go into that. Do you miss Glasgow at all?'

He thought about it for a few moments. 'Yes and no. Glasgow is where I was born and brought up. As such, it will always be a large part of me. But we're happily settled here now. Glasgow's the past, Dagenham is the present and future. Tell me, as we're talking about Glasgow, what of the Belgrave? Is it still the same?'

'To be honest, I haven't been there for ages. It lost its appeal after you left. But it was certainly the same the last time I visited it.'

'Did you gamble?'

'Of course. And won. As usual.'

He shook his head. 'You always were incredibly lucky at the tables. I used to marvel at that.'

She smiled secretively. 'Freddy and I, God rest his soul, were frequently at Monte Carlo and other such places. You soon get to know what you're doing. How to calculate the odds. When to bet, and when not to. But yes, luck does come into it and Freddy always said I had the luck of the devil.' A twinkle came into her eyes. 'And maybe he was right, seeing I had the good fortune to marry him.'

'You must miss him a lot,' Tom said quietly.

'I do. And Robert of course. I miss them both terribly.'

The smile she gave Tom was a real heartbreaker.

The evening passed in a flash, and all too soon it was time for Dolly to leave.

Robin was asleep, Dolly having assisted in putting him to bed. She had read him a story, with Brigid looking on, until he'd nodded off. If it had reminded her of when Robert was a child she didn't mention it.

'Will you come and see us again some time, Dolly?' Tom asked in the hallway. 'You're always welcome.'

'Always,' Brigid emphasised.

'You have my word on it.'

'And next time let us know in advance so I can get some sherry and wine in,' Tom added.

Dolly laughed. 'I'll hold you to that.'

'Come on,' Tom said. 'We'll walk you to your car.'

At the car Brooks was standing holding open the door, having turned up precisely at the time he and Dolly had agreed. Like Smith, the butler, he'd been in Dolly's employ for many years, though he was nowhere near as old as the butler.

They stopped by the car door and Brigid gave Dolly a peck on the cheek. 'I hope the meal wasn't too awful,' she said. 'I'm not much of a cook, I'm afraid.'

'It was lovely,' Dolly assured her. 'I thoroughly enjoyed every mouthful.'

It was Tom's turn to kiss her on the cheek. 'Goodbye for now, Dolly. Have a safe journey.'

'Thank you, Tom. You take care of yourself, and your family. Hear?'

'I will, Dolly. You can rely on it.'

She knew she could. Before getting into the car she stared at Tom for a moment, thinking, yet again, what a remarkable resemblance there was to her dead son. It was uncanny.

Tom and Brigid waved as the car drove off, Dolly returning their waves through the rear window.

'Well,' Tom declared, turning again to the house. 'That was a turn-up for the book.'

'Wasn't it just? I couldn't believe it when I answered the bell and found her standing there. What a surprise that was.'

'A lovely surprise,' Tom qualified with a smile.

Arm in arm they went back into the house. The two of them were happy as Larry, and very much in love.

'Have you ever been married, Bill?' Georgie asked. They were in the rear of the shop having the usual cup of tea during his delivery.

He shook his head. 'No.'

'Was that because of being in the army?'

Bill thought about it. 'Not really. I suppose the reason is that I simply never met the right woman. She just never happened along, that's all.'

What a pity, Georgie reflected, certain he would have made a good husband to some deserving female. 'Would you have liked children?'

'Oh, yes.' He smiled. 'I'm very fond of children. Mind you, it must be hard work bringing them up. Not easy at all.'

'It certainly isn't,' Georgie mused aloud.

'You have some then?'

'A boy called Ian. He's almost seventeen now and working with my brother down at the Ford plant in Dagenham, Essex.'

Bill glanced at Georgie's left hand, which didn't sport a wedding ring – a fact he'd previously noted.

'Ian was my first husband's,' Georgie explained, having caught Bill's surreptitious look. 'He died from leukaemia.'

'Oh, I am sorry,' Bill sympathised.

'His name was John and he worked on the railway. It was a tragedy he passed away so young. Ian was only a little shaver at the time.'

Bill had a sip of tea. 'You said your first husband?'

'I was married again to a chap called Charlie, a fireman. I left him a few years back.'

'I see,' Bill murmured.

'He was an alcoholic, amongst other things I don't wish to discuss. I'm well rid of him.'

'It seems I'm not the only one who's been in the wars,' Bill remarked.

Georgie gave a sour, bitter laugh. 'You can say that again.'

He regarded her with an expression of curiosity. 'Do I take it then you're still married to this Charlie?'

She nodded.

'Why haven't you divorced him?' Suddenly Bill was embarrassed. 'I'm sorry. I shouldn't have asked that. It's none of my business.'

'No, that's all right,' she assured him. 'I don't mind speaking about it. For a start, in Scotland you have to be separated for seven years before you can apply for a divorce, which we haven't been yet. Secondly, divorce costs a great deal of money which I don't have.' She paused to draw on her cigarette, then went on wistfully, 'I used to, but at one point Charlie's wages were cut and he was more or less drinking the remainder. I had to use my own savings to keep the house going, and there was very little left when we finally parted. So there you are.'

'This Charlie sounds a right charmer,' Bill commented sarcastically.

'Oh, he was.' A vision of Charlie sitting with a naked Avril on his lap came to her, and Georgie got to her feet. 'I'd better get back behind the counter, Bill. I've been gassing long enough. I don't want Mr Templeton to think I've been taking liberties.'

Bill drained his cup and got up too. 'Aye, it is time to get a move on.'

He could only wonder at the expression he'd seen cross Georgie's face. It had been one of great pain. And, if he was right, disgust.

Lena became aware of Hamish staring at her in the strangest way. He was at a filing cabinet looking for something, or pretending to anyway. It wasn't the first time recently she'd caught him looking at her that way. What on earth was going on, she asked herself. Had she suddenly grown horns, or whatever?

She shifted uneasily on her seat, not liking this one little bit. Should she speak to him about it? Demand to know what he was up to? Why he was staring at her in that manner?

When he walked past her a few minutes later she couldn't help but notice there was a glisten of sweat on his forehead, while his eyes had a dark intensity about them.

It was all very puzzling.

Dolly stood staring out of a window in the morning room at the well manicured lawn beyond, recalling her recent visit to Tom and Brigid, and how much she'd enjoyed it. Especially meeting the adorable little Robin, as sweet a child as there was.

Why not? she thought. It wasn't as if there was anyone else. In that moment she decided she would go ahead, her mind made up. It was the logical thing to do.

Tam was bursting with excitement when he arrived home from work carrying a bottle of whisky.

'What are you doing with that?' an astonished Chrissie demanded. 'It's the middle of the week. You don't buy whisky until Saturdays.'

'Great news, woman! McNair's is starting to gear up to full production again, and as a result they're taking on all the men they laid off. Starting Monday I'm back on a five-and-a-half-day week.'

'Oh, that's good!' Chrissie sighed in relief.

'Good? It's not just bloody good, it's fucking fantastic!' Tam exploded. Laying the bottle on the table he went to Chrissie, put his hands on her waist and whirled her round and round. Chrissie screeched with surprise, but loved it at the same time. She found herself breathless when Tam planted her on the floor again.

'I bought the whisky because this calls for a celebration,' he declared, and hurried across the room to get glasses.

'Does this mean you're back on full pay as from next week?'

'It certainly does.'

She closed her eyes. 'Thank God for that!'

Tam poured out two hefty ones, topping Chrissie's up with water which was how she liked it. Not that she was much of a drinker, but she did indulge from time to time. And this was certainly an appropriate occasion for her to do so. He handed her her drink. 'Shall we have a toast?'

She smiled, delighted to see him so happy. 'Of course. Go on, Tam.'

He thought for a moment, his brow creasing in concentration. Then he had it. Holding up his glass he said softly, 'Here's to all the poor buggers throughout the country still laid off. May they be back in full employment as soon as possible.'

Chrissie smiled. How typical of him to think of others at a time like this. It was a fine and suitable toast as far as she was concerned, and she thought it was a lovely sentiment. 'Amen,' she whispered.

'You spoil me, so you do,' Bill declared, having just finished a beautiful pastry he'd been given to accompany his cup of tea. 'That was absolutely delicious.'

'I'm glad you enjoyed it.'

'I most certainly did. Your Mr Templeton is very good to his staff, I must say. Not every boss would be so generous.'

Georgie knew that to be true enough.

'Can I ask you something, Georgie?'

'If you wish.'

'It's a bit personal, so I hope you don't mind.'

Oh God, she thought. What was he going to come out with? 'On you go.'

'Your voice, it's got a wonderful husky quality to it that I've never heard in a woman before. It's . . .' He paused to smile. 'Most attractive.'

'You like it, then?'

'Oh, yes.'

'Well, I wasn't born with it this way,' she explained. 'I sort of accidentally acquired it.'

'Oh?'

'Years ago I worked in a bleach factory. There was a terrible fire one day. Horrendous, it was.'

'People killed?'

She nodded. 'And I was very nearly one of them. I was overcome by smoke and fumes while trying to escape the building, and was rescued by the fire brigade, which is how I came to meet Charlie.'

Bill frowned. 'The chap you're still married to?'

'That's right. He saved my life that day. If it hadn't been for Charlie I'd have been another of the victims. We started going out together shortly afterwards.'

'I see,' Bill murmured. 'And the voice?'

'The result of smoke and fume inhalation. It completely changed the way I sound.'

'Well, well.'

'I couldn't smoke cigarettes for a long time. Even a single drag made me cough and splutter. Then one night, when I'd had a gutful of Charlie, I tried again. And on that occasion it was fine, so I've been smoking ever since.'

Bill wondered if he dared. Not yet, he decided. It was still early days. He'd wait a while yet.

But he would. He damned well would when he considered the time to be right.

Chapter 25

Lena closed the office door firmly behind her before rounding on Hamish, who was poring over some papers. 'All right, what the hell is going on?' she demanded, but not loudly enough to be heard by the other women outside.

He blinked at her in astonishment. 'What are you talking about?'

'You and the queer stares you've been giving me lately. You obviously think I haven't noticed, but I have.'

'I've no idea . . .' he began to bluster, then broke off in confusion.

'You're not going to deny it, are you?'

'I'm not aware of having been staring at you,' he said meekly.

'Not just staring at me, but looking as if I was some sort of meat laid out on a butcher's slab, and you one very hungry man. Well?'

'I'm sorry, Lena, truly I am.'

'I don't want sorry, Hamish. I want an explanation.'

'There isn't one. I mean . . .' Again he broke off in confusion, seeming to cower behind his desk.

'I'm still waiting, Hamish,' she persisted. 'And I'm not leaving this office until you tell me what's going on.'

He took a deep breath, then another. 'All right,' he croaked.

'I'm listening.'

'Not here. This is neither the time nor the place. Can you meet me in the Swan after work?'

She studied him, wondering if this was some sort of ruse to get rid of her. Couldn't be, she decided. He must know that if he didn't turn up at the Swan she'd be right back here in his office tomorrow morning.

'I'll be there,' she declared.

'I'll explain everything then. I promise.' He hesitated, then asked, 'Was I that obvious?'

'To me you were.'

'I just hope no one else noticed.'

She treated him to a sharklike smile. 'It's your problem if they have.'

'Oh, shit,' he muttered to himself after she'd gone. But this meeting had been on the cards anyway. He'd planned to have it out with her, just hadn't so far got round to arranging it.

Well, for better or worse, it was arranged now. He wondered what her reaction was going to be.

'There you are, gin and orange,' Hamish declared, setting a glass down in front of Lena and sitting down opposite her. He glanced around, having deliberately chosen a table where they wouldn't be overheard. He just hoped no one came in and sat close to them.

'Now, the first thing is I don't want you to take offence at what I have to say. I mean, please don't get angry or slap my face in public. That would be awful.'

His words immediately caught her interest. 'Go on, Hamish.'

'Promise me?'

She nodded.

Hamish gave a sigh of relief, and had a swallow of whisky. 'This is embarrassing for me, Lena. It really is.'

She didn't reply, instead lighting a cigarette, her gaze riveted on his face with an intensity he found disturbing.

'It all started when Celia had the twins,' he said. 'You'll

remember how huge she got before giving birth?'

'I remember.'

'Well, naturally I thought that afterwards she'd slim down again. Or at least attempt to. Which simply wasn't the case. She's still as huge now as she was then.'

That surprised Lena, who hadn't seen Celia since she'd come to the office to speak to Hamish while very pregnant. 'Why's that?'

Hamish shrugged. 'I don't know. I've pleaded with her time and again to do something about her weight, but she totally ignores me.'

Lena frowned. 'You mean she's happy to be that large?'

'Seems so. Not only large, but a right mess to boot. She never wears make-up any more. Never goes to the hairdresser. Buys the most outlandish clothes that make her look even bigger than she is. And . . .' He shuddered. 'And she sometimes goes for days on end without washing or bathing. To be blunt, there are occasions when she smells. Ripe as a piece of French cheese.'

Lena couldn't help herself. She giggled. 'Surely you're exaggerating?'

'I wish I was.'

Lena simply couldn't picture the beautiful Celia in such a state. The idea was mind-boggling.

'She was so pretty too.' Hamish sighed again. 'With a figure to match. Now . . .' He trailed off, and shook his head.

'I'm so sorry.' Lena was genuinely sympathetic.

'Not half as sorry as I am, I can tell you. Every time I look at her nowadays I have the distinct urge to vomit. It's a nightmare, Lena. An absolute nightmare.'

'I had no idea.'

'Well you wouldn't, unless you'd seen her. Which of course you haven't as she hardly ever leaves the house.'

'What about her father? Hasn't he said something?'

'Not that I'm aware of. There again, that doesn't necessarily mean he hasn't.'

'And what about her mother?'

'Again, I don't know.'

'You'd have thought her mother would. I've seen her at several official dos and she's always struck me as a well-turned-out woman. And the chairman himself is smart as a new pin.'

'I hate going home at night now, Lena. Absolutely dread it. I sometimes come in here and sit by myself, just putting off the evil hour when I have to see her again. She's become totally repulsive to me.'

Lena had a sip of her gin, sad to hear it. Poor Hamish. He deserved better.

'Her personality has changed as well,' Hamish went on. 'Where before she was outgoing and fun, she's now quiet and secretive.'

'Secretive? In what way?'

Hamish stared into his drink, his face contorted with emotion. 'In all manner of ways. It's as if she's forever hiding something from me. Though God knows what.'

They sat in silence for a few moments. Then Hamish said quietly, 'There's more.'

'Oh?'

He took a deep breath, and slowly exhaled. 'Sex. Or more precisely, the lack of it.'

'I see.'

'Again, it stems from the birth of the twins. She wasn't particularly keen afterwards, which I thought would eventually right itself. Things would get back to normal, so to speak.'

'But they didn't?'

He turned an anguished face towards her. 'Not only that, they got worse.'

'Oh, dear,' Lena murmured.

'It got to the point where she just didn't want to know. Ever. It would suit her down to the ground never to have sex again.'

'Have you suggested she sees a doctor? There must be something wrong.'

'I have, but she won't hear of it. Simply tells me to F off.'

Lena couldn't imagine the well-bred Celia swearing. She just wasn't the type. 'Really?'

'Oh, she uses words worse than that at times. The C one is quite a favourite.'

Lena was amazed. There again, maybe she was being naive. She didn't really know much about the so-called upper classes and their habits. 'Are you telling me you don't get any sex at all?' she asked.

'On occasion. But I literally have to beg for it. And I mean beg. When she does grant me the favour I've no sooner started than she's urging me to hurry up. Hurry up, she says non-stop until I'm finished. Honestly, it's almost as if she was saying you've got a minute, starting now!'

Despite herself, Lena had to smile. 'If it wasn't for your expression I'd think you were joking.'

'I'm most certainly not, I can assure you. It's humiliating.'

Lena had another swig of her drink while she thought about Hamish's revelations. No wonder he had been staring hungrily at her, considering how his sex life had been. 'What about prostitutes?' she queried. 'Have you considered those?'

A guilty look came on to his face. 'To be honest, I have. Not only considered them, but tried a few.'

'And?'

'I didn't find them very satisfactory, I'm afraid. On one occasion I was so bloody nervous I couldn't even get it up.' He shook his head. 'No, pros are not for me. I want there to be more to sex than that cold-blooded procedure.' He finished his whisky. 'I'm going up for a refill. Do you want another?'

'Just a single this time.'

'Right. Won't be a mo.'

Poor Hamish, she reflected as he made his way to the bar. He'd thought he'd won the jackpot in marrying the chairman's daughter, which hadn't proved to be the case at all. She'd also guessed by now what might be coming next, and why he'd asked her not to get angry, or slap his face in public. A fool could see the proposition a mile off, and she was no fool. Not by a long chalk.

'What was Celia's attitude to sex when you first got married?' she asked curiously when he re-joined her.

'Loved it. Anywhere, any time, swing from the chandelier if you like. Couldn't get enough.'

Lena could well understand what a shock Celia's change of attitude must have been to Hamish after the birth of their twins. His now being desperate was only too understandable. Especially as Celia, by the sound of it, had completely let herself go into the bargain.

Hamish cleared his throat. 'There's something I want to ask you. A sort of favour.'

Here it comes, she thought. 'What is it?'

'Is there any chance, any possible chance, of us taking up again where we left off?'

Lena pretended not to understand. 'How do you mean?'

'The, er . . . arrangement we had.'

'You mean, the one Saturday a month at your place?'

He nodded eagerly. 'That's it.'

'You want to start it again?'

'Please, Lena,' he begged.

'But you don't have a place any more,' she pointed out. 'You live with your family in a different house. I can hardly turn up there on a Saturday afternoon, can I? Nor can we use my house, as I live with my parents and sister.'

'Ah!' he exclaimed. 'I've already thought of that.'

Lena smiled wryly. She just bet he had. 'I'm listening.'

He twiddled his thumbs, obviously nervous as all get out. 'I have a friend who owns a small private hotel. We could go there once a month. And I promise you, he'd be completely discreet.'

'A sort of Mr and Mrs Smith, is that it?'

'Right,' Hamish enthused. 'So what do you say?'

Lena lit another cigarette, her mind racing. This was an offer that needed careful consideration. She certainly wasn't going to turn it down out of hand.

'You've caught me a bit by surprise, Hamish. I wasn't expecting this.'

'I had intended speaking to you soon. And to be honest . . .

well, I've been trying to summon up the courage to do so. It's not easy to . . .' He trailed off. 'You know?'

She arched an eyebrow. 'What?'

'Let's just say I wasn't sure how you'd react. I even thought you might laugh at me.'

'And why would I do that?'

'Marrying the chairman's daughter, only to come crawling back to you with such a request. You might have taken deep offence.' He suddenly looked at her in alarm. 'You haven't, have you?'

Lena shook her head. 'No.'

'Oh, thank God for that.'

If anything, she was rather flattered, she thought. More attractive women might well have taken offence, but not her. 'Tell me,' she asked quietly, slightly changing tack. 'Have you ever considered leaving Celia?'

Hamish glanced away. 'Of course I have. But I never will.'

'Even though she's causing you so much unhappiness, not to mention frustration? You could leave her and start over. I appreciate the chairman might sack you if you did, but there are other firms, you know.'

'There's more to it than that.'

'Oh?'

'You may think this soft of me, and I won't blame you if you do, but I love my children very much. It would break my heart to lose them.'

Lena sat back in her chair and studied him. This was a side to Hamish she'd never seen before. 'I don't think it's soft. Not in the least. If anything I think it's admirable, and applaud you.'

He blushed. 'Thanks.'

'I mean that, Hamish. I truly think it's admirable of you. You've gone up in my estimation.'

'Thanks again. But true as that reason is for staying with Celia, there is another. This one, I have to admit, quite mercenary.' He paused, then went on, 'It's not generally known yet, but I'm to be promoted to vice chairman in a few months' time. I don't merit it, of course – you appreciate that better than anyone –

but it's going to happen all the same. Call it nepotism if you will, but I have the chairman's word on it.'

'Was it his idea?'

'Of course. He wants me to take over the company when he retires in a few years. My being vice chairman is a way of being trained up for the big job when it finally comes.'

'I see,' Lena murmured. 'Lucky old you.'

'In a way. But the price is Celia. The opportunity would go flying out of the window if I left her. And, there's no denying it, I am ambitious. Always have been.'

'Then I wish you good luck, Hamish.'

'It's your good luck too,' he said quickly. 'If you wish it to be.'

Lena frowned. 'How so?'

'I'm taking you upstairs with me. You'll be my right hand, so to speak. As you've been ever since I became a department head.'

She stared at him in astonishment, momentarily thrown. 'You mean when you become vice chairman?'

'Exactly.'

'But your duties will be totally different from what they are now.'

'Maybe so,' he admitted. 'But whatever, I want you there by my side to ensure I don't muck up and make a fool of myself. I'd probably be out of my depth otherwise.'

Lena had to admit that was probably true. Even as a department head he was out of his depth most of the time. It was because of her that the department ran smoothly. 'It's very honest, not to mention brave, of you to admit that, Hamish,' she said.

He shrugged. 'It's true though, isn't it?'

'Yes,' she stated bluntly. 'It is.'

'So what do you say?'

Lena regarded him shrewdly. 'Does my elevation depend on my answer about resuming our affair?'

'It does not,' he replied emphatically. 'I swear to you it doesn't. Turn me down and you'll still go upstairs with me. Nor am I being kind, or anything like that. I simply need you, and that's the long and short of it.'

Working for the vice chairman as his right hand? She liked the idea of that. And the chairman's right hand given time. 'Will I get more money?'

Hamish smiled. 'Absolutely. Don't you worry, I'll make it worth your while. You'll do very nicely out of it, thank you very much.'

It was a lot to take in at once, Lena told herself. She needed to give it some thought.

'Well?' Hamish demanded.

'There's no problem about me working for you when you become vice chairman. On the contrary, I'll jump at the chance.'

'And the other thing?'

'That needs thinking on, Hamish.'

His face fell. 'You're going to turn me down, aren't you?'

'I never said that. Simply that it needs consideration. I'll give you my decision in a couple of days' time. How's that?'

He nodded. 'It'll have to do, I suppose.'

'Yes, it will. Now let's leave it at that for the time being.'

Tom glanced over at Ian, who'd come for Sunday dinner as he invariably did, although he was now living in a house which he shared with three other bachelors from Ford. 'Have you written to your mother recently?' he asked.

Ian shook his head. 'I just never seem to get round to it.'

'Then make an effort. She'll no doubt be worried about you.'

'All right.' Ian nodded. 'I'll do it tonight.'

'See that you do. I'll be asking you tomorrow at work if you did.'

Ian sighed. He hated writing, it was such a chore.

Tom's eyes twinkled mischievously. 'And tell her about that lassie you're courting. Georgie's bound to be interested in that.'

An embarrassed Ian blushed beetroot red.

'You've decided then?' Hamish asked. He and Lena were in the Swan, at the same table they'd sat at three evenings previously.

'I have.'

'And?' He was certain she was going to turn him down.

'The idea of the hotel is out, Hamish. That would be just too degrading, I'm afraid. Going to your place was one thing, an hotel quite another.'

So, he'd been right. She had turned him down. Disappointment welled within him. 'I'm sorry to hear that, Lena. I had hoped . . .' He trailed off, and shrugged his shoulders. 'Never mind. It was worth a try.'

'But I do have a suggestion to make.'

'Oh?'

'A suggestion I believe to be a lot better than yours.' She took her time, teasing it out, taking a sip of her gin before continuing. Enjoying the look on his face.

'Lena?' he urged impatiently.

'Why only once a month? Why not more? Once a week, say. Or even twice. What do you think of that?'

His Adam's apple bobbed up and down as he gulped. This was the answer to his prayers. 'And how would we manage that?'

'Simple, really. I move into a house of my own where you can visit me whenever you like.'

'A house of your own.' He frowned. 'You're prepared to leave home?'

'Well, that's what it would mean. At my age I should have left years ago, but never did because there wasn't any reason to. But now there is. Or could be, if you agree.'

Every week, twice a week! He almost drooled at the thought. It would certainly solve his problem. By Christ and it would!

'There are terms, though,' Lena added quietly.

'Such as?'

'You buy the house, or pay the rent. Also pay to have it furnished. I can't afford to do that by myself, Hamish. I'll need help. You'd also have to stump up for the gas, electric if it's installed, and maintenance,' she added.

'And what do you pay?' he croaked.

She treated him to her razored smile. 'I pay by being your

full-time mistress. That's what. Yours whenever you want me.'

Full-time mistress! That certainly appealed. 'And how long would this last for?'

'As long as you like. That's a promise.'

Hamish closed his eyes and pictured Celia, shuddering at the vision he conjured up. True, Lena was no oil painting, but neither was Celia nowadays. And Lena was terrific in bed, as he knew from past experience. Enthusiastic was too tame a word to describe her.

'The question is, can you afford it?' she asked.

Hamish started mentally doing sums. It sounded a big outlay, but it wasn't really. What was more, once he became vice chairman his salary would jump enormously, and that was only months away. He nodded. 'I can afford it.'

'It's agreed then?'

'It's agreed.'

Lena knew it was probably the best she could ever achieve where a relationship with a man was concerned. With her face no one was ever going to marry her, so being a mistress was the next best thing.

She'd settle for that. And be grateful into the bargain.

Chapter 26

'I was wondering,' Bill Bailey murmured, staring at Georgie over the rim of his teacup. He hadn't thought he'd be nervous at broaching this, but he was. '. . . if you'd care to come and meet my mother one night?'

Georgie wasn't entirely surprised. She'd guessed over the past weeks that he was leading up to something. All the signs had been there. 'Oh?'

'I've told her about you. I hope you don't mind?'

'Not at all, Bill.'

'She'll lay on a bit of a meal. That sort of thing.'

'A meal?' She was playing for time.

'Aye. Nothing fancy, mind. Boiled ham, no doubt. That's what my mum usually gives guests.'

Georgie pulled out her cigarettes and lit up, not failing to notice how increasingly nervous he was becoming. 'What's your mum's name?'

'Florrie. Short for Florence.'

'Is she old?'

'Fairly elderly. She's just turned seventy.'

'And your father's dead, is that right?'

'Quite a while ago now. My mum was glad of the company when I came out of the army. She'd been lonely without him.'

'They were close, then?'

'Very. They absolutely idolised one another. He's a great loss to her.'

Georgie could well imagine it would be the same with Chrissie should Tam pass before her. The difference was, Chrissie would still have Lena and herself at home.

'I don't even know where you live, Bill?'

He told her.

A short tram ride away, she thought. Not that far.

'If you come I'll show you my medals,' Bill proposed, tongue half in cheek.

'You have medals?'

'Oh aye. Sometimes they give you one for just having been there. I've got several of those.'

'Any for bravery?'

His eyes took on a peculiar look. 'I have one. But please don't ask me about it.'

'Bad memories?' she sympathised.

He nodded, but didn't elaborate.

It was that little exchange which made up her mind for her, though why, she couldn't have said. 'I'd love to meet your mum,' she declared. 'When?'

'How about this Friday?'

'Suits me.'

He beamed. 'I'll be looking forward to it.'

Georgie just hoped she wasn't making a mistake. There again, where was the harm in meeting his mother? It didn't mean anything.

'A place of your own!' a shocked Chrissie exclaimed.

'That's right. It's high time I left home, don't you think?'

'But . . . but it's so unexpected.'

'What brought this on?' Tam asked, taken aback.

Lena shrugged. 'Seems a good idea, that's all. You don't want me kicking around under your feet for the rest of your days, do you?'

Tam began studiously packing his pipe. This was a turn-up for the book. Lena kicking around under their feet for the rest of their days was precisely what he'd believed would happen. Now here she was, proposing to fly the coop.

'Have you found somewhere?' Chrissie queried.

'Not yet, Mum. I haven't started looking. But I will shortly.'

'Tam?' Chrissie prompted.

He shook his head. 'There's nothing I can say. She's old enough to go if she wishes. I can't stop her. And why would I try, if that's what she wants?'

Chrissie abruptly sat down. 'This has made my head spin, coming out of the blue as it has.'

'Sorry, Mum. Shall I put the kettle on?'

'Please, Lena. I could do with a cup after that.'

'It'll cost you to get furniture and the like,' Tam commented.

'I plan to use the second-hand showrooms. I should be able to pick up some bargains there.'

Tam grunted his approval. She'd obviously thought this through. But then, he'd expect nothing less from Lena. She'd always had her head screwed on the right way.

'You intend living by yourself?' Chrissie asked with a frown.

'That's right, Mum. I'll enjoy it.'

'Are you sure?'

'Oh, yes. I have no doubts in that department. None at all.'

'What about cooking and cleaning?'

'Don't worry, Mum, I'm quite capable. I'll neither starve nor live in a pigsty, I promise.'

'It just seems queer to me.' Chrissie shook her head. 'Lassies don't usually do that sort of thing.'

'Well this lassie intends to.'

'Don't argue with her, Chrissie.' Tam smiled. 'You know Lena. Once her mind's made up that's it. Arguing will only make her even more determined. That's the way she is.'

Lena laughed. 'You know me only too well, Papa.'

'Aye, well I would, you being my daughter.'

Lena was still laughing as she went to lay out the cups and

saucers. That had gone more easily than it might have, she reflected. Which was something of a relief if she was honest.

'Just call me Florrie,' the old woman said, extending a heavily veined hand covered with liver spots to Georgie.

'Pleased to meet you, Florrie. And I'm Georgie.'

'Pleased to meet you, Georgie. I hope you like boiled ham, for that's what we're having.'

'Love it.'

'Good.'

How stooped she was, and frail, Georgie noticed, as Florrie shuffled over to the gleaming range, which had been newly black-leaded.

'Will you have a seat?' Bill asked, indicating an easy chair.

'Thank you. But perhaps I should help Florrie? Give her a bit of a hand?'

'I may be ancient but I'm not decrepit,' Florrie retorted before Bill could reply. 'If I want your help I'll ask for it. Now, the pair of you sit down, otherwise you'll be in my way.'

Feisty, Georgie thought approvingly. Florrie was certainly that. Already she'd taken a liking to her.

'Tell me all about yourself, young woman,' Florrie demanded from where she was busy at the range. 'Bill has mentioned a few things, but I'd like to know more. If you don't mind, that is.'

Talk about getting right to the point. Georgie smiled to herself. 'I don't mind at all,' she replied. 'If you'll tell me about yourself afterwards.'

Florrie shot her a look, then nodded her agreement. 'Get on with it then. I'm all ears.'

'Is it true what your mother said about me being the first female you've ever taken home?' Georgie asked, when she and Bill were on the way to her tram stop. She coughed, for there was a lot of fog about, interspersed with thick chimney smoke. If she'd spat into a hanky the spittle would have been black.

'Aye, that's right.'

'I'm honoured.'

He chose to ignore that. 'So what did you think of my mum?'

'I liked her. Liked her a lot, actually. She certainly doesn't pull any punches.'

Bill laughed. 'You can say that again. She can be a proper tartar when she gets going. But her heart's in the right place.'

'I can imagine.'

'She took a shine to you too. It was obvious.'

'Really?'

'Oh aye. I could tell. The fact that she offered you a second helping of boiled ham was the proof. She rarely does that to any of our guests. Not that we have many.'

Georgie glanced sideways at him. 'I don't suppose you've got many friends locally, having been so long in the army?'

'A few pals from the old days before I joined up. I bump into them from time to time in a pub I use.'

Thinking of Charlie made her ask, 'Do you drink a lot, then?'

'Not really. I enjoy a pint and a dram as most men do. But I can take it or leave it. Why?' And then the penny dropped. 'I'm not a drunk, like your husband, Georgie. You have my word on that.'

'Sorry for asking,' she apologised. 'It was rude of me.'

'Not at all. I can well understand why you'd want to know after what you went through with that man.'

Georgie smiled gratefully at him. 'I really enjoyed tonight. Thank you, Bill.'

'My pleasure, I assure you.'

How easy-going he was, she thought. There didn't appear to be any side to him whatsoever. 'You forgot to show me your medals,' she teased.

'So I did.'

'You never wanted to in the first place, did you?' she accused him light-heartedly.

'I offered.'

'But didn't produce them. I don't think you have any at all.'

'I do,' he stated emphatically. 'I have some all right.'

282

She believed him. But then she had when he'd first told her.

'Hey, that's your tram!' he exclaimed as they were approaching the stop. They broke into a run, arriving at the stop just as the tram clanked to a halt.

'Thanks again,' she said breathlessly, and clambered aboard.

'See you next delivery day, Georgie.'

'See you then, Bill.'

Georgie found a seat and slumped into it. She wondered if he'd been going to ask her out again, only to be prevented from doing so by the arrival of the tram. She was not at all sure what her reply would have been.

There again, there was always the next delivery day.

'Lena!'

She glanced up to find Hamish beckoning her into his office. Once she was inside he closed the door behind them.

'This is for you,' he declared, picking up an envelope from his desk and handing it to her. The envelope was open and contained a wad of notes, a number of them white ones. 'To get you started with your house,' he explained. 'Have you found anywhere yet?'

She shook her head. 'I've been watching the ads in the papers but haven't spotted anything that might be suitable. Not so far, anyway. But when I do I might need time off from here to view. And then, when I have the house, more time off to arrange matters.'

Hamish nodded that he understood. 'Just speak to me first, then go and do what you have to. Understand?'

'Thank you, Hamish.'

'Do you fancy a drink in the Swan after work?'

'For any particular reason?'

He gave a dry, bitter laugh. 'Because I'd much rather spend an hour with you than with Celia. That a good enough reason?'

She was strangely touched. 'It's enough.'

'Good.' As she was turning away he said, 'Lena?'

'What, Hamish?'

'On the other hand, we could spend a few days at that hotel I mentioned. Get the ball rolling, so to speak.'

She could hear the pleading in his voice, and realised how desperate he must be. She also noticed that a sudden faint sheen of perspiration had appeared on his brow during the past few seconds. Be that as it may, she wasn't going to stoop to acting like a common tart, even if she did want sex as much as he.

'We'll stick with the drink, Hamish,' she replied. 'I've already made plain my feelings on going to that, or any other, hotel.'

He sank back into his chair, his disappointment obvious.

'Don't worry, though. The time will come soon enough. You'll see.'

She felt immensely powerful as she left his office. It was a sensation she liked. Very much.

'You're getting very friendly with the delivery man,' said Janet, during a lull when there weren't any customers in the shop.

Georgie affected surprise and innocence. 'Am I?'

'It looks that way. You have your tea break with him every time he comes. The pair of you sit in the back shop nattering away like a couple of old fishwives.'

'He's easy to talk to,' Georgie prevaricated with a smile.

'Is there anything in it?'

'In what?'

'The pair of you? He certainly fancies you all right. That's clear enough.'

'Not to me it isn't.'

'And you seem quite keen yourself, I've noticed.'

'Have you now?' Georgie replied coldly.

'He's not bad-looking, either. Rather handsome, really.'

'I suppose.' Georgie grudgingly admitted. 'If you like that type.'

'Which you obviously do.'

Georgie glared at her colleague. 'Aren't you taking a lot on yourself saying something like that?'

284

Janet was instantly contrite. 'Sorry, Georgie. I didn't mean to upset you. I was only commenting, that's all.'

'Then I'll thank you to mind your own business, and I'll do the same.'

Further conversation was interrupted by the arrival of a customer.

Little madam, Georgie thought later. How dare she presume? Even if she was right.

'Is this a new boyfriend Georgie's got?' Tam asked Chrissie one night when they were alone. Lena was out somewhere, and Georgie had gone to the pictures with Bill.

'She says not. She says they're only friends. Nothing more.'

'Hmm,' Tam grunted.

'Why do you ask?'

Tam folded the newspaper he'd been reading and dropped it to the floor. 'Because she's had two bad experiences, I suppose,' he said quietly. 'I wouldn't like her to get her fingers burnt again.'

'No,' Chrissie replied slowly. 'I wouldn't either. But she's a grown woman, and a mother, Tam. She'll know her own mind. It's certainly not up to us to interfere.'

'I have no intention of interfering, woman. But I can be concerned, can't I? She is my daughter, don't forget.'

There was silence between them for a few minutes, then Tam asked, 'What do we know about this chap anyway?'

Chrissie sighed. 'You won't let it go, will you?'

'I'm simply curious. Surely there's no harm in that?'

Chrissie laid her darning aside. She'd had enough of it anyway, and her eyes were hurting. Not for the first time she wondered if she should visit the optician for a test.

'Well?'

'Well what?' She frowned.

'What do we know about him?'

Persistent, Chrissie thought. That was Tam all over. 'Not a lot really. Just a few bits and pieces.'

Tam was clearly irritated. 'Which are?'

'He's ex-army. Joined as a lad, and came out only recently. He lives with his widowed mother and works as a delivery man servicing Templeton's, where he met Georgie. That's it.'

'How old is he?'

'No idea. Georgie has never mentioned it.'

'Has he been married?'

'Again, Georgie has never mentioned it. Though I did get the impression he hasn't. Honestly, Tam, stop worrying. Georgie's quite capable of looking after herself.'

'Aye, like getting herself hooked up with that pervert Charlie. She looked after herself there all right.'

'Aye well. We all make mistakes.'

'And I just don't want her to make another one.'

'Let me remind you, Georgie said they were only friends. Nothing more.'

Tam eyed his wife balefully. 'In my experience that never works between a man and a woman. It simply isn't natural. One thing is eventually bound to lead to another. Unless he's queer, that is.'

Chrissie was genuinely shocked. 'How could he be that when he was in the army? What a suggestion!'

'Take my word for it, lass, not all queers flounce and walk around with limp wrists. Some of them can be hard as nails, believe me.'

'And how would you know about such a thing, Tam McKeand?'

'I just do, that's all.'

'Huh!' she snorted.

'Don't huh me! I hate it when you do that.'

'Huh!' she snorted again, taking a rise.

'Huh yourself.'

She made a mental note to tickle him when they got into bed. If he hated her snorting then he hated that even more, being ticklish in the extreme.

'I've had a thought,' she declared.

'Oh aye?'

286

'This Bill invited Georgie home for tea to meet his mum. Why don't we suggest to her she invites him here for tea to meet us? A sort of return gesture, you could say.'

Tam considered the suggestion. 'What an excellent idea,' he enthused. 'Then I can judge him for myself.'

Chrissie was alarmed. 'You won't put him off, will you? Or start quizzing the poor man?'

'I promise.'

'A promise I'll hold you to, Tam. I'll be furious if you subject him to some kind of interrogation.'

'I can ask questions, can't I? What it was like in the army, and so on?'

'As long as you keep it to that sort of thing.'

'I will.'

'Anyway.' Chrissie shrugged. 'Georgie might not want to invite him.'

'Why not?'

'She might just not want to, that's all.'

'I don't see why she wouldn't. She went to his house, surely it's only polite for her to invite him to ours?'

'We can only suggest it to her. The decision will be hers.'

When they spoke to Georgie later that evening she was all for it. Bill was to be asked to tea.

Lena went to the large window dominating the room and stared out, thinking what a lovely area Hillhead was. Far smarter than where she currently lived with her parents, and where she'd been brought up.

The 'apartment', as the factor so grandiosely called it, was light and airy, with large rooms and high ceilings. She'd fallen in love with it the moment she'd walked through the door.

There were trees in the street, she noted, and the street was devoid of any rubbish or debris. The facing terrace, which was identical to the one containing her 'apartment', was constructed of stone that positively shone in the sunlight.

Her apartment, she realised she'd thought. And so it would be, for there and then she decided to rent it, knowing it would be a place where she'd be happy.

Hillhead! Who'd have ever thought she'd be moving into such a posh area? Certainly not her. But why not? With Hamish funding her she could afford it easily.

'Right,' she declared out loud. It was straight back to the factor and sign whatever had to be signed, and pay whatever had to be paid as a deposit. Hamish's envelope stuffed with cash was burning a hole in her handbag.

She was euphoric as she locked the front door behind her and hurried off down the stairs. She'd found her new home. And it was an absolute cracker!

Chapter 27

L ena closed Hamish's office door behind her, then whirled to
face him, her eyes blazing with excitement. 'I've got some
wonderful news!' she declared.

He came to his feet. 'So have I.'

That threw her slightly. 'You first, then.'

'My promotion has been brought forward. I start as vice
chairman next Monday.'

'Oh, Hamish!' she breathed, delighted for him.

'You'll be starting your new job then as well. I've decided that
your title will be personal assistant to the vice chairman. What
do you think?'

'I . . .' She broke off, lost for words.

'Pleased?'

'Of course I am. But shouldn't a personal assistant be able to
type and take shorthand? Neither of which I can do.'

He shook his head. 'I'll have a secretary who'll do that. No,
your duties will be more or less to check everything that arrives
on my desk. Keep me on the right lines, so to speak. Ensure I
don't make any balls-ups.'

Which was precisely what she did now. 'I see.'

'That all right?'

'Fine.'

He then mentioned a sum that far exceeded what she currently earned. 'Big promotion, big pay rise. For both of us.' He beamed. 'Any complaints?'

She knew he meant the latter as a joke. 'None.'

'Sure?'

If they hadn't been at work, she'd have given him a hug. 'Absolutely, Hamish. Absolutely!'

'I can't tell you how thrilled I am, Lena. I'm bubbling inside with it.'

'And so you should be. You're very lucky.'

'Aye.' He nodded. 'I'm well aware of that. On two counts. One, marrying Celia. And two, having you to rely on. For which I can't thank you enough.' He suddenly remembered something. 'Oh, and by the way, you'll have your own office right next to mine. An office all to yourself.'

'Really?' She was amazed.

'Really. It's not long been refurbished, either. Tastefully, too, in my opinion.'

'And your office?'

'Twice the size of this with a carpet on the floor and a drinks cabinet.' He laughed. 'Imagine, a bloody drinks cabinet! Can you beat that?'

'When's the announcement going to be made about your promotion?' Lena enquired.

'A memo is being put round this afternoon which'll cause quite a stir, I shouldn't be surprised.'

'And about me?'

'No memo. You just report upstairs next Monday and that'll be that. I'm sure we'll both settle in fairly quickly.'

Lena, frankly, couldn't wait. She rather enjoyed her present job, but the new one should be far more interesting. And certainly far more financially rewarding.

Hamish's eyes twinkled. 'I'll tell you what. As soon as we can we'll christen the drinks cabinet. I'll enjoy that.'

'I'll bet you will,' she teased.

'There's another thing. As from next Monday the chairman is going into semi-retirement in order to play more golf. He intends coming in only one day a week from now on, and probably only half a day at that. In other words, I'll be more or less running the company.'

Better still, she thought. Hamish's cup was certainly running over. 'When was all this decided?'

'At the weekend. Or at least that's when I was told. Celia and I were over there for Sunday lunch, and the chairman dropped his bombshell in the middle of it.'

'Well, you did know it was coming,' she pointed out.

'I did. What was so unexpected was bringing forward the date. That took me completely by surprise. You could have knocked me over with the proverbial feather.'

'I've got some good news as well.'

'You said. What is it?'

'I've found the most perfect place. At least I think it is. I'm certain you'll love it.'

'When are you moving in?'

Lena laughed. 'Hold your horses. It needs doing up first. And then I've got the furniture to buy. It'll take a few weeks at least.'

'Where is it?'

'Hillhead. A lovely street. I fell in love with the apartment the moment I walked into it.'

'"Apartment".' Hamish chuckled. 'Sounds very posh.'

'The factor's description, not mine. And yes, I suppose you could call it that. Certainly a lot posher than I'm used to.'

'There are going to be a lot of changes to what you've been used to.' Hamish smiled.

Lena could only agree, well aware she was about to move into a whole new lifestyle, including the increase in salary coming her way. It was going to be lovely.

'Tell you what,' Hamish said. 'Why not a drink in the Swan after work to celebrate both sets of news?'

'I'll be there. Now I'd better get on. There's plenty to be done.'

A little later, as was his habit, Hamish skived off to the coffee shop to meet up with the regulars.

'I insist. This round's mine,' Lena declared, pushing a ten shilling note at Hamish. 'Think of it as a sort of thank you for what you've done for me.'

'A lady shouldn't pay for the drinks. But in this instance, I gracefully accept your offer.'

Lena studied him as he went up to the bar. He'd changed considerably since they'd first met. The sexy blue eyes were the same, if a little duller than before, while his hair was definitely thinning, and had begun to show the first strands of grey at the temples. He'd also put on weight, though not drastically. All in all, he was still a damn good-looking man.

'So, how's Celia?' she asked when Hamish re-joined her.

He pulled a face. 'Fatter than ever. She's now so portly she's started waddling like a duck.'

Lena laughed. 'Surely you're exaggerating?'

'Nope. She waddles just like a duck.'

'Is she taking any better care of herself?'

'Hell will freeze over first. Fat and unkempt. My darling wife who used to be so beautiful.' A catch came into his voice. 'It's a tragedy, that's what it is. One of Greek, or Shakespearean, proportions. As I said, my price for getting where I am today. And a heavy price it is too.'

'You've still got the twins to be thankful for,' Lena reminded him.

A smile crept across his face. 'I wouldn't change them for anything. Not for all the tea in China. And that's a fact.'

When they finally left the Swan they were both slightly tipsy, Hamish even staggering a little.

'I enjoyed that,' he slurred.

'So did I.'

His eyes narrowed in concentration. 'You know something, Lena?'

'What?'

'You really are terrific company. A man feels relaxed in your presence. Very . . . relaxed.'

She was touched. 'Thank you, Hamish. Shall I call you a taxi?'

'You do that and I'll drop you off.'

'Are you sure about that?'

'Absolutely. It isn't any trouble.'

'But what if we're seen?'

'That could have happened any time in the Swan. Besides, what's wrong with the boss taking a colleague out for a drink? Or dropping her home in a taxi after they've both been working overtime? I don't see anything wrong in either.'

Neither did Lena, albeit they hadn't been working overtime. Just then a taxi came into view which she promptly flagged down. Having given the driver her address she sank on to the leather seat beside Hamish. As the taxi moved off, to her surprise, he took her hand and held it, at the same time giving her a smile in the darkness.

For the first time in her life Lena felt cherished by a member of the opposite sex.

It was a glorious feeling.

'Come in, come in.' Chrissie beamed, ushering Georgie and Bill into the kitchen, where the table was already set for the meal that was to follow.

Tam rose from his chair. This was a moment he'd been waiting for: meeting his daughter's new 'friend'.

The first thing he noticed was how completely at ease Bill was. Not nervous in the least. Confident in himself, Tam thought, unsure whether he liked that or not.

Introductions were made all round, then Tam offered their guest a dram, which Bill accepted. Georgie glanced at Lena, who gave her an almost imperceptible nod of encouragement.

'I'm told you were in the army,' Tam began. 'And in the war?'

'Bill doesn't like talking about the war,' Georgie put in hastily. 'And don't ask why, he just doesn't, that's all.'

'Sorry,' Tam apologised. 'I didn't know.'

Not a good beginning, Georgie thought. Damn!

Georgie clicked the front door shut behind Bill and returned to the kitchen, where Chrissie and Lena were already busy at the sink.

'Did you have to give him the third degree, Papa?' she said. 'For a while in here it was like the Spanish Inquisition.'

'I didn't give him any third degree,' Tam blustered. 'I was only making conversation.'

My arse! Georgie thought angrily, though she didn't say so in front of her parents.

'You were a bit harsh, Papa,' Lena commented over her shoulder.

'Nonsense.'

'You were, Tam,' Chrissie declared grimly. 'I felt right sorry for the poor chap.'

'Then you should have said something.'

'I tried to, several times. But you just weren't listening.'

'We all tried to steer the conversation in different directions,' Lena added. 'Except you kept coming back to whatever you were droning on about at the time.'

Tam was upset. He hadn't realised he'd been that bad. 'I was only doing my job,' he replied gruffly.

'And what job's that?' Georgie demanded.

'Being your father. Trying to protect you, that's what. I thought you needed it after the almighty mess you made with Charlie Gunn.'

Georgie burst into tears and fled the room.

'Idiot!' Chrissie snapped. 'Bloody stupid idiot.'

'I'll go and talk to her.'

'Leave her for now,' Lena advised. 'And for what it's worth, I liked Bill. I thought him a genuinely nice bloke.'

'Me too,' Chrissie said.

Tam dropped his head to stare at the floor. He too had taken a shine to Bill, but only after he'd got to know a bit about him, and been in his company for a while.

Taking out his pipe Tam slowly began the procedure of filling it and lighting up. Bill's visit wasn't mentioned again for the rest of that day.

Chrissie exclaimed in delight and waved the letter that had just arrived at Tam and Lena, who were having breakfast. 'It's from Tom,' she explained. 'Brigid's expecting again.'

Tam's face lit up. 'Is she, by God? That's wonderful news.'

'How far gone is she?' Lena asked.

'Four months, it says here.' Chrissie shook her head. 'I couldn't be more pleased.'

'A wee lassie would be nice this time,' Tam commented. 'A sister for Robin.'

'Aye, true enough,' Chrissie agreed. 'Unfortunately we don't have a say in such matters. What comes along comes along.'

Georgie appeared in the kitchen. 'What's all the commotion about?' she demanded.

'Brigid's going to have another baby,' Chrissie informed her.

'Good for Brigid.'

'I'm sure Tom had something to do with it,' Lena observed.

Georgie laughed. 'I'm sure he did.'

Suddenly Lena was depressed, knowing she'd never have any children of her own. Marriage would never happen for her. Pushing her plate away, she came to her feet. 'I'd better get going or I'll be late. It's a big day for me, don't forget.'

'Good luck then,' Tam declared.

'Aye, good luck, Lena,' Chrissie added. Crossing to her daughter she kissed her on the cheek. 'You can tell us all about it when you get in tonight.'

Lena stared around her, having just entered her office for the first time. It was a little male for her taste, but lovely all the same. As Hamish had said, it had clearly only recently been refurbished.

Crossing to her desk, she sat behind it. It was a larger desk than she'd previously had, and the chair was far more comfortable.

295

'Personal assistant to the vice chairman,' she said aloud, and smiled. She'd certainly come up in the world.

'What do you think?' Hamish asked from the doorway that connected their offices.

'It's wonderful.'

'Come and see mine.'

His was just as large as he'd said it was, the Wilton underfoot a pattern of blues and reds. Her desk might be big, but his was positively enormous. There was also a pretty chaise longue, presumably for him to lie on should he feel like doing so.

'Look at this,' he declared, and led her to an ornately carved cabinet which he opened to reveal myriad bottles and glasses. 'Nothing but the best, eh?'

'I'm impressed.'

He leant closer to her and whispered, 'So am I.'

He was like a kid with a new toy, she thought. And why not? It was a huge achievement on his part. Even if he'd had to marry the boss's daughter to get there.

'We'll have that drink I promised you before going home tonight.' He smiled.

'I'll look forward to it.'

He suddenly became all businesslike. 'Now, we'd better at least appear busy. Make a start, eh?'

'What would you like me to do?'

He gestured towards some files on his desk. 'We'll go through those and see what's what. And when we've done that we'll take it from there.'

'Right.' She nodded, and added, 'Just one word of advice, Hamish, if you don't mind.'

'What's that?'

'Forget the coffee shop for a while. At least until you get settled in and everything's running smoothly.'

'Good idea, Lena.'

She was pleased he'd agreed, for she was safeguarding her own job as well as his.

* * *

'We've had a letter from Dolly,' Brigid announced to Tom when he got in from work. 'She's over the moon at our news.'

Tom beamed at his wife, whose bump was now quite obvious. From the look of things it was going to be a large child. 'I thought she might be.'

'She's promised to come and see us again after the baby's born. Which would be marvellous. The only worrying thing is she says she's been unwell. Nothing too serious according to her, but the doctor's advised she stay in bed for a while until she recovers.'

Tom frowned. 'Does she say what's wrong with her?'

'No, only that she's been unwell. She thinks the doctor's being a bit melodramatic, but has decided to stay in bed just to be on the safe side. According to her it's driving her mad.'

'Well, it would do,' Tom said. Dolly wasn't the sort of woman who enjoyed being inactive. 'Anyway, what's for tea and where's that son of mine?'

Later that evening Tom wrote back to Dolly, telling her he hoped she'd be better soon. And to let him know once she was up and about again.

Georgie glanced at the wall clock, thinking Bill was late with his delivery. This would be the first time she'd seen him since he'd come to tea.

Half an hour later she began to worry as he still hadn't shown up. Usually Bill was prompt to within five or ten minutes.

He arrived a quarter of an hour later. 'Sorry, I can't stop for a cup of tea today, Georgie,' he apologised. 'I'm having trouble with the van.'

She watched as he bustled in and out several times until the delivery was complete. Then he was gone with a wave of a hand, and a muttered 'See you next week.'

Her heart sank as she heard his van roar off. There didn't appear to be anything wrong with it to her. In fact it sounded just as it normally did.

Georgie bit her lip. Had it simply been an excuse for not joining her for a cup of tea? Had he taken offence when he'd visited them? In her opinion Papa had been rude; was this a consequence of that rudeness? In other words, was her friendship with Bill over?

She sighed. There was nothing for it but to wait till next week and see what happened then.

It was going to be a long week.

Hamish came awake to the realisation that he was alone in bed. Where the hell was Celia? He lay there for a full ten minutes before deciding to get up and investigate.

He found her in the kitchen guzzling the substantial remains of a steamed pudding she'd dished up earlier. She stared at him, a heaped spoon halfway to her mouth, her eyes blazing hate and loathing. Unblinking eyes that narrowed as she continued to stare.

Pig, he thought. That's what she'd become. A pig!

He said nothing, nor did she. Turning on his heel he left her to her gorging.

'That'll be one and threepence ha'penny,' Georgie said. The customer she was serving handed over the money and she rang it up on the till. She was about to have a word with Janet when a bobby came into the shop.

'Mrs Gunn?'

She was taken aback. 'Yes?'

'You're Mrs Gunn?'

'I am.'

'Is there somewhere we can talk privately?'

What in God's name was all this about? 'Come with me,' she said. 'You all right by yourself for a few moments, Janet?'

'Of course.'

In the back shop, Georgie turned to face her visitor. 'So what can I do for you?' she asked.

'I understand you and your husband are separated, Mrs Gunn. However, you are still his next of kin.' The bobby paused for a moment, then went on, 'I'm sorry to have to tell you that your husband was killed in the early hours of this morning whilst in the performance of his duties.'

Georgie's mouth went dry. 'Killed?' she echoed.

'He and a colleague, when a section of wall collapsed on them.'

Charlie dead? She was stunned by this bolt from the blue. 'I see,' she muttered.

'Would you care to sit down?'

'No, I'm fine, honestly.'

Charlie dead! She didn't know whether to laugh or cry.

Chapter 28

'**A** telephone as well?'

Lena was nervous about her mother's visit, but had felt she had to agree when Chrissie had all but insisted. 'I'll need it for work, Mum,' she lied.

'Is that a fact?'

'It was Mr Murchison's idea. My boss. The company are paying for it.' Lena was only too horribly aware of how unconvincing she sounded.

'My my. You really must be important now,' Chrissie commented, a trace of sarcasm in her voice.

Lena shrugged, and didn't reply.

'And most of your furniture appears to be new. I thought you were going to be buying from the second-hand showrooms?'

'That was before my big promotion, Mum. Don't forget I'm earning a lot more now.'

'Aye, that's true enough. But you've hardly started the job and couldn't possibly have saved up enough money in the time to pay for all this.'

'I did have savings.'

'Must have had a lot, then.'

Lena felt wretched, hating having to lie to her mother. 'Would you like a cup of coffee?'

'In a minute. I haven't seen everything yet. Now, where's your bedroom?'

'This way. I'll show you.'

Chrissie followed Lena into the bedroom. Like the rest of the 'apartment', it was newly decorated, Lena having had the painters in. Immediately, Chrissie eyed the brand-new bed, which hadn't yet had its wrappings removed. 'A double, eh?'

'More comfortable, wouldn't you say, Mum?'

'Oh aye, no doubt about it. Though you've never complained about the single you've been used to all these years.'

Lena couldn't hold her mother's piercing gaze, and dropped her own to stare at the floor.

Chrissie crossed over to the bed and sat on it. 'Come here, lassie. Join me.'

Lena did so.

'Will you tell me what's going on? For there's something here that isn't right.'

Lena, again staring at the floor, didn't reply.

'Well? I'm waiting.'

'What makes you think something isn't right?'

Chrissie sighed. 'I'm your mother, and know you through and through. Just as I know Georgie through and through. So, are you going to explain?'

'There's nothing to explain.'

'Lena, don't lie to me. I may be a poor, uneducated working-class woman but I didn't come up the Clyde on a bicycle. Nor am I as green as I'm cabbage-looking.'

Despite herself, Lena smiled.

'I'm still waiting,' Chrissie stated patiently after a few seconds had ticked past.

Lena knew then she'd have to tell her mother the truth, that there was nothing else for it. In her heart of hearts, it was what she really wanted to do.

'Mum,' she said, starting off slowly. 'It's never mentioned in the house, but we all know I'm ugly as sin.'

'That's not true!' Chrissie protested vehemently. 'I admit, you're no great beauty. But ugly as sin? Never!'

'That's very kind and loyal of you, Mum, but you know it *is* true. I wish it wasn't, but the fact remains that it is.'

A hint of tears crept into Chrissie's eyes. 'So what's that got to do with this so-called "apartment"?'

'I'd love to get married, Mum, and have babies, but that'll never happen. No man will ever propose to me.'

This maternal side of Lena was new to Chrissie. 'One might,' she argued.

'It's highly unlikely. And the idea that I'll end up as an old maid isn't exactly an appealing one, I can tell you.'

Reaching across, Chrissie took hold of her daughter's hand, and gently squeezed it.

Lena took a deep breath, and went on. She told Chrissie everything, with the exception of having blackmailed Hamish into having an affair in the first place.

'So there you have it, Mum. I'm to be Hamish's mistress. A kept woman.' Shaking slightly, Lena detached her hand and crossed to the small fireplace where her cigarettes and lighter were on the mantelpiece. Taking out a cigarette, she lit up. 'I suppose you're ashamed of me now?' she queried in a small voice.

Chrissie studied her daughter. She hadn't known what to expect, but certainly not this. Life certainly was full of surprises. 'Is this Hamish Murchison a good man?' she asked quietly, not replying to Lena's question.

Lena couldn't yet look her mother in the face. She was too embarrassed. 'It depends what you mean by good. He's not the brightest spark around, and only got where he is today by marrying the chairman's daughter. And with help from me, I have to add. But yes, I suppose, on the whole, he is a decent enough chap.'

'And his wife won't . . . well, you know . . . any more?'

'Only rarely, according to him. And then he's had to plead with her first. Go down on his hands and knees, so to speak.'

Chrissie shook her head. 'That's awful.' She sounded genuinely sympathetic.

'And, as I just said, she's let herself go dreadfully. Fat as anything nowadays. Sometimes he even has to tell her to have a wash because she smells.'

Chrissie made a face. 'How disgusting.'

Lena wished she had some drink in. She could certainly have used one right now. 'It's my one chance to have anything like a normal life, Mum,' she choked. 'Can you understand that?'

'Aye, lass.' Chrissie sighed. 'I can.'

'I appreciate I'll only be second fiddle, and that I'll never have children. But surely that's better than the alternative? That's how I see it, anyway.'

Chrissie's heart went out to her daughter. The ugly duckling who'd never turned into a swan. She and Tam had often wondered where she'd got her looks from and never succeeded in coming up with an answer. 'Will this set-up make you happy? For surely that's the important thing.'

Lena considered the question. 'Yes, I believe so, Mum. As happy as I'll ever get a chance to be.'

'And he's paying for everything?'

'That's right. It was part of the deal.'

'Have you . . .' She broke off, and coughed. She was still unclear on this particular point.

'Lots of times, Mum. I lost my virginity to him quite some time ago.'

Chrissie's face flamed. She was unused to talking about such matters, particularly to members of her own family. 'I see. Was it . . . agreeable?'

'Very. We get on exceptionally well in that department. If you know what I mean.'

Chrissie did, only too well. She and Tam were just the same, if perhaps not as frequently as they'd once been. 'Your father must never find out about this,' she said. 'He'd go off his chump if he knew.'

'He'll only find out if you tell him, Mum.'

'Have no fears about that. He'll never hear of it from me.'

'That's fine, then.'

Chrissie got to her feet. 'I think I'll have that cup of coffee now. If it's still on offer, that is?'

'Of course it is, Mum.' Lena looked Chrissie full in the face for the first time since her explanation. 'I don't ask for your approval, Mum. Just your understanding.'

Chrissie went to Lena and took her into her arms. 'You have that, lass. I don't condemn you for what you're doing. It's your decision, after all. As for approval, let's just say I don't disapprove. You're entitled to a wee bit of happiness just like everyone else. And if this is the only way for you to get that happiness, then so be it.'

'Thanks, Mum,' Lena said huskily, a huge wave of relief washing through her.

'It feels like a comfortable bed,' Chrissie commented as they left the room.

Which made Lena laugh.

Georgie glanced at the wall clock. Bill should be showing up any minute now and she would find out what was what about their friendship.

The door opened, but it was not Bill who came in. Instead, Wally, the previous delivery man, appeared carrying a tray. Georgie stared at him in surprise.

'Morning, Georgie.' He beamed. 'How's tricks?'

'Where's Bill?'

'Oh, very nice,' Wally retorted. 'No nice to see you again, Wally, how's your leg sort of thing.'

'I'm sorry,' Georgie apologised. 'I was just expecting Bill, that's all. Anyway, I thought you were retired?'

'I am.'

'So what are you doing here?'

He rested his tray on the counter. 'I've been asked to take over the round for a while as this Bill is ill.'

'Ill?'

'Aye, the influenza, I hear. Bad with it too. He'll be laid up for several weeks, I expect.'

Alarm flared through Georgie. Influenza could be a killer. She'd read somewhere that fifteen million people had died from it during the great worldwide pandemic of 1918 to '19. 'He's bad, you say?'

'That's what I was told. Now, I'd better get on. I take it I'll still be offered a cup of tea when I'm finished?'

'Tea and a sticky bun if you like.'

'That's the ticket, Georgie. You're a real gem.'

She stared at his retreating back as he headed for the rear of the shop, worried sick about Bill.

'What's wrong with your face tonight?' Tam demanded. 'Have you got the bellyache or something?'

Georgie shook her head. 'No, I'm fine, Papa.'

'Then cheer up, for God's sake. You've been a right misery since you got in from work.'

'Sorry.'

'Hard day at the shop?' Chrissie enquired.

'Not really, Mum. It's Bill. He's off with a bad dose of influenza.'

Chrissie's expression immediately became one of concern. 'I've heard of other cases recently. Mrs McGuire, further up the street, has it. I understand she's in a right old state.'

'Why don't you go and see him?' Tam suggested.

'I've been considering it, Papa.'

'And?'

'You don't want to catch it yourself,' Chrissie warned. 'Best to keep away. At least until he's over the worst of it.'

'Sound advice.' Tam nodded. 'I should have thought of that.'

Georgie couldn't make up her mind whether to go or not. 'I'll leave it for a few more days,' she said rather unconvincingly, wondering how Bill's mother was coping. She was quite an old woman, after all.

And what if Florrie was down with it as well?

* * *

'How much longer before this "apartment" of yours is ready?' Hamish asked.

Lena smiled. 'Getting impatient, are we?'

'Just a bit.' From the hungry look in his eyes it was obvious to her just how randy he must be. 'Surely you've got everything more or less organised by now?'

'I have, and shall be moving in, lock, stock and barrel, this weekend. So how's that?'

'Excellent,' he enthused. 'When can I pay a call and be shown round? I'm dying to see what it's like.'

'I'll be in a mess unpacking, but how about Sunday night? Can you manage that?'

'Try and stop me. Shall I bring anything?'

'A bottle would be nice.'

'I'll bring several as a house-warming present.'

She laughed. He was keen. There again, if she was honest, so was she. It had been a long time. 'Will you have any trouble getting away?'

'I'll make up some sort of excuse for going out. Not that Celia will enquire. She's always more than happy to see the back of me.'

How sad, Lena thought. 'Between seven and eight. Will that be all right?'

'I'll be there. With bells on,' he added meaningfully.

'I'm sure you will.'

'Ting a ling.'

Lena couldn't help but laugh again. Ting a ling. How ridiculous! Yet somehow apt.

Georgie stood looking up at the tenement where Bill lived. Should she visit or not? He was a friend, after all, so why was she holding back?

It wasn't fear of catching flu herself; that wasn't it at all. It was to do with her and Bill and the possibility that he might read more into her visit than she intended.

Somehow it had been easy when she'd been married, for there

could be nothing between her and Bill other than friendship. Even though she was separated, she was still a married woman. But that state of affairs had abruptly changed with Charlie's death.

She was confused by the situation she now found herself in. And even a little scared, if she told the truth, though what there was to be scared about regarding Bill was beyond her. You couldn't have found a nicer or more gentle man. There again, hadn't she thought that about Charlie? She had only found out differently after they'd wed.

She hadn't gone to the funeral. Hadn't wanted to. It would have been hypocritical of her if she had. Anyway, she hadn't known when it was taking place, or where, though she could easily have found out if she'd wanted.

She presumed Avril had gone to live with her Aunt Betty; hardly a big change for the girl, who'd spent most of her time there as it was.

No, she'd leave her visit for a few more days, she suddenly decided. Turning round, she retraced her steps back up the street, but she had only gone a hundred yards or so when she stopped. This was nonsensical, she told herself. She was being downright daft. Bill was her pal, and her pal was ill. That's all there was to it. Turning again, she headed back to his close, plunging inside when she reached it.

'Oh, it's you, Georgie,' Florrie declared on opening the door. 'Come on through and I'll put the kettle on.'

'How's Bill? I hear he's got influenza.'

Florrie sighed. 'He has indeed. But he's now on the mend, I'm pleased to say.'

Florrie looked awful, Georgie thought. Tired and drawn, and even frailer than she recalled. 'That's good. How have you been coping?'

'Surprisingly well, considering. The neighbours have been a great help, mind you. In and out all the time to see how I am, and if there's anything they can do. I don't know how I'd have managed without them.'

'There's nothing like a decent neighbour.' Georgie nodded. 'We're fortunate like that ourselves.'

'The worst bit was when Bill was delirious,' Florrie said quietly. 'Thrashing around, sweat pouring off him. Out of his mind most of the time. But that's past now, thank God.' She gave Georgie a shrewd glance. 'He'll be pleased to see you. He's mentioned you on a couple of occasions.'

Georgie was surprised. 'Has he?'

'Aye, when he was delirious. At one point he called out your name as if he thought you were in the room with him.'

Georgie glanced away, not knowing what to make of that. Florrie smiled.

She put the kettle on, then set out cups and saucers. 'Would you care for a slice of fruit cake?' she asked. 'One of the neighbours handed it in earlier.'

'No, thank you. The tea will be fine.'

'Watching your figure, are you?' Florrie teased.

'Not at all,' Georgie protested. 'Why do you ask?'

'Relax, lass, don't fash yourself. I'm only having a wee joke.' Florrie ran a hand over her forehead. She was dreadfully tired. Bill's illness had taken a lot out of her.

'Are you all right?'

'Aye, fine. There's nothing wrong with me. Strong as a horse, even if I don't look it.'

Georgie could only wonder if that was true.

'Shall I take you ben, and bring the tea on through when it's ready?' Without waiting for a reply Florrie led the way. Georgie followed.

Bill's face lit up when he saw who his visitor was. 'Georgie!' he exclaimed in delight, struggling into a sitting position.

If Florrie looked awful, he looked ten times worse, Georgie thought. He'd clearly lost a lot of weight. His collar bones were protruding, and his face was almost emaciated.

'This is kind of you,' he said with a smile.

'So, how are you, Bill?'

'Getting better. Getting better. That right, Mum?'

'Aye, he is. This time last week I thought he was at death's door, and that's a fact.' She sighed, a sigh that came from deep within her. 'The doctor said things might have turned out differently if he hadn't been so fit.'

'At least that's one thing I can thank the army for!'

'I'll get the tea,' Florrie declared, and left them to it.

'Sorry I'm unshaven,' Bill apologised. 'I just couldn't face the thought of a razor on my skin. For some reason it's become extremely tender.'

'Don't worry about that. I'm used to seeing men first thing in the morning.' Oh dear, she thought. Maybe she shouldn't have said that. 'I do have a brother and father after all,' she added lamely.

'I still feel embarrassed. You haven't exactly caught me at my best.'

'You've been ill,' she said. 'What else would I expect?'

He smiled, but didn't reply.

'Do you mind if I sit down?'

'Of course not.' He patted the edge of the bed. 'There isn't a chair, I'm afraid, so will this do? How's the shop?'

'The same. It never changes. Oh, by the way, Wally has been hauled out of retirement to do your round while you're off. It was him who told me you had influenza.'

'I just hope he doesn't think he's getting his old job back on a permanent basis, that's all.'

Georgie could see he was concerned. 'I wouldn't worry if I were you. The job will be there waiting when you return. Which you mustn't do until you're fully well again. Hear?'

He grinned sheepishly. 'I hear you, Georgie.'

'Return too soon and you could have a relapse or something. People make that mistake all the time.' She suddenly flushed. 'Sorry, I shouldn't be telling you what to do. It's none of my business.'

'But I like it. Shows you care.'

Their eyes locked for a few seconds, then she glanced away.

'It's good to see you again, Georgie,' he said, his voice loaded with sincerity.

'And you, Bill.'

'I've missed you.'

'I've missed you too, Bill,' she confessed, and meant it every bit as much as he did.

'I'm pleased about that.' Reaching out, he touched her hand, then drew his own away again at the sound of his mother approaching with their tea.

Georgie felt strangely elated when she walked to the tram stop. It was as though she'd suddenly won an unexpected prize.

Chapter 29

'Well, you've certainly made a good job of this,' Hamish declared in admiration. They were in the sitting room, which had been painted cream throughout, including woodwork and ceiling. There was a burgundy-coloured carpet on the floor, and the combination was quite striking. Lena thought it worked a treat, and so too, apparently, did Hamish.

'Modern furniture,' he noted. 'Goes well in here.'

'Thank you.' She smiled. 'I'm glad you approve.'

He glanced at the drawn curtains. They too were cream, sporting swags and tails with flashes of burgundy to match the carpet. 'You've been quite adventurous really.'

'I've always hated the flock wallpaper you get in so many houses. And old Victorian furniture you need two strong men to move.'

Hamish laughed. 'You've just described the chairman's house to a T.'

'And yours?'

'Somewhere in between, I'd say. Celia is a little more traditional than you.'

'And how is she?'

'Immersed in a novel when I left her. Didn't even look up when I said goodbye.'

'What did you tell her about where you were going?'

Hamish shrugged. 'I didn't. Merely said I was off out, and that was that.'

Lena was already excited at the thought of what was going to happen, and had been for most of the day. She was almost twitching with it.

'Shall I open the champagne?' he asked. He had brought two bottles.

'Please. I'm afraid I don't have any proper glasses. In fact, all I have are tumblers.'

'That doesn't matter. You get a couple while I do the honours.'

'Don't spill any, now,' she warned.

He grinned. 'Don't worry, I won't spoil your nice new carpet. Now on you go.'

Quite masterful, she thought. She liked that.

He waited till she returned with the tumblers before popping the cork, and she exclaimed excitedly as he poured the frothing wine.

'A toast, Lena?'

'What to?'

'Us,' he declared firmly. 'And your "apartment".'

They drank.

'Christ!' Hamish swore softly. 'That was unbelievable. Out of this world.'

Lena couldn't have agreed more. It had been indeed. 'You were heroic,' she purred.

'Was I?'

'Absolutely.'

He ran a hand over her thigh, thinking about what had just taken place. So far the 'apartment' had cost him a pretty penny, but it was going to be worth it.

Bending his head, he flicked a nipple with his tongue. 'I don't know about you, but I'm exhausted.'

'Not too exhausted, I hope.'

'Why's that?' he teased, knowing exactly what she meant.

'A lady's expectations, Hamish.'

He laughed. 'You're insatiable. Always were.'

She took it as a compliment. 'Why don't I get us another drink while you revive?'

'Good idea.'

He watched her slip from the bed and throw on a brightly patterned kimono. 'That's pretty,' he commented.

'Glad you like it.'

'I like what's inside it even more.'

Her eyes twinkled with amusement. 'What a silver-tongued smooth talker you are, Hamish Murchison. You could quite turn a girl's head.'

He continued to watch as she padded from the room. By God, she was a terrific shag. Fabulous in fact. It made him shiver just thinking about it.

Lena returned with more champagne and sat alongside him. 'When will you come again?' she asked.

'I haven't left yet!' he protested.

'I'm aware of that. But when will you come again?'

'Keen, aren't you?' he teased.

'As mustard.'

Pushing the flap of her kimono aside he began stroking her leg, which was still sweat-slicked from their recent exertions. 'How about Wednesday night?'

'If you come straight from work I'll cook for you.'

'Are you any good?'

'Try me and find out.'

'I've already tried you and found out.'

She laughed. 'Cooking, idiot. Not the other.'

'Well, if you're half as good at cooking as you are at that then I can't wait.'

'I'm good at all manner of things,' she said. 'You might be surprised.'

He studied her, then shook his head. 'I don't think I would, Lena. You're an extremely talented woman, especially at work. I'd be lost without you there.'

'Thank you,' she whispered. 'I appreciate that.'

He thought of what Celia had become, and then of Lena. There was just no comparison. None at all.

He laid his champagne aside, then took hers and did the same with that. 'Guess what?'

'What?'

'That revival you were hoping for. It's taking place.'

She glanced down. 'So it is. In such a short time, too.'

Moments later they were again locked in each other's arms.

'So how was Bill tonight?' Chrissie enquired when Georgie arrived home after her second visit. Tam was still at McNair's, overseeing a big order that had to be filled urgently.

'Much improved, I'm happy to say. Out of bed and sitting in the kitchen. He's also put on a little weight, I noticed.'

Chrissie didn't fail to hear the enthusiasm in her daughter's voice. 'Does he know about Charlie?'

'He hasn't mentioned it. So I presume not.'

'So why haven't you told him?'

Georgie shrugged.

'There must be a reason, Georgie. It's as plain as the nose on your face, at least it was to me, that the man dotes on you.'

Georgie still didn't reply.

'Don't you care for him that way? I thought you made a splendid couple. There again, I thought the same about you and Charlie.'

'Aye, me and Charlie,' Georgie said. 'That was a mistake if ever there was one.'

'You can't let that mistake ruin the rest of your life,' Chrissie told her. 'It seems to me you have another chance here, so why not grab it while you can?'

Georgie thought about it. 'Bill has never said anything to me about an intimate relationship. Not really.'

'That's because he believes you to be a married woman,' Chrissie pointed out.

Georgie became agitated. She lit a cigarette, blowing the smoke

314

fiercely away. 'The truth is, Mum,' she said at last, 'I'm scared. Scared and confused.'

'Scared and confused about what?'

'Oh, I don't know!' Georgie exclaimed. 'I just am.'

'Scared of Bill?'

'Not in any physical way. But on an emotional level, I suppose.'

'And confused?'

'Because I don't know my own mind.'

'Hmm,' Chrissie murmured.

'I've only ever thought of him as a friend, you see. Nothing else. I couldn't because of my situation.'

'But now you can, Georgie. Your situation's changed.' Chrissie studied her daughter for a few seconds, then asked, 'Have you ever kissed him?'

'No, I haven't.'

'Then maybe you should. It could well be the indicator you're looking for.'

'Indicator?'

'Come on, Georgie, don't be so dense. A kiss can tell you all manner of things. It certainly did me the first time I kissed your father. I felt . . .' She hesitated. 'Well, we won't go into that. But I'm sure you understand what I'm getting at.'

'And what if it leaves me cold, Mum?'

'That's an answer, isn't it?'

'And what if it doesn't?'

'Then that's another answer. But I think in your heart of hearts you already know which one it's going to be. Don't you?'

'No,' Georgie lied. 'Now if you don't mind I'm going through to my room. I've a few things to do there.'

Like think, Chrissie mused as Georgie left the kitchen. Not that she was trying to get rid of her daughter, not at all. But Georgie was too young to remain a widow for the rest of her life. That would be a tragedy.

In her opinion, if happiness was round the corner, then get walking.

* * *

'You weren't joking when you said you could cook. This is delicious,' Hamish enthused.

'Thank you.'

'What exactly is it?'

'Veal with orange. It's got all sorts in it. Stoned raisins, currants, nutmeg, oranges, and so on and so forth.'

Hamish shook his head in amazement. 'I don't mean to be rude, but how did a woman from a working-class Glaswegian background learn to cook a dish like this?'

'What were you expecting, mince and tatties?'

He laughed. 'Not quite. But the question stands.'

'I went to evening classes for a while some years back. No reason, really – it just appealed. Afterwards I thought it had been a waste of time as I could never have served up anything fancy to my parents. They're strictly plain food people. Especially my father. His favourite meal is toad in the hole, would you believe. No disrespect to Papa, but to him that's the height of culinary achievement.'

Hamish laughed again. 'Doesn't know what he's missing.'

Lena tasted the red wine, a fine claret she'd laid in for the occasion. 'What's Celia like as a cook?'

Hamish also had a sip of wine. 'To be honest, she's quite talented. When she puts her mind to it, anyway.'

Jealousy stabbed through Lena. 'Oh?'

'Never been taught, but just seems to know what to do. She's particularly brilliant at sweets. Makes a wonderful thing with fresh cream and brandy snaps. I always make a glutton of myself when that turns up on the table.'

Lena's jealousy intensified. 'Just cream and brandy snaps?'

'Sherry is involved as well. She turns the whole business into a sort of log.'

'I see,' Lena murmured.

Hamish stared at her, then glanced down at his plate. 'Sorry. I shouldn't have told you that.'

'Not at all,' Lena protested. 'I'm only pleased she's good at something.'

There and then Lena decided she was going to work very hard at her cooking, improving her knowledge and her ability. She was damned if fat Celia was going to be better than her in the kitchen.

As for the bedroom, she had no worries there. None whatsoever.

'I shall be reporting back to work on Monday,' Bill declared. Florrie had gone to a neighbour's for a cup of tea within minutes of Georgie's arrival, her intention being, as Georgie and Bill had both guessed, to leave the pair of them alone.

Georgie frowned. 'So soon?'

'I asked the doctor when he was here yesterday and he says that'll be fine. I'm quite recovered.'

'You still need to put on more weight.'

'Aye.' He nodded. 'You're right there. But that'll come, given time.'

'Wally won't be best pleased. He's enjoying himself doing the round.'

'Wally can take a running jump,' Bill said vehemently. 'The job's mine, and I'm keeping it. He can go back into retirement where he belongs.

Georgie smiled.

'I have to say, Georgie, your visiting me has done me a power of good. I can't thank you enough.'

'You're more than welcome, Bill.'

'I just wish . . .' He trailed off, and shrugged.

'What, Bill?'

'Nothing. Pipe dreams, that's all.'

Her heart began hammering. She was suddenly aware that this was the moment she'd been waiting for. 'I've something to tell you, Bill,' she murmured, in a voice that was only just above a whisper.

'There's nothing wrong, is there?'

'No, nothing wrong.' She took a deep breath. 'Charlie's dead.'

Bill stared blankly at her. 'Dead?'

'Killed while attending a fire. Apparently a section of wall fell on him and a colleague, killing them both. It was covered in the papers, but you wouldn't have read about it as you were ill at the time. If Florrie saw it the name clearly didn't ring a bell.'

Bill was stunned. 'So you're a widow again?'

'That's right.'

'Free?'

'I suppose so.'

'If you're a widow again, then you're free.' He wanted to say it was brilliant news, but he thought it would be tasteless. A man was dead, after all. Even if he had been a bastard who'd caused Georgie a load of grief. 'How do you feel about it?' he asked tentatively instead.

'Relieved. It means Charlie isn't lurking in the background any longer.'

Bill nodded at her honesty. 'So what about us?'

She glanced away.

'Georgie?'

'That depends on you.'

'No it doesn't,' he contradicted her. 'It depends on us.'

True, she thought.

'Well?'

It was time to put it to her mother's test. Was it mere friendship between them, or could it be more? At that point she remained undecided. 'I'd like you to kiss me,' she said in a voice huskier than usual.

Bill didn't need to be asked twice. Going to her, he took her into his arms, gazed deeply into her eyes, then did as she'd requested, aware of her trembling as their lips met.

'I've wanted to do that for a long, long time,' he said when the extended kiss was finally over.

Georgie sighed with contentment. She'd stopped trembling and her insides were positively glowing. It felt so right being in his embrace, so warm and comforting. She knew now, without the shadow of a doubt, that they could be a couple.

'I think you'd better do that again,' she said. 'Just to be certain.'

He frowned. 'Aren't you already?'

'Of course. But I'd like to play a little hard to get.'

'I thoroughly enjoyed that,' she declared as they left the Variety Theatre. 'I haven't laughed so much in ages.'

'Me neither.'

'Some of the jokes were rather blue, though. I found myself blushing more than once.

'You're not some sort of prude, I hope?' he teased.

She blushed again at the suggestion. 'I don't think so. At least I've never considered myself one.'

'That's good. For I'm certainly not.'

She glanced sideways, wondering what it would be like with Bill. He'd never been married, after all, and she'd never thought to question him about past experiences, of which she was sure there must have been some.

She hooked an arm through his, and drew closer to him. 'As it's such a lovely night why don't we walk for a wee bit before catching a tram?' she suggested.

He looked up at a cloudless sky dotted with stars like so many diamonds winking down. It was indeed a lovely night. 'We'll walk if you wish. It'll do us both good.'

He and Georgie had been seriously courting for a number of months now, seeing one another two or three times a week. Learning more about one another, building and strengthening their relationship. Their previous friendship had deepened into something much more than that.

They walked a little way in silence, each savouring the other's company, revelling in just being together.

'I've had a thought,' Bill said finally.

'And what's that?'

'I'm fed up with feeling sad every time I have to say good-night to you.'

A sense of warmth blossomed inside her, and she pulled herself even closer to him. 'I feel the same way.'

'Then perhaps we should do something about it.'

She glanced at him again, a tightness replacing the warmth in her belly. 'Such as?' she queried softly.

'Get married.'

She came to a sudden stop to stare at him. 'Are you proposing, Bill Bailey?'

'Well, don't look so surprised. You must have guessed I was going to at some time.'

She had, of course. 'Then do it properly.'

He raised his free hand and placed his fingertips against her cheek. 'Will you please marry me, Georgie?'

'And if I say no?' she teased.

'Then I'll shoot myself.'

She laughed. 'Dope.'

'So, what's the verdict?'

Georgie couldn't have been more certain of anything. She and Bill were made for one another. It was, in her opinion, a perfect match. She considered herself extremely lucky to have a third chance with someone. 'I'll marry you, Bill,' she breathed. 'I'll be delighted to.'

Neither cared that they were in the street with people passing in both directions.

They kissed, oblivious of everything around them.

'Getting married!' Florrie exclaimed.

'That's right, Mum.'

'Thank God for that. Off my hands at long last. I thought I was never going to get rid of you.'

Georgie laughed, knowing the old woman was joking.

'Thank you very much,' said Bill, pretending to be hurt.

'Mind you, I've seen it coming for a while now. I'd have had to be blind not to.'

'You approve, then?' Georgie asked.

'What do you think, lassie?'

'Thanks, Mum.'

'Don't thank me. Thank Georgie for taking on a big lump like yourself. She must be mad.'

'I'd be mad to pass him up,' Georgie declared, eyes shining.

Florrie beamed. 'Now, when's the big day?'

'We'll have to organise a house first,' Bill replied. 'We'll name the day after we've found one.'

'Well, you already have. If you want it, that is.'

Georgie frowned. 'I don't understand.'

'This house. It's yours. And more or less everything that's in it.'

'But what about you, Mum?' Bill protested. 'Like Georgie, I don't understand. Are you staying here or going somewhere?'

'I shall be going to live with your Aunt Pru in Helensburgh. She'll jump at the chance of having me there – she's been lonely ever since your Uncle Archie was killed in the war. And I'll enjoy being by the sea, which I've always rather fancied after a lifetime in dirty old Glasgow.'

Bill turned to Georgie. 'What do you think?'

'I'm all for it. And I can't thank you enough, Florrie.'

'That's settled then,' Florrie declared enthusiastically. 'I move out and you two move in. Perfect.'

Georgie thought so too. Absolutely perfect. It was the icing on the cake.

Chapter 30

'There's a letter come for you,' Brigid told Tom on his arrival home from work.

'Oh aye?'

'Official-looking, too. Your name and address have been typed. Posted in Glasgow according to the franking.'

Who could be sending him an official letter from Glasgow? 'Where is it?'

'On the sideboard.'

'Daddy, Daddy, Daddy!' Robin yelled, careering into the room and heading straight for his father. Tom grabbed hold of the lad and swung him aloft, tipping him from side to side as Robin squealed with delight. It was the nightly ritual when Tom got in from Ford.

'One of these days he's going to be sick all over you when you do that,' Brigid prophesied.

'Never. You wouldn't be sick over me, would you, son?'

'No, Daddy.'

'See?' Tom smiled at Brigid, who raised a disbelieving eyebrow. 'And how's my daughter?'

'Sleeping, I'm happy to say.'

Sarah was now two months old, and a lovely child, at least according to Tom and Brigid.

'Has she been fed?'

'Half an hour ago, so she'll stay down for a little while.'

Tom put Robin back on the floor, then crossed to the sideboard to find out what the letter was all about.

'I'm hungry,' Robin announced.

'Tea will soon be on the table. You'll just have to wait.'

Robin pulled a face, then ran from the room.

'I don't know where he gets his energy from,' Brigid declared, shaking her head. 'It makes me tired just watching him.'

Tom picked up the letter, which indeed had a Glasgow postmark. He ripped the envelope open and extracted the single sheet it contained. Quickly he scanned the contents.

'Oh, dear,' he whispered.

'What is it?'

Tom glanced over at his wife, whose expression was one of concern at the tone he'd used. 'Dolly's dead.'

Brigid's hand flew to her mouth. This was dreadful news. 'How?'

'The lawyer doesn't say. It seems she's left me a substantial amount of money and this Mr . . .' Tom looked again at the letter, 'Mr Bird wants me to go up to Glasgow to sign some papers.'

'Go to Glasgow?' Brigid frowned. 'Can you get time off?'

Tom thought about it. 'We are a bit slack at the moment. If I go to management and show them this letter it should be all right. They're usually fairly reasonable about matters concerning bereavement.'

'Poor Dolly,' Brigid whispered. 'She was such a nice woman.'

'And good to us. It was lovely the times she called in to see us en route to London on her shopping trips.'

Brigid nodded her agreement. 'Substantial amount,' she mused. 'I wonder how much?'

Tom exhaled heavily. 'I have absolutely no idea. But whatever, it was kind of her to remember me in her will.'

Dear Dolly, he thought. He was going to miss her.

*   *   *

'Lena, I'm off out now,' Hamish said, putting his head round the door of her office. She knew that meant the coffee shop. 'And I won't be in for the rest of the afternoon as I'm playing a round of golf later.'

'Well, enjoy yourself.' She glanced at the window where sunshine was streaming in. 'You've got a lovely day for it.'

'Exactly. Now, is there anything you want me to do before I leave?'

She smiled indulgently at him. 'There's nothing, Hamish. You just toddle off.'

He lowered his voice. 'I'll call in this evening, if that's all right by you?'

'Of course it is. I'll be waiting.'

'Good. See you then.'

Lena sighed when he'd gone, and leant back in her chair. The chairman might still be the chairman, and Hamish vice chairman, but it was she who literally ran the company nowadays. The thought gave her a great sense of achievement. Naturally, only she and Hamish knew what the real situation was, but so what? As far as she was concerned that didn't matter.

Who would have thought she'd ever get into a position like this? Certainly not her. She was a woman, after all, and women were kept pegged to a particular level, not allowed to advance into positions of power. Those were strictly men only.

Taking out her cigarettes, she lit up. By God but it felt good to be where she was. Fulfilling, too. The boss in all but name.

She couldn't help but laugh to herself.

'Surprise!'

Chrissie's eyes popped out on stalks, or so it felt like to her. She couldn't believe what she was seeing. 'Tom,' she croaked.

'In the flesh.' He pulled her into his arms and hugged her tight. 'Hello, Mum. How are you?'

'Why didn't you warn us you were coming?'

'I wanted to surprise you.'

Detaching herself, Chrissie wiped tears from her eyes. 'Well, you've done that all right.' She patted her bosom. 'My heart's jumping about like billy-o.'

'Can you put me up for a couple of nights?'

'Aye, of course. Silly to ask. Now come in. Come in.' She shouted through to the kitchen. 'Tam, it's Tom. He's home!'

Tom picked up the small suitcase he'd brought, and the bottle of whisky he'd bought nearby. When he entered the kitchen it was to see Tam standing beaming at him.

'Hello, son.'

'Hello, Papa.'

They shook hands, and Tom gave the bottle to his father. 'I thought we might have a dram?' he suggested.

'Grand idea.'

'So what brings you here?' Chrissie wanted to know. 'Or is it just a visit to see your old mum and papa?'

'A substantial amount of money, you say,' Tam repeated a few minutes later. 'Any notion how much?'

'None at all, Papa. A few hundred, I should imagine.'

'A nice little windfall.'

'Mrs Mulherron was a good woman,' Chrissie commented. 'I fair took to her. How old was she, do you know?'

Tom shook his head.

'And you're seeing this lawyer tomorrow?' Tam said.

'That's right. Half past eleven. He's got offices in Gordon Street.'

Chrissie had a sudden thought. 'Are you hungry, son? I haven't much in, but I could do you an omelette if you like.'

'That would be smashing, Mum. I am a bit peckish.'

'Right then!' She began bustling about.

'It's grand having you back, son,' Tam declared quietly.

'It's good to be back, Papa. Though we are well settled in Dagenham. We enjoy it there.'

'No religious problems, I take it?'

'None.'

Tam nodded his approval.

'Now tell us all about wee Sarah,' Chrissie commanded from the sink. 'There's only so much you can put in a letter. I want to hear everything from your own lips.'

Tom was completely stunned. 'How much?' he eventually asked in a tight voice.

Mr Bird, the lawyer, repeated the sum he'd just mentioned.

'Jesus Christ,' Tom gulped.

Mr Bird, bald, spectacled and in his early forties, smiled at Tom. 'I did advise you in my letter it was a substantial amount.'

Tom shook his head in amazement, still unable to fully take this in. 'A substantial amount to me is obviously very different from a substantial amount to you, Mr Bird. I thought we were talking hundreds, not a bloody fortune.'

'You are her main beneficiary, Mr McKeand. And Mrs Mulherron was an extremely rich woman. By the way, that figure doesn't include the house and contents, which will realise considerable equity in their own right.'

The house as well! Tom couldn't believe it. His mind was reeling. 'But . . . why me?' he stuttered. 'Are there no relatives?'

'I'm afraid not. Mrs Mulherron was quite alone in this world.'

'I see,' Tom murmured.

'Now,' Mr Bird went on, 'there are certain arrangements that have to be made, papers to be signed and so on. So shall we make a start?'

When everything had been completed for the time being, Tom left the lawyer's office and headed straight for the nearest pub. He badly needed a drink while he tried to absorb the bombshell that had just exploded in his life.

Why, he need never work again if he chose not to do so, he realised. In fact there were all sorts of things he could choose whether or not to do. From now on almost anything was possible – financially, anyway. His head was still spinning when he reached the pub and plunged inside.

* * *

'So how did you get on?' Chrissie queried anxiously when he finally returned to his parents' house. He wasn't drunk, but not exactly sober either.

'You'd better sit down before I tell you, Mum.'

'Oh aye. A disappointment, eh?'

He waited till she was ensconced in an armchair before relating his conversation with the lawyer.

'Oh, son,' Chrissie whispered when he told her the amount he'd inherited, her face draining of colour. 'Are you sure there's no mistake?'

'Quite. That's what Dolly left me. That plus the house and all its contents.'

Chrissie shook her head in wonder. It was simply incredible. 'Aye, well, you won't be short of a bob or two from now on,' she said. Which must have been the understatement of the year.

'Mr Bird, the lawyer, informed me it was a heart attack,' said Tom.

Smith, the ancient butler, smiled sadly. 'That's correct, sir. Madam was in the morning room and had asked me for her usual glass of sherry. When I returned with it she was sitting with her eyes closed, as if she'd just dropped off to sleep. Thinking that to be the case I left her to it. It wasn't until later that we discovered the truth – that she had in fact passed on.'

'There wouldn't have been any pain, then?'

'I shouldn't think so, sir. It must have been all over in a moment. At least that's what I'd like to believe.' The butler turned away so Tom couldn't see his expression, which was one of profound grief. After a moment he turned back to Tom. 'Sorry about that, sir.'

'That's all right. I understand.' Tom cleared his throat. 'What's going to happen to you now, Smith?'

'Oh, I'll be absolutely fine, sir. Madam was kind enough to leave me a sum that will see me through to my final days. She was extremely generous, I have to say.'

'And the rest of the staff?'

'The same with them sir. Everyone received something. No one was left out.'

'That's good.'

Smith glanced sadly around the morning room, a thousand memories flitting through his mind. 'Can I enquire what you intend to do with the house, sir?'

'Sell it, I'm afraid. I live in England now, as you know, and have no intention of returning to Glasgow. So the house is surplus to requirements.'

'I thought as much, sir. We all, the staff that is, did.'

'I shall be having valuers in to appraise the contents, which will then be sold, or auctioned off. When that's done the house will go on the market. It's so beautiful I shouldn't imagine it'll take long to be snapped up.'

'No, sir,' Smith agreed.

'In the meantime I wish you and the others to stay on until such times as you find new employment, or the house is sold. Whichever comes first.'

'That's kind of you, sir.'

Tom regarded the ancient butler. 'I presume you won't be looking for another job, but retiring?'

'Quite correct, sir.'

'Where will you go?'

'I've already considered that, though I haven't yet come to any decision. But I shall find a place all right, don't you worry about that.'

'You're going to miss being here,' Tom said softly. 'It'll be an awful wrench to leave. I can only say I'm sorry, being the cause of it.'

Smith shook his head. 'You're not the cause, sir. Madam's dying is.' He hesitated, then said, 'It never crossed my mind that she'd go before me. And yet she has. One of life's little ironies, I suppose.'

'Yes,' Tom agreed.

'It was a lovely funeral, sir. All the staff were there, plus a few of Madam's friends. It was a tearful farewell right enough.'

'Dolly was buried before I found out about her death, otherwise I too would have attended.'

Smith nodded that he understood.

'There's something I'd like to do before I go,' Tom declared.

'Which is, sir?'

'See round the house. Is that possible?'

'Of course, sir. It is yours now, after all. You're perfectly entitled. Where would you care to begin?'

'I'll let you decide that.'

'Very good, sir. If you'll just follow me.'

It turned out to be even bigger than Tom had thought. Absolutely huge, in fact. What a pity he had to sell, he mused on leaving. But he had no intention of returning to Glasgow and its religious bigotry. No, he and his family were settled down south, and that's where they'd stay.

'So what are you going to do with all that money?' Tam asked. He and Tom were having a drink in a local pub.

'I have no idea, Papa. And that's the truth.'

'Will you keep on working at Ford?'

'Maybe, maybe not. One thing's certain, I'm not jumping rashly into anything. That would be stupid.'

Tam nodded his agreement. 'Very wise of you.'

'Once everything's settled and the money's in my account, I want to send you and Mum a cheque. I hope you're not going to be all stiff-necked and say you'll refuse?'

Tam had a swallow from his pint while he considered that. He had his pride to think of, after all. There again, Tom was his son, and he wanted to share some of his good fortune with him and Chrissie.

'Well, Papa?'

'For your mum's sake, eh? Maybe make life a wee bit easier for her.'

'Exactly.'

Tom extended a hand and the two of them shook on it.

* * *

'I have to admit, you've made a beautiful job of your "apartment",' Tom said. He had arranged by telephone to pay Lena a visit.

'Thank you.'

He stared at her, thinking there was something different about his sister. Something he couldn't quite put his finger on.

'Drink?'

'Please.'

'Whisky or gin?'

He smiled. 'Whisky, please. I hate gin.'

She hadn't known that. 'Have you seen Georgie and her new husband since you got back?' she asked, busying herself with the glasses.

'Last night, as a matter of fact.'

'What did you think of Bill?'

'Seemed a decent enough chap to me. It was obvious the pair of them get on well enough.'

Lena handed him his whisky. 'I like him too. Georgie seems to have landed on her feet this time after the one she had before.'

'Aye,' Tom muttered. 'That Charlie was a bad lot right enough. Bloody pervert.'

Lena raised her glass in a toast. 'Here's to Georgie and her new marriage, may it be a long and happy one.'

They both drank. 'Now, what about you?' Tom queried.

'What about me?'

'Well, for a start, how are you getting on living alone?'

If only he knew, Lena thought. If only he knew. Hamish was with her three evenings most weeks nowadays. She might not be married like Georgie, but she had the next best thing. A lot more than she'd ever thought would come her way. And she was profoundly grateful. It was enough to satisfy her.

She smiled. 'Just fine.'

'That's good.' He didn't add that it wouldn't have suited him. 'And how does it feel to be Mr Moneybags?'

He laughed. 'I still haven't really got used to the idea. I certainly don't feel any different.'

'No?'

'Not really. I half expect to wake up one morning and find it's all been a dream.'

'And what does Brigid think?'

'She had hysterics when I told her on the phone. I had quite a job convincing her I wasn't pulling her leg.'

'Understandable, I suppose,' Lena mused. 'It's not every day you're left a fortune completely out of the blue.'

'No, it isn't,' Tom agreed.

How much more relaxed his sister was than he recalled, Tom thought. Previously she'd been permanently wound up, on edge, bad-tempered. But all that had now seemingly disappeared. There again, maybe he'd just caught her on a particularly good night.

'You've put on a little weight,' he commented. 'It suits you.'

'Thank you.'

He noticed her bust was fuller too, but didn't mention that. The Lena of old would have snapped his head off if he had, telling him to mind his own bloody business. She would have thought it was far too personal a remark to make.

All in all it was a very pleasant visit, and then it was time for Tom to leave. At the door they hugged, and kissed cheeks, she telling him to take care, and give her love to his family, he wishing her all the very best for the future.

How strange, Tom thought as he strode off down the road. Why on earth had there been a man's collar stud on Lena's dressing table? If she had a chap in tow why hadn't she mentioned it?

How very strange.

Tom carefully laid the wreath he'd brought along on Dolly's grave, which already boasted several other wreaths and flower arrangements.

'I just wanted to say thank you personally, Dolly. You were a wonderful human being and I'll miss you.'

He stood there in silence for a few minutes, remembering the Belgrave and how good she'd been at gambling, and other things.

There was a choke in his throat, and a hint of tears in his

eyes, when he finally left the graveside and made his way out of the cemetery.

Tom was on the train home again when the idea suddenly came to him. An idea which instantly appealed. Appealed a great deal. In fact, an idea he considered inspirational.

He'd set up his own business, a manufacturing one. He'd produce nuts and bolts as Freddy, Dolly's husband, had so successfully done. Start small, and then, as he got established, expand. With his contacts at Ford surely he could become a supplier to them? He'd told his father he wasn't going to rush into anything, nor would he. There would be a lot to learn before striking out on his own.

No, not quite on his own. He'd take Ian, Georgie's son, with him. Eventually put him into a managerial position. Georgie, not to mention Ian himself, would love that.

Oh yes, what a brilliant idea. And one, he was sure, of which Dolly would wholeheartedly have approved.